UNDER PRESSURE

UNDER PRESSURE

MOONLIGHT DETECTIVE AGENCY™ BOOK FOUR

ISOBELLA CROWLEY   ELL LEIGH CLARKE
MICHAEL ANDERLE

DISRUPTIVE IMAGINATION

LMBPN Publishing
PMB 196, 2540 South Maryland Pkwy
Las Vegas, NV 89109

First US edition, December 2019
eBook ISBN: 978-1-64202-621-4
Print ISBN: 978-1-64202-622-1

THE UNDER PRESSURE TEAM

Thanks to the Beta Readers
Nicole Emens, Mary Morris, Kelly O'Donnell, John
Ashmore, Larry Omans

Thanks to the JIT Readers

Dave Hicks
Jeff Eaton
Jackey Hankard-Brodie
Diane L. Smith
Dorothy's Lloyd
Micky Cocker
Deb Mader
Lori Hendricks

If I've missed anyone, please let me know!

Editor
The Skyhunter Editing Team

To Family, Friends and
Those Who Love
to Read.
May We All Enjoy Grace
to Live the Life We Are
Called.

CHAPTER ONE

Taylor's House, Harrison, Westchester County, New York

Silent and alert, she crept down the length of a long, dark tunnel. She knew she was in danger but exactly where the threat lay was beyond even her advanced perception.

The fog of malevolence—the increasingly less subtle vibes of haughty viciousness and murderous intent—had spread gradually over the entire city. It seemed to grow stronger as she moved south, across the island of Manhattan.

She had departed alone, not knowing quite what to expect and acting on a tip from Dr Alexander Thomas, the former vampiric thrall whose life she had spared in exchange for his aid. The residues of his deadly and burning link to his former mistress had granted him access to her mind, and he'd told Taylor that he'd seen this place in her plans.

Her experience stretched far beyond the limits of humankind. Despite that, it had been a long time since she'd seen anything quite like this.

Usually, she could sense when a powerful foe—especially another vampire—wanted her dead. Their hostile intent emanated like radio waves from their person to provide some clue when she was near them.

She normally only perceived negative vibes of this intensity when she was right on top of them. And in those cases, the signals clearly came from a specific point.

But now, in this subterranean labyrinth and not far from her own secret sanctuary, she felt that same malefic energy, only it was equally intense everywhere she turned. Her foe, the Egyptian elder vampire Moswen Neith, had somehow blanketed New York with something almost like a curse upon the very air.

Taylor knew her own capabilities and that she was far from helpless, even against adversaries who could easily crush most beings. She was also not readily given to fear, but this was unnerving.

It unsettled her because she knew without a doubt that she faced a degree of evil power beyond anything in recent memory—possibly beyond any she had ever dealt with.

And because the low, maddening buzz of her opponent's aura was omnipresent, there was no shift and no waxing in its power when Moswen herself attacked.

A grasping hand came out of the darkness of an alcove that lay barely out of sight, its claw-like nails aimed at the white flesh of Taylor's throat. Decades of combat experience and a sixth sense honed even beyond what vampirism granted were the only reasons she survived. She vaulted aside toward the opposite wall.

All her senses, already pulsing in a state of heightened

alertness, now kicked up to the maximum as her larger adversary pressed after her with a powerful leap.

Moswen said nothing and made no snarl of rage but moved in almost total silence. There was only the miasma of her hatred, the flashes of yellow light from her eyes, the sounds—which would have been imperceptible to human ears—of her feet on the tunnel's metal, and the air parting before her passage.

As Taylor impacted with the far wall, the other vampire was there on top of her and her hands clamped down on her shoulders. The smaller woman buckled, summoned all her strength, and fought back. The two half-crouched, half-stood on the wall, gravity ignoring them as they hung laterally into empty space.

She had hooked her arms under Moswen's, seeking to break her grip, push her hands aside, and strike straight at her heart. But her adversary was stronger—and with not only the natural advantage conferred by her greater height and mass. She possessed an eldritch power that had percolated over centuries beyond even Taylor's long experience.

Finally, she broke free, using her attacker's own inertia against her to shove her against the wall and launch herself back.

Moswen was, somehow, already on her again.

Everything became a flurry of pain and rage and violence. Taylor clawed at her assailant's throat, punched her face, wrenched her limbs, and kicked at her legs and stomach.

The Egyptian responded in kind. Fierce, battering blows rained down on the smaller vampire, knees struck her ribs and jaw, and the long and terrible fangs bit at any vulnerable flesh they could find.

The blood of both women, dead and yet not dead, soon flowed, then gushed and splattered. Both began to take amounts of damage that slowed them, yet a rage that had seared its way through entire generations of humankind drove them on in their struggle.

Taylor had, for a time, not even felt or truly registered the damage she sustained in the battle. Instead, with the blind fury of a trapped animal, she had devoted everything to simply ripping Moswen apart.

Her nails raked strips of flesh from the other vampire's back and shoulders, her fangs briefly tore a chunk from her neck, and when the Egyptian knocked her down with an elbow, she sank all ten fingers, as well as her teeth, into the calf of the other woman's leg and peeled most of the muscle from it.

That was when Moswen screamed with such bestial anger that Taylor was momentarily shocked and drew back. The pain of her own various wounds swamped her all at once.

The howl wavered, then formed itself into words. "You know not!" Moswen shrieked. "You know not what you've done. I've only been toying with you."

"No—you're finished."

She hissed defiance and braced herself. Her black eyes, already large within her small white face, grew huge as Moswen reared, trembling, and seemed to summon a dreadful power as if out of the depths of the earth. Sinister golden light shined from her eyes and played about her body.

Taylor knew what was happening now. She'd wounded her foe badly enough that she would soon have to retreat, but this development meant that she needed to kill Moswen now.

The other vampire had changed. She no longer resembled a tall, regally beautiful Egyptian queen. Her appearance now perfectly reflected the tomb-spawned monstrosity she was.

She had grown in height and bulk, and her dusky skin had taken on a leathery, almost scaly quality. Hair had sprouted from her neck and shoulders and appeared in the center of her palms. Her jaw had distended and elongated while her nose had flattened, and her ears had risen to points high on her head. The black pupils of her brown eyes had changed from orbs to slits.

Many vampires, particularly old and powerful ones, possessed the ability to shift to a more bestial form with even greater strength at the cost of their reasoning abilities. Moswen, horrifyingly, was now an awful hybrid of woman, serpent, and jackal.

"No!" Taylor cried and flung herself at her enemy, totally committed to taking her head, or her heart, or both and sending her to the abyss before she could take full advantage of her powers.

Somehow, she wasn't fast enough. Moswen's hands were now outright talons, clusters of five knives, and one of them sheared into her midsection.

The smaller vampire doubled over, spitting blood, and harnessed all her strength and self-control. The pain was overwhelming and unbearable.

Her eyes flew open. Black within white, round and staring at the ceiling of the cave above her with the mindless intensity that only a nightmare can bring.

"Oh," she gasped, her lips parted slightly to permit the faint expulsion of air and sound. "My God. I would never have thought…"

It was rare for her to have nightmares. For a while, in her early days, she had not even realized that vampires could have them. But as time wore on and the months and years and decades spun away into the oblivion of the past, the function of dreaming had returned to her.

When it happened, it usually portended something. Or, at least, served to remind her of some fact of massive importance.

She closed her eyes again and allowed her usual frosty calm to return. The tension shook its way free of her slight, slender body to dissipate amidst the darkness. Here in the real world, there were no signs of immediate danger and she had healed her wounds from that fight.

Satisfied with the control she'd regained, she rose to a standing position within the rectangular niche dug into the earth.

Most days, she slept in her coffin. But at times, she could not rest as well and did not feel as secure, guarded as she was only by the stone sarcophagus within her mansion's cellar which enclosed the wooden box.

So, years before, she had added a trapdoor to the bottom of the coffin and dug a hole in the floor to the cave below. She'd added carved stairs for good measure although it was a simple matter to float to the ceiling and push her way through to the basement.

The vampire did so now and the air parted as she levitated and the horizontal portal opened before her hands. She climbed through the coffin and emerged into her cellar.

Judging by the faint reddish glow of the window slits at the tops of the walls, it was barely dusk. The nightmare had woken her early. Her house was designed to be dark, though, so she ought to be safe from what little remained of the sun.

When Taylor ascended the stairs and stepped into the hallway, her loyal butler was already prepared to wait on her needs. Presley was a werewolf who usually wore the form of an elderly English gentleman and dressed the part in a black tuxedo, complete with white gloves.

"Good evening, Miss Steele," he greeted her. "Shall I warm up one of your cars? The 2017 Tesla, perhaps?"

She knew why he asked. Usually, if she rose before full dark, it meant that she intended to drive to the Brooklyn offices of the Moonlight Detective Agency without delay in hope of arriving there before the day staff went home. The agency's business hours were officially listed as ending at 6:30 but in practice, it was open twenty-four hours a day.

"No, Presley, but thank you," she said. "I will be here for now. Bring my tea to my bedroom, if you would, please. I would benefit from privacy right now."

The old man nodded. "As you wish, madam." He turned and strode back toward the kitchen.

The vampire, her black silk robe trailing along the wooden floor, climbed to a room at the end of the hall on the second floor. It was where she spent much of her time when staying in at night unless she chose to read in the first-floor sitting room.

Now that Remington had moved into the guest room on the upper story, however, she found that she preferred the first floor more and more.

But he did not seem to be there and was likely still out working. She'd assigned him a messy if only minimally dangerous case that ought to keep him busy.

Taylor entered the room and sat on the bed for a moment. She did not sleep in it, of course, but simply having one in her "bedroom" seemed appropriate. It created a cozy sense of normalcy and would throw off suspicion in the unlikely event that uninvited, uninitiated humans gained entrance to her home.

Within her brain were vast stores of information, and over the many long years of her preternatural existence, she had learned how to organize the stores, sort through them, and re-order them as needed.

Her mind rapidly produced a list of everything she would require for her trip. There wasn't much, really. It would be better to travel light, and she could pick up some things at John F Kennedy International or at her destination.

She stood up to begin packing.

Presley's footsteps, so regular and familiar, climbed the stairs and he knocked gently on the door.

Taylor paused, flitted over, and opened it. "Thank you, Presley." She accepted the cup and saucer from him. Within it was her breakfast, known for reasons of tradi-tional politeness as red salt tea.

She, like most vampires who preferred discretion and had adapted to the more civilized modern world, had an under the table arrangement with a blood bank. She paid them very reasonably for their goods and services.

Not to mention that, in exchange for their silence, she had put the word out on the street that any vampires—or their servants—who might try to raid or attack their establishment could expect swift and merciless retribution.

Her nature was not overly vicious and she was willing to be reasonable with those who extended her the same courtesy. But swift and merciless retribution was something she did rather well when the situation called for it.

She sipped her tea and found it good. Before the butler could ask if she needed anything else, she spoke.

"I have some things to contemplate, so please do not disturb me. And when Remington comes home, especially if soon, relay the message to him."

Presley inclined his head forward, the movement half a nod and half a curt bow. "Of course, Miss Steele." He turned to leave her in peace and closed the door himself.

She retrieved a single suitcase from her closet, into which she began to fold a few clothes, for starters. It was easiest to eliminate the simple tasks first and quickly leave herself with a smaller number of chores.

Midway into the process, she paused. Before she completed gathering and packing her things—even though it would only take perhaps an hour at most—she decided that she ought to do something very important. Book her flight.

Airline tickets were always bothersome to secure on short notice. If absolutely necessary, she could call in a favor or two from some of her contacts or use her powers of command on the airport's personnel. It would be easy to compel them to give her someone else's seat on her desired flight.

But there was no reason to use her valuable favors or to cause a public scene and inconvenience some unfortunate humans when instead, she could simply check the flight availability.

She turned her laptop on and reviewed her paper receipts from the blood bank while the device booted up. When it was ready, she sat in the black leather chair before it and immediately checked for any flight going to her desired location within the next twelve hours or so.

Her brain took in and processed information more quickly than a human's could. It took only a minute or two to locate what she sought—a single first-class seat on a plane departing New York in four hours. The cost was considerable but perfectly doable.

Numbly, Taylor went through the process of punching in the pertinent information and transferring the necessary funds. Soon, her ticket was secured. She only had to make it to the terminal in time, and she had no doubt whatsoever that, barring some bizarre contingency, she would arrive early.

The ticket would be via El Al, Israel's flag carrier airline which, due to terrorism concerns, was known for its stringent security procedures. She would have to pass an interview, a thorough baggage check, and a scan that compared her personal information against the databases of various major intelligence agencies and police forces.

None of which concerned her much. The one potential

risk was that Kendra Gilmore, her contact in the FBI, might have allowed her superiors to begin investigating the mysterious Ms Steele.

But even if that were the case, she had ways to convince mortals to do as she wished.

As she considered the trials to come, Taylor resumed packing. Well before the night was over, she would board a plane en route to Ben Gurion Airport, El Al's headquarters, which was partway on the road between Tel Aviv and Jerusalem.

Moswen had invaded her rightful turf. Now, she would return the favor, but only long enough to get what she needed.

CHAPTER TWO

Taylor's House, Harrison, Westchester County, New York

Presley stood beside Taylor's ebony china cabinet, which was tucked discreetly into the far left corner of the kitchen, and dutifully polished the windowed doors with a rag and a bottle of glass cleaner.

The case probably could have gone another week or so before it really needed touching up. But the old man had caught up with all the other household chores for the moment, and cleaning things pleased and relaxed him.

A security device set into the first-floor ceiling emitted a low beep and outside, he heard a car coming up the driveway. That would be Remington, returning home from work. He must have had a long day.

The butler finished his task and returned both rag and bottle to their usual abode under the sink. Then, he stood in the doorway between the kitchen and the foyer, his hands folded behind his back, and waited to deliver Miss Steele's instructions.

Footsteps approached the front entrance and the door

banged open. In trudged David Remington, scion of one of New York's wealthiest families—albeit *nouveau riche* by society standards—or, as the young man preferred to be known in his professional capacity, Remington Davis.

Remy stank heavily of sweat, despite the chilly weather, not to mention the other fluids soaking his suit—mainly blood and a foul, pungent black slime. His hair was mussed, his jaw seemed to trail slackly, and his gait was slow and shuffling.

For a moment, Presley tensed. He feared that something might truly be wrong—that their enemies might finally have transformed young master Remington into something unthinkable.

"Christ on a cracker with extra shit-sauce," the young man blurted, his voice ragged and almost fading with exhaustion at the end. "Where the fuck is Taylor so I can thank her for giving me such a fun, fun, fun case to work?"

The butler sighed with relief. Clearly, everything was normal. He cleared his throat.

"Miss Steele is here but is occupied with important matters of an unspecified nature," he explained in his leathery yet dignified Old World English accent. "As such, she has quite specifically requested that I ask you not to disturb her until further notice."

As Remington crossed the foyer, the butler saw that he carried a sword—Holy Roman Empire, Oakeshott Type XVIa, by the looks of it. It smelled enchanted and a slight residue of some repulsive black ichor lingered upon its blade.

"Yeah." Remy sighed. "Well, that's fine. Whatever. I need

a goddamn shower first before I deal with anything—and I mean anything—else right now."

Presley nodded. "That sounds like a splendid idea, sir. Do, however, leave the sword where all that mess won't get on the carpets, if you would, please."

He made a vague grumbling sound and continued down the hallway toward the staircase and presumably, the second-floor shower.

Of course, he'd left the door open, and his bodyguard, Conrad Warfield stepped through it. Like Presley, he was a lycanthrope.

"Hello," Conrad said, waved a hand, and smiled his customary proper, public-relations-friendly smile. "We did have our work cut out for us today, so try not to mind him too much."

The old man nodded. "Quite all right."

The bodyguard looked about twenty-eight or thirty by human standards but was in fact almost thrice that age. He was tall, fit, and handsome, with a neatly trimmed goatee and a pleasant, professional manner, having gone to America's best schools during their heyday. He even spoke with a slight Mid-Atlantic Accent.

As the younger werewolf traipsed past, he added, "I heard what you said about Taylor. I won't bother her."

"Splendid." Presley did not move from his position in the kitchen doorway. "It might be best if you simply found your way to Mr Remington's room to finish your last hour or two of bodyguard duty in seclusion there, as Miss Steele may require the run of the house."

Conrad hesitated for only a moment, as though curious

as to what was going on. Finally, he gave a faint shrug and followed Remy up the stairs.

The butler returned to the kitchen and double-checked to ensure everything was in order—which, of course, it was. He contemplated reading a book from their considerable library before retiring for the night himself.

Soon, the shower upstairs began running.

A moment later, a door opened, the sound gentle, and light, almost imperceptibly soft footsteps moved down the second-floor hallway before descending the stairs.

It was Taylor, of course. She had waited until Remy and Conrad were safely out of the way, her sensitive hearing picking up their every movement before emerging.

He looked over his shoulder and saw her wearing her coat, scarf, and sunglasses and carrying a single heavily laden suitcase. Clearly, her current course of action involved slipping out undetected. Or, at least, undetected by Remington or Conrad.

The vampire turned her head slightly and inclined it in his direction, the movement subtle and casual. She did not break stride. In almost total silence, she glided across the carpet of the foyer and passed out through the front door and into the night.

She could have taken the interior door to reach the garage, so she probably wanted to make a quick security inspection of the mansion before she departed.

Presley made no effort to pursue her and ask where she was going. Taylor always had her reasons. He trusted that, when the time was right, he would discover exactly what they were. For now, he wasn't troubled.

They had been together, both professionally speaking

and as friends, for a long, long time. Extended, wordy exchanges were seldom necessary anymore. He knew her moods and her ways, and she knew he would not ask silly questions.

Something was afoot. But, as always, she would deal with it in her own way and at her own pace.

Besides, at one hundred and eighty-two years of age, he was far too old to be wrapped up in this kind of potential drama. Slaying dwarven mobsters and vampiric thralls recently was about enough excitement to last him the next decade. Maybe two.

Taylor's House, Harrison, Westchester County, New York

Remington allowed the hot, steamy water to run over his head and shoulders for a moment longer and soaked up the warmth. Not only that, he wanted to be sure that every last trace of that crap was washed out of his hair and off of his skin.

Finally, he turned the water off, peeked around to make sure Conrad wasn't nearby, and stepped out to wrap a towel around his waist almost immediately. He dried himself off with another and noticed that he'd need to do laundry in another day or two.

Conrad's voice called from somewhere across the hallway. "Oh, are you getting out of the shower, sir? Presley asked me to stay in your room until my shift was over. I wanted to warn you since I know how you are about nudity."

Remy frowned. "Only when you're around. It might not be so bad if you shapeshift into a canine monstrosity. Can you shapeshift into a woman, by any chance? No, wait, forget I said that."

The lycanthrope replied with one of the annoying fake laughs of his and Remy ignored it.

Quickly, he dressed in fresh underwear, socks, slacks, and a shirt and didn't bother to put a tie on. He almost always wore one in public but when hanging around Taylor's house—his new home away from home—there wasn't much point.

While he freshened up, he pulled his phone out, opened a music playlist he'd recently made, and set it to random shuffle. "Wolves of Chernobyl" by Municipal Waste began to play. The music calmed him immediately and dissipated the stress of the day's labor.

He emerged from the bathroom feeling almost human being again. The sword leaned against the wall just outside, its tip on a bed he'd made of empty plastic trash bags. Fortunately, it wasn't overly sharp so he was fairly confident that none of the minimal remaining gunk had found its way onto the carpet.

Remy picked it up. By now, Taylor probably ought to be done with whatever Presley had said she was busy with. He wanted to talk to her about a few things. The conversation might not be friendly, but it needed to happen.

"Ugh," he muttered and again tried not to think about that...thing he'd had to kill earlier.

He descended the stairs and went to the door leading into the basement. After one sharp knock, he opened it. "Taylor? Hi. Mission accomplished, but I think we need to—"

The cellar was dark and he squinted in an effort to see.

Taylor's coffin stood open, but the vampire herself was nowhere to be seen. He descended and checked behind the wine cases to be safe but found nothing.

"Hmm. Sitting room, or her so-called bedroom, I would assume." Still holding the befouled sword a safe six inches from his body—and clothes—he checked the first floor.

The sitting room was empty, although it looked like Presley was leaving it to perform some errand.

Shrugging, Remy went back upstairs and knocked on the door to Taylor's nominal bedroom.

"Taylor, hi. All objectives completed. We need to talk, though. Like, what was—"

He turned the knob. The door opened to reveal the dark, silent, and definitely empty chamber. He poked his head in to make sure. Again, he found nothing.

Disgruntled, he turned away and stood at the top of the stairwell, leaning on one of the intricate banisters. "Hey," he called down the steps, "Presley. Where is she? You said she was still here. Did she leave for work already?"

"Sir," the butler's voice replied, "do please come down here rather than shouting."

With a weary sigh, the young man did as he was asked and managed to corner the elderly lycanthrope in the no longer vacant sitting room, where he now reclined with a rather dusty and weathered book. It looked like the type written by someone with no sense of humor and printed by someone who used eight-point font to save production costs.

The title was as uninspiring as the cover. *Proper Maintenance of Topiary Gardens.*

Presley looked up from the tome and spoke first. "Miss

Steele was compelled to leave early, and I'm afraid she didn't say when she would be back. I am inclined to suspect she will be gone at least for the full duration of tonight."

"Oh," Remy acknowledged. "Dang."

With a frown, the butler gestured to the black-stained blade. "Ah, we really must do something about—"

"Right!" He cut him off. "This. It's exactly what I wanted to ask you about. Or Taylor, rather, but I suppose either of you will do. What I mainly want to know is why the hell did she throw me against...that...thing without sufficient warning?" He glared at the old man.

Breathing in through his nose, Presley set the topiary book down on the end table. "You'd have to ask Miss Steele to be positive, sir, but I would guess it means she had faith in your competence."

"Welllllll," Remy responded and took a moment to bask in the implication that he had finally received some proper recognition, "that sounds fairly accurate. But all she said was, 'Remington, I'm sure you can handle it. You're not in much danger.' Danger. It's not a question of how likely I am to die. It's the fact that those godawful abominations are disgusting. I don't even want to think about how my mother would react if she were to find out that they so much as exist."

"Someone," said Presley, "has to deal with them. And the agency has to make a profit, does it not? Besides, judging by the spell on that blade—I assume Taylor procured it recently and without telling me—I'd imagine you made short work of the beast once you found it."

His jaw clenched in frustration. The butler was so calm

and composed all the time. He was almost as bad as his mistress.

"That's not the point. Besides, finding it is bad enough. Do you realize what kinds of conditions that thing lives in? It makes me wonder how the client even found out the damn thing was there, to begin with. I'm merely glad it's still winter. In the summer, there would have been...bugs. Hundreds and thousands of bugs."

The old man looked tired. "Kudos to you for your valiant achievement in vanquishing it," he stated in a monotone.

"I mean," Remy added and raised one hand to adjust his tie at the neck, only to recall that he wasn't wearing one at the moment, "it wasn't really all that life-threatening. Especially with the big, impressive magic sword and all. I can see why Taylor actually trusted me to deal with it single-handedly. Well, me plus Conrad."

Usually, when the agency's affairs required someone or something to be killed, Taylor handled it herself.

"But," he went on, "simply because something is easy doesn't mean it's...pleasant. In the slightest." He shuddered and ran a hand over his face as though trying to wipe the memory from his brain with the same motion.

Presley, to his great irritation, smiled. "That is quite understandable, sir. Of course, that is also why she entrusted the task to you. Now, we must do something about that sword."

"Oh, right," Remy agreed. He shoved the blade sideways toward the lycanthrope. The old man almost flinched but accepted it gingerly. He tried not to get any of the trace amount of hideous slime on his white gloves.

The young man smiled. "Thanks for letting me borrow it. Or thank Taylor, I guess. I already wiped the worst of it off, but I'm very sure that it'll need further cleaning, sadly. I'm sure you're the perfect man for the job."

With that, he spun on his heel and strode away before the butler had time to protest or try to give the sword back to him. He couldn't imagine Presley would much look forward to the task but then again, Remy had already more than earned his pay for the day.

In fact, as he traipsed up the stairs toward his room, he realized that he'd have the house all to himself for the night.

Taylor was gone. Conrad would only be there for maybe another hour at most and then he'd have the privilege of driving back to his apartment on the Upper East Side and doing whatever it was he did at night. The butler would pass out soon after that.

Life was good.

"I still have a good three, maybe even four beers in the fridge," he recalled out loud to better savor the sweetness of the words. "And there ought to be at least, say, two pizza places that will be open for another couple of hours. If I time it right, it ought to arrive a little after Conrad leaves."

His bodyguard probably heard him say that, not that he cared. It wasn't like the fastidious bastard ever ate anything other than kale, Greek yogurt, and protein shakes anyway. Unless he was in werewolf form, of course. Then he suddenly developed a healthy interest in red meat.

Remy pushed the door to his room open. Conrad had, horrifyingly, changed out of his usual dark suit and was now wore casual sportswear while doing some fairly impressive stretching exercises.

"Conrad," he said and slammed the door behind him. "Is there any chance you could bring me a beer from the fridge?" He picked the remote up and turned the TV on.

The lycanthrope turned and looked at him with a blank expression.

"Yeah, going up and down stairs is good exercise," he continued. "But I had to stab that thing, like, thirty-seven times and the hydraulic suction effect when trying to pull the blade free made it into a hell of a workout. Plus, my next mixed martial arts class is tomorrow, so that'll make up for all the liquid carbs I'm about to drink."

The werewolf returned his limbs to a normal configuration. "Actually, sir, if you don't need me for bodyguard duties at the moment, I'm a little busy. Technically, my contract only applies to activities that protect you from harm."

"Fine," he grumbled and shook his head. "Do you have any pizza topping requests? I don't know if you even eat that stuff anyway but might as well ask."

As he returned his attention to his next set of stretches, Conrad merely said, "Thank you, sir, but I try to stay away from pizza."

With a shrug, Remy whipped his phone out and called the nearest pizzeria while he wandered down to the refrigerator. It occurred to him that he probably ought to get a mini-fridge or at least a cooler so as to reduce staircase trips when beer was involved.

"Hi," he said into the speaker in response to the young

lady's tired-sounding greeting. "You guys are still open, right? And you still deliver to…" He gave the address

There was a short silence and he could almost hear her cringe. They must have a new guy doing the driving. Taylor's house lay at the extreme rear of one of those awful, labyrinthine rich-people neighborhoods and was not easy to find.

"Yes," she admitted reluctantly.

"Huzzah," he said. "I'll take an extra-large, regular crust, regular sauce, three-toppings. We'll say, pepperoni, sausage, and…uh, green peppers. With a side of ranch. Not the Lite kind, please, and thank you."

The young woman confirmed his order and told him that he could expect his pizza in about forty or forty-five minutes.

"Thanks." He hung up. He had about two dollars in cash, which ought to be enough for a tip. And, although he was trying to keep his drinking under control lately, forty-five minutes seemed like a long time to wait for food.

He took a deep breath and opened the fridge. "Two beers tonight," he told himself. "That's all."

CHAPTER THREE

John F. Kennedy International Airport, New York City

Taylor strode briskly and purposefully but with a cool relaxation through the bright halls of JFK. She did not wish to attract undue attention so she employed one of her subtler powers.

Simply by concentrating on the vibe she sent out and moving in certain ways, she could make herself less conspicuous. Humans were somehow compelled not to look in her direction, not to take notice of her, and not to look twice if they glanced once.

No one bothered her.

Of course, at other times, the opposite was advisable— commanding the attention of certain mortals. Knowing this, she had dressed to impress.

Her coat, slacks, shoes, and dark glasses all were the height of New York fashion, not as pricey as some accouterments but far from cheap. They were classy and all in black, of course. It was rare that she felt even the slightest need to dress in any other color. It matched her hair and eyes.

The stylish monochrome of her appearance was broken only by the smooth ivory skin of her neck and face. She wore black gloves to cover her long red nails, which no one would find suspicious given the frosty weather.

At one point, a rather muscular man eyed her suitcase. It was big and obviously packed full, yet she carried it in one small hand. She saw him shrug and go about his business, likely assuming that she'd simply stuffed it with clothes.

Soon, she spoke to a morosely polite young man behind a desk. "El Al, right? Just so you know, they have a rigorous procedure of their own in addition to the standard Transportation Security Administration stuff, so you can expect to have your luggage searched, a background check run on your info, and to be interviewed face to face."

"Yes, I know," she confirmed. "Thank you. I'm not terribly worried about it."

He nodded and punched a few things into his computer and tried not to look at her. She had, of course, allowed him to notice her and to be impressed with her sophisticated beauty and her air of mystery. If he thought she was incognito royalty or something to that effect, so much the better.

No problems materialized as the last of the red tape was taken care of and the young man provided her with her ticket. He directed her toward check-in with the good people responsible for El Al Israel Airline Ltd's famously tight security.

Two men came out to greet her. One was tall and

broad-shouldered with a big square jaw, the type of individual whom most mortals would have found intimidating. The other was a more modest size, but something about the grim calm of his face and the careful nature of his movements suggested that he was the more dangerous of the two. He was almost certainly a former member of the IDF or Mossad. Both men, like her, wore dark glasses.

"Madam," said the larger one, "your luggage. It must be inspected."

She smiled gently and handed the suitcase over. The big man accepted it with one hand and although he had no trouble lifting it himself, a slight arching of his right eyebrow revealed his surprise at its weight. Or, more to the point, at the fact that she had carried it so easily.

As he turned to take her luggage away, the smaller one extended a hand as if to place it on her shoulder, although he stopped halfway.

"If you please," he began, "your interview. You know that we do this for every passenger, yes?" He'd probably been born in Russia and come to Israel somewhere in his teens, she guessed, since his thick accent was something of a hybrid between the two nationalities.

Taylor inclined her head. "Of course. Lead the way."

He directed her to a small office and gestured for her to sit in a simple but cushioned chair, while he sat behind a sparse desk. She imagined that it contained extra weapons above and beyond the large-caliber pistol he wore concealed on his person.

"Now," the officer began, "we talk about your information and your intentions to visit Israel."

"Certainly," she replied. She kept her demeanor cool but

faintly pleasant. For good measure, she even sent out a very subtle vibe of nervousness. It was, after all, normal for people to be a tad jittery when some kind of armed authority figure interrogated them. It was best to seem neither too nervous nor too calm.

Besides, she did not, in fact, have anything to hide as far as the security of the plane or the state of Israel was concerned. If anything, succeeding in her goal would do them a favor.

The man continued. "These are all standard questions, but it is important that you answer them honestly. To hide something is very suspicious. Of course, we are already checking the information from your passport, so to lie is pointless."

Taylor allowed her next smile to look ever so slightly more worried but simultaneously projected a vibe that said *I know everything will be fine, so let's get through this.* She didn't expect that she would have much difficulty.

The officer proceeded with the interview and delivered various questions which, she knew, had as much or more to do with her attitude as with the content of her answers.

She told him that she was a private investigator—there was no sense in lying—but that this was more of a bucket-list tourist trip than anything. While she'd expected to be busy, she had suddenly found some time off and had purchased her ticket on a whim, reasoning that it might be months or years before she had another chance to finally visit the beautiful eastern Mediterranean.

While she spoke, she also beamed suggestions into the man's mind to signal that she was someone relatively wealthy and important and not to be trifled with, and ensured that he noticed how good she looked in her svelte-cut black coat.

Everything went fine initially.

"Yes," the officer murmured after a few more questions, "there is one thing, however. It seems you were recently involved in an investigation by the FBI. Agent Gilmore. Could you please tell us about that?"

Taylor would have preferred to avoid having to discuss this at all, but she had expected it and had her story ready.

"Of course. We had a break-in at our offices early last December. One of the suspects seemed to be a transient with a criminal record who had caused trouble across both New York and New Jersey recently. Because of that, it was technically an interstate crime spree so naturally, the FBI paid me a visit to confirm what I had already told the NYPD."

The man nodded. He had an excellent poker face, but she could tell he was satisfied. She'd passed the interview.

Soon, her suitcase was back in her hand and she boarded the plane. The tall, broad-shouldered fellow would have found nothing save clothes, toiletries, traveler's checks, a bottle of water, and a book on archaeology. And sunscreen.

Her seat was beside another woman, which was probably for the best since some ultra-Orthodox men were known to object to having to sit next to female passengers. She had no desire to deal with even the mildest commotion.

As the plane readied to leave, a stewardess approached her.

"Madam," the lady said quietly, "we have been told that

you are not Jewish and we wanted to make you aware that we only serve kosher meals. We hope that this is acceptable."

She smiled. "That's fine. I'll wait until after we land to eat."

Taylor's House, Harrison, Westchester County, New York

Remy slouched in his beanbag chair and tried deliberately to look as slothful and useless as possible. The idea was to convince Conrad not to bother him since he was deep into relaxation mode.

Fortunately, his bodyguard was completely absorbed in doing burpees. He'd managed a good twenty of them so far. Remington suspected he'd continue with the awful things without pause until the very moment his shift ended.

The pizza had arrived about five minutes before. In that span of time, he had already polished off the first slice and was halfway into his second beer. He could actually feel the carbs and calories undoing whatever recent progress he'd made toward being almost as fit as Conrad.

Well, he reassured himself, *after that bullshit earlier today, I'd say I deserve a little indulgence. Besides, it's Thursday, which is only one day away from Friday. It's practically the same thing.*

An awful entertainment gossip show was on the television in front of him. He had no idea why he was watching it except that it seemed to fit tonight's theme of not giving a crap.

An attractive woman in her mid-twenties wore a top that was revealing enough to be titillating but without being too vulnerable to accusations of sexism or whatever. She stood smiling next to a tall guy a few years older who chortled endlessly at his own jokes.

"And," the woman went on—he realized that he hadn't paid any attention to what they were saying until now —"according to no fewer than three of his colleagues, including a set designer, hairdresser, and sound engineer, it was only a boom mic in his pants after all, anyway. Apparently, the supposed 'grinding' happened while he bent over to pick up a packet of sugar substitute."

The guy laughed again at this and a kind of smug swagger rippled through him as he gestured vaguely at the camera. "We've all heard that one before," he remarked. "But time will tell, won't it? Okay, guys, hold on and we'll be right back."

The program cut to commercials.

First was an ad for a startup called BuzzDash that hired desperate college students and recent male divorcees to deliver alcohol, painkillers, and medical marijuana directly to people's doorsteps. Remy nodded with approval, impressed that the city, state, and federal governments hadn't united to shut the company down yet. He gave them three or four months until that happened and maybe also a few civil lawsuits.

Next up was one of those bizarre breakfast scenarios where everyone was getting ready for work or school in brightly-lit conditions while a properly dressed and made-up household matriarch cooked a highly nutritious meal for her bumbling husband and attractive, well-behaved children.

"Christ," he quipped. "Even I don't remember weekday mornings being that picture-perfect, and I'm rich."

He missed out on what the commercial was selling, though, because a loud, obnoxious, electric whining sounded behind him. He snapped his head toward the sound. Conrad had finished his evening workout and was now liquefying fruits and veggies in a portable juicier.

Remy blinked. "You know, that might have come in handy earlier today against the one appendage that kept thrashing around even after I stabbed the brain."

"Oh," Conrad responded, "ha, yes. I really do prefer to keep it clean, though." He took an enthusiastic drink of juice. "Anyway, my shift is up so I'll head home. Have a good rest of the evening."

"You too," he replied. "Remember—ten Kegels at every traffic light."

Nodding his approval of this advice, the lycanthrope departed.

And Remy took a deep breath and simply chilled. Things were okay, for the moment. Finally.

The only thing that threatened to undermine his growing relaxation was one simple fact—Moswen Neith was still alive. Or undead. And she didn't seem like the type to forgive a grudge.

Still, she might be the type to be scared off by a superior show of force. She and Taylor had finally met not long before and Taylor was good at superior force.

Optimism isn't always wrong, he decided. *Okay, it usually is but not always.*

He basked in the warm and fuzzy glow created by the half-digested pizza, not to mention the beer, that settled in his stomach and worked their magic on his brain—and liver, probably. In that moment, he very nearly felt like peace and normalcy was returning. To the extent, of course, that slaying monsters, spying on adulterous gnomes, and bribing fairies could ever be normal.

Yes, maybe Taylor whipped Moswen's ass hard enough that the sadistic bitch reconsidered her little plan to take over New York. She might be packing her bags even now and deciding to return to Israel permanently to rule over whatever hole in the desert she came from and calling it good.

Just maybe, she's decided to leave us alone once and for all.

He wasn't very drunk. Most of his powers of reason still remained to him. It was, therefore, only for a brief, overly-hopeful moment that he actually believed that was true.

Basement of a Warehouse, Flushing, New York City

Moswen Neith reclined on her throne. She had a way of sitting, learned over long years of aristocratic experience, which was at once languid and alert, simultaneously casual and filled with the dignity of command.

It was her preferred way to be seen when receiving guests. They instantly grasped that she held power and authority over them. And yet, at the same time, they would not make the mistake of assuming that she somehow regarded them as important.

In this instance, there were two guests. They had not come together and the business she had with each of them was separate. Although, naturally, both would work toward her overall agenda in their own ways.

She extended a hand and pointed at the first one with a long, black nail, then made a curling motion with the finger to beckon him forward. He stepped toward her grand chair.

Most of her thralls were away on various errands, advancing her interests according to her commands. She had retained a small honor guard as well as enough staff to see to her daily needs, fourteen persons in all.

Of these, ten had lined up to form a human corridor with their bodies, five on each side, which led the first guest directly to the foot of Moswen's throne.

"My friend," she intoned, "welcome."

It was a man, fifty-five or sixty in human years, who wore a crisp military uniform and a beret. He was tall and thin, bespectacled, and dour-looking, although people had once complimented him on the bright twinkle in his eyes.

Lately, however, his eyes looked dead and glassy, and those same people assumed he was merely tired.

"Mistress," he replied. "It's good to be here. What can I do for you?"

She crossed one long leg over the other and sat a little straighter to convey the importance of her coming request.

"I wish for you and your soldiers to capture a group of people. Their leader is a woman, Taylor Steele. At her right hand is an old man, Presley. With them also are three young men, all around thirty years old, who are called Remington, Warfield, and Thomas, and a short man, some-what older, called Volz. There is also a girl known only as Riley, and another woman called Diaz."

She paused as the officer nodded his head and ran the names through his head again.

"All of them," she continued, "are dangerous criminals. They will make great problems for us if they continue to go free. If possible, I want them captured and brought to me alive. But you have my permission to kill if you must. It is better for them to die than to escape. Is this clear?"

He gave a sharp, forceful nod. "Yes, ma'am—I mean, mistress. Your wish is my command, and my commands will be obeyed. By my men, that is. We pride ourselves on our competence and efficiency."

She detected a trace of sullen rebelliousness in him and contemplated igniting his brand for a moment, the better to completely dominate his spirit, but decided against it. Let him sulk and try to hide his secret thoughts. For now, he would do as he was told.

Besides, a man in his elevated position was far too useful to her to simply be discarded or punished arbitrarily. Soon, she would have the power to do as she wished with her servants, as was her birthright, but she would proceed cautiously.

For now, the world was still upside down and traitorous upstarts like Taylor were determined to keep it that way. Until she and her pets were out of the way, Moswen would have to be prudent.

Her wounds had long since healed but the memory of the pain was fresh. The seething anger it inspired only hardened her resolve to see her adversary broken, humiliated, and utterly destroyed.

"Good," was all she said to her waiting thrall. She waved her hand. "You are dismissed."

The man bowed and spun to march from the chamber, giving her a glimpse of the insignia patch on his sleeve—an eagle with outspread wings holding a clutch of arrows in its talons.

As he walked away, he slipped a cell phone out of his pocket and quick-dialed a number. "Hi," he said into the phone, his words clear to Moswen's hearing even as he stepped out of the chamber itself. "It's me. How are you doing, Lieutenant? Listen, since I'm now officially retired, I thought we should have a drink...maybe talk a few things over..."

Moswen pointed to the other guest and beckoned him forward.

The second man was about the same age as the military officer but otherwise, the two could not be more different. Where the soldier was tall, thin, and dour of face, the second man was short, fat, and possessed a nervous energy mixed with a slight arrogance.

"Good evening, mistress," he greeted her in his pleasant if unctuous fashion.

"Good evening," she replied, "Congressman."

CHAPTER FOUR

Abandoned Lot Near a Warehouse, Flushing, New York City

Don Gannon fumbled under his dashboard and retrieved a packet of gum. There were only two pieces left, unfortunately. He'd chewed through almost the entire pack in the course of a single day. No one had ever said that quitting smoking was easy.

"Hell," he muttered under his breath, "it'll give me a nice strong jawline again, I suppose." He removed and unwrapped one of the sticks of gum and popped it into his mouth.

The day wasn't too cold. Winter was on the wane and spring was already sending out feelers to determine if it was time to return yet. Of course, there would be more chilly weather, a little more snow here and there, and maybe one last blizzard that came out of left field simply to punish the good people of New York for being too presumptuous.

But the worst seemed to be over. And on a relatively

mild day like today, Don thanked whatever higher power might have existed for that.

He was getting old and could feel the frost in his bones. If he had saved his money better, he might already have been on his way to retirement in the legendary "Sixth Borough" of New York City, the one known as Miami, Florida.

Sadly, he couldn't keep the car running. It made a noise and generated perfectly visible smoke. That would have been counterproductive, to put it mildly.

Granted, his car wasn't all that well hidden there. Parked as he was beyond a fence and a half-wall with a miniature billboard-style sign to block most of the vehicle, it was not as though he were in plain sight from the warehouse, at least.

Still, a cursory examination by anyone who noticed a car parked across the lot would not pass muster.

But if that were the case, he could simply claim to be lost and in need of some time to himself, besides. Past sixty, haggard, unkempt, and poorly dressed, he knew he was a man who could easily pass for a borderline derelict, a barely functional old alcoholic who slept in his car more often than in his wife's bed. In fact, the kind of person one would expect to hang out in an abandoned lot for no identifiable reason.

Sometimes, there were advantages to looking like a crusty douchebag. No one ever assumed he was a journalist. He scratched his greying beard stubble and reached for his binoculars.

Today was Day Three of his stakeout. One of his sources had tipped him off that he ought to keep an eye on anyone coming and going from a particular seemingly boring and useless warehouse in northern Queens.

Of course, he had not watched the place at the same time of day each time. On the first day, he'd been there for a few hours in the afternoon. On the second day, he had borrowed a friend's car and staked out the lot in the morning.

And today, he had his own vehicle and had waited until after dark to arrive. In all three cases, he'd noticed guests coming and going.

There was a story there, and he would find it.

Once, he had been something of a rising star at the New England Inquirer. Sure, it was usually dismissed as a cheap, paranoid, gossipy type of publication and they'd never hit the big leagues.

But that wasn't the point. He'd broken his share of stories which had caught the attention of the so-called respectable press, which had gone on to commit their own, greater resources to further investigations. In a couple of cases, he'd even been cited and credited. Thanks to him, the Inquirer had gotten its day in the sun.

That day could come again.

He looked through the binoculars. A nearby streetlamp cast a cone of pale yellowish light on the walkway before the warehouse's entrance, and thanks to it, he'd noticed when two men had arrived about half an hour before. Their backs had been turned and he couldn't identify them.

The first one had already left. The second ought to be along at any moment now.

For another three or four minutes, he waited. Finally,

the door opened and a short, rotund man in early middle age slipped out. When he crossed to the street, he waddled through the light.

"Oh ho." The reporter chuckled, the sound faint and raspy. "That gentleman looks familiar, doesn't he? I'll be damned if it isn't US Representative Abel Dusek, in the flesh. Now, what could a politician of his caliber possibly be doing waltzing—alone—into an old warehouse like this? It's almost like he's meeting someone."

Don glanced at the pad of paper in his lap, picked his pencil up, and jotted the congressman's name, the location, the time, and the date.

All this information came at the end of a short list—that now spanned about two of the pad's pages—of other names and places and times he'd recorded over the last three days. The entry above it was simply *Unidentified US Army Officer—Colonel?*

And above that one were others, not as juicy but still rather interesting. A veritable cornucopia of people had visited this inconspicuous locale recently, most of them people he did not recognize.

But some seemed connected to certain others, on whom he had already collected dirt in the past.

Something was definitely going on. Quite possibly something big. He didn't really know anything yet. But despite his advancing age, he still had his instincts, his intuition, and his "reporter sense" that tingled when a conspiracy seemed to form before his eyes.

The Inquirer had—perhaps due to all the weird stuff happening lately—increased its circulation and its profits but not by much. It was still a small paper with a small staff. They had only five full-time reporters. Don Gannon got along well with all of them but one.

Unfortunately, that one was Jenny Ocren, who also happened to be their most popular and prolific writer, mainly because she was insane.

He knew that some people thought the Inquirer and its audience were as loopy as hell, but he also knew there were strange things in the world that needed to be investigated. For his part, he had always tried to strike a balance between probing the unknown and staying mostly within the realm of common sense.

Ms Ocren, however, seemed to actively court the loonies. As the old sayings went, birds of a feather flocked together or like attracts like and so forth.

Increasingly, Ocren's stories were the ones driving the uptick in sales. And Don, although nearing the age at which he ought to simply retire and be done with it, still had his pride. He'd be damned if he let the newspaper he'd worked for all these years go completely down the drain, increased sales or no.

He aimed to combat the decline the only way he knew how—by chasing the best scoops, uncovering the strangest and most attention-grabbing stuff, but coming to conclusions that weren't paranoid LSD trips in print form.

Besides, he knew a thing or two about LSD trips, anyway, although that was long in the past.

The aging man looked around him and double-checked with his binoculars to ensure that no one was watching him, coming toward him, or preparing to follow him. The lot and street were as quiet as a tomb—by New York standards, anyway.

He waited until he saw two cars drive past on the adjacent street. As the sounds of their motors drew closer, he turned the key and allowed his own engine to grind to life, glad that his day's work was done. He was even more glad to be able to run his heater.

The car might take a little extra abuse from accelerating right after starting it in chilly weather, but he didn't want to linger there. He pulled out after the second of the two passing cars and merged easily into the avenue.

No one followed him. He hoped that they—whoever they were, exactly—didn't have a lookout who'd glimpsed his license plate. But if that were the case, he might be screwed anyway.

The drive home proceeded in peace. He switched on the radio, frowned at most of what he heard, and finally settled on a classic rock station. They played the usual roster of songs that everyone had heard six hundred times by now, but he didn't mind. It was the musical equivalent of comfort food.

Absent-mindedly, he wondered how that Remington boy was doing. He was a recovering addict too, if Don recalled correctly, and had proven to be a fairly good source of tips, leads, and halfway decent hunches. He'd have to call him soon and maybe do coffee again.

Hopefully this time, though, Remy wouldn't try to role-play a scene from a goddamn spy movie or stealth shooter game. Even for a young person, he seemed to have a slightly tenuous grasp on reality.

"Kids these days," he mumbled, and reached for his last stick of gum.

Taylor's House, Harrison, Westchester County, New York

Remy's eyes flicked open before his brain was ready to comprehend anything they saw. It was too busy dealing with the horrible sound of his alarm.

"Uhhh." He drooled while one of his arms flapped outward, compulsively seeking the clock and the magical switch upon it which would make the noise go away. "Fuckin'...ugh. What?"

His fingers brushed the knob and he jabbed it fiercely. It clicked and the awful blaring returned to the depths of hell from whence it had come.

With an extended groan, he rolled onto his back, spread his arms, and stared at the ceiling. His room was still mostly dark—aside from the comforting glow of his neon beer sign, of course. There was also a slight nimbus of light coming from the windows. It was barely dawn.

He dragged himself forward, hauled his torso up through force of will, and assumed a seated position. Blearily, he rubbed the crusty gunk from his eyes and surveyed the room before him.

Three empty beer bottles stood on the floor instead of two like he had promised himself.

"Goddammit." He grunted. "At least that means that there are now zero in the fridge. It removes the temptation and shit."

Deep within him, something cringed and wheedled at the thought. He was left entirely without booze for the weekend. The immediate urge was to buy more as soon as he was done with work later today.

"No," he said and forced himself to stand. "I think we'll be perfectly fine for a few days. Sobriety isn't that bad."

Besides, he had martial arts lessons tonight. That ought to distract him and might even be inspiring or something. He had to admit he got a slight high from intense exercise.

He walked across the room, scratching himself. "So that's the deal with Conrad. Wonder Boy is a junkie, after all. Deprive him of exercise and health food for forty-eight hours and he'll be foaming at the mouth and offering hand jobs in a back alley in no time flat."

By now, he'd been there long enough for a sense of routine to settle in, so his hand reached out, largely without him having to think about it, and snatched his bathrobe off a hook as he passed it.

Remy stumbled into the bathroom, leaned over the sink, and turned on the hot side of the faucet. The water that emerged was cold at first, so he splashed it in his face and let it run a minute to bring the heated liquid to the upper floor of the house. After cracking his neck, he shut the faucet off and turned the shower on.

Months before, when he finally started to get serious about trying to live like a responsible adult for once, he had discovered that leaping more or less directly from the bed into the shower helped to wake him up more efficiently. It got his blood moving and blasted him out of the daze of half-consciousness more quickly.

Ideally, though, a shower should be followed by coffee. It was a good thing he now had a butler.

He stepped out of the bathroom and descended the

stairs. The pale glow of the early-morning sun seeped through the windows and made the house a touch less cavern-like than usual.

A short walk to the kitchen revealed Presley, who seemed to have been awake for a good hour already and who pressed the *On* button on the coffee pot as Remy entered.

He waved to the old man. "Morning there, Jeeves old boy. May I have some of that coffee? Also, where is Taylor? It's rapidly approaching Barbecue Hour for members of her species, so I kind of assumed she'd be back by now."

With a sigh, the butler turned toward him. Somehow, the steaming and burbling of the coffee maker seemed the perfect leitmotif to the old man's movements, even if, being British and all, he was probably more partial to tea.

"My name, sir," he observed, "is Presley, not Jeeves. Perhaps I ought to completely ignore you when you persist in behaving as though that were somehow still funny, as I can only assume you want attention."

Remy blinked. "What? Nonsense. I merely forgot your name, is all. I'm sure it happens all the time. Also, you should answer my other two questions."

"I will," Presley retorted, "be having a single cup of coffee myself, if you don't mind, and you may help yourself to the remainder. As for Miss Steele, she never returned after her early departure last night. I suspect she's left town."

"Left town?" he exclaimed. "What the hell for? That's...odd."

The old lycanthrope had opened a cupboard and taken out two ceramic mugs to set them on the counter beside the pot. "She did not bother to inform me where she was going or how long she'd be away, I'm afraid. Miss Steele invariably has good reasons behind the things she does."

The young man's mouth hung open a second. "But she didn't even tell me."

He almost winced when he realized how pouty and even hurt he'd sounded. For the moment, though, he couldn't really help it.

"I mean, I'm actually...you know, important to the stuff she's been doing lately." He coughed. "No offense, old boy. We all appreciate you manning the coffee pot and polishing stuff that mostly sits in dust-proof cabinets, anyway."

Presley sighed as he splashed milk into one of the mugs and added a spoonful of sugar. "Do you come up with these kinds of comments in the shower, sir, and then stash them away for later?"

"No, of course not." He stretched for the other, empty mug. On general principle, he preferred not to put sugar in coffee and to keep the cream to a minimum. "I merely do what comes naturally."

Both men poured themselves a cup and stood holding the steaming mugs, waiting a minute for the beverage to cool off enough to drink it.

"Presley," the younger man added, "sorry about the... shower comments. I stupidly had three beers instead of two. And I'll try to, you know, use your actual name."

The butler nodded. "Thank you, sir."

Remy sorted through his thoughts. Stupid and ridiculous though it was, Taylor running off for God knew how long and not even mentioning it to him made him feel almost…abandoned?

Hey, now, he chastised himself, *you specifically told her that she wasn't your mother, so don't start acting as though she is.* He nodded. That really was good advice.

He took a not quite scalding sip of the coffee. "Well, then. With her gone, at least I don't have to listen to her telling me to be careful and other such nonsense when she's also the one who thinks it's funny to send me after things that resemble sentient toilet clogs. Thanks for the coffee, J—er, Presley. I'll throw some clothes on and head into the office. There's shit that needs to get done."

The butler acknowledged this with a brief raise of his hand.

Remy trotted up the stairs, careful not to spill any coffee, and returned to his room to dress properly. He thought about having breakfast but decided he could always get Alex, the intern, to fetch some after he arrived. The poor bastard lived at the office so it wasn't as though he had anything better to do.

Once his shirt, tie, slacks. and jacket were back on his body where they belonged, he headed down to the garage. Presley noticed him but did not react. At least, not at first.

"Sir," the butler called as he stepped through the door at the end of the hallway. "Allow me to remind you that your car is parked outside, not in the garage."

He tried not to rub his hands together with glee. If by some chance Presley wolfed out and tried to physically stop him, he could always claim that he was merely opening the garage to move his car into it since Taylor was gone and all.

His actual plan, however, was to take one of her cars.

He snatched one of the keyrings off the wall, pressed the remote start button, and checked to see which car's headlights flashed. One of the myriad black Teslas responded although the lights were almost imperceptible under the heavy cover.

With a quiet chuckle, he strode over to the vehicle, threw the cover back, and was reclining comfortably in the driver's seat by the time Presley appeared in the doorway.

"Mr. Remington," he snapped, now visibly irritated, "Miss Steele did not give you any such permission."

Remy flapped a hand dismissively. "It's okay. What she doesn't know won't hurt her."

He pulled the door shut, but the butler yelled something, so he rolled the window down. "What?"

"I said," the old man snapped, "Mr. Warfield hasn't arrived yet and there are no guarantees that you'll be able to intercept him. It would be unwise to travel without his protection as per Miss Steele's instructions."

"Oh." He sighed. "Conrad. Right. Well, how much protection do I really need for simply going to the office? It's not like we'll go on another vampire hunt. Besides, he worked really hard yesterday, standing there waiting to wipe me clean after I killed that abomination and sweating all over my carpet while wearing disturbingly tight sportswear. Tell him to take the day off if you see him."

He rolled the window up and pulled out of the garage in time to clear the rising door. The black Tesla cruised down the driveway, down the hill, and out onto the street.

Once he was in the city, he realized that he still felt a little resentful. Somehow, it seemed as though Taylor still didn't consider him an equal partner. Still, he supposed it wasn't fair to take it out on Presley.

"Well," he mumbled, "I'm sure he's used to it by now."

For no real reason, he decided to take an alternate and slightly slower route into work. It wasn't like anyone was around to stop him.

CHAPTER FIVE

Moonlight Detective Agency Offices, Bushwick, Brooklyn, New York

Remington arrived at work about ten minutes later than usual. Given that it was a good forty-five-minute drive on a regular day, this meant he'd been on the road longer than he'd have liked. But at least he'd taken the scenic route for once.

"Randalls and Wards Islands. The conjoined islands. It's almost as if they were a single island. Mm, yup," he exclaimed as he pulled into the office's small parking lot. "And...uh, Maspeth, I guess. Such fascinating vistas of sights undreamed of. I wonder if Alex already thought to get donuts?"

He eased the Tesla into his usual place. Judging by the other vehicles present, they had no customers who currently demanded face-to-face service, which was probably just as well. However, both Andrew Volz, their dwarven tech specialist, and Roberta "Bobby" Diaz had already arrived.

When he stepped from the car and locked it, he noticed that it was shaping to be another cold, nasty day. Yesterday had been relatively tolerable. Not that he'd been able to appreciate it much while bathing in hideous slime during his exterminator duties.

Remy pushed through the front door and made eye contact with Bobby, who was seated behind the reception desk. She was an attractive blonde with a truly epic pair of business assets and, as usual, wore a tight, low-cut top to make the best of them. She looked surprised and even confused to see him.

"Oh," she stammered and frowned. "Uh...hi, Mr. Remington? I saw the car pull in so I kinda thought you were Ms Steele. Where is she, anyway?"

He shrugged in an exaggerated, dramatic way. "I dunno. I think she ran off with an old boyfriend or something. No, she didn't, I made that up. Her butler said she left last night on business of some kind and she isn't back yet."

Bobby nodded, not greatly troubled.

"Okay," she went on as he hung his coat and scarf, "we have a pile of messages and stuff to go through. Honestly, it'd probably be easier if I put the answering machine on the speaker so you can listen to them all yourself while you get coffee. I still have to type the reports up anyway."

"Sure," he agreed. "I don't suppose the intern has procured breakfast of some kind?"

"Um..." Bobby looked doubtful. "I'm not sure what 'procured' means, but last night, I think Taylor sent Alex off to do some kind of overnight errand so he isn't here. Does that answer your question?"

It did and he nodded. He frowned and reminded

himself bitterly of how terrible and unhealthy donuts were, anyway, and especially when he'd eaten two-thirds of a pizza the night before.

He trudged toward his personal office in the far corner and resolved to wait for a couple of minutes before he downed his second cup of coffee of the morning. Bobby, meanwhile, flipped a couple of switches and the answering machine disclosed its secrets to the entire office.

Beep.

"Uh...hi." The voice of the first caller floated from the ceiling's speakers. "I'm George Bilansky. I was in about three weeks ago? I was wondering...did you ever, you know, get the photographs and chatlogs I requested? I mean, obviously, you can't take a picture of her if she didn't actually go there, to begin with, ha-ha. But I kinda wanted an update as to whether you've found anything."

Remy sniffled as he stepped into his office. "Don't worry, George," he muttered. "If we discover that your daughter really is falling in with the ol' Beelzebub worshipers up on 21st, you'll be the first to know. Downloading black metal albums and the new *Doom* expansion doesn't really count, though."

He dumped his minimal gear on the floor beside the desk and booted his computer up. In addition to the various cases they had in progress, there was also still accounting-type stuff to deal with. That was not his favorite task, although at least he was good at it. His parents' business acumen had rubbed off on him over the years.

Beep.

"Okay," said the next voice, which Remy identified as

belonging to the third-party, conventional private eye to whom they'd outsourced menial tasks, "about the whole missing persons case."

The investigator sat and spread the papers Bobby had left on his desk so he could view each one individually while the PI's message continued.

"It seems like many of these people are either from northern Queens, or they were last seen in that vicinity before they disappeared. Also, one of my contacts reported seeing a group of suspicious characters—you know, dark-suit types dressed way too nicely for the neighborhood—standing around at an old warehouse in Flushing. I'd rather give you the address in person so you can look forward to me stopping by soon."

"Awesome," Remy quipped. He stood and left his office, deciding the time had come to venture to the coffee machine.

Beep.

"Hello," a silky, almost ethereal female voice said, and Remy froze in place. "I wanted to thank you for doing such a good job taking care of my...plumbing problem. I'd like to settle our bill via conventional mail if that's okay."

He shuddered. Honestly, he should have expected that such a nice, beautiful Elven lady would end up being responsible for what he'd had to deal with yesterday.

"Of course," he muttered.

As he passed through the lobby area, Bobby waved to him. "Mr. Remington. That last one reminded me of something I thought you'd like to hear about. I read about it yesterday after work."

Remy wasn't sure he was in the mood but he slowed enough for her to at least begin to speak.

The receptionist had never been initiated into the preternatural. As far as she knew, Taylor was simply a pale woman who preferred to work nights, Riley the fairy was a perky girl who showed up occasionally as a freelancer, and Volz was merely short.

Curiously enough, however, she was an avid reader of The New England Inquirer and therefore believed in all kinds of loopy stuff, only not the correct loopy stuff, even when real evidence was all around her.

But she was not the sharpest tool in the proverbial shed, anyway, so he wasn't too worried about it.

"So," she began, "there's this guy over in the East Village. He flushed his toilet and turned on the shower, and all this blood came out. He thought maybe an animal was stuck in the pipes or something. But he took a blood sample to a biologist at the college, and this doctor can't even identify the species."

Uh-oh, Remy thought. *That fucking blood golem a couple of weeks ago got farther than I thought before it dissolved. It sounds like we need to mindwipe a normie—except, of course, Taylor isn't here to handle it.*

Ms Diaz continued to prattle away, essentially repeating what she'd read in the latest Jenny Ocren story.

"...that when the Saturnians first made contact, they taught mankind how to genetically engineer androgynous warrior-angels out of blood that was contaminated with various STDs. Well, the people who are in the know suspect that this is tied to how the ODESSA organization was developing a new super-strain of AIDS and preparing to—"

"Yes, intriguing," Remy interrupted hastily. "I'll have a look at this week's Inquirer a little later. If you'll excuse me, I need coffee now." He hastened toward the break area in the back.

As he rounded a corner, he passed Volz. The dwarf, relatively thin for his species but still short and as solid as a boulder by human standards, chuckled quietly as he plunked away on one of the general staff computers.

"Hi, Volz," he said. "How are all the improvements coming along? Usually, I don't even notice when you add yet another one, which means you must be doing a really good job."

"Splendidly," the dwarf rumbled. "I'm removing the ability of bumbling human hackers to acquire access to any of the audio recorded by our security systems. It's quite easy. I simply hadn't gotten to it before now."

Remy nodded and finally approached the short table where the coffee machine stood. He took a cup from those provided. "That sounds potentially useful, I think. By the way, it occurred to me that you never really commented on the matter of us...uh, you know, completely massacring the Surrly-Greyhammer cartel. No hard feelings, right?"

A low grinding sound emerged from somewhere in Volz's throat.

"Hard feelings, yes, but not toward you or Taylor. Members of that very cartel were the ones responsible for ruining my prior business, as you ought to recall. It is not pleasant to see so many dwarves get themselves killed, but..."

He trailed off and shook his head, then resumed. "If they play stupid games, they must expect to win stupid prizes. Such as death and destruction, for example. I thought they'd know better than to sell preternatural drugs to humans, not to mention declaring war on Taylor. Allowing that barbarian Greyhammer to lead them simply because he looked impressive was their first and last mistake."

The investigator considered this and decided he believed it. Volz wasn't the lying type. Besides, the entire reason he worked for the agency these days was a direct result of the cartel's perfidy.

"So," he added, "have you seen Riley? We haven't really needed her but I get curious as to how she's doing, et cetera." He added a single packet of non-dairy creamer to the bottom of his cup and poured coffee on top of it.

Volz replied at once. "I have not. I assumed she had returned to her nest, and I have been busy with other things."

Remy frowned. The fairy had...problems. He thought he'd helped her out of the worst of them, but it was tough to be sure.

"Well..." He sighed. "The last I heard—as in a couple of days ago—she wasn't home, so who knows what she's out doing? I'll check on her later. We've all been fairly busy lately."

As he strolled to his office, stray thoughts began to weave themselves together within his mind. Months before, he would have thought this was paranoia, but with all he'd learned since autumn, reality was a far more likely explanation.

Moswen Neith was still out there. They did not know what she was up to yet and Taylor, Riley, and Alex were all unaccounted for.

He didn't want to get to his accounting work yet and also didn't want anyone to hear him spamming Taylor with nervous check-in calls. It would look bad. So instead, he left the building via the side exit and wandered outside.

Their office was positioned in a relatively disused part of town. The car park off to the side still enjoyed a little business, but not much. As he walked toward it, he saw only a couple of empty vehicles there.

He pulled his phone out and dialed Taylor's cell number.

It rang, which was a good sign, he supposed.

"Come on," he muttered after the seventh ring. "Pick up, Taylor."

After the twelfth, the ringing stopped and was replaced by a prerecorded female voice. "The number you are trying to reach has been disconnected and is no longer in service. Please try again."

"What?" He snapped. "Try again when you literally said that it'd be pointless to do so? Who wrote the script for that recording? For fuck's sake."

He slipped his phone into his pocket again. If he smoked, which he didn't, he'd probably need a cigarette right now. He wouldn't have minded a drink, either.

Shaking his head in the cold air, he turned back toward the building to get to work.

At that moment, something exploded. Vivid blue light flashed in front of him, above, and around him and streamed through the office's windows. From within the structure came a rumbling boom.

"Holy shit!" Remy yelled. Before he even knew what he was doing, he broke into a sprint and barged through the door. There was no obvious damage that he could see outside.

As he burst into the building itself, the part of his brain responsible for things like rational thought reminded him that he might well have hurled himself directly into a trap.

Despite the inner caution, he jogged down the hall and into the main central floor area, then he forced himself to a stop. His eyes attempted to scan everywhere at once.

Everything looked essentially normal.

Volz lay on the floor, though, having fallen backward in his chair. The computer he'd been working at was still on and the dwarf himself was alive and not visibly injured.

"Volz," he said and leaned forward with a hand extended to help him up, "are you okay? What the hell was that?"

The dwarf's big, strong hand engulfed his and he began to heave himself upward. "Uhhh…" He uttered what could have been a moan. "That…was…weeeeiiiird…" His eyes rolled and almost glazed over.

Remy squinted. Something wasn't quite right, but his best guess was that Volz was discombobulated. It happened to everyone, especially when caught in the middle of a strange explosion of light.

Leaving the dwarf to recover, he jogged toward the reception desk to check on Bobby. She, too, looked more or less okay. From what he could guess, she must have kick-rolled her chair back when the blast had struck and was now perched awkwardly against the wall behind her desk.

A parcel delivery guy stood near the entrance. His back was propped against the other wall, opposite Bobby.

"Huh," he mused, tapped his lips, and surveyed the scene.

The delivery boy was someone he hadn't seen before but judging by the stunned look on his face, whatever had happened had surprised him as much as everyone else. He must merely be a new guy.

Logically, there was also a parcel on the reception desk. It was half-open and he walked toward it.

"You," he said to the parcel courier, "are dismissed. Thanks." If by some chance they needed to check in on him, they'd have footage of him on the security cams and could go from there.

The young man blinked. "Uhhhhhhhhh…" He stretched the sound out so long that Remy was afraid he might drool on the floor.

With a sigh, he took his arm and more or less helped him out the front door. There was no delivery truck visible out front, so he must have parked around the corner. With him sent on his way, he hurried back into the office.

By now, Bobby had rebalanced herself and regained her composure, although her eyes bulged and she looked around constantly as if this was the first time she'd ever seen their lobby—or any other lobby, for that matter.

"Are you okay?" he asked.

She nodded so he turned to the package.

It was unremarkable—brown paper around an oblong cardboard box about a foot in length like something a thermos would come in. Within the box was absolutely nothing. It looked like there was a small coating of royal blue powder smudged against the inside in a couple of places, but that was it.

"Shit," Remy mumbled. Was it some kind of gift from a client that had accidentally teleported itself to its home dimension? An anti-vampire neutron-bomb-type weapon sent by Moswen that didn't harm other species? If that was the case, Taylor was right to be far away.

He was still considering the possibilities when Bobby wheeled herself to the desk and contributed to the examination.

"Wait," she said, her voice sharper and more hurried than usual. "I get it! Seriously, it's obvious when you look at it. Look—no postmark. This was never processed by an actual parcel delivery service, let alone the post office. And that return address is bullshit. That ZIP code doesn't even exist. It's a Jersey ZIP but they attached it to a town in upstate New York. And last but not least, I've never seen that delivery man before. We were targeted by someone who tried to cover their tracks."

Remy's mouth had fallen open in the middle of her spiel and for a second, he was afraid that he, like the parcel guy, was on the verge of drooling.

"Bobby," he asked, "are you...on something? No offense, but—"

"Shit!" she exclaimed and pointed out the front door, "he's getting away! We should question him."

He spun and barged out the door, but the unmarked pickup truck containing the delivery gentleman was already rumbling out into the road. It wove alarmingly as it barreled down the street as though the driver was drunk.

Irritated, he smacked himself on the forehead. Bobby was right, he should have pursued him. He'd merely been so surprised. Normally, Ms Diaz couldn't deduce that a hamburger had once been a ground beef patty and now, suddenly, she'd deduced what had happened even before he had.

And, he marveled, *since when is she an expert on ZIP codes? When we first put her on the payroll, she screwed up her own address.*

Back inside, Bobby had come out from behind the reception desk and held her head in her hands. "My God." She gasped. "It's all coming together. This isn't a regular detective agency, is it? That crap I read about in the Inquirer—half of it is true and you guys are the ones who deal with it!"

Remy stared at her for a moment. *Ohhhhh, hell.*

"Bobby," he stated, "since you…ah, no offense, but seem to have suddenly gained a considerable number of IQ points, I think we need to have a talk. Will you step into my office?"

She took a deep breath. "I can tell from your body language, timbre of voice, and facial micro-expressions that you're probably not lying and it's not a ruse to kill me for having discovered the truth," she said, "so okay, sure."

They flipped the sign on the front door to *CLOSED* and sat in his office. He told her everything, basically. Not the juiciest details—particularly those that might have made him look bad—but enough.

"Taylor, you see," he concluded as he twirled a pen

between his fingers, "has essentially kept a lid on all the preternatural stuff in the Greater New York Metropolitan Area for, like...I don't know, a few decades, at least. I'm not even sure how old she is. In any event, this agency is her front. And all of us—especially me, of course—are on the front lines, keeping order, maintaining plausible deniability, and protecting the good people of this fair city or whatever."

He paused and exhaled. "Welcome aboard."

Bobby nodded. She seemed to be taking it well.

"So," she surmised, "Taylor must have hired you as bait since you're good at doing irresponsible things that draw tons of attention. And you must have hired me to distract any male human officials who come in."

Remy suddenly broke the pen in half and showered his right hand with spilled ink. "I—whuh...no," he stammered. "You don't—fuck—ahhh..." He trailed off and hung his head. "Never mind."

"It's okay, whatever," she went on. "That package must have contained some kind of...magical bomb, a spell triggered by opening it, which affected the cognitive abilities of everyone in the building. I... God, I feel like I've woken up from a really good dream."

She grinned openly. "And I knew it. I knew that there was way more going on in our world than most people think. Most people always thought I was fairly dumb but I was right, goddammit! Okay, the Inquirer has to be wrong about some of it but at least I was on the right track."

Remy had to smile. "True."

Bobby's face fell back into seriousness as her souped-up brain returned to overdrive. "But who could have sent it?

Moswen? It augmented me with no negative effects, at least not so far. Why would she help us?"

Their eyes met and apparently, they both reached the same conclusion at the same time.

"Man the front desk," he instructed her. "I'll check on Volz."

She nodded and hurried to her post. He rushed around the corner to the computer desk where the dwarf still sat and no longer typed and flicked through tabs but instead, stared dumbly at the glowing screen.

I don't like where this is going. Not at all.

"So, Volz," he began. "Were you able to bypass the encryption sequences that were circumnavigating the defibrillation autoimmune destabilizers? Or the...uh, pseudo-disetablishmentarian neuroinhibitors determining the elliptical non-Euclidean framerates of the...carburetors?"

Dammit. I ran out of big words, he cursed himself. *Wait, I should have used 'polysaccharides' somewhere in there.*

Volz turned and looked at him, his brow furrowed and jaw slack. "Whuh? I don't...speak that. Does that mean this thing? I like the light it makes." He gestured at the computer screen.

Remy raised a hand to his face and pinched the bridge of his nose. "Fuck," he stated.

CHAPTER SIX

Fluttershire Fairy Colony, Fort Washington Park, New York City

Remington was grateful to have one of the vaunted Steele Estate Teslas today since it occurred to him that his Lincoln was becoming a too-familiar sight at the park.

By now, someone had to have noticed that he visited constantly, parked in the same place, and walked over to a particular mound of earth right next to the base of the George Washington Bridge.

He'd developed an alibi months before. "Well," he'd planned to say, "according to Wikipedia, the George Washington is the world's busiest motor vehicle bridge, with total traffic of one hundred and three million vehicles in 2016 alone, that being the last year for which we have reliable statistics, for some reason. I simply have to come and see it in person every once in a while. I'll never stop being awed by things that are superlatives in their respective categories."

Fortunately, he'd never had to use it, at least so far.

Another thing he had never needed to do, though, was seek help from the Fair Folk in determining how to undo a malevolent curse that bumped everyone in a building into opposite brackets of the intelligence spectrum. The preternatural slowly made more and more sense to him, but true magic was still mostly uncharted territory.

"Okay," he muttered as he stepped out of the car and made sure his special care package was in hand and concealed behind his back. "Let's go argue with all the little flappy dickheads. Again."

The mild weather over the last couple days had melted the inch or so of snow they'd had previously. Unfortunately, that meant he had to trudge through mud instead of snow.

He reached the usual place but no fae were in sight. It was only a matter of time, so he waited.

After a moment, one of the guards noticed him. "Cease! Desist!" a tiny voice snapped. "Do not think you can sneak up on us."

"Yes," added another voice from the other direction. "Oh, how clever you think you are. You probably imagine that we don't know why you're here. We know well."

Like one half of an elderly couple who have the same argument once a week, year after year, Remy took a deep breath, released it slowly, and resigned himself to his fate.

"Hi, guys," he said.

Two humanoids about the size of his hand, both with iridescent dragonfly wings, floated toward him from each corner of his field of vision. One had blue-tinted skin and the other's coloration was a bright orange.

"So," the blue one stated waspishly. "You've come to

inculcate Riley in your devious outlander's ways again. And without even having the courtesy to bow."

That's a new one.

"Okay, I'll—"

"No," the other cried. "Bowing alone will not buy you our trust after all the nothing you've ever done for us."

Aside from bringing you a gift every single time I come here. He bit his tongue to keep from blurting that little fact out loud.

"You know, guys," he drawled, "I'm really not in the mood today. Let's skip the informalities. I have a treat for you and you can have it if you bring me Riley or at least tell me where she is. The End."

The blue one drew back in midair and made scoffing noises. "You dare? Riley has slept for almost two days after too much time spent in the world of humans!"

The orange one had fluttered around Remy's right elbow. "You speak of treats, yet you hide the proof? What is in that bag? Deceiver."

"I was getting to that," Remy pointed out. He brought the bag out where both could see it. A few other fairies had floated up as well and they all stared at him. "Bring me Riley and it's all yours."

He reached in and produced not only the usual two bottles of honey but also a rectangular cardboard box.

"This," he announced, "is microwaveable New-York-style pizza. Your favorite. Assuming someone in your colony can magically replicate microwaves, you can use this to make your very own pizza whenever you want it. It's not as good as the real thing, but still, this is the expensive kind from the fancy part of the frozen foods aisle."

For a moment, there was silence. Then, it seemed the entire colony reacted much like a typical Times Square crowd when the New Year's ball dropped.

"Oh! Ha-ha! Heeeee!" one of them shrieked and darted up to kiss Remy on the forehead, while the others swarmed him and snatched the food items out of his hands.

"Long live Remyyyyyy!" another cheered.

It only took about two minutes for them to retreat to their lair with their new treasures, and for Riley to emerge.

She wafted out of the ground rather slowly, he thought. And even if she had slept for the last eighteen or twenty hours, she still looked wasted.

"Riley," he greeted her. "It's good to see you. Are you okay?"

"Hi, Remy," she replied and fluttered her tiny eyelashes. "I'm sleepy."

He frowned and tried to keep himself calm. She was still beautiful, of course, with a shapely figure, symmetrical face, and thick platinum hair, but she looked like she'd been on an extended drug binge or alcohol bender.

He'd been on many of those himself over the years.

Goddammit. I thought we already had this discussion. I tried to help her. Clearly, I didn't do enough.

Trying to sound firm but warmly concerned, he asked, "You haven't been going to the mall, have you? We both agreed that you'll be much happier when you don't keep doing that."

The fairy was not addicted to any chemical substance, he had learned, but to attention. A few weeks before, she'd almost been arrested with her constant, almost desperate exploits to get men to flirt with her, buy her shit, and lavish praise on her.

"That," she retorted, "is none of your business."

"We'll see," he murmured. "But please talk to me if you have a problem, okay? Anyway, I have a problem myself and you're the only one who can help me right now."

She perked up a little. Feeling needed always seemed to improve her condition. "What's wrong?"

He swallowed. "You might not believe this, but…"

To the best of his ability, he summed up everything that had happened since he'd awoken that morning—Taylor's absence, Alex's absence, and the stupidity-affecting mail bomb.

"Wow," Riley gasped. "Boobs is smart now? That's so weird. I want to see."

"Come along, then. Without Taylor around, I don't know who else to turn to." His stomach clenched at having to admit that.

She requested a short intermission to improve her condition and he agreed since technically, he'd rolled her out of bed. She flitted into the nest.

It took about five minutes. Even when she had lived with him for a few days on end here and there, he'd never entirely understood how her species kept themselves presentable. Whatever they did, it seemed to work.

She emerged looking lovely. Somehow, there was almost no trace of the wan, haggard look she'd developed, and her hair and dress were smooth and shiny.

"Mkay, nicely done," Remy commented.

"Thank you," she responded and beamed.

"Now, let's get moving. I'm not sure I trust Volz, in his

current state, not to stick a fork into a wall socket or something. I only hope Bobby is keeping an eye on him."

Moonlight Detective Agency Offices, Bushwick, Brooklyn, New York

During the half-hour drive to the office, they mostly talked about minor things. Remy discussed stuff that had happened at Taylor's house lately and Riley discussed her current preoccupations and the course of the weather.

He'd hoped to get some information out of her regarding whether or not she'd been on another shopping and flirting spree but she dodged around the subject.

Later, I'll come down harder on her, he resolved, *but for now, I need her a little too much to risk pissing her off or sending her into an emotional breakdown.*

When they arrived, he immediately blew out his breath in relief to see that the building had not burned down. That was always encouraging.

Bobby greeted him as he stepped through the door. "Hi again, Mr Remington. So far, so—holy shit! Is that..."

It took him a moment to realize that she was referring to Riley. She'd never seen the fairy in her true form before, only when she'd shapeshifted to human size. The preternatural was often invisible to humans who hadn't been initiated or lacked the necessary perception.

"Riley," Remington said. "You met her before, but she was bigger. This is actually her normal state so you might as well get used to it."

"Hello!" the fairy said cheerfully.

Bobby stared for a minute before her face broke into a

grin. "I've loved fairies ever since I was a little girl. Aww, she's so cute."

"Later," Remy began, thinking of all the important things going on, "I'll let you two get better acquainted but for now, we really need her to focus on unraveling what the hell happened with the big blue flash."

The receptionist's face went serious again. "Right. I understand. By the way, Volz seems to have been struck with...well, some fairly serious cognitive impairment. I have him in your office with a few markers and one of my coloring books, so he should be fine."

He nodded. "Good." He and his tiny companion faced one another.

"Riley, I'm sure you can already see or smell the magical residue in here. What I'd like you to do is analyze the nature of the spell. What, exactly, did it do and how? Where did it come from? Who cast it? Stuff like that."

The fairy's nose was already twitching and she glanced at patches of the walls that looked perfectly normal to human eyes. "Yes, there's considerable magic here. Powerful stuff, too."

That already answered one of his questions.

Riley set to work. A faint silver glow appeared around her hands and behind her eyes as she floated about the office to touch, peer at, and sniff things. She paused occasionally to think and in this way, conducted a thorough inspection in general.

While she worked, he went into his office and spent about fifteen minutes chipping away at invoices. Volz was on his hands and knees on the floor, ravaging Bobby's coloring book with a green Sharpie.

Finally, the fairy floated in through the door. "Okay," she reported, "I think I know most of what's going on. I worry that it's...hard to talk about, though." She glanced at the dwarf, who ignored her.

Remy looked up from his computer. "Right. Hey, Bobby? Could you come in here and...uh, escort Volz to the other side of the building for a few minutes? We need a little privacy."

The receptionist walked in and took Volz by the arm, talking to him the way one would coax a young child and convincing him, after a moment, that she had something even more fun to do in the break area.

"But," she quipped, "let me know once you have all the facts and I can help put them together now. God, this is so exciting. I can't wait to do advanced deductive reasoning. I think I've already guessed most of it."

She closed the door behind her with her foot and left him and the fairy alone together.

"Right," Remy stated briskly. "Give it to me raw, I guess."

She spread her hands. "The spell was designed to reverse everyone's thinking abilities. I think the idea was that since we're all fairly smart, it would turn us into...well, like how Volz is. For some reason, though, it had the opposite effect on Boobs."

My God. Remy shook his head. It was truly amazing and he could not say a word for a moment. *Bobby was so stupid, to begin with, that the dumbification spell backfired on her. If you ask me, there ought to be an official world record for that.*

"I see," he acknowledged and kicked himself mentally

for his thoughts about Bobby. She'd never been anything but nice to him. "How long will it last?"

"I have no idea." Riley shrugged. "Spells like this are really hard to understand when it comes to stuff like that. It was prepared by someone who's even better than I am. Someone scary-good."

Dread crept up his spine at that while his abdomen clenched. "As in morally good, or did you mean 'so good at magic that it's scary?'"

"The second one," she clarified.

He ran a hand through his hair and adjusted his tie. "Yeah, that's what I was afraid of. But why? What did we do that provoked this, and to whom? Of course, Moswen is the obvious answer, but I'm not sure this is her style. She's more the brute-force type."

They sat in silence for a moment before he stood. "Well, let's get Boobs in here since apparently she's now the smartest person in the office."

Volz was completely absorbed in watching one of those surreal cartoon-pig videos on a streaming website that she had pulled up, which freed the receptionist to contribute to the investigation.

"Wow," she commented. "This is heavy stuff. It's not that complicated but it's still mind-blowing in a way."

By now, Remy had summed up everything the fairy had told him. Although, of course, he'd omitted any specifically judgmental-type comments on Bobby's mental abilities prior to being ensorcelled.

She tapped her lips with two fingers. "Well, I basically surmised most of that myself based on the clues plus what I've read over the years. And as it so happens, I noticed some fairly suspicious threads running through those messages this morning. In fact, I put most of it in my reports. They're done already, by the way."

He raised an eyebrow, genuinely impressed. "Excellent. Can I have the short verbal preview right now?"

"Sure." Bobby put her left hand on her left hip and gestured with her right as she spoke. "So, that private detective, Detullio, has already traced some of the activity we're looking at to Flushing in north Queens. And he previously interviewed this guy—I put his name in the report—who said he saw something suspicious."

Nodding, Remington waited for the bombshell or at least a halfway-decent conclusion.

"But the really interesting thing is that I think Detullio is holding something back. Like what he said about wanting to come in and talk to us in person. Either he saw something weird—something preternatural—himself, or the other guy did. I suggest that you should study my reports, talk to Detullio, and then ask him where you can find Mr Weird Interview. You know, so you can corroborate all the information."

He took a moment to run his tongue along his teeth and his gaze went distant as he turned this over in his mind. "Yeah, that sounds like a plan. Frankly, I can't think of anything better."

Riley buzzed over. "Will you take me?"

"Aye," he affirmed. "You're kind of necessary. Since the office was magic-bombed, though, I don't want to leave Bobby and Volz here unprotected, even considering her advanced brainpower. So…"

He pulled his phone out and dialed Conrad's number.

"Hi, Conrad. Are you available?"

The lycanthrope responded at once. "Yes, sir, do you need me?"

"We do. Riley and I need to go investigate something and someone targeted the office with a cognitive-inversion spell cleverly disguised as a thermos box. You know how it is. I'm sorry about calling you in halfway into what I previously said would be your day off but at least you won't have to deal with me, though."

The man hesitated before he spoke. "That's...true, yes. I'll be right in."

"Beautiful, thanks." He hung up and looked at the receptionist. "Conrad is a werewolf, by the way. Yes, he can be somewhat annoying at times, but if anyone fucks with you, he'll rip their head off. And I mean that literally. I've seen him physically remove heads. So, you'll be safe."

She looked a little uncomfortable at that but nodded.

Everyone drifted out to the lobby, and he checked on Volz quickly, who drooled slowly into his reddish whiskers as awful, Flash-animated talking animals pranced about on the screen before him.

"Riley," Remington intoned, "we'll leave as soon as I've read those reports and Wonder Boy gets here."

"Okay," she replied. She looked somewhat distracted. Less delay would be better so as to keep her mind from wandering toward the mall.

Before they left, though, he headed outside again and attempted another call.

The phone rang a dozen times, as it had earlier, and kept ringing. He didn't get a robotic voice telling him that

Taylor's cell was out of service but he didn't get an answer, either.

"Dammit, Taylor," he grated. "This is not the time for you to visit your great-uncle in Carfax Abbey or what the fuck ever."

He stepped inside in time to see that they had a visitor.

Someone backed through the front door, a blond man about Remy's height and age, who held a couple of boxes that appeared to be brimming with donuts.

"Afternoon," Alex announced in his Australian accent. "I'm a little late for breakfast, aren't I? Not that it's ever too late for donuts. Taylor had me out chasing my fellow members of the Oz ex-pat community. I have no idea why, unless she thought it would be funny to remind me of how arse-backward your seasons are up here."

He set the baked goods on the reception desk and looked at everyone. His brow creased into a frown when he realized that something was off.

"So," he asked in a quieter tone and his gaze grew a tad shifty. "What did I miss?"

Remy raised a hand, palm outward. "Hold on a minute," he instructed, "while I try to think of where to begin."

CHAPTER SEVEN

Ben Gurion Airport, Israel

Shortly before her plane landed, Taylor excused herself to the bathroom, where she'd applied sunscreen lotion to her exposed face and neck. The flight had eaten up the remainder of the night and the sun was recently risen, although she had managed to mostly shield herself from it with her hat and scarf.

But there was still a certain amount of pain. She'd also had to apply subtle command powers to the people near her to keep them from noticing the rather severe sunburn she'd begun to develop.

Now, finally, her feet were back on the earth, although the deadly fireball was already rising in the sky and threatened to make her efforts that much more difficult.

Emerging from her flight and navigating the airport had not been difficult. There were a few routine security procedures, but the fact that El Al had permitted her to board in the States, to begin with, carried enough weight to expedite the process. It was little more than a passport check, customs, and an official reading her the basics.

Now, she stood near the curb and waited for a suitable taxi to drive past as she gazed at the landscape through her dark-tinted glasses.

There was grass there, but she perceived the dry, rocky soil beneath. It wasn't full desert—the land was not totally barren until one pressed farther inland and more to the south—but still, it was so different from the moist, temperate, and sometimes chilly landscapes around New York.

Or England, for that matter.

A cab approached and something about its driver gave off the right vibration. Relieved, she flagged it down and it slowed to a stop directly in front of her.

She'd been about to simply climb into the back seat and pull her suitcase in with her, but her phone buzzed in her pocket at that precise moment. During the brief distraction, the driver exited, took her luggage, and loaded it into the rear compartment while she slipped the cell from her coat.

She glanced at the screen, frowned, and returned the device to its abode almost immediately. Then, she seated herself and allowed the driver to close the door for her.

He returned to his position behind the wheel and looked at her with an inquisitive arch to his thick eyebrows. A portly, olive-skinned man in late middle age, he struck her as a reliable, professional sort, although something about her exotic appearance had intrigued him all the same.

"Hello, and thank you for taking my bag," she said. "Do you speak English?"

She had a rudimentary grasp of Hebrew and was moderately fluent in Arabic, but sticking to English would fit better with her assumed travel persona.

"Yes," the man confirmed. "Where are you going?"

She gave him the address of a hotel west of Jerusalem where she'd booked a room during the flight.

"That is long drive," he remarked, "but I can take you." He pointed to a sign which displayed a detailed breakdown of the cab company's rates.

"Yes," she responded. "That is fine."

As expected, he ventured a few friendly questions during the trip but only enough to satisfy his basic curiosity. He did not pry beyond that. Taylor gave him the same story she'd told the security officer at JFK. It wasn't too far from the truth, anyway.

When they arrived at her destination, she asked a question of her own before she stepped out.

"There is another place I must go," she began. "Can you wait ten or fifteen minutes for me to check in at this hotel? I can pay you for it."

She calibrated her voice with the right mixture of undertones. A small touch of imperious confidence, a dash of feminine vulnerability, and the suggestion of an appeal to his professional duties. She was unsurprised when he agreed.

"Thank you. I will get my own suitcase if you open the boot. Trunk. Rear, whatever."

He chuckled and nodded.

Taylor climbed out, retrieved her luggage, and approached the hotel, an off-white building of understated elegance hemmed in by lovely palm fronds. As she climbed the broad steps and entered the reception area through the front doors, she could feel the driver's continued fascination. He wanted to know where she was going next.

It was almost a shame that, after he'd taken her there, she would have to ensure that he forgot. He might dream vaguely of a small, dark, woman who had stirred his curiosity, but none of the details of her visit to his country would remain in his memory.

Most definitely, it would be safer for everyone that way.

The hotel's lobby matched its exterior. It was bright, clean, modern, subtly beautiful, and somewhat minimalistic. In a surprisingly wistful mood, she could not help contrasting the place to the older, European style of ornate luxury she was once accustomed to.

At the reception desk, she showed her reservation credentials to an energetic young woman who spoke excellent English and seemed rather distracted. She must have had plans for the evening. As such, the girl did not bother to ask unnecessary questions about sunburn and the check-in process took only a few minutes.

Taylor accepted her keycard with a nod and a smile and went to find her room, which was on the second floor. Sleeping away from the earth might prove difficult, but it also gave her a small amount of extra security since the hotel's only side exits were fire escapes, complete with alarms.

The vampire wasted no time. She examined the room quickly—nice, unspecial, and serviceable—and retrieved a couple of things she might need from her suitcase. Briskly, she closed and locked the case, slid it into the back of the closet, and returned to her cab.

The driver gave no sign of being irritated by waiting for her. She'd taken only ten and a half minutes, well within the range of time she'd suggested.

"Thank you," she said again. "Now, the place I need to go to is in Jerusalem itself. Again, I am sorry for the long drive, but I am willing to pay and you're helping me so much by doing this."

The man half-smiled. "Yes. Where in Jerusalem? I may not be able to go all the way to far eastern part…"

She gave him the address.

"Ah," he acknowledged, "that is in the west. Good. Only a few more kilometers."

They passed close to the Jerusalem Forest on the slopes of the Judean Mountains, en route to the small, relatively out of the way commercial district that was her ultimate destination. It wasn't too far from the Old City, either.

For a moment, she wished she had more time to simply explore the area and take in its rich if turbulent history. It was rare for religious iconography to have any adverse effect on her unless it was specifically enchanted to do so. Otherwise, she liked feeling a connection to things from the past and Jerusalem had no shortage of those.

The cab driver glanced up. "We are almost there."

"Ah, good." Taylor smiled. "I think it would be nicer in the evening. The sun does not agree with me, I'm afraid."

The man squinted, and she realized that he'd probably taken the phrase "agree with" literally and needed a moment to process what she'd said. Then, he nodded.

"There is more danger after dark, any place you go," he pointed out. "So day is best. Still, you should be careful."

"Oh, I will." She adjusted her sunglasses.

The driver glanced at her again and she spared a moment to thank fate that the myth about vampires casting no reflection in mirrors was indeed a myth. It would have made certain types of interactions far more hazardous if it were true.

"I must say," the man began and his voice thickened, "you are very beautiful. Please, do not take this the wrong way. I do not mean to...how you say, flirt. I only speak the way you would...praise a painting or a sunset."

For once, she decided to allow herself to be flattered.

"Why, thank you. That is a nice thing to say." Her understated but pleasant smile, in this case, was entirely genuine.

The last few minutes of the drive passed in comfortable silence. The old, closely-crowded white and tan buildings, rose around them and the streets narrowed. Not many people were about, and only a few cars drove past.

The driver slowed, and she could tell that he wasn't really sure of the exact address, although they were on the correct street.

"Do not worry," she said to him. "We're close. You may just drop me off here and I can find the place myself on foot."

He raised his thick eyebrows. "Are you sure?"

"Yes." She added a touch of finality to her tone.

The man brought the cab to a stop at the edge of the street. She paid him and tipped him generously, and he accepted it almost with sheepish embarrassment.

There was one more thing, though.

The vampire stood beside the driver's door and the

man rolled down the window to drink in the sight of her. She made eye contact and held it.

"Most of this," she said in a voice that was barely a whisper, "you will forget. The shadow of a pleasant dream shall remain. But none who mean harm to me or you will discover the slightest detail of our encounter."

The dark brown of his eyes almost vanished as the pupils grew, seemingly swallowed by her own black irises. This was followed by a curious sensation of soft light, deep-red, and she snapped her eyelids shut. That ended it.

By the time the driver returned to normal perception and blinked in half-dazed confusion, Taylor had already turned away. He could not see her face.

"Thanks again," she said and altered her voice slightly from its usual pitch, "and enjoy your drive back to Ben Gurion to pick up your next fare."

Then, she was gone.

She heard the car drive away slowly as though the man within it tried to determine where he was and how to get back to the airport. By then, she'd already slipped into the shadows between the buildings, the shadows cast by lampposts, and even the shadows cast by strolling people who barely noticed she was there.

Soon, she found the place she sought—an antique shop, whose sign bore the image of a Coptic Cross. A single light burned within. The proprietor was open for business.

The vampire smiled and stepped through the door.

Flushing, Queens, New York
Remington straightened his tie, adjusted his cufflinks,

and wiped the sweat from his palms with a rag before he ran a hand through his hair. It had, to the best of his memory, been a while since the last time he ran through that many nervous reactions in so short a time.

In fact, it was probably because he wasn't nervous. He was merely "in the zone."

"Okay," he told his minuscule companion, "this appears to be the place."

Specifically, it was the abode of the man whom Bobby had referred to as Mr Weird Interview Guy.

Before they'd left the agency's offices, Remy had called Detullio, the private detective to whom they'd outsourced a little of their workload.

"Heyyyyy there, buddy," he had greeted the man. "You're not on your way over here already, are you? No? Good, because we need to head out anyway, so I thought we'd save you a trip by meeting to discuss things...uh, somewhere. Your place? Or maybe a café? Or if all else fails, we can simply drive around the block in Taylor's—I mean, my car."

The man had been a little irritable and flustered since he wasn't overly confident in the security and privacy of the circumstances, but given that he seemed busy enough himself, the advantage of not having to drive to Bushwick had finally convinced him.

Remy had picked him up at a corner shop near his house down in Gravesend—he refused to reveal his home address—and they'd driven to a deli about half a mile away. Having filled up on donuts, he didn't order anything. But Detullio looked like a man who had a great fondness for large sandwiches, so the trip would have looked profoundly un-suspicious to anyone who might have taken an interest.

"Okay, so," the rotund PI had said between mouthfuls of cold cuts and mayonnaise, "this guy I spoke to, his name is Singh—you know, a Sikh, a nice enough fella. I lied by omission, though, when I said all he'd seen was guys in dark suits standing around."

He had raised an eyebrow at that. "Oh really? Go on, then. And don't be shy. Some of the shit we've dealt with is weird enough that nothing—and I mean nothing—will shock me."

Detullio hadn't exactly made him a liar, but he'd tested his honesty when he described the man as having also seen something else. Judging by the description, it was clearly a person mutated into monstrousness by Snow White.

"Ugh," he had quipped when his contact finished his story, "I can see why you didn't want to say that over the phone." His skin crawled at the memory of having been attacked by junkies who'd shot up with that crap.

"Yeah, no shit." The PI had grunted and finished his sandwich in one final huge bite. A little of the mayo and meat-juice fell onto Taylor's car seat, but neither of them had paid it any heed. "Word on the street is that Snow White is everywhere now and that she makes bath salts look like pot. Remember bath salts? It practically turned people into zombies."

Remington remembered. He'd come close to trying them himself once.

Their discussion over, he'd taken Detullio to where they'd met up and after he'd settled his fee, he'd given

Remy Singh's address so he could conduct his own follow-up interview.

He'd returned to the Tesla and informed Riley that they'd drive directly to Flushing.

"Okay," she'd agreed. She had lain low in the back seat during the trip to the deli. As he'd suspected, the PI was unable to see the preternatural. "Where's that?"

"North Queens." He'd sighed. "Of course we hired a PI who lives basically on the complete opposite side of western Long Island."

Traffic wasn't too bad, relatively speaking, on either Belt Parkway or 678, and they made it in about thirty-five minutes.

Now, he stood before the housing block where Singh apparently lived. Riley floated behind his shoulder. As a precaution, they'd decided she should stay behind him and out of sight, at least at first. If the man had indeed seen a mutated druggie, it might have opened his eyes to the preternatural realm.

Remington approached the door of number six and knocked. When no one answered after about forty seconds, he rang the doorbell for good measure. After a moment, he heard footsteps approaching from within.

A muffled voice beyond the door asked, "Yes, hello?"

"Hi," he replied, "I'm Remington Davis, an associate of Mr Detullio. You spoke to him a day or two ago, right? I wanted to follow up on that and ask you a few questions." The man was probably watching him through the peep-hole, so he kept his physical demeanor as businesslike as his tone of voice.

The individual responded with a groan. "Oh, no." This

was followed by a stream of low muttering that he couldn't make out. It may well have been in the man's native language. Fortunately, at the end of the grumbled spiel, the locks clicked and the door itself swung open.

Standing just beyond the threshold was a tall man, sleepy-eyed with a well-groomed black beard and mustache and a blue turban wound around his hair.

"Hi," said Remy and grimaced in an officious kind of way. "Are you Mr. Ranj Singh?"

The man nodded. "Yes. And you said your name was Davis. May I please ask, on whose behalf are you here?"

Clearly, it seemed to Remy, merely saying he was an associate of Detullio's wasn't quite good enough. Then again, for all Mr Singh knew, he might be a mob hitman come to silence him for what he'd witnessed. He was brave to have even opened the door.

"Moonlight Detective Agency," he said and produced a card from his jacket's breast pocket. "A private investigation firm. We're actually the ones carrying out the investigation and outsourced some of our work to Mr. Detullio due to being overburdened lately."

Singh blinked and took the card, read it, and checked both sides. "I see. Very well. Come in, please, although I must ask you to remain in the living room."

Nodding, Remy stepped forward as Singh moved aside. He motioned behind his back for Riley to follow him but to remain out of plain sight. It occurred to him that even if Singh could see her, she probably had some kind of spell to make herself invisible. He only prayed that she wasn't too distracted by thoughts of the goddamn mall to think of that.

The tall man's apartment was dark but tidy and filled with the rather appetizing aromas of recent cooking. Singh shut the door behind him, circled, and motioned to a nearby couch.

The investigator seated himself. "Thanks." As he settled, the other man pulled a chair closer.

The man took a long breath of air. Something about his demeanor was strangely resigned as though he had hoped to be done with this business but knew, now, that he'd have to answer more questions about it. "What is it you would like to know, Mr Davis? And would you like a cup of coffee?"

He held a hand up. "No, thank you, I had coffee earlier. And I'd like to know exactly what it is you saw and where. As Detullio probably mentioned, we're running a missing persons case and we suspect that this mysterious ware-house may be connected to it."

"Yes," the man answered him, "of course. The ware-house is not far—perhaps one half of a mile or less. I often take walks in the evenings in that direction, and that is when I saw it."

His almost narcoleptic demeanor changed. He'd grown more alert in his sudden discomfort.

Remy maintained the gentle, but firm demeanor of professionalism and nodded while he motioned for the man to continue his story. "Don't hold back, sir. I'm not here to judge you for what you've seen. And it's absolutely necessary for me to hear the entire story."

Somehow, he got it right. Singh related the rest of his tale and relaxed a little while he also recognized that he wouldn't have to leave out all the juicy details.

He explained how, while he strolled down the sidewalk in a less-traveled direction a little past twilight, he froze where he was when he noticed a scene that simply didn't look right. Although he was very sure he was concealed as he barely glimpsed the warehouse's lot between a damaged fence and a tree, he was still immediately seized with fear.

Four men in dark suits and glasses had stood in a group and it looked like at least one of them carried a gun in two hands. Singh wasn't sure what type but the whole picture was of something seriously bad about to take place.

Then, worse yet, two of the men had guided a…thing—humanoid but not fully human—out of the back of a truck and into the warehouse itself. It bulged, hunched over, and its skin seemed to give off a faint, chalky-white radiance as though its veins were lit with moonlight. The creature struggled, moaned, and growled and seemed barely controllable in its bestial fury.

He had glimpsed all this in the space of about one second. Then, he'd turned away and hurried back the way he'd come, moving as fast as he could without making too much noise. Since then, for the next few days, he'd barely left his apartment, terrified that the men might have seen him.

Remington dusted his trousers as the Sikh gentleman finished. "I see… Thank you, Mr Singh." He made direct eye contact. "I'd like to reassure you that your story is known to no one except Detullio and myself unless you've told anyone else. Have you?"

"No," he responded immediately. "I have not even told my wife or my parents."

"That's probably for the best." He stood. "If these people

did know you saw them, they probably would have already acted by now. Go about your usual routine as though everything was fine. My people and I will deal with this problem directly. I can assure you of that."

Singh exhaled as he, too, rose to his feet. "That will be a great relief."

"I would imagine so." Remy glanced at the business card still in the man's hand. "The card is yours. Keep it on your person but don't show it to anyone. If anything happens, call us. Now, which direction is this warehouse in and on which street?"

The tall man told him as they walked to the door with Riley wafting surreptitiously behind. On the threshold, Remy shook his hand.

"Thank you, Mr Singh. Again, be careful but try not to worry. We have things well in hand. Enjoy the rest of your day."

"I will try. Good luck." He nodded and closed the door.

The investigator ran a hand through his hair again as he strode away from the building toward the parked Tesla. The interview had gone well, all things considered, and he looked forward to being able to fulfill his promise to Singh and be done with this crap.

As he opened up the car, he noticed that Riley was smiling. Beaming, rather. She looked overjoyed or at least extremely amused.

"So," he inquired, "what has you so happy all of a sudden?"

"Um…" She blushed and shrank back as though trying to get out of having to answer.

He didn't feel like letting her off the hook. "No, I'm curious. Tell me."

"It's only," she began, "the way you acted with that man. All serious and smart. It's like that expression I heard— you've 'got your shit together,' I think is how it goes."

Remy, to his own surprise, burst out laughing. "I suppose I do, at that. I'm capable of it when I must."

She nestled against his neck as he closed the door and settled into the driver's seat. "And you're good at it. It seems weird to me in a way, but being around humans, I can see how it's a good thing."

"Thanks. In fact, hell," he confessed, "the poor bastard probably thought I was from a Three-Letter Agency and the business card was only a front. It makes me wonder if getting some sinister black shades might make me even more dashingly effective as an investigator than I already am."

The thought glowed warmly within him like the after-effects of a good meal. There was no time for daydreaming, though. They had a scary abandoned warehouse to investigate.

CHAPTER EIGHT

A Warehouse in Flushing, Queens, New York

"Well," Remy said in an almost inaudible voice, "if sketchy characters are indeed corralling Snow White victims in this neighborhood, I suppose this would be the place for it."

Riley made a low humming sound. She hovered close to his ear so he barely heard it. "Yeah, I think so. It smells bad here."

He sniffed. "Your sense of smell has never let me down. All I smell is…wet sidewalk, I guess."

The warehouse was a few hundred yards away. There were, fortunately, no men in dark suits and sunglasses standing around with violin cases, nor any mutated drug addicts. Both Remington and the fairy were crouched behind a low wall in a nearby parking lot, well out of sight. Unless the potential criminals had a well-camouflaged sniper or something up on the roof, they should be able to conduct their surveillance without risk.

The car was safely and inconspicuously parked another couple of hundred feet farther back behind a hedge.

Riley came to rest on Remy's shoulder. She still seemed rather tired. "What's strange, though," she said, "is that the smell isn't only coming from the building. It's all over here. It seems like some of it is under us."

His tongue moved over his teeth and he rubbed his jaw. "That's...intriguing. I don't particularly look forward to another sewer adventure, but it might be better than barging headfirst into the lion's den. Either way, my clothes will probably get fucked."

And either way, they had to know more about the warehouse.

It hadn't been all that long ago when he would have been perfectly comfortable with the whole headfirst-barging tactic. He still had half a mind to attempt it now, actually, but bitter experience had begun to teach its lesson.

"Riley"—he glanced at her—"can you fly over and around the building and do recon? Determine if anyone is in there or if there's any change in the smell or any magic emanating from the place. Stuff like that."

"Yes," she replied, although she did not sound or look enthusiastic.

He couldn't blame her. "If there's any danger, fly up and out and meet me at the car. I don't want to risk you need-lessly. The whole idea is to make sure we don't blunder into a trap again."

She seemed to gather strength from the air as she spread her wings. "Okay. I'll be right back."

Remy crept over to a thick juniper bush nearby and

stood behind it. That looked less suspicious than crouching under the rim of a low wall and it still offered him good concealment and a halfway decent view.

He watched as the small, greenish-silver form of the fairy drifted through the air toward the brooding, dilapidated building and became almost invisible when she reached it. Five or six minutes elapsed with no fireworks.

Footsteps alerted him that someone was coming down the sidewalk and he looked up. A guy in a sweater and earmuffs walked his Pomeranian. Remy pulled his phone out and pretended to be checking it but ignored the man, who took his dog out into the empty street to go around him.

Keep walking, my friend. He wished he could say it aloud. *Neither of us wants your dog to flip out at one of the Fair Folk buzzing toward my shoulder.*

Both man and canine were safely a couple of hundred yards away when Remington caught sight of Riley again. She flew in a straight line but didn't appear to be *fleeing*—a good omen.

"Okay," the fairy stated, "there's no one in the building, but it seems like some people were there recently. And the awful smell is even stronger. I could kind of taste magic around, but I would have to examine it more closely to know more than that."

"Hmm." He ran a hand through his hair. "I'm tempted to suggest that—"

To his surprise, she interrupted him. "No, I don't think we should go in there. Not when it's only you and me. It's hard to explain, but...even if no one is present, that's a bad place. Please, trust me on this."

A little startled, he said, "So be it. Instead, let's go after these other traces you mentioned. The ones under our feet."

Five minutes of searching led them to a rundown brick building, little more than a shed, which was mostly hidden behind trees, bushes, and strategically placed debris. Behind the rusty door was a staircase leading down.

"Yes," said Riley, "it's coming from down here. It seems to be empty, though."

"Empty means safe, right?" Remy adjusted his tie. "I don't see a condemned sign, so if a ceiling falls on us we can always sue the city of New York. Down we go. It looks like an old service entrance. I wonder what this leads to."

They closed the door behind them and descended four flights of stairs to what he decided was an abandoned subway tunnel. The fairy generated a soft silver glow to light the way before they finally paused in a place that looked unpleasantly familiar.

Everything was made of rusted metal, the ceiling high enough to accommodate a train, although none had passed through there for a long time. Gashes were visible in the surrounding iron and curious dark stains on parts of the walls and floor.

Remy brooded over the scene. *Yeah, I've definitely been here before. No, scratch that, we were here before. Myself, Riley, Conrad, Presley...and even Taylor. And about eighty pissed-off cartel dwarves and vampiric thralls. What a jolly soiree that was.*

"The bloodstains," Riley continued, "smell like vampires, more or less. But we already saw these when we were looking for Taylor, didn't we?"

"Yeppers," he conceded. "It's so strange, though. We must have missed something. Taylor hasn't been herself since she came back from that incident. It makes me worry that Moswen...did something to her before we joined forces."

An icy nausea rose from the pit of his gut at the prospect. There was no way that Moswen could have turned her. He refused to even consider such a ridiculous thought. If Taylor were now the servant of a hostile vampire, he would already be dead.

But what, he mused, if it was something subtler? A curse or a disease or something similar that had slowly eaten away at her. It might explain how she'd grown aloof and chilly, even by her own standards. Not to mention morose, hesitant, and willing to foist unpleasant tasks onto Remington's shoulders.

And, of course, the fact that she had disappeared to God only knew where without telling anyone about it.

The fairy looked ready to lower herself onto his shoulder and call it a day. But as Remy stared at the old bloodstains and shivered in the darkness and cold of the tunnel, an idea came to him.

"Riley," he almost sputtered and snapped his fingers, "remember when we were looking for Surrly's missing dwarves and we found them all ripped apart in that other tunnel? You were able to do that...uh, thing you did where you generated a hologram of what happened there in the past?"

"Yes." she agreed at once. "I could do it again. Although I'm so tired."

"That is understandable," he conceded. "But if you'll do

it anyway, I'll buy one of those awful sugary beverages masquerading as coffee and let you have a couple of sips."

That prospect seemed to perk her up.

The fairy waved her hands in alternating patterns and finally clapped sharply. A section of the tunnel about forty feet square was suddenly illuminated in what looked like pale starlight. After a moment of haziness, two figures cast in similar frosty light materialized on the scene.

He stepped back and decided to get out of the way of the holographic encounter. It couldn't harm him, but it'd be easier to observe it from the sidelines.

From behind, a slim, dark-clad form—undoubtedly Taylor—walking into the center of the shining space. Another larger form exploded from the edge with such speed and ferocity that he flinched, despite knowing that he was merely an observer.

Remy held his breath as he watched the two humanoid figures battle, their movements impossible for the human eye to follow half the time. Both landed blows and their fight strayed beyond the edge of the glowing arena and returned to it.

As the spectacle progressed, he noticed two odd things. First, where he pressed against the wall to the side, he felt the gashes in the metal and wondered if mere fingers—even those of vampires—could have caused such damage. Had they perhaps used weapons?

Second, he could not make out the faces of either combatant. The transparent silver light thickened into a golden-amber haze around the head of the larger vampire and a deep crimson fog over Taylor's face.

He glanced at the fairy. She struggled to maintain the

spell and he saw that she squinted and trembled at the same time that the image fuzzed like an old-fashioned TV set whose antenna needed adjustment.

"Wait..." Riley breathed heavily as the two foes separated in the center of the phantasmal hologram, both bleeding, and seemed to shout at one another. "I can't... I'm losing it..."

A crackling sounded and the forms went indistinct seconds after the larger vampire seemed to grow even more and to change somehow. In the next moment, the holograph flashed out like a dying light bulb and the entire picture vanished when the spell came to an end.

"Shit," he said. "Well, this is certainly where Taylor and Moswen finally went toe to toe. But what the shit was all that? I couldn't tell what was happening at the end."

"I'm sorry." The fairy panted, obviously both half-exhausted and embarrassed. "It started to...not make sense, and I couldn't keep watching it. Something went out like a candle."

He motioned her over to rest on his shoulder. "You did what you could, and I appreciate it. But now. it looks like we'll have to switch to Plan B. Once we decide what Plan B is, anyway."

They emerged cautiously from the tunnel, took their time, and peered through the rusty door at the top of the staircase to ensure that no one was watching them or waiting for them. To their relief, the coast was clear and they hurried back to the car.

Remy suddenly wondered how wise it had been to take one of Taylor's vehicles. Someone with the proper talents or connections might be able to observe the license plate and find out who the owner was. And if they thought that she herself was snooping around, they'd be much more likely to bring out the heavy artillery.

For now, though, things seemed to be fine. He retrieved his phone once they were safely in the Tesla.

Riley rubbed her eyes as she watched him. "Do you really think she'll answer?"

With a frown, he tapped the appropriate speed-dial icon. "I've always been an optimist by nature. It gets a man through the winters and such."

After a pause, the phone rang and continued to ring. His companion had drifted over to the far end of the dashboard and didn't really hear the details when the ringing changed to a message before the phone went quiet altogether.

She glanced at him. "What is it? Anything?"

He sighed, pinched his nose, and re-pocketed the device. "Confirmation of the inherent stupidity of optimism—an international dial tone. Not only is Taylor unable or unwilling to answer, but she also isn't even in the United States. At this point, I'm fresh out of ideas as to where the hell she is or what she might be doing."

Disgruntled, he leaned back in the car seat and allowed his head to tilt back and his eyes to roll toward the heavens. It took about a minute before he could bring himself to start the car.

Riley rolled over on the dashboard and caught his eye. "Okay, so what do we do?"

"Work the case." He shrugged. "I don't think we're up to invading that place's basement yet, especially since we don't know what we're dealing with yet. The other option is to do what we always do. Go places worth going to and talk to people who might know something until it all makes sense."

Jerusalem, Israel

The shopkeeper had clearly been surprised to receive such an unusual request. His initial reaction was fear and hostility, exactly as she'd expected.

But Taylor was the persuasive type. It did not take long for her to make progress with him and soon, she would have what she wanted.

"Madam," the man said when he began to calm, "it will take me a short time to find this, but I will find it. Please be patient."

He was a slight man, physically speaking, but despite his diminished size, he gave off a vibe of alertness, intelligence, and a kind of wily energy—the type who might well kick the shit out of a gang of young toughs who tried to mug him, much to their astonishment. He wore spectacles and had a neat silver beard.

Judging by the minutiae of his dress and the symbol he displayed on his shop sign, he was very likely an Egyptian Coptic Christian, perhaps with Jewish relatives, come to the holy city to escape the political turmoil in his native country.

She gave a slight smile and a minor inclination of the head. "Of course. I am not in a hurry."

In fact, the sooner she had the object, the better. But with herself now half a world from her home, an extra ten minutes of waiting made little difference.

The vampire busied herself by examining the curious items all around her. Much of it was basic and ornamental, of slight interest due to being old or obscure but of little value beyond that bestowed by sentimentality or curiosity.

Other objects were more interesting. She identified ceremonial vestments and chalices that had been used in medieval-era churches and synagogues and mosques, chairs and headdresses, and wands or scepters that had belonged to magicians of real power. The traces of their arcane talents still wafted from their possessions like steam from a hot spring immediately after the sun had set.

The shopkeeper returned. His wary eyes scanned the storefront before he came around the counter, holding a small item bundled in sky-blue cloth in his right hand.

He held his left hand up. "One moment, please."

Taylor waited, alert but relaxed, as he ambled across the shop and turned the sign in the front window to the *Closed* position. He drew the curtains, locked the door, and turned slowly, now holding the blue-wrapped object with both hands.

"Madam, do you know what this is?"

She intuited immediately that he was entirely aware of its true potential but he would not mention that until she said something to indicate her own degree of understanding. If she gave a wrong answer, he would respond by saying that it was merely old and valuable or that it had been passed down through many generations and required fastidious care.

Both of those statements were true, of course, but they did not tell the whole story.

"That," she began, and pointed gingerly at the bundle

with a red-nailed finger, "is the ritual dagger used by the tenth-century magician Teremun al-Harb. He employed it in a ceremony thought to be a mere legend in which he and his followers overpowered and defeated a vampire who had ravaged the Sinai."

The proprietor's face might as well have turned to stone.

Taylor continued briskly. "It is said—pardon me, it is known that to this day, it retains some power when properly activated to bind the evil undead—*vampiri, lamia, ghul, vukodlak*, the walking corpses who feed upon the blood of the living."

Phrasing it that way made her deeply uncomfortable, but she gave no indication of her feelings. Besides, she had made peace with what she was long before. And she held herself to certain standards. She was civilized.

Slowly, the man nodded. "Yes, this is true. I see that you are knowledgeable. And I suspect that you are interested in this relic for reasons that are more than mere curiosity. You are not only a collector of rare things. Yes?"

She smiled lightly. "Yes. What is your name, friend?"

"Hossam Totah," he stated, and she had no doubt he told the truth. "And yours?"

"I am called Taylor Steele. In my country—America—I am often called upon to deal with certain problems that no one else can resolve. I have seen many things. I know that there are things which are real and true, even if the modern world has forgotten them."

With a nod, Totah stepped closer to her and motioned for the two of them to relocate to the back of the store.

They sat at a low table on comfortable cushions and

drank a small pot of tea while they continued the discussion of the al-Harb dagger. And, of course, its price. Taylor would have been willing to pay much of her entire fortune for it, at this point, but she did not bother to reveal that fact. Still, her opening offer was quite generous.

After a cursory effort to haggle a little, Totah pretended to consider her bargain and diverted the talk instead to the object itself. He asked permission to switch from English to Arabic, which she granted. She was more familiar with the Egyptian dialect than any other and she had little trouble understanding him.

"The magic in this dagger," he explained, "is dormant. It has great power but it is useless to you without a spell to awaken it."

"I see," she acknowledged. "And how would I acquire this spell or find someone who can cast it?"

He finished his tea and set the cup aside. "Yes, I know of one who can give you the text and perhaps the components. But he is not capable of casting it himself. For that, you will need a true sorcerer—a witch, perhaps. I understand the West has witches of significant talent."

"True," she agreed, "but not as true as it once was."

The shopkeeper wrote down the name and address of the individual he had alluded to and handed it to her. He apologized for his sloppy script, although she found it legible enough.

"Ms Steele," he went on and his deep, dark eyes gazed into hers, "there is one more thing. Although this dagger is intended to be used for good, one who would wield it must descend into a realm of dark and evil magicks. There is great danger. If I sell this precious object to you, are you certain that it will be worth the price? Not only the money, of course, but the toll that it may extract from your very soul?"

Taylor closed her eyes for a few seconds. She knew of what the man spoke but hadn't quite expected him to state it so frankly. "Yes. It is of the utmost necessity. Many innocent lives are at stake."

The old man nodded. "So be it."

She paid him slightly more than her opening offer, as expected. It was a handsome sum but not one that would cripple her in the months or years to come.

They both stood and moved out toward the entrance. She tucked the still-wrapped dagger into her clothes.

"Sir," she said, "thank you for this important item as well as for your hospitality and advice. May you prosper in peace and safety."

He smiled. "May you as well. Take care."

She stepped outside into the ancient streets. The modern technology of lamps and vehicles seemed almost incongruous, even in a part of Jerusalem that could not be that old. New and flashy cars drove past now and then or parked along the street, and groups of young people—mostly Copts and Armenians and Muslim Arabs, it seemed—strolled past, speaking many different tongues. The air was warm and dry and fragrant.

It took a few minutes to hail a cab, this one driven by a woman who was polite but seemed tired and uninterested in conversation. This suited Taylor perfectly, as her thoughts and emotions roiled within her and demanded attention as she reclined in the back of the taxi.

The battle. It replayed in her head as it had almost every day since that terrible, bloody evening in the tunnel. She vividly recalled the almost overwhelming evil force that Moswen Neith projected, the pain she had inflicted, and the thing she had become.

And, of course, the effect the whole experience had on her. Since then, she had been afraid. Fear was not an emotion she felt much of, these days.

When the memory reached the point at which Moswen transformed, Taylor cut it off as cleanly as if pressing the button on a monitor. She refused to see that again. But it stayed with her regardless and drove her forward, and her hand clenched around the slight bulge where the dagger rested.

She intended to put that fear to rest, once and for all. Soon.

CHAPTER NINE

Moonlight Detective Agency Offices, Bushwick, Brooklyn, New York

Miss Roberta "Bobby" Diaz sat behind her desk in the lobby, twirled a pencil between the fingers of both hands, admired the perfect hexagonal structure, and realized that she knew almost nothing about graphite. At least she'd discovered that it wasn't actually lead.

It used to be that her tasks and chores—she was effectively the agency's secretary as well as its receptionist—took her all day to complete, and she was often slightly behind.

Today, everything seemed easier. Patterns had emerged, shortcuts had suggested themselves, and although at times it felt like her brain reeled and scooted ahead of itself, she managed to keep up.

And, of course, she mentally reviewed every case they'd handled that she could recall, teased out the preternatural elements and wondered, with a kind of subdued shame, how she could have missed some of the glaring clues.

It was strange and even a little frightening but incredible, in a way. If indeed she was under some kind of spell, she wasn't sure she wanted to be cured of it.

A figure appeared at the front door and pushed its way in, ringing the little bell. It was a tall, old man in a shabby brown coat but aside from that, he looked like he'd done a hurried but effective job of freshening up—shaved, showered, and put on the nicest clothes he had. He took the coat off as soon as he was indoors.

"Hello," Bobby greeted him. He looked familiar.

"Good afternoon, miss. I'm a friend of Remington's. You might say even a business partner. Although this is the first time I've been into the office so I don't believe we've met. I'm Don Gannon."

She recognized the name and Remy had shown her a picture of him. He was taller than she'd imagined, although his posture was a little stooped. And of course, he'd gone the extra mile today in the hygiene department.

"Hi, Mr Gannon. Yeah, Mr Remington told me all about you. How can I help you?"

To be safe, she opted to give no indication of her current level of intelligence. First, she'd wait to hear what he had to say and try to see what, exactly, he wanted.

Remy had told her about their informal deal to exchange information. He and Riley had returned about an hour before but they were busy in his office, going over information and making plans. She decided not to mention that he was present, either.

"Oh," Don said and smiled with mostly genuine warmth, "I only wanted to drop off a few tips I thought Mr Remington might find useful—word on the street and all that. And, naturally, check to see if you good people have anything for me in return."

In the corner of her field of vision, she saw Conrad saunter along the far side of the lobby to ensure that everything was alright. He waited there a few seconds before he drifted out of sight, although still close at hand.

"Okay," Bobby replied. She wanted to look cheerful and a little vacant but found it difficult to emulate her past persona in a conscious fashion. "Um, why don't you start by asking if there's anything you want to know about from us? Specifically."

Don rubbed his chin and seemed perplexed by its smoothness. "Well, my personal investigations of late have turned up a few faces. And I'm fairly sure I have names to go with those faces. What I'd like is to know if your agency has had any dealings with those names or any record of their activities."

The young woman nodded. Mr Gannon's gaze had begun to drift gradually toward her cleavage. Clearly, he wasn't that old.

"I see." She jiggled her mouse to wake her computer. "So, what are the names?"

He leaned against the reception desk. "For starters… Abel Dusek. Yes, the Congressman. I only want to know if you've had any business dealings with him. Or, if possible, with anyone in his employ since a man in his position might act through intermediaries."

Bobby allowed her face to show legitimate surprise at that and she wrote the name down. She remembered, to her own satisfaction, how it was spelled.

"Wow. Okay. Looking into his associates might take some time, though."

"That's fine." He waited for her to finish scribbling. "Second, Colonel James Russel of the New York National Guard—Army branch, not Air Force. I believe he retired recently—or so the official story goes—but can't confirm that yet."

She added the name to the same post-it note as Dusek. "Is that with one or two S's and L's?"

"Uh...two S's, one L." He seemed taken aback by the question.

"Okay, so," she explained, "I can run the names through our customer databases quickly and at least tell you that, but anything else will definitely take a while." She punched both men's names into the computer and leaned back while it worked its magic.

It took only about two seconds. *No results found.* She told Mr. Gannon as much.

"Damn," he mumbled. "Well, please get back to me if you find anything later." He produced a business card from within his shirt pocket and handed it to hr.

"Sure thing," she said.

Don plucked a piece of candy out of the complimentary bowl. "Is Remington in right now?" While he enjoyed the sight of her, he clearly would rather have this conversation with a person he knew well.

"Nah," she lied, "I can take a message, though."

Again, the man fondled his stubble-free jaw. "Well, I happen to have completed some rather daring investigative work on a stakeout last night, near a locale known as a hotspot for shady, dangerous characters."

She nodded as if impressed. "Ohh, I see. Really? What did you find?"

His ego stimulated, Don proceeded to divulge more than he probably intended to.

"Oh, you know"—he chuckled—"the kind of thing that might well crack certain cases wide open. What they like to call 'visual evidence.' It's not always easy to come by, but I pulled it off. It might even be related to some of those missing persons you folks are looking into."

"Hmm, that could be," Bobby interjected. "Go on. I find this kind of stuff fascinating."

He smiled. "Based on my intel, it seems there's some kind of...cult, afoot. That's what people are saying and I can see it being true. They're aggressively recruiting members with real influence in society—politicians, entertainers, police and military officers, that kind of thing. Perhaps trying to get a foothold in DC, even. It might also be related to this Snow White business. Some people have even said that this little cult is run by a vampire. I don't know about that, but it seems like something Remington might be intrigued by so he should definitely talk to me, and soon."

"Wow," she drawled. "I will relay the message, Mr Gannon, no problem."

Satisfied, Don took one last look at her breasts, then said his goodbyes, retrieved his coat, and sauntered to the exit.

Once the man had stepped out the door, she counted the seconds until either two minutes had passed or she heard his car start, whichever came first. The engine started after ninety-six seconds.

She immediately punched the names of Dusek and Russel into both a conventional search engine and another, secret database that Volz had set up before the spell-bomb had all but incapacitated him.

The conventional search turned up nothing of interest, aside from normal political information about Rep Dusek and an announcement in a military publication that Col Russel had put in for retirement about three weeks before. She was surprised that Gannon hadn't found it himself, but he might not have had time to look.

The other search would take longer. She set it to send the results to Mr Remington's email. While she waited, Bobby stood and walked to his office. She knocked on the door.

"Bobby?" he asked. "Come in. This is about Don Gannon, isn't it?"

"Yes, it is." She opened the door and stepped through.

Remy pored over documents she'd given him earlier between glances at something on his computer screen. Riley was asleep on top of the overturned coffee cup he always kept on his desk.

So that's what it's for. I always assumed he turned it upside down to keep bugs out and forgot about it whenever he went to get coffee.

He looked at her. "I heard him out there. Well, kind of. Thanks for running interference since I don't really feel like dealing with him right now. What did ol' Don have to say?"

She recounted their interaction in detail and finished by handing him the post-it note with the two men's names written out.

"And," she concluded, "the results of Volz's DarkSearch should be in your inbox at any minute now. If we're lucky, we can probably get this colonel's address or some kind of personal info that will help you track him down and talk to him."

Remington scratched beside his nose. "Nicely done. And—yup, there it is." He glanced at his PC screen and clicked on something, presumably the search results. "So, do we think this Russel guy is an intermediary, a major player, a defector from decadence, or what?"

Bobby placed her left hand on her hip and gestured with her right as she spoke. "I've thought about it myself since Don came in, and I honestly suspect that Moswen turned him into one of her thralls."

He raised an eyebrow. Judging by his grim expression, he'd quickly grasped the implications of their nemesis having a slave who happened to possess high-level military contacts.

"The thing Don said about this cult led by a vampire is probably true," she went on. "She's trying to infiltrate DC via the official channels leading out of New York. And she failed to kill you guys before using brute force, so trying to do it with 'respectable' agents might work better for her. He has to be either a thrall or, like, she's holding a member of his family hostage until he does her bidding."

"Ugh," he commented, "I think you're right, unfortunately. No offense, I simply mean that if that's true, things could get even uglier than they already are. And, yup, I found his address."

He wrote the new information on the note beside

Russel's name. That done, he used his pencil to gently prod the sleeping fairy on the cup.

"Riley, wake up. Sorry, but I really need to ask you something."

With a tiny sound of protest, she rolled over, yawned, and returned to consciousness. "What is it? I was sleeping."

"Yeah, my apologies. Something kind of important has come up, though. We have a lead on one of Moswen's chief lackeys. The problem is, he's quite possibly a thrall. Taylor was able to remove that enchantment from Alex, but she... uh, you know, kinda isn't here. Do you think...your magic could handle it?"

The fairy sat up, rubbed her eyes, and sighed. "I'm not sure. I...give me a moment to think. I just woke up."

Bobby frowned and imagined how the fairy must have felt pressured. She thought about suggesting that he wait until later, but he was right about one thing—this was important.

"Okay," he said and his expression softened. "Personally, I never take naps since they screw up my sense of time, so I can...uh, see how you'd need a minute. Do you want some coffee? I'll even force myself to put sugar in it for you."

She held a hand up, stretched, shook her head, and sat in silence for about twenty seconds before she spoke.

"Okay, I'm better. I need more sleep, but that helped. Um...I don't know, though. Vampire magic is different from fae magic. It's stronger in some ways and weaker in others. Of course, I could try, but we might get hurt in the meantime." She frowned and blushed.

While Remy considered this, an answer leaped into Bobby's brain and she relayed it immediately.

"You could take Conrad," she suggested. "That way, you'll have backup muscle if things go south. Based on what you said previously, at least between him and Riley, you could probably restrain him and maybe capture him until Taylor comes back and can deal with it herself."

"True, yeah." He nodded. "But then you and Volz would be left unprotected. Actually, let's check on both of them, shall we? I need to get out of this goddamn chair, anyway. Sitting for more than an hour at a time is insufferable unless video games or beer are involved."

He stood, stretched, and the three of them headed into the rear of the office suite, where Conrad kept an eye on Volz.

The well-groomed lycanthrope half-sat on the edge of the desk, a patient, slightly indulgent smile on his face as he watched the dwarf go about his activity of the day.

Volz had acquired a cluster of freshly sharpened pencils and threw them one by one, dart-like, at the ceiling. His tongue hung out of his mouth to funnel drool into his red facial hair. Six of the pencils had stuck and ten or twelve lay scattered on the floor.

Conrad looked up. "His aim is improving, actually. And I'm surprised at his persistence. He's been at it for a few hours now, and all those that are sticking are only from the last hour since you guys got back. It's all in the motion of the wrist, I'd say."

His eyes glazed and vacant but oddly focused, the dwarf aimed another one. His hand flicked up and the projectile shot heavenward in an almost perfectly straight line. The point sank into the plaster of the ceiling but the pencil wobbled and fell with a gentle clack.

"Oh, dear," Bobby muttered.

"Wow," Remy said. "That's great, Volz. Truly impressive wrist action, as Conrad would say. Are you doing okay there, buddy?"

The dwarf turned to look at him. "Whuh? Oh, yeah. This is fun. You wanna try? I bet I can do better than you. I'm better..." He picked up another pencil.

The investigator motioned for them to turn away and huddle.

"Well," he whispered, "I had kind of hoped that he'd have recovered enough to hack into traffic cameras and do a facial recognition check to help us determine where Russel was last seen, but noooo. I don't think that'll work out. We'll have to do this the old-fashioned way and ring the man's doorbell."

"Okay," Bobby added, "but we're not too far from closing time, so that makes me think if you don't need Volz or me, we could maybe go to that bar you mentioned—the one where preternaturals hang out? You told me about it briefly and said the bartender was really nice and always agreed with you on everything. Would that place be safe?"

He adjusted his cuffs. "That's a good idea, actually. Por's Bar, in Lower Manhattan. It's a safe zone, a neutral territory. If Moswen's henchmen tried to start shit there, they'd have a war on their hands. Yes, go there and take Volz with you. But...uh, don't let him jump onto the pool table while other dwarves or werewolves are playing."

Conrad wandered over. "Pardon me, but I overheard most of that. Does this mean you'll need me, sir?"

"Correct," Remy stated. "You're the backup muscle. If Riley can't handle this guy, you bite his ankle or whatever."

"Ah," the werewolf responded, "yes, of course. Something like that."

They made a few additional preparations—such as having Riley sip a little coffee, with Remy and Conrad sharing the remainder—then waved goodbye and left.

By now, it was getting dark. Bobby assumed she could get away with closing the office earlier but opted to do a little research before she departed.

She set the sign out front to *Closed* and booted up one of the computers in the back so that she could keep Volz nearby while she worked.

Specifically, she looked up the fastest route to Por's Bar. Once she found that, she quickly planned a different, circuitous route—one which would probably throw off anyone who tried to follow them and which avoided all the traffic cameras of which she was aware.

With the route fresh in her mind, she shut the PC down and stood. "Okay, Volz. Sorry, but it's time to leave. We'll go someplace fun."

He looked up, a pencil poised for javelin duty. "But I'm already having fun," he protested.

CHAPTER TEN

Bayside, Queens, New York

"You know," Remy quipped, "this is a nice neighborhood. I don't know how much colonels get paid but that's, like, one of the higher ranks, isn't it? Anyway, I should have known. The point being that I'm glad we have Taylor's nice posh Tesla. A lower-class car would have seemed too conspicuous here."

"That's a good point," Conrad agreed.

The three of them—human, werewolf, and fairy—sat parked at the curb, a couple of hundred yards down from the townhouse where James Russel apparently resided. Getting here had taken about thirty-five minutes, a little longer than Google Maps suggested, as usual, due to the whole rush hour situation.

Annoyingly, this also meant that other people returning home from their jobs constantly pulled up and walked around.

"Let's wait," the investigator continued, "until no one is around, shall we? Besides, we need a minute to decide exactly how we'll handle this. We can't be sure if we'll have a friendly ten-minute chat or if this entire block will be ripped apart and burned down."

Conrad flexed his hands and loosened his suit, the better to discard it if he needed to make a sudden shift. "We can start by having Riley place another soundproof magical shell around Russel's townhouse," he suggested. "In case things get physical and therefore noisy."

"Good idea," he agreed. "You and Bobby both are full of ideas today. And we need them." He slumped and sighed, the sound of it long and ragged. "It's one of those kinds of days."

The nap and the sip of coffee seemed to have helped Riley slightly, but she was still more lethargic than usual. Remy, used to focusing on the details of her small face, could not help noticing the dark circles under her eyes.

"I can do that," she informed them in reference to the anti-sound spell, "but it will use some of my energy and make it harder to…um, remove the enthrallment spell."

"Well, shit," he grumbled. "Okay, how about this. Don't cast it right away but do cast it the instant it looks like things might get ugly."

She and Conrad agreed. They also agreed to let him do most of the talking, which pleased him.

I've always had a way with people, he reminded himself and smirked as he stepped out of the car.

The fairy again kept out of sight in the rear. If Russel had truly been made a thrall, by definition, his eyes would have been opened to the preternatural. Remy walked in front and Conrad hung back a couple of feet behind his elbow.

The townhouse was quiet as they approached, and the post-rush hour human traffic had mostly dropped off. The investigator took a deep breath, raised his fist, and rapped against the door four times.

It opened after only about ten seconds. Standing beyond the threshold was a tall, thin, dour-faced man with prominent bags under his eyes as though he hadn't slept more than four hours a night for the last two weeks.

"Yes?" he said. The word was crisp and to the point, about what was expected for a military officer. If he recognized them, he did not indicate as much yet.

Remy's gut clenched. If the colonel had widened his eyes and reached for a weapon, at least they'd know what was going on. As it was, they were still in the murky realm of uncertainty.

"Hi," he greeted him. "You're James Russel, right? We're from a debt collection agency and were told to have a chat with you. There seems to be some confusion as to whether a certain sum is owed by you or another individual with the same name."

The man's frown deepened. "I see. I don't have any outstanding debts. You'd best move on to one of the other James Russels."

Shit, he's about to slam the door in our faces, he realized.

"Uh," he said and inched forward and in an effort to stall the man, "are you sure about that? You are Colonel Russel? Only one of the guys on our list is a colonel. So... uh, that's you, I think?"

Out of the corner of his eye, he thought he could see Conrad wince at such a crappy lie.

But, oddly, Russel didn't slam the door. Instead, he

froze, then seemed to jerk in place as though he'd had a nasty acid burp and tried to hold it in. His eyes remained wide open the whole time.

Before Remy could say anything else, the man beckoned. "Come in, please. We can get this all sorted out in only a couple minutes, I'm sure."

"Oh," he replied and blinked in surprise. "Good."

They stepped in and Conrad closed the door behind them before the colonel could.

The investigator suddenly wished that he'd told Riley to ride on his back collar or under his coat. That way, she could have warned him if she smelled any dark magic in there. He'd simply have to hope that she'd at least warn Wonder Boy if need be.

Russel led them into his living room, which was tidy but strangely dark as though he hadn't bothered to turn the lights on yet. He turned around to face them.

"Your name," he stated, "is Remington Davis, isn't it?"

For about a second, it seemed that time froze while Remy was forced to confront the inescapable fact that they really, really hadn't planned this as well as they should have. In the next moment, chaos erupted.

Russel lunged with inhuman speed at the same moment as Conrad, who surged into him, both men suddenly snarling. An end table tipped and spilled a flowerpot onto the floor.

"Riley!" Remington cried. "The spell!"

The fairy had already levitated toward the ceiling and she waved her hands as soft, silver light encased the outer walls and ceiling of the townhouse.

He had already sidestepped toward the fight. Conrad

had tackled Russel through the door to the kitchen, only for the colonel, grunting and raging, to hurl the younger man back out.

"Whoa!" Remy exclaimed and hopped back to avoid the lycanthrope plowing into him. Instead, the airborne man careened into a bookcase and knocked it over.

Before the investigator could consider his next move, Russel was on him.

"You're dead," the colonel declared, his voice hoarse. "And I won't even need the team to finish the job."

He started to grab at the man's arms to throw him to the floor but Russel was too fast and strong. His hands slid around his throat and his left foot swung behind his legs, and as he toppled, his attacker's right knee came down on his stomach.

"Fuck," he croaked. "Riley—"

The colonel's demeanor had changed completely. He bared his teeth and had a desperate, sweaty, crazed look that was horrifyingly familiar. Remy had seen it on Alex, and on all the other poor bastards under the direct, sorcerous control of Moswen Neith.

A bestial growl sounded somewhere beyond his head and a dark, hairy form bulldozed into the man to hurl him off Remington and into the couch. Conrad had come through, after all. He and the other man wrestled and clawed at each other's faces while cushions and stuffing erupted everywhere.

Remy rolled aside and found his feet. He looked everywhere for the fairy.

She floated down again and trying to read Russel to

gain enough of an idea of how Moswen's magic worked in order to counteract it.

"Riley," he panted, "there's a brand on his chest—over the heart, remember? That's how Moswen spurs them on. Deactivate it or whatever. Do something!"

"I'm trying," she protested, and in the silver light that shone from her hands, he finally saw the strain on her face. She looked like a ninety-eight-pound human trying to bench-press a three-hundred-pound barbell.

Oh, hell, we're in over our heads again. Unless Conrad can kick the guy's ass.

Remy spun toward the battle between the magically-augmented human and the fully transformed werewolf. Both had braced their feet against the floor and strained against the other's hold, raw strength against strength, but neither had the right leverage to hurl the other against wall or floor.

Something had to give and he decided it ought to be Russel. He ran at the man in a swooping circle and aimed a fist toward the left side of his jaw.

Three things happened at once. He threw his punch, their adversary moved his head to dodge it while he attempted a return blow, and Conrad saw his opening and headbutted the colonel in the chest.

The investigator tripped over his feet and fell back as Russel careened into the wall. He raised himself on his elbows and saw Conrad, poised for the kill, but holding back. They needed the colonel alive.

A flash of light immediately followed. First, a soft silver glow burst from the man's chest, but it quickly turned to a blazing amber-golden color, and finally a weird pale yellow as the hues blended and struggled.

A fast, sharp glance upward and back confirmed that Riley had accomplished it. She'd hacked her way into Moswen's brand and begun the process of deleting the fucking thing from Russel's system.

The colonel was having a near-seizure. He clutched at his chest and his eyes rolled back in his head, most likely in terrible pain. Which at least meant he wasn't attacking them for the moment.

"Ha!" Remy laughed. "You're on a roll, Riley! Keep at it! Shut that shit down! Ha-ha—"

His triumph faded quickly, though, when the fairy uttered a thin, wavering scream. "I can't do it!" she wailed. "I can maybe…only…block her from—*aaaahhh!*"

The light changed again. Now, it seemed that a diagonal gash traversed the middle of it to divide it into two halves, gold and silver before it winked out.

Behind him, something thudded to the floor.

He whirled to where Riley had plummeted and now lay crumpled on the bunched carpet, trembling but otherwise inert, her wings wilting over her.

"No!" Russel gasped and staggered forward a step. "It can't—I can't risk it. You sons of bitches have to die. You—"

Conrad's paw lashed out. He struck the colonel across the face with his palm, and his head struck the wall again as he was flung back. He slumped, drooling, and fell still.

Remy groaned and turned over to wipe a hand down his face as his brain struggled to catch up with all that had happened. He crawled over to the fairy.

"Riley, are you okay? Jesus—"

She wasn't dead and he thanked whatever powers

might exist for that much. Neither was she entirely uncon-scious. The strain, especially in her already-tired condition, had simply been too much for her.

Something hot and red prickled all over his face, neck, and shoulders, and he realized it was shame. He'd pushed the poor creature so hard that she'd practically killed herself. He made a swallowing motion, bit ruefully on his lip, and picked her up gently, then turned.

Conrad shifted to his human form and the wolf hair vanished mysteriously from his body as he gathered his discarded clothes.

Remy turned his head toward the lycanthrope long enough to deliver hasty instructions. "Get him into a bed and tie him up or something." He rushed into the kitchen with the fairy in hand.

Frantically, he rifled through Russel's cupboards, found a mug, tea bags, and a jar of sugar. He made quickie microwave-tea, extra sweet, and gathered a little of it in the smallest spoon he could find.

"Riley," he said softly, "can you hear me? Drink this. It will help you feel better." He moved the spoon toward her face, annoyed by the slight trembling of his hand. The spoon also seemed awkwardly large. It was about the same size as the fairy's entire head.

She twitched and rolled over on the counter. "*Unnghhh*...okay..." She grasped the spoon with both hands, sipped its contents, and drained most of it.

He allowed himself to breathe. If the fairy was lucid enough to do that, she had to be mostly okay. Probably.

Peace and order soon returned, at least to the extent

that was possible when they'd broken into someone's residence, assaulted him, and commandeered his house.

Conrad had moved the colonel into his bed and secured him to it with duct tape and electrical cable. Remy found a washcloth, restored the toppled end table to an upright position, and let Riley lie on the cloth while she recovered. He also made a couple more mugs of tea for himself and the werewolf.

"Well," he remarked, "that was an adventure." He sipped the hot beverage.

Conrad grimaced. "We're very lucky, sir. I think Riley managed to...I don't know, interfere with Moswen's brand, somehow. Otherwise, she would have simply used it to burn his heart out by now, and he's definitely still alive."

"Good," he stated. "Thank you for kicking his ass, by the way. Riley, are you doing any better? I'm sorry this happened, and I mean that."

The fairy sighed and raised herself to a seated position on the washcloth. Her wings were still limp but at least she moved them again. "I think," she said. "And...I'm sorry I couldn't do it. I let you down—"

"Not quite," he corrected. "You might not have removed the brand but it sounds like you at least broke Moswen's link to it."

She shook her head. "It won't last. She'll be able to get through it in another day or two. If I was...at my best, I think I could have made it permanent. This"—she covered her face with her hands—"is all my own fault."

Her voice broke at the end, and he was afraid she'd start crying.

"No," he reassured her, "it's my fault. Like I said, I—"

"No, you're wrong," she protested and her voice rose to an almost squeaky pitch. "You're only trying to do your job. I'm the one who keeps going to the mall and wasting all my time and energy with those men and being an idiot. You even told me not to and said you'd help me, and I kept doing it anyway." She shuddered and might have been weeping.

Remy saw that Conrad was about to say something, so he held a hand up, palm outward. Then, he turned to the fairy.

"Well," he began, "Moswen is one hell of an old, powerful vampire, so it's not like you failed against a run-of-the-mill schmuck who's only been undead for, like, twenty years. I suppose you're right, though, but the fact that you've admitted there's a problem is a good sign. Most of those twelve-step programs put that as Step Number One, if I recall."

"Good for them," she replied in a small voice. "I don't know. Maybe I can get better. I don't think I can get any worse."

He'd never seen her like this, so that might have been true. Rather than push the point, he gave her a moment to herself and turned instead to the werewolf.

"Conrad. I think it might be best if we spent the night here, actually. There is less chance of us being seen and we can keep an eye on the colonel so he doesn't do...uh, whatever it was Moswen wanted him to do. Kill us, obviously. But what he said about 'the team' concerns me. He might have other guys still under his command—or close enough since he's technically retired—who also went over to the dark side. If we wait until daylight to move out, that at least that reduces some of the risk."

The lycanthrope agreed, although only on the condition that he be allowed to head outside and check to ensure that the street wasn't a tow-away zone beyond a certain hour. A quick recon trip to their car and back assured him that it wasn't.

By now, Riley had begun to recover and she felt more talkative.

"Remy," she implored, "I'm serious about this. I need to get better. You guys almost died because I couldn't stop him in time. I can't...I can't let my friends be in danger because I'm not able to do what I normally can."

He nodded. *I've heard many addicts say that before. No— stop it. She's trying. Maybe she really will bounce off the bottom this time and keep moving up. Give her a chance.*

The fairy continued. "And I'm tired of feeling bad all the time. It's like you said. I keep feeling terrible because I can't feel as great as I did the first couple of times. I can't ever get it back. It's like chasing something that always gets away. It isn't worth it. I'm done. This is it, I promise."

She reached a hand out. Remy extended his pinkie and let her grasp it.

"I am glad," he replied, "to hear you say that. And I'll help if I can. Starting tomorrow, you'll need to prove it, though, and I think you can."

She smiled. "Okay."

CHAPTER ELEVEN

Por's Bar, Lower Manhattan, New York

Bobby watched as Volz's facial expression changed over the course of a couple of minutes. At first, he'd wrinkled his mouth and brow at what he called the "piss-weak taste" of non-dwarven beer. But after he'd downed the first one, the warm glow seemed to settle in and a goofy look of contentment crept over his broad features.

Porrillage, the bartender, spared him a quick glance before he returned to his work. "Weird," the gnome commented. "I have never seen a dwarf enjoy regular beer that much. He must have fallen off the wagon."

She smiled and immediately grasped all the implications of what the small man had said. That meant she'd understood the joke without any difficulty. It was a new experience, as jokes often went over her head.

With a watchful eye on her companion, she sipped her beer. It wasn't bad. She pondered all the craftsmanship and refinement, not to mention trial and error and sheer dumb luck that must have gone into beermaking over the centuries.

It was incredible that people had perfected all these discoveries. And yet, she wondered, for what?

Someone came up beside her, a slender man with smooth, fine features, silky hair, and pointed ears. "Hello there," he said in a smooth voice. "I don't believe I've seen you here before. We get some humans but not enough, in my opinion."

Bobby half-smiled. The guy was good-looking, albeit in a slightly swishy way, but she really wasn't in the mood right now.

"Hi," she countered. "Are you an elf? If so, I'm really sorry, but I'm not interested. I dated an elven guy once and it was a bad experience. You know, because of the differential aging factor. Most guys don't want to be with a woman long-term if she'll be sixty while he still looks like he's in college, you know? I'm sure you can imagine how that kinda cramps a girl's style."

"Oh," he replied and looked slightly uncomfortable. "Well, I wouldn't necessarily say that."

She shrugged. "I suppose you could try…I dunno, a gnomish chick? I assume they live about as long as you guys do."

Por passed under the bar again. "Not quite," he quipped.

"Too bad," Bobby said, turned away from the elf, and focused on her brew.

Her would-be suitor, sulking, stepped over and pretended to ask Volz a question or two, but the dwarf merely made confused grunting sounds, so he sashayed over toward the arcade games.

Bobby took another sip. She was only two-thirds of the way into her first beer. She didn't drink much, though, and already, the alcohol was loosening up her mind. It freed it to roam and explore.

She'd concocted the story about dating an elf on the spot and out of thin air, and it had clearly worked in persuading the guy to leave her alone. She never would have been able to manage that in the past.

Then again, before everything changed, she might not even have realized that he was simply trying to get into her panties.

It almost made her squirm with discomfort when she thought of how many things she must have missed over the years. She was only twenty-seven, but that was still slightly more than a quarter century's worth of knowledge and insights—and squandered opportunities.

And the mention of aging and lifespans had set off a chain reaction of other notions and ideas and questions. What was the meaning of all this? How could people live blissfully unaware in such a multi-faceted universe—which included the preternatural alongside the natural, when the natural was already complex enough?

"Hey," she said, "Por, could I get a refill here? It's okay, you can charge it as a second beer."

The gnome was hooking up another keg. "Sure thing, ma'am. Give me a second." He finished the task and hurried over to climb his makeshift wooden steps to reach the bar.

"So, sorry to ask," she began as Por extended his hand toward her mug, "but did you hear the story about why I'm here? Probably not, since Remington's busy. Let's simply say I've gone through some major changes lately and I'm not sure if I'm...dealing with them as well as I could."

The gnome's face shifted into something that was half a grimace and half gentle sympathy. "You got initiated into the preternatural, did you? It's okay, humans usually need a couple of weeks—or years—to really absorb it all." He snatched her mug and bounded toward the tap.

"Yeah," Bobby confirmed, "that's it. Part of it. There's more. My eyes have been opened in more ways than one... it's like I'm seeing and hearing and thinking of things that are completely new—I've never experienced them in my life until now."

It irked her that she couldn't express herself more clearly. Why hadn't she learned to talk better? She'd have to teach herself to speak like one of those erudite professor types, given that she had the brainpower for it now.

While she tried to organize her multitudinous strains of cognition and emotion into something that made more sense, a man to her left stepped out of her field of vision. Another man stepped into the same place—or was it the same person?

She turned her head toward him as he sidled up.

"Hey there," he said. "Did you get cheated on? Sorry, ha, but that's the first thing I thought of when you said your eyes had been opened."

Bobby gave him a quick examination. The first man she'd seen—before the second one stepped in—had almost exactly the same body proportions as this one but his facial features were different. His skin tone slightly darker, hair lighter and wavier, and his jaw stronger, and he had five o'clock shadow.

It was the same man, she concluded.

A shapeshifter? He must have observed her for a while and tried to gauge her preferred type, then subtly altered his appearance to appeal to her. She had to admit, he looked good. But what she saw right now wasn't really him, was it?

"No," she told the guy flatly. "See, I never allowed it to get to that point because I caught him lying to me. It was like he was one person one minute and a completely different person five minutes later—like I could never tell who the real person was and he became merely a number of different masks that he wore to suit the occasion. I like people who are genuine."

The man stared in astonishment for a moment and nodded slowly. "Oh, right, I completely understand. Hell, everyone has different sides to their personality, but…they should at least try to be consistent. Not completely different."

It occurred to her that he was setting her up. He would continue his attempt to flirt and when the time came to drop the bombshell that this wasn't what he actually looked like, he could argue that it least it was close to his real appearance.

"Maybe," she said. "You know, I almost think you'd look better with darker, straighter hair. And if you shaved a little closer."

The man sighed, exasperated, and pushed away from the bar. "Well, I tried," he grumbled and wandered off to play pool.

Volz chuckled. "Who's that guy? He was funny…"

Por climbed up to the bar and pushed her mug across the surface, once again filled with foaming golden lager.

"Nicely done," he told her. "That guy tries that shit on basically every new good-looking girl who comes in here. Half the time, it works and the other half, they're usually not sure how to react. Hell, maybe the sonofabitch will go home tonight and rethink his life or something."

"Well," Bobby almost stammered, "life is...something that bears thinking about. I only said what seemed obvious, you know? And none of this would have even occurred to me a week ago. I notice so many more things but it makes me wonder—is this all there is? Is life really a group of people and other entities fumbling around trying to fool each other so they can fool themselves into thinking there's a...a meaning to it all?"

The gnome paused and stared at her with a hard but not unfriendly squint, and he put his fists on his small round hips. "It sounds to me like you're having one of those existential crisises...crises? Whatever the word is. Hey, we all have them sometimes, right? It's okay."

"I suppose," She sighed and frowned as something occurred to her. "And I think it would be 'crises,' based on the way the Latin roots work. Or Greek. I...uh, would have to look that up to be sure, but based on my memory of how other words work, that sounds right. Like, there's a pattern here. To the...suffixes. Do I make any sense?"

"Kinda," said Por. "I'll be right back."

He ambled over to serve another patron, an apparently female member of a bulky, tusk-mouthed, green-skinned species who tried very hard not to look at Bobby. Perhaps she was envious of her looks or maybe simply contemptuous of her attempts at intellectual discussion.

The green woman's boyfriend—or husband, perhaps—came out of the bathroom and sat beside her. His head snapped toward Bobby and something about his gaze reminded her of a hungry dog.

"Crap," she murmured under her breath.

The green guy, even more muscled and yet ungainly than his paramour, extended a big arm in her direction and actually yelled at her. "Hey! You. Wanna come over here? We're lonely. You look like you could use some fun."

He made the word "fun" sound like it involved violently cathartic acts of anger management. His girlfriend, meanwhile, gritted her huge teeth.

Some of the ambient noise in the tavern died down. Bobby felt gazes drifting toward her. Even Volz looked uncomfortable, having snapped at least partially out of his complacent stupor.

She inhaled through her nose. "Well," she called across the bar, "I might consider it but what does she have to say? Sorry, but among my...uh, species, threesomes have to be agreed on by everyone."

"What?" The man snarled belligerently. "What she says doesn't matter. You come over here now!"

His woman shoved him hard off the barstool and he sprawled across the floor. "Shut up, Ugluk! Look at her. She looks like some fairy whore anyway. You have no taste. Fucker! I'll tell everyone about this. You're going soft."

Ugluk responded in his own native tongue, which sounded like chunks of concrete forced through a wood-chipper. Soon, the couple growled and swatted at each other as they argued their way out the door, much to the relief of the entire bar.

Por chuckled. "Miss Bobby," he proclaimed, "the next one is on the house. We have a non-discrimination policy, of course, but orcs and alcohol don't mix. You probably saved me considerable business. Maybe you should give lessons on some of this shit."

She shrugged. "Well, it was obvious that the two of them had a rocky kind of relationship. It wasn't really about me so there was no reason for me to be involved. I let them deal with their own problems."

It was nice that Por seemed to appreciate her, but even as he slid her a free extra beer, she was glum. There she was, twice as smart as she'd ever been, and yet she barely understood what was happening.

"I wonder," she began aloud, "are most misunderstandings because so many people are average? It makes sense when you think about it. Most things in society are meant for the majority who fall in the middle. People who are either too dumb or too smart must...you know, be confused most the time." She almost laughed. "Not like I'd know or anything."

Por listened to her with one ear while he conferred briefly with one of the waitresses on a complicated cocktail order from a table full of what might have been aliens. Once he was done, he turned to Bobby again.

"I tell you what," he began in a low voice that would have been inaudible to the other patrons. "I can tell you're having a rough evening, despite making mine even better. And from what you told me when you first came in, Remy

—who, to be honest, is kind of a dipshit—has landed you all in trouble yet again."

"That's the long and short of it, yeah," she admitted.

The gnome fished around under the bar, found something, and laid a small hand flat on the wooden surface.

"This," he explained, "is a key to the guest room. Around the corner back there"—he gestured with his head—"is a staircase that'll take you to it. You and your dwarf buddy can spend the night. You'll feel much better in the morning after a good sleep, trust me. Wake up to a fresh start and some of those thoughts will have sorted themselves out in your head, all by themselves, while you were dreaming."

Bobby hadn't expected that. "Okay, sure, thanks. Shit, I am getting tired. It's been a long day." She accepted the key and drained the rest of her beer in a long gulp.

Volz looked at her, his eyes dull. "Sleep," he dribbled. "That sounds...good."

Por had been about to return to work, but he lingered a moment longer. "Oh, there are two beds with a curtain you can pull between them. And if that still isn't enough to put your mind at ease, look under the one closer to the door, where you'll find a baseball bat. Ain't nobody gonna try anything after you whack him a few times with that."

She laughed and it felt good. "Thanks, Por. I'm fairly sure Volz meant it, though. He's already barely conscious as is."

Then a chill went through her as she contemplated the multiple ways in which that statement was true.

CHAPTER TWELVE

Remington extended his index finger and used it to pat Riley gently on the back. "Okay. Do you feel better? You can do this. We believe in you and stuff."

The fairy inhaled audibly and her wings perked up as she spread her arms and closed her eyes.

Outside, the sun was up, although only a little of its light penetrated the cracks in the blinds. Remy and Conrad stood on either side of James Russel's bed, while the fairy stood on the nightstand next to it, in full view of the man's chest.

When Russel had awoken in the middle of the night, mostly delirious, they'd given him water and sleeping pills. Now, he was technically awake but in some kind of drowsy fugue state that was likely the combined results of the drugs, exhaustion, confusion, and whatever the hell Moswen's brand might still be doing to him.

The time had come to take care of that last problem.

The fairy clapped her hands and held them pressed

together, and silvery light erupted from the colonel's chest. He'd mumbled wordlessly and shifted his position while his head lolled from side to side. Now, however, he stiffened and his eyes snapped wide open.

Conrad exchanged a glance with Remy, and it occurred to both of them that, if the fairy's spell failed, their captive might die of a heart attack or a stroke even before Moswen could kill him herself. Then they'd have to deal with the unexplained death of a retired officer under circumstances where a few witnesses might have seen them approach his house.

And Taylor still wasn't around to perform a mindwipe. If they fucked it up, there would be no clean slate.

Particles of golden light, the residues of Moswen's power, began to filter through the silver, but Riley's aura held.

"You got this," Remy assured her and hoped he was being encouraging and not pressuring her. "You already cut the bitch off from having full access. The job's half done. You only need to remove the part that's left."

She made a humming sound and trembles rippled through her minuscule body as she concentrated to channel her power into the body of the man tied to the bed and do what she could to purge him of the Egyptian vampire's malevolent influence.

Colonel Russel's mouth fell open and strangled gasps emerged from it. His eyes were glazed and his hands clawed at the sheets. While he thrashed helplessly in place, the starlight glow on his chest intensified, solidified, and became a cloud that blotted out the golden sparks.

Finally, a long sigh rattled from his lungs and all the

magical light winked out at once. He slumped on the mattress, breathing hard and sweating.

Riley fell to her side and moaned, shuddering but conscious.

Remington gestured to Conrad and pointed to the colonel. "Check his vital signs or whatever it is that you're supposed to do with old people and see if there's still a hieroglyph on his chest."

The werewolf nodded and set to work. Remy, meanwhile, examined the fairy.

"Are you all right? I think you did it. Goddamn, it worked."

She rolled onto her back, released a long sigh, and rose to her feet. "Yes, I...I'm much better than last night. And I did. I...crushed it out of existence. There's nothing of Moswen's left on this side of the cut I made yesterday."

"Ha!" Remy gloated, grinned, and looked skyward. "I knew you had it in you. Beautiful work. Later, we'll get sweet potato pie, if I can remember."

The fairy smiled and wiped her brow. "I'd like that."

Conrad looked up from the bed. "He's okay, mostly. It's been a rough twelve hours, but he doesn't seem to be in any serious, medical danger."

"Even better," the investigator quipped. He ran a hand through his hair.

Russel stared into space and sweated onto his pillow and still looked like he needed a whiskey with hot lemonade followed by a shower and about ten hours of sleep. But for now, he was vaguely awake and conscious.

Remy addressed both his companions. "We'll give him five or ten minutes to recover before we interview him.

How about we help ourselves to more of his delicious tea in the meantime?"

The trio sat in silence in the kitchen. When they'd drained their cups about halfway, Russel's voice spoke from the bedroom, forming coherent words for the first time since the fight.

"Hey," he called, his voice weak and ragged. "What the hell is going on here? Who are you people and what are you doing in my house? I…ughhh— Jesus, it's coming clear again now—"

Remy and Conrad nodded, and they headed into the bedroom. Riley followed at a slight distance and remained out of obvious sight. They weren't sure if the de-thralled colonel would still be able to see her.

The investigator took the lead and tried his best to look confident and officious. It helped that he and the lycanthrope were both dressed in suits. And, thankfully, he'd had all night and morning to think things over and practice how he'd handle this.

"Colonel James Russel?" he asked.

The middle-aged man on the bed frowned. "It's probably no use to deny it. If you people have tracked me down, you know who I am."

He nodded. "Good answer. I can't tell you exactly who I work for but believe me on one thing. We are on the same side. Tying you to the bed was necessary for your own protection since you haven't been yourself lately. And you said a minute ago that memories were coming back to you. We'd like to hear more about them. This is all off the books but you can still consider it a formal debriefing."

The colonel took a couple of deep breaths. "Can I have

a cup of tea?"

"Sure," he said. "Wonder Boy, get on it."

"Yes, sir," Conrad acknowledged and strode away to the kitchen.

Remy pulled a chair up to the bedside. "Right. Now we basically know what happened, but we need your version. Unusual things have occurred lately, haven't they? Start from the beginning and tell us everything."

Russel tightened his jaw, his face uncertain. "What's the date today?"

When he told him, he had to hold the man's phone up to prove as much.

Shaking his head, the colonel started talking. "A little over three weeks, ago, then. I was on my way into work and this...woman accosted me—all good-looking, and spoke with a Middle-Eastern kind of accent, although I couldn't quite place it. Normally, I never let a stranger lay a hand on me, but something was...wrong. Different. She touched my chest and I can't remember anything after that for a while."

Conrad returned with a steaming mug and once they'd released his hands, handed it to the colonel, who nodded his thanks and took it with both hands.

"Then," he continued, "things were...kind of a blur. I can't recall everything. I felt confused much of the time and saw myself doing things without intending to do them —like my brain floated there helplessly while someone else controlled my body. Someone was giving me orders..."

"Drink some tea," Remy suggested as the colonel trailed off. "More of it ought to come back as the effects wear off."

Russel took a long sip. He looked at Conrad and

gestured with the cup. "It's good," he stated.

"Thank you, sir," the lycanthrope responded with a smile.

The colonel focused on Remington. "You mentioned effects. Is this a drug thing, then?"

"Affirmative," he said. "By the way, Colonel, are you aware that you're technically officially retired from the Armed Forces and the Department of Defense now?"

The man looked startled and altered his posture subtly. "No...what? Wait—yes. I remember now. I applied for retirement without even knowing why."

He drank more tea, gathered his thoughts, and continued. "And I also remember"—he fixed Remy with a hard stare—"your face from the photos they showed me. I was... I was supposed to assemble a team for a black op and eliminate you."

Remy nodded. He wasn't exactly shocked. "Who's they, Colonel? Who showed you these photos and gave you these orders?"

His gaze went distant as more of the truth unveiled itself within his mind. "That same woman. As far as I knew at the time—or seemed to know—she was one of ours, acting off the books. She said you were a dangerous criminal and an accessory to terrorism. I seem to recall thinking in the back of my mind that this was all as suspicious as hell. The Army National Guard doesn't conduct domestic covert operations like this, for fuck's sake. But somehow, I couldn't help myself. It seemed right and official, and yet it didn't."

That's interesting, Remy thought. *With Alex, Moswen used a simple brute-force approach—"Do what I say or I'll hurt you," basically. Now, with her plans growing in scope and complexity, she's become more subtle. Her top thralls operate under layers of deceit and illusion.*

The colonel's eyes hardened, and the muscles along his jaw went tight. "If I find out," he rasped, "that they were right and we're not on the same side, and you have any intent to misuse this information, you'd better kill me right fucking now or I'll rip your throat out the second I get out of this bed."

Conrad tensed and kept his gaze focused on the officer.

Remy was a poker player, and it took most of his considerable powers of self-control to keep a calm face at that statement. Russel definitely meant what he said.

"No, Colonel," he replied, "there will be no need for that. The people who tried to brainwash you, to begin with, are the criminals here. And, together, we'll stop them."

Russel snorted and leaned back in the bed, shaking his head. "This is Company shit, isn't it? Anytime you guys get involved, it's all smoke and mirrors."

He smirked a little and shrugged. "Well, sir, if you're still confused, let's review the facts, shall we? You were approached by someone—clearly a foreigner and possibly from a country with elements that are, shall we say, not aligned with American interests."

After a small pause for effect, he continued before Russel could interrupt. "Then, you find yourself in a state that matches the description of several experimental psychotropic drugs, in which you're persuaded to do strange things like suddenly retire, and perform a *de facto* hit on persons such as, for example, the two of us."

He pointed to Conrad and himself. "Ivy League douchebags, aka the Company's favorite recruiting pool. This foreigner specifically targeted you, a high-ranking officer. And all of this happened at a time when everyone knows that New York's streets are flooded with new drugs from somewhere overseas."

The man remained impassive, but Remy spread his hands. "You do the math, Colonel. Do you really think that we're the terrorists or transnational criminals here?"

His face took on a droopy, sullen look. "I damn well better see some kind of official proof, and the sooner the better."

"You will," he promised and immediately wracked his brain for ways to deliver on that. They'd be able to concoct something, he was sure.

Briskly, he stood up. "Finish your tea and take a minute to think it over. Then we'll talk about what to do next and even let you get out of bed."

"Gee, thanks," Russel snarked. "There isn't anything else in this tea, by the way, is there?"

Remy snapped his gaze toward Conrad. "Wonder Boy. You didn't put sugar in this man's tea, did you?"

"A little," the lycanthrope admitted as they strolled casually to the kitchen. "I thought it would help to perk him up."

He threw his hands up. "For fuck's sake, man, I told you not to do that anymore."

In the kitchen, the trio conferred in low voices. Riley started off by asking what had happened. "Is he better?"

"He's free," Remy whispered. "He's suspicious of us but I'm fairly sure we've got him."

"You know," Conrad interjected, "I did once have a gentleman from the CIA try to recruit me. I didn't fancy the idea of them finding out about lycanthropy, so I turned him down. Still, that Ivy League comment was a nice touch, sir."

He gave his bodyguard a thumbs-up. "Thanks, Conrad. And it's too bad. You would have made a great CIA guy. Anyway, we now merely need to make sure this man doesn't immediately run and tattle to the government. That would result in our operation being blown out of the water, while Moswen slips back into the sewers and keeps mentally enslaving people until she wins."

Riley remained to rest while the two men headed into the bedroom.

"Colonel," Remy said, "I'd like to exchange phone numbers and I'd like you to tell this team you contacted to stand down but also stand by. Within the next few days, we'll get back to you on the latest developments, and your help would be appreciated."

The man still looked somewhat skeptical, but then the investigator thought of something.

"Our contact with the FBI—a senior special agent named Gilmore—might be the one who makes contact with you. With your help, we can expose these pricks and shut them down once and for all."

Russel nodded toward Remy's pocket. "You already took my phone. If you want to exchange numbers, you don't exactly need my permission. Let me out of this bed so I can take a piss and a shit, though, and I'll consider cooperating. For now."

He smiled. "Deal."

CHAPTER THIRTEEN

Moonlight DetectiveAgency Offices, Bushwick, Brooklyn, New York

The black Tesla pulled up to the office at 10:02 am.

"Hey," Remy observed, "it looks like Bobby's car is here. That's a good sign, I think. Unless someone stole it and is laying a trap for us. Ugh, why did I say that out loud?"

Conrad frowned. "I have no idea, sir."

Riley looked out the windshield from her usual position on the dashboard. "I don't see or smell anything unusual. I think we're probably fine."

"Excellent." He drew into his usual spot, shifted into park, and shut the engine off. As they emerged from the vehicle, though, he had to admit that he was disappointed to be the first and only driver of a black Tesla in the lot.

Remember what Presley said. Taylor always has good reasons for the seemingly bizarre things she sometimes does.

He pushed the door open, stepped into the lobby, and instantly noticed Ms Roberta Diaz.

"Bobby," he greeted her. "It's so nice you could make it

in. Por didn't say anything nasty about my drinking habits, did he? If so, I guarantee he merely made it up to make it sound like he's selling even more booze than he already is. Pure propaganda."

"Hi, Mr Remington," she responded. "And Conrad, and Riley. Did you guys sleep in your clothes? No offense, but I've always seen you looking sharp, so it's...uh, you know, weird to see you all rumpled. Oh, Volz is here also—he's fine—and Alex is back."

Yesterday, they'd sent Alex to buy pipe bomb components from multiple different stores across the Tri-State Area using cash. Buying all they need from one place with a card would have probably resulted in Agent Gilmore needing to interview them yet again.

"Good," said Remy. "Our date with the colonel went..." He sighed. "Fairly well. Are there any developments on your end?"

"None," she reported and ran her fingers through her hair. "I took a route that made it difficult to follow us, and we avoided traffic cameras, so I think we stayed off the radar and obviously, we're still safe."

He nodded. Not that he'd ever disliked her previously— she'd always been nice and mildly entertaining—but he was growing fond of the new, genius version.

"Good job. As for the business with Russel, we'll tell you all about it in a moment. Is that donuts I smell?"

"Yes." Bobby smiled. "Volz and I picked some up on our way in. Alex did the same, so there's, like, four boxes back in the break area."

"Can I have one?" the fairy asked.

He glanced at her. "Sure, although I'm not sure all that

fried bread will fit in you. Maybe in human form. If you go that route, though, make sure you stay embiggened until you're done digesting it—and preferably, passing it too. Unless the spell also transforms the size of foreign substances in your digestive tract?"

Conrad cleared his throat. "Mr Remington had a long night. He seems to have trouble keeping his thoughts to himself."

"Silence, Conrad," he responded. "You're...uh, kind of right, though. Sorry. Let's get some coffee."

En route to the break corner, they bumped into their favorite Australian intern.

"G'day," Alex said. "Or not so good, depending. I bought all your pyrotechnics. They're in the back storage room with the components well separated, so there's no chance of them going off accidentally unless someone walks in there and flame-throws the whole lot."

"Spectacular," Remy congratulated him. "Too bad about not being able to bring my flamethrower in to work, though. By the way, have you had any brand activity? We probably pissed Moswen off again."

The Australian grimaced and his right hand went involuntarily to his chest. "A few palpitations, some stinging, and a half-arsed impression of anger, but nothing too overwhelming. What did you do this time, anyway?"

He smiled. "Remember when we removed your brand to stop Moswen from killing you and made you our trusty, donut-fetching intern? Well, we did basically the same thing to this Colonel Russel guy. Riley handled the magic."

"Really," he marveled. "It almost makes Taylor a mite redundant, doesn't it? Don't tell her I said that."

"Of course not." He patted the man on the back and proceeded toward the coffee machine and the stacked pastry boxes.

Once everyone's belly was filled with caffeine, sugar, and fat, they reconvened around the corner from the lobby. That way, they could quickly greet any customers who came in while still being out of the immediate sight of the front door.

Remy found the murder board, as they'd taken to calling it—a large, wheel-mounted poster board that handled erasable markers and sticky notes equally well. He pushed it into the center of the floor, while the others arranged themselves in chairs in front of it.

Bobby, seated closest to the lobby so that she could perform her reception duties if need be, stared at the board with heightened interest.

"Huh," she remarked, "I never realized you guys actually used that thing. I saw it with the sheet over it a few times or pushed into the corner facing the wall, but I thought it was simply...there. Extra." She almost looked embarrassed.

He shrugged. "The More You Know. We mainly use it to keep track of info we've gathered on especially sensitive cases, hence the necessity of keeping it a secret. Since you weren't initiated into the preternatural at the time, it would have obviously raised too many questions."

She waved a hand. "Fair enough, I guess. Now, are we gonna get on with the show here? I'm curious about Russel."

Volz made an "ooh" sound, followed by, "Show? I wanna watch a show. The one with the colors. It was funny."

"Later," Remy said. "Actually, Conrad, give him your phone and let him play Candy Crush or something."

With a sigh, the werewolf did as he was told and winced when the dwarf's thick, strong-fingered hands closed around the screen.

"Okay," the investigator began, "let's review. Each of these notes represents a different important fact or a major player in the Moswen case. They detail everything we know about her or her operation. I'll get to where Russel comes into all this in a minute."

He quickly summarized the stakes of the game. Mostly, they all knew this stuff—even Bobby picked up most of it at a rapid pace—but there were a few threads that needed weaving into the overall fabric.

His summary complete, he moved on to emphasize the new information that they'd gleaned from the colonel.

"Basically," he stated, "Moswen is doing the next best thing to putting a bounty on our heads, which is to use subtler forms of enthrallment combined with half-assed cover stories to make it seem like we need to be wiped off the planet. Or at least captured, which might be even worse."

He tried not to shudder at the thought as the memory of how Alex had almost died under Moswen's burning brand raised itself in his head. He didn't particularly like the pompous, whiny bastard, but it had still been... unpleasant. And he had little doubt that the Egyptian vampire would do the same, or worse, to all of them if she could.

"We've temporarily neutralized the threat from Russel and his team," he pointed out and moved the sticky note with *Russel* on it to the side. "And we might even be able to use them as allies. Although first, we'll need to legitimize ourselves, which will probably involve talking to Agent Gilmore again."

Bobby raised her hand. "We might want to stall on that, though, since Gilmore mainly deals with Taylor and she'd start asking questions about where she is. I don't think she'd react well if we said we didn't even know."

"Yes, good point." He tapped his lips thoughtfully. "We'll give it, say, forty-eight hours. I'll stall Russel with a text or two, and that'll give us time to think of something else, perhaps."

He went on to point out to all of them that there might be more hits on any of them ready to be executed by brainwashed minions, but they had no real way to know until they made progress on their current leads.

"And so, in conclusion," he announced and felt rather like a respected Cambridge professor presenting a thesis on the mating habits of katydids, "we really fucking need a new plan of some kind. Something that ties all this together, that keeps us from getting out heads bitten off, but also allows us to act and move things forward, at least until Taylor gets back. Whenever that might be."

Uncomfortable silence reigned for a moment, the only sound being the high-pitched sound effects that emanated from Conrad's phone as Volz plunked away at it, engrossed in a game or video.

Again, the receptionist raised her hand. "Honestly, Mr Remington, I can't really think of much else we can do at this point, besides maybe have someone shadow Representative Dusek. I can keep working on assembling a list of his contacts and associates, and we can trace some of them and follow them in the hope that they'll bring something new to light."

Pursing his lips, Remy gave an appreciative nod. "Yes, that's better than nothing, at least while we wait for things to develop with Kendra and the colonel. And, hopefully, for the good vampire to return and help us in dealing with the bad vampire. All things considered, though, I'd say we're doing fairly well even without her."

Riley, her enthusiasm for helping the agency seemingly bolstered by her resolution to stay away from the shopping district, applauded. The sound of her tiny hands striking each other resembled someone trying to light a gas stove on the other side of the building.

"Thanks." He pointed to her and grinned. "After Boobs —uh Bobby—finishes our list of contacts for Dusek, I'll probably take Riley and handle that myself. In which case, Conrad, you'll be on guard duty again. Also, we really need to do something about Volz."

The dwarf looked up. "Whuh? Leave me alone." He returned his focus to the screen.

Conrad reached for his cell gently. "Okay, Volzy, you had a nice long time to play...whatever that is. Uncle Conrad needs his phone back."

"No!" the dwarf protested. "Mine. You can have after I sleep. When's lunch?"

Remy looked at everyone in turn. "Any other comments, questions, or concerns?"

There were none.

"Right." He pushed the murder board back against the side and facing the wall, and tossed the sheet over it for good measure. "So, uh, you can all return to your posts or whatever. I'll make some fresh coffee…"

For a moment, it looked like Boobs was about to offer but she shrugged and returned to her desk. She had more important tasks to do, so Remy didn't complain.

He needed a minute to think things over, anyway. They were stuck in limbo. Although closer than ever to cracking Moswen's foul operation, there was, for the moment, almost nothing they could do except wait. He hated simply waiting for things to happen.

"Well," he muttered quietly, "there's always the other cases. What's-His-Name with the Baphomet-phobia and so forth."

When he reached the break area, he stared at the greasy rings on opened boxes where donuts had been and realized that he'd been slack in working out lately. And he'd had to miss another martial arts class. They might try an intervention with him soon.

Shaking these minor concerns from his head, he approached the coffee machine.

Another insight struck him. Until yesterday, he'd never really thought of Bobby as a serious player and a true member of the team. Granted, she'd never been filled in on what was really going on but had the deception been necessary? Given her interest in the goddamn Inquirer, she probably would have believed everything and been happy to help. Even with a less-generous loadout of IQ points.

And now, there she was, grasping implications and repercussions and doing important research. So much so that he didn't want to distract her from her work and now performed mundane tasks like coffee preparation himself.

Well, someone has to do it. There is no way in hell we could run this operation without a steady supply of perfectly legal stimulants.

Coffee-making had the advantage of being a task that almost anyone could do competently. He considered this and weighed it in light of the fact that, as vice-president of the company, he was officially in charge during Taylor's absence. He now had real, actual leadership responsibilities.

It was kind of terrifying, but he liked to think he was doing okay at it.

Still, the example of Bobby makes me wonder. It's kind of a conundrum, isn't it? Other people have intrinsic value and all that, yet different people are better suited for particular tasks than others. Being head honcho, for the time being, I need to keep that in mind along with corny stuff like treating everyone with respect. Which I suppose I never really thought about much until now. But it's also knowing how to allocate the labor.

And if all-out war with Moswen broke out before Taylor returned—which was possible—his margin of permissible error would shrink to almost nil. Not only everyone's self-esteem and career satisfaction, but their very lives would be in his hands.

The coffee pot burbled as he stared blankly at its lighted button. Suddenly, and for the first time ever, he missed the days when Taylor merely used him as bait.

CHAPTER FOURTEEN

Moonlight Detective Agency Offices, Bushwick, Brooklyn, New York

The office's front reception area would soon close for the evening, and Remy was no closer to finding a solution than he had been hours before. He was in the break area again, seeking refuge while he guzzled more coffee—a three-to-one ratio of decaf to regular, at this hour—when two things happened.

First, Riley fluttered through and waved to him as she approached, probably wanting to talk about something.

Second, Bobby pressed the intercom and made a brief announcement. "There's a taxi pulling up out front and officially, we're still open for another nine minutes."

"Damn," he muttered. "Couldn't they have gone to a restaurant and ordered a well-done steak three minutes before closing time? That way, they'd be annoying someone other than us and they'd still end up with a steak."

As if anticipating his reaction, Bobby added, "So I'll let

them come in and state their pitch. I'll be clear that we're almost closed, though, and won't let them take too long."

That's better, he reasoned. He finished his pseudo-coffee and motioned for the fairy to join him. She complied with a small smile.

She put her hands on her hips while she floated in front of his face. "Remy, are you okay? I feel a little better, so it makes it easier to see things, even if I still don't understand all human behavior. I can tell you're having a rough time. I think you're doing good, though. Like the way you handled things yesterday and the way you summed things up today."

He gave a kind of sour half-smile. "Thanks, Riley, it's nice to hear you say that. Having to take over our whole operation, though…it's not easy. There's much more to leadership than the stuff in action movies, where it's all barking orders and looking cool. I have to…take care of you guys in addition to making everyone pull together and get things done."

"Aww," the fairy replied. She came closer and patted him on the earlobe. "Well, I don't think you're doing badly at it. Not at all."

Before he could reply to this, the front door opened and footsteps strode in—quick, purposeful, and surprisingly silent. To his surprise, they did not stop at the reception desk but continued through the lobby and toward the main office floor.

"Oh! Hi," Bobby's voice exclaimed. "We—ah, wondered—"

Remy brought the fingertips of both hands to his

temples before he hurried out of the break room. "You have to be kidding me. Not even an 'I'm on my way' text."

Taylor walked into the office. She was dressed in a black jacket, black gloves, and black shades, and carefully removed a small, oblong object bundled in blue cloth from her handbag. Something about her skin looked unwell, as though she'd recently been exposed to the sun and was only now recovering.

As usual, her face showed no identifiable expression or feeling.

By now, everyone else had scuttled over to offer their greetings—or at least to confirm that the agency's undead proprietor was well and truly back.

Conrad reached her first and his handsome face revealed a mixture of concern and relief. He had strongly discouraged anyone from going home early this evening, mostly out of fear for their safety.

"Miss Steele," he said, the words hurried, polite, and a tad awkward, "we were all worried. Is everything all right? I've kept a close eye on the crew this whole time."

About the same time that he opened his mouth, Alex appeared from somewhere out of the office's depths and looked at her askew with his usual undercurrent of embittered trepidation. He stood a few feet to Conrad's right.

"So you're finally back, are you?" he stated gruffly. "I didn't get much from the Australian ex-pat community here aside from continual bitching about the weather. What was the actual purpose of that little errand, anyway?"

Midway into his ramble, Bobby hurried over, leaving her desk but remaining where she could see the reception area. Her face was drawn with anxiety, probably over how Taylor would react to the news of the magical IQ bomb.

"Miss Taylor, we have a few things we need to talk about," she interjected.

As the words left her mouth, Volz trudged up, pushed into the space between Remy and Alex, and stared at the vampire with a vague and curious recognition. His mouth hung slack.

"Hey," he drawled, "it's...you. You're a...friend." His face split into a large, dopey grin.

Taylor was now completely surrounded. She stopped and the twist of her mouth registered subtle displeasure. Calmly, she removed her glasses, folded them, and slid them into a pocket. Her dark eyes were calm but clear.

"It would seem," she stated in a low voice, "that there have been developments in my absence."

While all this was happening, Remy felt as though he were slowly regurgitating a tangled ball of frustration, confusion, wounded ego, and self-righteous indignation. His hands formed into weird grasping claw shapes and they trembled.

His gaze locked on hers. "Where the fuck have you been?" he sputtered, his voice almost cracking. "You slipped away without even the slightest indication of where you were going or when you'd be back. And this at a time when we're in the midst of one hell of a serious investigation that's on the verge of turning back into all-out war!"

He threw his arms up, allowed himself to sway in a melodramatic fashion, and gestured at her with his right hand.

"I've barely held things together all this time. And developments is putting it goddamn mildly. Jesus Christ. Normally, I don't go around making demands, I think, but I am very sure that you owe us an explanation. Like, right now."

The barely perceptible expression of her mouth moved another notch in the direction of sourness.

"I was in Israel," she stated flatly. "I had to go there post-haste in order to acquire something that we'll need in order to defeat Moswen."

Remy calmed, at least a little, and his gaze wandered down to the curious azure-wrapped bundle in the vampire's hand. "Oh. Well, you could have—"

She cut him off by holding her hand up, the palm outward, probably abetted by some preternatural ability of hers. He simply stopped talking as quickly as if someone had pressed *STOP* on the audio file in his brain.

"For now," she interjected, "we need to discuss what's going on here and all that has occurred lately. It's clear to me that there is some situation with you all that requires further management."

He bristled inwardly. She assumed that he had not been able to handle things without her when in fact, Riley had complimented him on how well he'd done.

Still, he didn't intend to argue with the main gist of her words.

"Kind of." He sighed.

And, for a moment, he was on the verge of breaking down and blathering about how he'd missed her, he needed her, he wasn't sure what to do without her—and how none of them felt like they could handle things without her there as a backup, a secret weapon, or an insurance policy. Taylor was everyone's ace in the hole.

Thankfully, he stopped himself because that wasn't true. It was good to have her back, but they'd held things together. The point of absolutely needing her had not yet come.

"Well," he began, steeled himself, and regained his dignity and composure, "we're all still alive and the agency is still functioning. We're not at the point of catastrophe."

The vampire almost smirked. "Well, then, you must have done something right. My compliments."

"Thanks. I hope you didn't hurt yourself, saying that. Still, it's good to have you back because some serious shit has gone down, yeah," he confirmed.

She nodded. "Let's sit and discuss it, then. Do not omit anything or color the facts." She glanced around at the other employees. "That goes for all of you. Feel free to contribute in any way you think might be useful. The more accurate my information is, the better I can help."

Remy scratched his nose. "Fine."

He spoke first and kept his account both as detailed and as objective as possible. A few times during the story, Bobby or Conrad raised their hands to inject commentary of their own—or to politely correct him on his exact inter-pretation of events, much to his annoyance.

While he talked, he noticed also that Taylor looked at both Bobby and Volz in a strange way. Clearly, she'd picked up on the fact that something was different about them. Of course, as the revelations continued, they reached the part with the enchantment via mail bomb, and her face settled into calm, if stern, realization.

Of course, he glossed over things a tad with regard to that particular incident. He didn't want to insult either Bobby or Volz. Especially since the former was probably now well aware of how much less intelligent she used to be, while the latter now lacked the brainpower to deal with hurt feelings in any kind of mature way.

Toward the end of the powwow—at the moment when Remy had reached the murder board conference they'd held this morning—someone else came into the office through the front, having apparently walked in off the street.

Bobby departed the instant she heard the door open and positioned herself behind the desk in time to greet the new arrival.

He glanced into the lobby in mid-sentence. Their guest appeared to be an average fortyish man with an air of uncertain hesitancy.

"Excuse me," he said to the receptionist in a phlegmy voice, "are you still open? Judging by the sign, I wasn't sure."

"Yes," Bobby answered, "although we're about to close. If you're here about a case, we wouldn't have time for a full interview. But if you'd like to ask a question or two or schedule an interview for tomorrow, we can definitely take care of that."

Even as he spoke to Taylor, Remy nodded his head, pleased with her appropriate response.

The man went on with his pitch in the background and partway into it, everyone around the corner in the main office area tensed and, in the next moment, froze.

"Well," he began, "I...uh, I'd heard that this place deals

with...paranormal investigations. I'm inclined to be the skeptical type, but—this is embarrassing—I think I might have a problem with exactly that kind of thing."

He cleared his throat in the sudden, tomb-like silence and continued. "I think I may have a problem with a... werewolf killing animals of mine around the time of the full moon. This is the third month in a row. It sounds crazy, I know."

Even Taylor looked prepared to rush the man, kidnap him, clamp a chloroform-soaked rag over his mouth, and give him a good mindwipe, hoping that no one on the street would see what transpired through the windows.

But Bobby, playing her usual dumb blonde persona, defused the situation almost immediately.

"Oh, ha...um, it's okay," she replied and managed to sound perplexed but sympathetic. "While...uh, we don't exactly believe in the supernatural, we're willing to investigate weird occurrences with no judgment."

A brief pause followed broken only by the sound of her pen scribbling notes onto a piece of paper as she always did with new clients. A moment later, she resumed speaking.

"What I mean is that werewolves aren't real, but there are people who act like them—or unusually large animals with rare diseases, things like that. Give me your name and contact information and I'll put that, along with your problem into our system. They'll review it first thing in the morning and get back to you."

The man breathed a sigh of relief. "That would be great. I feel like I'm losing my mind here. At the end of the day, it doesn't matter if it is a werewolf or a rabid dog or even a neighborhood kid off his rocker. I simply want to know what's going on and put a stop to it."

Taylor smiled gently as they listened and the tension in her shoulders melted away. She was impressed at how well Bobby had handled a potentially delicate matter. She exchanged a brief look with Remy.

We're in agreement, finally, he surmised. *My decision to hire her, to begin with, is even more correct than it already was, now that she's one hundred percent a valuable member of the team.*

A moment later, the customer was on his way and Bobby locked the front door after him, flipped the sign to *CLOSED,* and turned the front lights off. She joined the others where they sat in the center of the floor spanning the main office suite.

"Clearly," the vampire began and addressed them all, "we have a number of things to deal with. Thank you—and I truly mean this—for having held things together as best you could while I was gone. I might not have left if I'd thought you couldn't handle the ins and outs of our business."

Remy tried not to smirk as he basked in the implications of the statement.

She continued quickly. "Soon, I will help each of you address some of your individual issues. But first, I need to explain why I left in the first place. It has to do with our friend Moswen, of course. The rebuke we dealt to her last time was only a minor setback. She is as dangerous as ever and we must take action to stop her at once."

"Awesome," he remarked. "So, what do you have there? An anti-vampire homing missile?"

"Not quite." She sighed. "Over the course of my research into our adversary, I learned of the possible resting place of an ensorcelled dagger that once belonged to a man called Teremun al-Harb. As it so happens, it lay in the same country that Moswen most recently came from—Israel—and originated in the same country that was her first home—Egypt."

"Okay," he extrapolated, "so it's an anti-vampire homing knife."

She pretended he hadn't spoken at all. "The dagger, when activated by a sufficiently skilled practitioner of the arcane, has the power to bind vampires and evil undead spirits. Rendering her helpless is as good as killing her, the point being that she can no longer harm anyone, not only us."

"But," Riley interjected and drifted up a little as she spoke, "will the magic bind you when we wake it up?"

Taylor's mouth almost frowned. "I am not sure yet. We need to find a talented witch to cast the spell, anyway, so when the time comes, we can ask her."

"All right," said Remy. "I'm sure you have binders full of witches. Let's choose a good one before we call it a night and go see her in the morning. Or...uh, evening, if you prefer."

Now, the vampire did frown. "Unfortunately, traditional witches of true power are relatively rare in America. They mostly remained in the Old World rather than come to the New. Back in Europe and Asia and Africa, some still fear them but they are appreciated. The infamous events of the Salem Witch Trials sent a strong message that the emerging civilization on this continent did not want them here and witches tend to have long memories."

Conrad frowned and raised a hand. "But if I may, Salem was only a small incident. Unpleasant, yes, but nothing compared to the witchcraft persecutions in Europe during the Early Modern Period. Are they aware of that?"

"Yes," Taylor explained, "but the common view is that those were a brief aberration in a period covering millennia. Salem happened during the inauguration of Euro-America. And with no familiar established tradition here, the majority of them simply decided that it wasn't worth it to practice their craft on the west side of the Atlantic. It might not be entirely rational, but it is what it is. Still..., there are a few."

She turned to Bobby. "Roberta, I gather that you are more confident in your abilities lately and that you've already done good work at turning leads up. I'd like you to begin searching for anything you can find about legitimate and respected witches in the vicinity of New York City. The sooner, the better."

The young woman smiled at being trusted with such a major responsibility. "Yes, ma'am."

"Now," Taylor continued and once more addressed the whole group, "there is one more problem I'd like to ask about. These congressmen whom Moswen has enthralled...do we know anything definite about them? Where are we on this? It's rather important."

Remington scratched behind his ear. "Yeah, well, we're working on that. We only received the tip from Old Boy Don yesterday, if I recall correctly. So much shit has happened lately that it's starting to all flow together in my head."

Before she could interrupt with some obvious comment about how they needed to get off their asses, regardless, he continued.

"I did think of trying to hack into traffic cam footage. I know it's kinda dystopian, but we have an emergency here. The problem is that there's only one man here who could pull that off, and he's not really up to it at the moment." He gestured with his head toward Volz, who paid no attention to the discussion and instead, picked chunks off a large rubber eraser. "I could do a stakeout."

Taylor drummed her red fingernails on the arm of her chair. "What about Kendra? You mentioned having her back you up to ensure Russel is on our side, anyway. It's one more excellent reason to call her in addition to the fact that you seem to enjoy her presence."

He was taken aback by this. Agent Gilmore had been helpful to them but he'd always had the sense that she had to be quarantined from half the details of what was really going on and might turn against them—with the force of the FBI behind her—if she found out too much. Although she was rather attractive, of course.

"What?" he stammered. "Really? You want to bring our friends from the government in on this in a direct capacity? You're not a shapeshifter simply pretending to be Taylor, are you?"

"Under the circumstances," the vampire replied curtly and ignored the last question, "I'd say that if she and her team can help, then yes. It's worth a shot."

CHAPTER FIFTEEN

Moonlight Detective Agency Offices, Bushwick, Brooklyn, New York

It was close to 9 pm and Bobby was still at the office.

Taylor, Remington, and Conrad had all departed for Taylor's house. Alex was in his makeshift loft, processing the office's mail before bed and hiding from Agent Kendra Gilmore, who'd arrived over an hour before. Volz lounged in Taylor's office, doing basically nothing.

Riley was there, too, but the last Bobby had seen or heard, she'd curled up to sleep under the overturned coffee mug Remy always kept on his desk. Plus, he had assured her that the fairy was invisible to most people even if she was technically in front of their faces.

"Okay, so," Kendra began and swallowed the last mouthful of pizza. A flat, empty box, originally containing the now-consumed meal, lay on the desk beside her. "We know that Moswen Neith has absorbed the remnants of that other mysterious organization that distributed Snow White. And, thank God, I haven't seen as much of that shit on the streets lately, but maybe this is the calm before the storm. We also know that she's trying to compromise public officials."

Bobby nodded. Taylor had decided to take the risk of leaving her to deal with Gilmore alone on the grounds that she was now looped-in on everything that was happening and had the augmented ability to deal with it. Still, the vampire had seemed nervous and had left her a fairly detailed protocol of what—and what not—to say or do.

"We're working on obtaining ironclad proof of that. I won't insult your intelligence by pretending to be all indirect about it, so if you can help us with that, so much the better—for everyone."

The Senior Special Agent gave a low chuckle. "I appreciate forthrightness. We're basically already on it, though. In fact, let me call my man on the street for an update. Then, it would be helpful if I could use your computers again to check something."

"Sure," the other woman agreed although inwardly, she was hesitant. There were many things they didn't want Kendra to see—at least, not yet. Not only because she was law enforcement but also because she was uninitiated.

But then again, from what Mr Remington had said, Gilmore and her team had already seen more than they probably should and continued to cooperate. And, supposedly, continued to deny that there were any preternatural elements at play.

Kendra woke her phone up and speed-dialed a number. A man's voice answered although the volume was too low for Bobby to hear exactly what he said.

"Mortensen, it's Gilmore," she stated crisply. "Do we

have those surveillance teams to put on the Representative and the City Council tomorrow?"

Agent Mortensen spent a minute or so replying, during which she caught only a few words and phrases, like "should be," and "oversight," and "deep shit."

Kendra nodded every few seconds. "Right. Okay, good. Yes, thanks to that bust we pulled off, they're taking us seriously, but that also means we're probably a hair's breadth away from other teams getting involved. Shit. All right, thanks. Over and out."

She powered down the device, leaned back in her chair, and sighed. "Getting anything done is like pulling teeth. I already have a slight reputation as the local 'cowboy cop' lately, I guess. I'm not sure how much longer we can keep our involvement with your company under the radar. People ask questions."

Bobby knew that something like this was coming and was grateful that Taylor and Remington had at least stuck around long enough to greet the agent and get things set up before leaving the whole mess to her for the evening.

"I understand," she said. "And watching our local politicians will help. But it's kind of a crapshoot, isn't it? What we really need is to know who's actually been visited by Moswen in the last month or two. That would help to narrow it down."

Kendra straightened again. "It would. If your computer system is as advanced as you say, let's agree that I'll turn a blind eye if it falls into the grey area of legality as long as it helps to crack this case. For example, the NYPD or the various county sheriff's departments might have records that can help us—things pertaining to Snow White or to mysterious recent arrivals from Israel or Egypt. I could obtain those the right and proper way, but it would take longer."

Bobby believed her on the grey area of legality issue, but there was still the question of the preternatural to consider.

Before he'd left, Remington had briefly lectured her on the importance of not letting anything slip to do with vampirism, lycanthropy, fairy colonies, or black magic. It could compromise everything. Gilmore might doubt their legitimacy, not to mention their sanity. It would jeopardize their relationships with their clients and might require exhaustive mindwipe actions on Taylor's part.

Not to mention, he'd gone on to say, that if Kendra believed it or was forced to believe it by hard evidence, who knew how she'd react? It could be psychologically damaging to a person to have their entire world suddenly turned upside down.

"Oh," Bobby had responded, "yes, I know. Trust me."

And he had. She could not help noticing his increased respect for her lately.

She stood and led the agent to another desk, one containing Volz's top-of-the-line computer. "Okay, let me boot it up and input the password—I have to ask you to look away for that part—and then you should be all set. The databases are clearly marked and right on the desktop."

"Agreed." Kendra paused and a wry look formed around her mouth. "And you don't have any objections to a federal agent poking around in your secret files?"

"Ha-ha. Well," she replied and tried to seem flippant and

none too bright, "I don't really understand how it all works anyway, but Mr Remington said he'd already gotten everything all ready to go for you. I wouldn't worry about it."

The woman sat and moved the mouse cursor toward the first database. She nodded toward Taylor's office. "What's the matter with your boy Volz? Normally, it seems like he'd be helpful in this kind of situation."

"He's sick," Bobby replied, frowned, and shook her head. "And we're starting to worry that he might be developing multiple sclerosis or something. He's had spells of these kinds of symptoms before—being out of it, exhausted, having trouble concentrating or with coordination of his movements... It's really sad. Of course, it might simply be a weird flu reaction. He's going to the doctor soon."

The agent pursed her lips. "A cousin of mine had MS. I could examine him and give you my not-professional opinion but yes, he'll need to see a doctor no matter what."

"Eh," she waffled, "I don't think that's necessary, but thanks for the offer. Right now, he doesn't really want to see or talk to anyone. Even Mr. Remington and normally, those two get along really well."

As she made that statement, she hoped Volz wouldn't choose to prove her wrong and emerge, blabbering incoherently about dwarven culture and dwarven magic, not to mention gems, jewels, precious stones, and more gems.

Fortunately, he didn't. Instead, Bobby watched Kendra for a moment and realized that the database program made more sense now than it had in the past. Before the bomb, she'd always felt like she barely got by with the office's tech.

Speaking of which, she had work of her own to do—finding a witch. She stopped in mid-stride, though, as a thought popped into her head.

Taylor had mentioned something else—something important. Kendra would need to know about the essence of it but not the literal truth and pulling that off would be a delicate balancing act. Still, as her brain's neuroelectric activity geared up and expanded to its full potential, she was fairly sure she could handle it.

"Oh, also," she quipped, "Taylor made some offhand comment that...uh, I think might be big when you think about it. About how she's mostly ruled out there being any other major suppliers of Snow White left in the city besides Moswen. So, like, if we deal with her and prevent her stash from being redistributed on the streets, that would, you know, break the spell, ha-ha. All the people affected by her drug-trade stuff will revert to normal."

The agent rubbed her eyes. "It's usually not that simple but then again, it's not unheard-of, either, for almost all of a particular type of crime to be linked to one key criminal. In any event, between the level of violence she's willing to use and the level of corruption she's trying to implement among elected officials, it's clear to me that removing Moswen from the picture is a goal we can all agree on."

"Definitely," said Bobby. "Also, do you have any updates with that military guy?"

Kendra frowned and turned away from the PC.

"This business with Colonel Russel," she explained, "could get as dicey as hell. All he'd have to do is make one phone call and the entire bureau would be involved, question me up and down as to what kind of cavalier shit I've done, why I haven't bothered to seek their approval or submit to their oversight, and fun stuff like that. We could all get in serious trouble. It's hard to promise anything."

"Hmm," she mused. "But since Remington told him you'd be in touch, wouldn't he be even more likely to call someone if he doesn't hear from you?"

The woman tensed. "Yes, that's possible. I'll deal with it in the morning. I was actually surprised to get that call from Remington because I almost thought he was…I don't know, afraid of me or something. He ought to relax. I should have known it was only because he needed help."

"Welllll," Bobby teased, "I thought maybe…oh, I don't know…there was kind of something between the two of you. Which makes me surprised that you're surprised. I mean, you have to have at least thought about it." She gave the other woman a suggestive glance.

Kendra only stiffened further and put on her business face. "I'm only here to do an important job," she mumbled.

"Well," the younger woman admitted, "I ought to get back to my job anyway. In fact—yeah, I can see the screen from here. It looks like I have a hit. I'll be over there if you need anything."

She returned to her PC, reviewed the information that had come up with an increasing sense of accomplishment, and her hands almost trembled with excitement. She snatched one of the office's landline phones off its hook and dialed the company's vice-president.

"Mr Remington," she said quickly when he answered, "great news. We have an address for a possible witch. Her name matched a few cryptic words and phrases that seemed unlikely to show up in conjunction with anyone who didn't know what they were talking about. The only problem is, it looks like she went off social media and such about five years ago, so she might not still be practicing. However, she has some good reviews from a few users of a forum that's all about spells and the occult and the most recent posts are from only...uh, a year or so ago."

"Huzzah," he replied. "Good work, Bobby. Tell Kendra I said hi, also. Let's plan on an early start tomorrow."

The receptionist sounded even more pleased than he did. "Thank you, sir. And that sounds great. We might have to spend the night here but we'll do what we need to. See you in the morning."

Moonlight Detective Agency Offices, Bushwick, Brooklyn, New York

Agent Gilmore stretched her arms and cracked her neck as Bobby returned to her computer.

Well, she thought, *if Miss Diaz here isn't going to directly need my help for a few minutes, I might as well actually do something. I hate feeling useless and lazing around. That's the kind of thing that Remington guy would do. Well, when he's not being daringly stupid. Or funny.*

She glanced around the office. The staff, holed up there for most of their time lately, was gradually turning the place into what looked like a college dorm populated by slobbish frat boys and the pizza they'd ordered and scarfed down hadn't exactly improved the situation.

Quickly, she told Bobby, so as to not seem too much like she was doing any unwarranted snooping. "I'll tidy things a little if that's okay but I'll stay out of Taylor's office so I don't bother Volz."

One downside of being an FBI agent was that people were always suspicious as to why she asked questions, why she went into a room, and in some cases, why she did or said anything whatsoever.

"Sure," the other woman acceded and turned her head slightly to make her voice heard although she didn't actually make eye contact. She seemed engrossed in processing the results of her query. Kendra hoped that the info she'd turned up would be worth the effort.

The agent stood and gathered the empty pizza box and grease-stained paper plates and napkins they'd used and pitched them into the trash. It was a start, but there was considerably more to do.

Then, as she walked farther back into the office, she was unsurprised to hear Bobby stand and move to a different computer, likely for privacy reasons. She sighed.

While she gathered a bevy of empty coffee cups, the receptionist made a phone call to Remington.

Most of their discussion was unintelligible, but she did hear "social media" and "good reviews," which made her curious. It probably had something to do with a different case of theirs. She didn't want to barge in on private matters with their other clients, so she let it go.

She crunched the cups so they'd take up less space, then stuffed them into the waste bin on top of the pizza box and its associated accouterments.

Once most of the surfaces were clear of trash, she located paper towels, dampened them with a splash of water and hand soap, and wiped the desks, counters, and any other surface that looked like it could use it.

In only twenty minutes, she had the main office floor at least looking presentable. She stood with her hands on her hips and admired her handiwork. It made her wonder why it had apparently been so difficult for the people who actually owned the place and worked there to take care of it themselves.

That line of thought led her to Remington's office. Volz wasn't resting in there so there was no reason why she couldn't head in and clean it as well.

She opened the door and stepped through. The place was, she noted with approval, in slightly better condition than the main floor. Still, there was a little dust here, a coffee cup there, and a forgotten jacket dangling from the chair. And that damn ceramic mug, for some reason.

Kendra threw the paper cup in the bin, brushed the dust away, and took the jacket over one arm to hang it on a proper coat rack once she left the office. Her gaze turned to the mug.

Each time she'd been in there previously, it had been turned upside down. It was probably a gift from a family member that he constantly forgot to use or didn't want to dirty, hence the empty paper cups for his daily percolated bean-water. Oddly enough, though, it was currently turned right side up.

She took it by the handle, lifted it and frowned. It seemed too heavy for its size, yet it appeared to be empty. It must have been made of especially dense ceramic.

Kendra took the mug and the jacket out, closed the door behind her, and put the coat where it belonged. She carried the cup and a few other non-disposable dishes over to the little kitchenette in the break area. Earlier, she'd noticed that the office had its own dishwasher.

When she opened it, however, it was already half-loaded with junk. She deposited the few plates, glasses, and knives and forks into the available slots and added the mug. As she turned it upside down to hook it onto the upper rack, it almost felt like something fell out of it.

"Weird," she muttered to herself. "I've been working too hard lately."

Without giving it a second thought, she slammed shut the door, set the dial to *Normal Rinse*, and turned the appliance on.

"There," she muttered. "That ought to restore a little normality around here."

CHAPTER SIXTEEN

Taylor's House, Harrison, Westchester County, New York

Remy slouched in his shotgun position, smiled in a vacant, subtly cocky way, and occasionally scratched the back of his neck, while Taylor lectured him from the driver's seat of the Tesla. It felt like being fifteen again and pretending not to care when his mother gave him a good talking-to.

"I will acknowledge," Taylor said, "that having to take only my car home rather than both simplifies our commute considerably, not to mention conserves fuel and slightly reduces our ozone emissions."

Hah! Remy laughed inwardly. *She actually admitted that I'm still right, after all.*

"But," she continued and her voice sharpened considerably, "I thought it was perfectly clear by now that you are not to take any of my cars without permission. I'm astounded that Presley failed to stop you, but it's not as though you're a child under his care. You are well past the age of responsibility for your own ignorant, hasty, ill-considered actions."

"Aww," he drawled, "I tried to ask permission, actually, but you didn't pick up the phone. Where were you in Israel, anyway, that you were physically incapable of answering? The Land of Nod or some shit?"

"Jerusalem," she grated. "And if I don't answer, that is the same thing as not granting permission. Any condition other than hearing me say 'yes, Remington, you may take my car' should be considered a no."

He adjusted his tie at his neck. "I'll assume that doesn't apply to emergencies where you need me to take the car to save your life, but otherwise...fine. Point taken."

"Good." Some of the tension fell away from her, and she drummed her nails on the steering wheel. "When we arrive home, there is something I'd like to tell you. An expansion, you might say, on the subject of my recent trip to the Levant. You were right about one thing—I owe you an explanation."

"That's good to hear," he replied. "I know you kind of already explained but not in much detail. Then again, I'm sure some of it is obscure arcane stuff that I have only a novice's grasp of, anyway."

"That," stated Taylor, "is mostly correct. But you should hear about it, nonetheless. Still, we ought not to spend too much time on it. There's not much we can do to help Bobby with the tech stuff, I'm afraid, so the best we can do is to get some rest so we're at full strength when we do find a proper witch to help us."

Remy squirmed in his seat. "Does that mean Conrad will spend the night?"

"Yes," Taylor said. "I might have to leave the house briefly, in which case, for your protection, I think we can agree that two werewolves are better than one."

She cut his protest off but, as it turned out, only to reassure him. "Although I see no reason why he can't sleep on the couch as opposed to in your room. Maybe even another guest room with its own bed."

He breathed a long sigh of profound relief.

Conrad was a slightly more conservative driver than Taylor was, but he nonetheless arrived at the house only about a minute later than they did. To all their delight and even relief, Presley had prepared a pleasant meal and a pot of tea for them.

As they sat to eat, he reflected on how his health was on the verge of suffering lately. He hadn't slept enough or had much exercise, and he'd mostly subsisted on coffee, donuts, and the occasional deli sandwich. As he enjoyed a fresh salad, boiled potatoes, and savory roasted chicken, he could almost hear his body thanking him.

Even Taylor seemed to enjoy the meal. She did not eat any of the food but appeared to savor its aroma, and she accepted a cup of regular tea with only a couple of drops of blood added to it from one of the bags in the fridge.

Remy gestured his thanks to the butler. "Thanks, Presley. I think we all needed that."

"Don't mention it, sir," he replied with a noticeable smile of sleepy satisfaction. "I'm well aware of your ghastly eating habits when you're distracted or hurried."

Conrad raised a hand. "You know, I can recommend some healthier than average drive-throughs that you might want to consider."

"Later," Remy said. "Taylor, you said we had to discuss something, right?"

"Yes." The vampire set her cup down and stood. "Come with me. Down to my crypt, if you please. I find it more private there than in the bedroom."

Consumed with curiosity, he followed her closely and didn't notice the odd, focused way the two werewolves watched the two of them leave.

"Mr. Warfield," the butler intoned behind them, "allow me to show you to your couch for the night."

They descended the stairs, closed the cellar door behind them, and walked to the sarcophagus-like stone structure that enclosed the vampire's old wooden coffin.

"David," Taylor said and stared at him with her black eyes, "do you recall when Gabriel's lackeys stole my coffin and you came looking for it to rescue me, only to discover that I was not even in it at the time?"

He put his hands into his pockets. "Of course. What does that have to do with...anything, though? Sorry, I'm merely wondering."

"Well, stop wondering out loud and I'll show you. Come this way." She beckoned and led him around to one of the back corners of the basement behind one of her wine casks, where an old-fashioned black iron candle holder was attached to the grimy stone wall.

Remy nodded with approval. "Ooh, spooky. This seems like the kind of thing a vampire should have in her cellar if you ask me. It's far more dramatic than the books on music and maths and all that stuff."

"You have no idea," she remarked and pulled down on the metal fixture. It scraped as it pivoted like a lever, and the section of wall beside it made a grinding sound and swung inward on secret hinges.

"Well," he had to admit, "this is even more haunted-castle-esque. Nicely done. What's down there? Three dudes in billowing white gowns to whom you feed the occasional baby?"

"No," she replied sharply. "And please don't joke about things like that. There are vampires who...truly behave that way. I am not one of them."

Without bothering to produce a light, she led him down a crude stone staircase. It spiraled around the walls of a roughly circular cave that was much like a dried well or cistern and ended in a pit filled with musty, chilly air and little else. Barely enough ambient light from the cellar above filtered down for him to faintly make out a rectangular hole in the earth at the very bottom. A shallow grave in a deep, dark tomb was the thought that immediately came to mind.

"I must say," he began, "I didn't realize you had this much extra space here. It's certainly...atmospheric."

Despite himself, he shuddered. The darkness, the claustrophobia, and the forlorn nature of the cave-crypt all served to remind him that the beautiful woman he was speaking to was, in fact, an animated cadaver.

Taylor stretched over his shoulder and touched a small iron brazier which he hadn't noticed at first. It burst into eerie blue flame, startling him but at least making the pit slightly more hospitable.

"Now," she stated, "I will tell you the full story of what happened when Moswen and I met in that tunnel beneath her warehouse. What you've heard thus far is only the loose outline. There are certain details which you must know."

He shrugged. "So be it. I'll try not to cover my eyes during the scary parts."

She told him everything. The way her enemy had taken her by surprise and the entire course of the fight. How the two vampires seemed evenly matched and inflicted severe damage on one another's bodies before they briefly reached a stalemate.

Grimly, she related that terrible moment when Moswen had shed even the pretense of being something like a human being at all to become a hideous jackal-serpent creature, losing the last vestiges of reason but gaining even greater strength and ferocity.

Remy shook his head slowly from side to side. "Well, damn. I didn't even know she could do that. I assume it's a unique thing that she—"

"No," Taylor interrupted. "She is not the only one. I can as well. And I did."

"Oh." He wasn't sure how to respond to that. "Uh…"

She laid a hand softly on his arm. "David, please don't tell anyone about this. You must understand that in order for a vampire to shift into an alternate form like that requires…how shall I put this?…the unleashing of ancient forces of darkness which are better left untouched. There have been some who shift to this form and never return. They live out their immortal lives as the kinds of monsters who are the reason nightmares exist."

"Do you mean," he asked and narrowed his eyes, "that you're worried that you won't be able to control yourself?" Something—almost a sixth sense—had informed him that she was half-hiding this from him, that she'd wanted to confess it but would need him to prod her before she did.

"Yes," she confirmed. He could recall only a handful of occasions when she seemed this vulnerable and almost bashful. "For most of my life—my second life, which has been far, far longer than my first—I have sought to control those urges. If I give myself up to them completely, I am no better than Moswen. That is her true form. The shape of a woman is the mask she wears for others' benefit. And, I must say also that even if I did, that would be no guarantee of victory."

It began to make sense, now. She didn't trust herself to overcome the Egyptian with her own powers alone.

"She wounded me very badly," the dark lady continued. "I was close to death, to be honest, although I gave as good as I got and she fled before either of us could finish it. It is fortunate that I had a few hours to heal before you led Greyhammer's posse to my doorstep."

"Aye," he said. "I'm sorry about that."

She waved a hand dismissively. "Anyway, I hope you now understand why I had to go to Israel. There is almost no way I can defeat Moswen without an unfair advantage. An ace in the hole. I'm simply not strong enough."

He shrugged. "Most people, myself included, would disagree, but fair enough. At least with the dagger, we have a chance, right?"

"Yes," she confirmed. "I have searched, with ever-increasing urgency, for a spell that can bind Moswen once more. We need something to return her to insensate impotence, lying forever in darkness as she did for two hundred and fifty years in the forgotten tomb she crawled out of.

I've done the research, pursued leads, and laid the foundations of our plan for months now."

Remy raised an eyebrow. "Oh, so that's what you've been up to all these nights when no one really knew what you were doing or where you were. And I suppose it ties into the infamous incident when you used me as bait."

The vampire did not respond right away, so he continued. "Well, at least we have Alex now. That is why you sent him off to randomly interview New York's other folk from Down Under, isn't it? I can't think of any other reason unless you merely wanted to get rid of him for a while. In any event, it's good to learn that you were doing something constructive."

Taylor folded her arms over her chest. "Yes, the whole endeavor has required considerable study, using resources that most people have never even heard of. Why, what did you think I did with my time? Simply sit around all night sipping red salt tea until dawn?"

He folded his hands in front of him and tried to look innocent. "Well...er, yeah, something like that. After all, why do any work yourself when you have us minions to take care of the dirty jobs you don't want?"

His gaze grew as distant as his mind and his jaw clenched even as his spine went cold. "Like that fucking... septic...thing a few days ago. Good Lord—"

Taylor gestured impatiently and chose not to respond to what was clearly a rhetorical question.

"Let us continue with the important part of this discussion, thank you. While the others continue with the search for a qualified magical adept, there is something else we can do. Namely, we can brainstorm a location where the deed should be done."

Remington's brow furrowed. He was now legitimately confused. "You mean, kicking Moswen's ass in private? It does seem like something that would require numerous mindwipes if too many normies saw it. I suppose her abandoned warehouse would work, although this being New York and all, you can never—"

"No," she interjected, "I mean a location for her entombment. The dagger's power will work in the place. It's not as though we can activate it here and coax her onto a barge destined for Antarctica before we finish the process under the Thiel Mountains, sadly. The Negev Bedouin had the advantage of encountering her in a forsaken desert where they assumed no one would ever think to look."

Her gaze was distant again, searching within rather than scanning the outside world. "This city is rather more densely populated, but there must be someplace where we can put her away forever—or as close to forever as possible. Some nook or cranny that will remain untouched for a long, long time."

Remy leaned against one of the stone pillars that braced the basement ceiling and looked up and around. By local standards, this house was practically ancient. By the standards of the region from which Moswen came, however, it was a different story.

"Well, that's a toughie," he admitted. "As I started to say a moment ago, there's never any real guarantee of privacy in this city or of permanency, either. Even in the most people-packed areas of the Old World, it seems like things remain as they are for longer periods of time. But here? Things are always changing."

"Yes," she agreed and grimaced. "I've noticed. Sometimes, that's a good thing. In this case, far less so."

His mind wandered to one of the companies his father owned stock in. "They're always rebuilding old stuff or making new housing for all our immigrants, or looking for ways to spend this year's public works budget on random improvements that sometimes delve deep underground. The real estate firms and construction outfits knock down buildings and dig up lots all the time. Even the darkest, most desolate sub-basement of an abandoned subway line might provide only ten or twenty years of isolation. Then, who knows? Hell, our oldest buildings are only two hundred years old, tops."

The vampire's fingers drummed against her opposite arms with an increasingly frenetic and aggressive tic.

"Yes, you're right. But we're running out of options. We cannot delay. Moswen must be overcome with all due haste. Sealing her away for even one paltry decade is better than nothing. What choices do we have?"

Remington suddenly felt the length of the day and the weight of its responsibilities upon him and clenched his hands into fists. The task suddenly seemed borderline impossible.

"I don't know," he grumbled. "Maybe a vault holding really boring technical reference manuals at the bottom of the New York Public Library? That's where the Ghostbusters did their thing that one time, isn't it? If it was good enough for them, ought to be good enough for us."

Taylor snapped an immediate response. "This is no time

to be flippant, Remington. Besides, I assume you refer to the 1984 film, in which case, that was the first ghost they encountered—the one they *failed* to take care of. Still..."

She paused and seemed to analyze the option and tease out what he'd said, even though he hadn't really meant it.

"Frankly," she said softly after a minute or so, "you may be on to something there. An esteemed library is the kind of place that's unlikely to be bulldozed to build more condos—or so we can hope—and provided that we can keep her physical body somewhere inconspicuous, it might be an excellent example of hiding in plain sight, so to speak."

Remy laughed. "See? Flippancy is practically my super-power. This reminds me of—"

His phone rang.

"Wow," he said and glanced at Taylor in much the same way he'd once looked at older kids who'd managed to acquire next-gen video game consoles a few days earlier than himself. "I'm impressed that we can actually get a proper signal down here." He slipped the phone out to examine the screen.

"Yes, yes," she riposted, her demeanor somewhat haughtily distracted and eyes hooded. "I have a booster tower well-hidden in the back yard. It's a great help to my phone service as well as my wi-fi router. Being a vampire is no excuse to live in a backward slum. We have amenities here."

As he raised the cell, Remy could not help noting the subtly elitist statement. Normally, she kept her vague sense of superiority under tight control. But with the strains of the present situation wearing her down and keeping them all on edge, the mask of civility had begun to slip.

In fact, something about her recent brusqueness and slight desperation almost reminded him of the aftereffects of addiction. Between himself and Riley, not to mention old friends who'd never recovered, it was easy for him to recognize.

But there was no time to discuss that now. His phone's screen displayed the identity of the caller. *Boobs / Office.*

He drew his finger across the green button. "Hi, it's me."

"Mr Remington," Bobby's voice said cheerfully, "great news. We have an address for a possible witch…"

"Huzzah," he replied once she'd delivered her whole explanation. "Good work, Bobby. Tell Kendra I said hi, also. Let's plan on an early start tomorrow."

The receptionist sounded even more pleased than he did. "Thank you, sir."

He ended the call and returned his phone to its lair within his pants.

Taylor was now seated on the rim of her open sub-grave. "I heard that. It's nice to finally have some glad tidings. I could track her down myself tonight, but it's possible she keeps to mortal, diurnal hours, and I think it would be best if you and I spoke to her together. We will go in the morning. Don't worry about me. I can survive the sun when I must."

Remy nodded. "Right. I'll go lose consciousness but I'll set my alarm for an hour earlier than usual."

"Good." Taylor looked thoughtful. "In the meantime, I will probe into this matter of the library."

He gave her a thumbs-up and trudged toward the stairs.

Taylor's House, Harrison, Westchester County, New York

Presley had found since Remington had moved in that his life and duties had grown more complex.

This wasn't only because he constantly had to remind the young man not to trash the place, not to disturb or annoy Miss Steele, and so forth but also because of the necessity of, for example, increasing the grocery budget and remembering to buy accordingly.

Remington often ate takeout of some kind, which simplified matters, but he also consumed extra milk and coffee, not to mention hand soap, toilet paper, and the like. After years of these things remaining perfectly static, it had required some adjustment.

Now, he walked down the main first-floor hallway toward the garage, intending to examine Miss Steele's cars. It would be prudent to see how suitable they were to have enhanced anti-theft devices installed. Perhaps a palm-scanner associated with the key rack.

He knew that things had escalated considerably of late and had even personally participated in a battle mere weeks before. And yet, on some level, his first responsibility was still to the estate. Caring for the house's vehicles was as important to him as ensuring that Moswen and her loathsome allies did not take over the city.

As he approached the door leading to Miss Steele's crypt, footsteps—too heavy to be hers—ascended the cellar stairs. The door opened.

"Hiya, Jeeves," Remy said in a dull, inattentive way. He was clearly tired and distracted.

Presley noted that the young man's tie was loose, his shirt half-unbuttoned, his hair mussed, and that his body smelled of relatively recent sweat.

Also, the butler thought it curious that Miss Steele had invited Remington into her personal sanctum and that they'd been there for a fair amount of time. Although hardly any major concern of his, he had to wonder exactly what they'd been doing.

"Good evening, sir. I can see that you've exerted yourself of late. I take it you'll retire shortly? Oh, and my name is Presley."

The old lycanthrope recalled Taylor's recent words about "lingering smell" but she'd been known to reverse her decisions on things before—she was still a woman, after all. Besides, her private activities were not something he'd allowed to interest him beyond what was necessary for his professional duties.

Remy blinked. "Uh…"

The young man suddenly looked a tad flustered. His

hand shot up to button his shirt and straighten his tie and for a moment, it almost seemed he would say, "It's not what it looks like," or something similar.

Instead, he blurted awkwardly, "I only—it's way bigger down there than you'd think—in terms of both volume and depth. I had no idea."

The butler nodded slowly, his face devoid of any indication whatsoever that he might have attached more than one potential meaning to the words.

"Yes, sir," he acknowledged, his voice as dry as his face was impassive. "Of course. The hidden nether regions sometimes are. Now, if you'll excuse me."

He walked past the rumpled young human toward the garage to complete his duties before he called it a night.

Hudson Heights, Manhattan, New York

Remy glanced at the clock set into the dashboard of Conrad's car. It was 8:52 in the morning—a little early to knock on someone's door, he supposed, but this was New York and according to the old saying, it never slept anyway. He hadn't slept nearly as much as he would have preferred, besides.

"Ma'am," Conrad inquired, "and sir. Will you need me to approach the door with you? I almost think it might be better if I stayed with the car. Still, if you have a safety concern…"

Taylor spoke first. "No, Conrad, thank you. Watch your vehicle and watch us but don't approach unless we—pardon, I—signal you to do so. A man and a woman asking to speak to a stranger will seem less suspicious or intimidating than two men and a woman. Three people are barely short of a mob. We don't want her to think she'll be arrested or press-ganged into a religious group who've heard about her activities and are trying to save her soul."

The werewolf responded with a slow nod. Remy had to admit that it was a good point. He could easily see how a genuine witch might be more suspicious or paranoid than the average person.

The bodyguard brought the vehicle to a stop near their destination—a small, almost quaint house like a miniature version of the Hudson View Gardens complex in the Scarsdale Tudor style. Despite winter having not yet fully departed, the ivy climbing one of the walls was green.

They weren't far from Fort Washington Park and absentmindedly, Remy wondered if their sorceress was aware that she lived within walking distance of an entire colony of the Fair Folk.

The vampire turned to the lycanthrope. "Assuming she lets us in, wait exactly thirty minutes before you come to check on us."

Conrad agreed. Much to his displeasure, Remy recalled the fact that Taylor and the werewolf had once been lovers —briefly and decades before. He shook his head to banish the image from the depths of his skull.

They stepped out into the bright morning sunlight. Taylor had applied a thick layer of sunscreen lotion before they'd left and she also wore black gloves, dark sunglasses, and a wide-brimmed black hat. In fact, she looked rather like a witch herself at that moment.

As they strode up the walk toward the little cottage, something else occurred to Remy and it gave definition to the strange sense of awkwardness that had crawled up and down his neck since they'd crossed Spuyten Duyvil Creek and entered the island of Manhattan.

"You know," he remarked in a low voice, "it isn't a common occurrence for the two of us to head out on a case together, is it? In fact, I can't specifically recall us ever having done so. Not counting moments like you showing up to the tunnel battle a few weeks ago or helping set the ambush for Alex before Christmas. Those aren't quite the same thing."

A wry twist appeared near the corner of her mouth. "Well, Remington, it doesn't make very good business sense to have a dog and yet do the barking oneself, now does it?"

He'd been about to retort with a canned reply—a cocky remark about how having him along meant she ought to feel safer and have an easier time of things—but the words were caught somewhere in his throat and died altogether. He made a brief, half-strangled swallowing sound.

Her mouth returned to its usual impassive set, but not before a slight sound escaped her—little more than a puff or two of air from the nose and the barest trace of a snicker.

"Ohhh, I get it," he said. "Trying to brighten the morning by getting a rise out of me. Well, with me along as your protection and eternal source of really good ideas, I suppose I can handle that extra duty as well."

"Ah," Taylor quipped. "Good."

By now, they were close enough to the house to stand in its shade. She hung back a step and after a moment's hesitation, he moved forward and banged his fist on the door. He made sure it was loud enough to ensure anyone in the house heard unless they were deep into a pair of headphones but not with enough force to be alarming.

There was no indication of any response at first but Taylor turned her head to the side. Her sensitive hearing must have picked something up. A moment later, footsteps approached, and the door opened a crack, secured by a short chain. A single eye peered out at them.

"Yes? Hello?" a woman's voice intoned. "Who are you and what on earth are you doing here this early?"

Remy flashed his best and most charming public relations grin. "Hiiii. We're from Moonlight Detective Agency and we wondered if you could help us."

Taylor stepped in. "You're Ms Alice Pendlebury, are you not?"

There was a vague sense that the person beyond the door scowled before she replied, speaking more slowly now. "Yes, and how do you know that?"

Remy was about to explain but Taylor laid a hand gently on his forearm and took control of the conversation herself.

"We're a private investigation firm. You might even have heard of us. We're looking for an expert in the occult, as we often deal with…esoteric and unusual cases and subjects. Paranormal investigations that other companies prefer not to deal with. Queries into what some might call 'supernatural' or 'preternatural' phenomena."

Remy allowed his grin to fade but kept his poker face on. Taylor had handled that well, he thought. Essentially, she had dropped a few code words, most notably preternatural, into what was otherwise a fairly reasonable statement. She'd even left sufficient room for plausible deniability.

"I see," said Alice. "I may be able to help you. But I'd need to know more of the details and even then, I can't make any promises. There are many people out there who cannot be trusted. I will not be taken advantage of or made a fool of."

The vampire nodded respectfully. "We understand, Ms. Pendlebury. We can offer you a generous sum of money merely for a consultation, with the prospect of more in exchange for further work. Currently, we're working on a fairly serious case, in which several innocent people may be in danger. Sadly, we cannot handle things entirely by ourselves, so it is imperative that someone be willing to aid us."

"Oh?" the witch countered. "And who'll aid me if the press gets involved and my business—which is already not exactly raking in the cash—suffers again?"

Remy, even being a mere mortal as he was, could sense the tension and heavily veiled hostility. Clearly, being taken advantage of and being made a fool was something Alice had personally experienced in the past. She would be loath to be of much help unless they could set her mind at ease.

What surprised him, though, was that Taylor seemed to miss it. She wasn't quite herself lately, and it was, after all, several hours past her usual bedtime. The vampire seemed to operate on a kind of driving cajolement, full of urging and insinuation but without much subtlety or consideration for the desires of the person to whom she spoke.

It was how she became when she was exasperated and growing desperate. Remy opted to intervene.

"Ms Pendlebury," he began in a soft voice, the kind a doctor would use while in bedside-manner mode, "we are aware of your reputation. We also appreciate that a woman in your position has to take into consideration her own social standing, pocketbook, personal safety—hell, even her feelings. As we understand it, you're in a line of work that, to put it mildly, doesn't garner much respect from the general public. Our whole business model revolves around respecting the dignity and privacy of our clients. And, at this point, all we are asking for is strictly confidential advice. That's all."

The eye narrowed as the woman beyond the door seemed to think it over. "At this point, you say. Hah! Well… advice, I can give. But if you plan to simply use that as a foot in the door so that later, you can ask me to place a death-curse on a business rival or personal enemy, nope. It shall not happen. I don't do things like that, thank you very much."

"Yes," Taylor responded, "understood. We are asking no such thing."

Remy wondered how true that was. The ultimate goal was to render Moswen Neith as good as dead. Then again, for someone like her, the witch might make an exception.

Alice sniffled. "That's a start. May I have your names, please?"

He glanced at Taylor. She made brief eye contact with him and nodded. "Taylor Steele," she stated.

Remy looked at the door. "Remington Davis."

Slowly, Alice's eye receded from the crack and into the darkness beyond, and he felt his lower gut clench. *Shit. We lost her. Somehow, we lost her. Does she know who we are?*

Before he could consider their failure any further, locks clicked as they changed position, the door swung open, and the woman flicked a light on. "Good. Come in, please. But don't try anything stupid. I have ways to protect myself, after all."

He flashed a calm, pleasant smile. His instinct told him that Alice would respond better to that than to a big, overbearing grin.

The witch did not look quite as he'd imagined. Somehow, he'd pictured an elderly woman—or late-middle-aged, at least—but Alice Pendlebury appeared to be in her early to mid-thirties. She was about Taylor's height, a good head shorter than himself, with wavy red hair and large spectacles. There was something pouty about the cast of her mouth, although her cheeks were rosy and her eyes twinkled.

The vampire crossed the threshold first, and his mind considered the old myth about how the undead had to be invited into a place before they could attack it. He was fairly sure that one was false, but receiving a formal invitation certainly didn't hurt.

Taylor inclined her head toward the woman again as she stepped in. "Thank you, Ms Pendlebury. I can assure you that we are not here to waste your time."

Remy followed a couple of paces behind his partner,

and Alice closed and locked the door behind him. He looked around the cottage. There were enough books and mysterious boxes stacked everywhere that he could see it as the abode of a witch, although in most respects, it seemed the normal dwelling of a woman who didn't mind clutter but was otherwise tidy and fastidious.

She led them through the living room and toward what seemed to be a combination of kitchen and dining room. Near the doorway, she stopped and looked at them.

"Would either of you like tea? Or coffee, if absolutely necessary?" She pushed her glasses up her nose and he recognized, for the first time, that she had a slight, vestigial British accent. Perhaps she'd come to the United States as a kid.

Taylor answered first. "No, thank you, I'm fine."

"I'll have tea if you're already making it," he said. "Well, if you have coffee, that would be even better, but don't make a pot simply on my account."

The witch shrugged. "Tea it is, then. There's half a kettle of reasonably hot water on the stove and cups and a bowl of sugar beside it."

Remy made himself a cup of plain black tea with no sugar. It was basic but fairly good. That done, he squeezed in at the small round table where the two women had already seated themselves.

"Ms Pendlebury," Taylor began, "let us get directly to business. Our client has come into possession of a rare list of ingredients and set of instructions for what they believe to be an ancient and powerful magical spell. Other persons —unstable and potentially dangerous individuals—covet this same information."

"Oh," the witch replied in a somewhat flat voice, "really. Do go on. Judging by your complexion, you look like the nocturnal kind, so I imagine you're eager to be off to bed soon."

Remy could tell that Taylor was miffed by this, but she hid it well.

"Too true," the vampire conceded. "What we would like for you to do is have a look at this formula and offer us your professional opinion as to its veracity, authenticity, practical application, and so forth. Again, we can pay you only for advice and possibly for further discussion or services later."

Alice raised the teacup she'd been drinking from before they'd knocked as if in a mock toast. "Further services, meaning you want me to cast the spell if I think it can be done. Right."

Remy stepped in. "We all have to protect our reputations, ma'am. You know how it is. Would you be willing to simply have a look at the recipe for starters?"

"Well..." She sighed. "It's not like I have much choice, do I? When the vampire who rules the city asks you to do something, it's usually wise to do it."

Both her visitors sat in silence for a couple of seconds while Alice sipped her tea.

Taylor, her hand still sheathed in a black glove, drummed her fingertips against the table. "I prefer to think of it as overseeing the city, rather than ruling it. I've not given you an order or a threat. In any event, we might as well drop the pretense."

"Quite right," the witch agreed and looked firmly at the other lady. "I know who you are and I have a fair hunch as to why you're here. I hear all the rumors, Ms Steele. Your reputation precedes you. Ever since you more or less usurped control of the Council and reduced it to an extension of your will, other and even worse types have coveted your position. You want me to help you retain it."

Remy was almost shocked. This woman had to know how dangerous his partner was, and yet there she was, saying stuff like that. Then again, he had probably said worse on multiple occasions.

The vampire was still calm but now frowned grimly. "Even worse would be a gross understatement, Ms Pendlebury. The preternatural world is volatile, and I wield a heavy hand only when it is necessary to keep the general peace. The rival to whom you allude would turn New York into their own private cattle farm, complete with slaughterhouse."

He leaned forward and added, "Hey, I'm still fairly new to the preternatural stuff, if the truth be told. I've only done this about half a year. And while I'll be the first to say that Taylor is someone you don't fuck with without good reason, I've also seen that she returns the favor. She's gone out on a limb multiple times, and virtually everyone we've —" He almost said killed but changed his mind. "Everyone we've fought against has actively threatened people, regular mortals and preternaturals alike. This isn't only about palace intrigue or whatever. It's about the common good."

Alice stared briefly at him and her bright eyes seemed to grow behind her spectacles.

"You're sincere about that, aren't you? Naïve and a little pompous, but I can tell you're not a complete prick. And somehow, I don't sense that Ms Steele is simply using you as her PR guy. Very well, then, I'll at least have a look at the spell. But if you want me to do any more than offer my professional opinion, I have a condition."

Again, they exchanged glances and again, she nodded.

"Okay. What is it?"

The witch smiled. Well, smirked, really. "You must provide me with something I want. Besides money, that is. And I'll only tell you what it is, young man."

Remy spread his hands. "Sure. Anything, at this point. We weren't lying when we said that innocent lives are at stake here."

Alice motioned for him to stand and follow her into the living room, while Taylor waited, impassive and silent, in the kitchen. The witch leaned close to his shoulder and whispered in his ear.

"Okay," he replied. "To the best of our ability, we'll deliver when the time comes. Now, please fulfill your end of the bargain."

"Of course, of course," Alice said and suddenly seemed pleased with herself. She almost danced back to the kitchen. Taylor had taken a slip of paper out of her pocket and laid it on the table.

The woman's spirits dampened quickly enough, though, after she looked at the spell and its list of necessary components. While her visitors sat, waiting and earnest, she sighed and rubbed her cheeks.

"Well, ladies and gents," she proclaimed. "It seems we have a true gourmet recipe here. This will require a little more than only a sprig of white sage. My goodness. these are special ingredients—the type I don't happen to have around the house."

Remy looked at the vampire.

"So be it," Taylor agreed. "I'd guessed as much. Where do we get them?"

CHAPTER EIGHTEEN

Taylor's House, Harrison, Westchester County, New York

Remy was developing a good feeling about the whole endeavor. From doubting that they'd even be able to get Alice to talk to them, they'd now convinced her to return to Taylor's house with them. It helped, of course, that the vampire possessed a vast library of esoteric literature. In addition, she already had a few of the necessary ingredients.

During the drive to Harrison, the witch had been curious about Conrad.

"So what are you, anyway?" she'd asked as she poked briefly in the satchel of things she'd brought from home. "You're not quite a normal human, I assume."

Wonder Boy had cleared his throat and stated politely, "Lycanthrope, ma'am. My name's Conrad Warfield. I understand you're Alice Pendlebury? It's nice to meet you."

"Well," she'd marveled, "isn't he a polite one."

Remy had almost drawn blood in biting down on his tongue.

He'd also been curious as to what, exactly, was on Taylor's spell ingredients list, but assumed it was pointless to ask before the two women had the opportunity to look through the vampire's motherlode of arcane tomes and decide exactly what they were dealing with.

The drive seemed to take forever, particularly since the conversation was only sporadic and mostly forced. Remy didn't feel up to trying to inject levity into the proceedings yet. He might still need his snarking juices for whatever lay ahead.

When they arrived at the estate, Presley had been unfazed by the presence of the strange lady, although a curious look of satisfaction crept onto his face when he realized she was another ex-Brit. He hadn't complained when Taylor asked that they be left undisturbed in the library.

The witch admired the antiquated yet tasteful style of the place. "It's a lovely house you have here. I must say, I'm excited to examine your book depository."

"Thank you," Taylor replied. "Unfortunately, we do not have time to peruse every single tome. Still, a quick review of the occult section ought to point you in the proper direction. Let me know if you need anything."

The library lay at the rear of the house. Remy had only been back there a couple of times. Although perfectly literate, he had to admit he wasn't a very avid reader. Plus, most of her collection seemed to consist of old, dusty nonfiction written either in stilted, archaic English or in other languages altogether.

The room was decorated mostly in dark greens and deep browns, with occasional accents of rich crimson and burnished gold. The wooden bookshelves reached almost to the ceiling, and a rolling stepladder stood in the corner.

Alice, her eyes sparkling brighter than ever, practically plunged into the room.

"Oh, this is marvelous." She chuckled. "I'm tempted to further alter our bargain to include a provision that I can come here simply to browse and read whenever I want."

"Hmm," Taylor hedged. "Forgive me if I don't specifically offer that privilege yet. Let us see how things go. Now, my collection of magical works is over here."

Remy followed as she led them to the far corner of the chamber. The vampire stepped back and stood beside him while the witch peered at the spines of the many books.

"My goodness," she remarked. "This is impressive but also, shall we say, somewhat disturbing. You have some dark stuff here in addition to very obscure material alongside the standard classics. Let's see…"

"Be careful," he warned her. "Presley has a book somewhere around here called *Proper Care of Topiary Gardens*. You wouldn't want to so much as touch that one by accident."

Ignoring him, Alice mostly spoke aloud as she examined the volumes and related her feelings on Taylor's diverse hoard.

"Yes, yes. Enochian magic…it's always nice to see some appreciation for good sir John Dee. Some ancient Egyptian stuff—fundamental. Hmm, I'm not sure I like the look of this one…what language is this? It's rare that I can't identify it. But the book feels cold to the touch so it's perhaps best left alone. Not that I'm a stranger to the blacker kinds of magic but it can get complicated if one isn't careful. Oh, and here's some Taoist alchemy…very nice."

She turned toward her host, her hands folded behind her back. "Yes, Ms Steele, your diverse and extensive library gets my stamp of approval."

Taylor smiled and Remy almost sensed that she was mildly taken aback. "That's quite a compliment, coming from you, Ms. Pendlebury."

"Oh?" She looked at the vampire with an expression that was neutral yet somehow intense and awaited further commentary.

Taylor folded her arms over her chest. "In truth, your reputation precedes you as well. It's surprising that we haven't met before today."

Remy raised an eyebrow at that. He didn't know if she was bluffing or not. Since it had taken Bobby's careful Internet search before Alice came up, he assumed she was at least partially lying.

Maybe she's referring to the stuff she read about our witch last night while I was sleeping? That would make sense. Even after all these months, I still can't read her as well as I ought.

"Yes," Taylor continued, "when my assistants produced your name, I thought I'd heard it before. You've successfully worked some rather powerful magicks—notably, the perimeter spell around greater New York. That's likely been almost as much a boon to the peace of our city as my own efforts have."

Perimeter spell? He made a mental note to ask about it later. First, though, there was something else he still wanted to know.

"So, Taylor," he enquired, as the witch pulled down

three books and set them on a small table. "Since I'm a big boy now, may I see that mysterious list of ingredients? I'm curious as to what's so obscure that Ms Pendlebury seemed to have developed a migraine over it when we showed her."

Taylor pursed her lips. "Hmm. Very well. I'll probably need you to help fetch some of them, anyway. Although not until Alice gives us the go-ahead."

She handed him the slip of paper.

He unfolded it and squinted at the flowery, old-fashioned handwriting, his eyes slowly scanning the list.

"Wow," he said. "I take it these ones you crossed off are what either you or Alice already have?"

"Correct." She pointed with a red nail. "The others are the ones that concern us."

The witch, overhearing them, smiled and patted her satchel.

Remy returned his attention to the uncrossed items.

"Fascinating," he remarked. "That only leaves, let's see here... One, apples from the Garden of Eden. Two, a piece of the Burning Bush. Three, fairy dust—that one I think we can manage. Four, a dead man's blood. Cute. And five, the blood of someone 'already under subject's control.' I assume that means one of Moswen's thralls."

He folded the paper again and handed it back, then commented, "Much of this stuff—the first two uncrossed ones, plus a few of the others—seems kinda Biblical, doesn't it?"

"Well, of course," Taylor snapped. "What did you expect? The spell is from Sinai, and those whom it's meant to affect come from the surrounding environs as well."

"It makes a certain amount of sense." He shrugged. "As

long as the last phase of the spell doesn't consist of some guy appearing out of thin air and trying to cajole us into joining his church group. What do you mean 'those whom it's meant to affect,' though?"

Alice looked up from the tome she was reading, turned her gaze to the vampire, and waited to see if she answered.

"Vampires originated from Egypt and the Holy Land millennia ago. Logically, therefore, the magic that can bind them—us—is equally ancient and comes from the same region."

Remy shook his head and pretended to be confused. "What? I thought you originated from England."

"Be quiet, Remington. You know what I meant. Vampirism originated there. Individual vampires, before we are turned, may vary." Her mind already appeared to have raced ahead to consider plans for their next course of action.

"Ohhh," he replied, "right. Of course. Mad cow disease is the one that comes from England. I had them completely mixed up in my head!"

Her eyes refocused on him. "You are truly astounding, do you know that? I wonder how many times, over the years, you rightfully should have had your ass kicked, but the person you opened your mouth to was simply too stunned at your audaciousness to act before you had time to flee."

"Um," he responded and squinted as he combed through his memory, "probably forty or forty-five. Maybe fifty, tops. The other nine hundred times everyone was simply won over by my good looks and charm."

Alice stared at him. "You're not bad-looking. But I'm not so sure about the charm, though."

Grinning hugely, Remy thrust his hands into his pockets. "Aww. Well, that's only because you don't know me well enough yet. Fear not. Everyone loves me once they know what's up."

The witch had already returned her attention to the tome before her. "We'll see, I suppose."

Taylor, too, had moved away from him to watch the woman, ready to offer aid or commentary. Feeling like a third wheel, he said, "Well, I'll leave you girls to your spellbooks and stuff. I happen to know a fairy personally, so I'll get in touch with her about the fairy dust. I could also use a shower…"

Trailing off, he turned and left, heading to the stairs to his second-floor abode. Halfway down the hallway, he pulled his phone out and called the office.

Bobby answered after the first ring and clearly noted the caller ID. "Hi, Mr Remington."

"Hi, Bobby. We found our witch and she's helping for now. How are things on your end?"

"Not too bad. Kendra and I ended up spending the night here since we were still working late and we wanted to be available in case anything happened. We could use some decent shut-eye, though."

"Hmm," he replied, "you might as well come on over to Taylor's. She has a few more spare rooms, and Conrad was nice enough to sleep on the couch."

Behind him, the werewolf commented, "Think nothing of it, sir."

Remy extended a thumbs-up in his general direction without looking at him and mounted the staircase.

"Also, we'll need Riley's help with things that are...uh, specific to...um, people like her." He wasn't sure if Kendra could overhear their conversation, so it was better not to mention the fae specifically.

"Oh, shit," Bobby breathed. "I almost forgot about her. Hold on one sec, okay?"

He stopped near the top of the staircase. All at once, he was worried. It would have been far too easy for the fairy to slip away while Bobby and Kendra were preoccupied and make her way to the nearest shopping center. While waiting for the receptionist to return, he loosened his tie with his free hand.

A moment later, Bobby picked the phone up again. "Okay, well, she's not here. She was sleeping under your coffee mug —that big one you keep on your desk—and I forgot that Kendra cleaned last night. I went to check the cup, and it wasn't there. And the dishwasher had been running."

Remy's hand stopped working at his tie as he froze in place and went cold.

"But," she went on, "when I opened it, there was no sign of Riley. She must have gone off somewhere. Maybe she went home to the colony?"

It occurred to him that he didn't know what happened to fairies when they were no longer among the living. For all he knew, they might vanish in a puff of vapor. "Let's hope that she's okay and that she hasn't gotten herself into anything she can't get out of..." He trailed off, thanked Bobby for updating him, and ended the call.

"Fuck," he rasped. His first urge was to rush to Fort Washington Park and check for her. But then, if something terrible had happened, would the colony know about it via some preternatural instinct? He didn't want to deal with that on top of his own potential grief.

Instead, he walked into his bedroom to finish the process of undressing and douse himself in copious streams of hot water.

His eyes bulged. "Jesus fucking goddamn shit," he sputtered.

Lying on his bed was Riley herself in her true, five-inch-tall form and her usual short silky dress, sleeping peacefully.

He drew a hand down over his face as he exhaled and his shoulders slumped with massive relief. Quickly, he took his phone out again and redialed the most recent number in his contacts.

"Never mind," he told Bobby, "she's here. She must have drifted in this morning while we were out."

"Oh." Bobby sighed. "Thank God. I'm really sorry about this. I'll tell Kendra to leave the coffee cups alone from now on."

He reassured her that it was fine, said goodbye, and hung up again. As the phone vanished into his pocket, the tiny fairy turned, yawned, stretched, and opened her eyes.

"Remy," she said in a small voice. "Hi. You wouldn't believe what a weird night I had..."

"Actually," he countered, "I probably believe it, based on what I just heard."

He sat on the edge of the bed, feeling tired again as the

tension left him and the ongoing stress of the last few days emerged in its place.

"I slept under the cup," Riley explained, "in case that lady from the FBI could see me. I don't think she could, but she's seen the people who were mutated by Snow White, so I wasn't sure. She scooped me up in it and almost put me in that chamber where you boil things with chemicals. I woke up and escaped while she wasn't looking seconds before she closed the door. Honestly, it scared me, and I thought I should come here instead."

Remy extended a pinky to ruffle her hair. "Well, I'm glad you're safe."

She smiled. "Thanks. I think we need to tell Kendra about...well, me and everything else. She'll find out sooner or later, anyway, you know. And that way, I wouldn't almost get melted." She shuddered.

He grimaced. "Ugh, you may be right. The thing is, Bobby at least believed in all those goony conspiracy theories even before we looped her in, whereas Gilmore strikes me as the rational, skeptical type. Not to mention she's a good decade older than Bobby anyway, so probably more set in her ways. She might refuse to believe in the preternatural even if we shoved it in her face."

For a moment, he was amazed in retrospect at how easily he'd accepted it. Doing considerable drugs in the not too distant past probably helped.

"Anyway," he continued and locked gazes with the fairy, "we'll need your help with something."

He explained the gist of the situation with the spell and the list of esoteric ingredients with an emphasis, of course, on fairy dust.

"Yes," Riley confirmed, "it does exist and we have some at the colony. We don't simply give it away, though. It's closely guarded by all the Fair Folk against any other species who might try to steal it. And I don't think you could change their minds by explaining about Moswen to them. As far as most of them are concerned, she isn't really our problem."

Remy stood again. "Crap." He finished, at long last, the aborted act of removing his tie. "Maybe we can give them stock in a sugar company—like, enough to possess a controlling share and a seat on the board of directors. Well, thank you for the info. One way or another, we'll think of something. But first, I need a damn shower."

Leaving his tie and shoes with the fairy, he walked to the bathroom, glowering in exasperation.

Because of frickin' course, things can never simply be easy for once.

CHAPTER NINETEEN

__Taylor's House, Harrison, Westchester County, New York__

Once he'd freshened up, Remy returned to the library and spread his arms to announce his presence.

"Okay, don't worry, everyone, I'm back. I had a nice, pleasant shower. Oh, and Riley didn't die in the dishwasher like I was afraid of for a minute. In fact, there she is, yeah."

The fairy fluttered behind him and perched on his shoulder.

The two looked up. They were seated side by side at the reading table and each flipped through a different old, leather-bound book.

"Good," Taylor said and returned to her reading.

Alice smiled, although he suspected it wasn't at him. "Hello there. You're very pretty. My name is Alice. What's yours?"

"Riley," the fairy replied. "Thank you. I like your hair. It's red."

The witch nodded. "She's a perceptive one. I take it

she's from the same colony where you'll ask about the fairy dust?"

"Yeppers," he confirmed. "They're…uh, temperamental —I've dealt with them many times before—but after a certain period of annoying bullshit, they always seem to come around, usually after I give them something that contains large quantities of monosaccharides. I hope I don't contribute to an epidemic of Type Two diabetes amongst their people."

She rested a fingertip against her chin. "I don't think it works that way with their species, although, if the truth be told, you seem to have more dealings with them than I do. Oh, but we're talking about the fae in the third person when one is right here, aren't we? What do you think, Riley?"

The fairy shrugged. "It won't be easy. We'll have to find a way to make it personal. Most of them don't really care what happens to humans or vampires. I'm one of the only ones who do, most of the time."

Without looking up, Taylor murmured, "Remington has a natural talent for improvisation. We can trust him to do his part while we focus on ours."

He grasped at once that this was Taylor-ese for "stop wasting time talking to them and do what I want you to do," but he decided not to let her get away with it that easily.

"So," he continued, "we can probably get the fairy dust, one way or another. But aren't we simply wasting our time if we can't procure all that other crap? I mean, apples from the Garden of Eden? You have to be kidding me. That can't be a thing. Meaning, you know, one that exists, and is real."

Alice arched her eyebrows. "What, like witchcraft? Fairies? Mad cow disease? The world is full of strange things. Eden-apples are certainly rare, for sure. But there are people—wealthy eccentrics and such—who collect things like that. It's merely a question of finding them and then, I suppose, either buying, renting, or stealing them."

Taylor looked up again, but she was curiously quiet and unresponsive. After a couple of seconds, her eyes hooded and distant, she said, "I have a lead on both the apples and the twig. Don't worry about them."

Remy hoped that was true. He also wondered how Taylor fared with the time of day now well into late morning. He'd suspected for a while that vampires did not biologically need sleep in exactly the same way humans did, but simply being active during the day for so long must have taken a toll on her.

The witch waved a hand. "Leads? Well, that's good. If you'll excuse me a moment, I'll rest my eyes and do my minimal unpacking."

She stood, took her satchel with her, and began taking things out to spread on the library floor.

"Wait," Remy asked, "you're spending the night here, too? Don't you want to get...uh, more than one satchel's worth of stuff from your place?"

"Ms Steele has informed me," she pointed out, "that she has very nice accommodations here, which ought to suffice for a couple of days. Besides, I only live half an hour away. You're lucky you found me across the brook there in Hudson Heights, aren't you? Otherwise, you might have had to go all the way to a *hexenmeister* in Pennsylvania Deutsch territory. That'd be an adventure, I'm sure."

He inclined his head in query. "Isn't it Pennsylvania Dutch?"

"Kind of, but only if you mispronounce it," said Alice. "Hence, the confusion. They're Germans with Old-World traditions, although of course the Dutch are their cousins anyway."

He shrugged. "You're the expert. Anyway, it sounds like you and Taylor have things under control here, so Riley and I will head out." He took a deep breath. "Wish us luck."

She looked up and smiled in a way that was almost... sympathetic? Pitying? "Good luck."

Fluttershire Fairy Colony, Fort Washington Park, New York City

Remy adjusted first his tie, then his cufflinks, and finally ran a hand through his hair. "You know," he told Riley, "I'm fairly sure this will be the first time you and I have ever negotiated with your people together for something. Usually, it's only me negotiating for your help."

"I think you're right," she agreed. "I'm not sure exactly how they'll react."

He patted the plastic shopping bag that dangled beside his hip. "This will help, I'm sure."

She peeked into the sack again. "It might. It looks good but this is normally the kind of stuff you use to barter for, you know, small things. Giving fairy dust to a mortal is really serious. It was one of those things I grew up knowing. No one ever does it, except maybe once every century or two."

The investigator grimaced, but he was fairly sure he'd

already done a few things that were once-in-a-century occasions. He might as well add another to the list.

They crossed the last few yards of the park's muddy ground and reached the dual mounds that indicated the blue and orange halves of the colony, which lay barely out of plain sight in the shadow of the George Washington Bridge.

"Halt!" a tiny voice commanded as usual.

"Hi, guys," he gushed. "I'm so glad to see you again. My old friends whom I love to give sweet things to every time I see them. It's fantastic that we have such a super relationship. Oh, and I have Riley with me. She and I would like to talk to you if that's okay."

Riley waved. "Hello. It's kind of an important thing. Please listen."

"What?" another voice squealed as the other guard joined the conversation. Both the blue and the orange sentries suddenly flitted into sight and converged about five feet in front of his face. "No. It's finally come to pass. The stinky giant plans to take her away and marry her without so much as an offer of recompense!"

"Uh," he stuttered, while his mind raced to dig himself out of this unexpected hole, "no, that's not—"

"How dare he," the other guard shrieked. "We've not even seen her in days. Now, she shall never again know the truth of the fae existence, and will have to subsist forever on the gruel of the mortal and submit to his boring, unimaginative desires."

Remy's eyes bulged at that. "Boring? Do you have any idea what kind of shit I've done at parties? I'll have you know that—" He made a choking sound as he forced himself to stop before he launched into a full-blown explanation.

His companion interceded on his behalf. "No, it's true. We're not getting married. Instead, we're trying to save everyone—the whole city, all the deep-dish pizza places and candy shops, and even the colony. Please, listen. We need help."

"Ha!" the blue guard scoffed, his hands on his hips. By now, another dozen of both colors had drifted out of their holes and formed a buzzing throng behind the sentries. "Another feeble attempt to use us as your personal army. You will never succeed."

Remy decided to cut to the chase. "I have marshmallow peeps," he pointed out and dangled the bag, and they gasped audibly, "but—you can't have them unless you hear our proposal. Deal?"

"You..." the orange one raged and literally trembled with frustration. "You cheap, rotten scoundrel! That's not fair. But so be it. We are not proud people. State your offer."

They did, taking turns to explain while their diminutive audience listened skeptically.

"Fairy dust?" A couple of them from the mingled crowd gasped. "Fairy dust? That is forbidden. Totally, absolutely—"

"Please," Riley urged, "remember that Moswen is a threat to everyone, including us. If she kills or enslaves all the humans, no one will be able to make marshmallow peeps or honey-roasted peanuts at all ever again."

This was followed by generalized chatter, rustlings, and murmurings as almost the entire colony had arrived by now and floated in midair. They'd formed a circle, almost a giant ball, to have their conference in their own strange language.

When it had gone on for five minutes and after two joggers had passed and glanced at Remy as he stood there staring at nothing—from their perspective—he coughed loudly and rustled the bag containing the box of peeps.

Finally, one of them—bigger than the others—turned to face him. "So, what's in it for us?" he asked.

"In addition," he began, "to a number of small birdlike creatures made of marshmallow and saturated with yellow food dye, I can also offer to bring you a fresh pizza sometime and a backup supply of honey, and…uh, the promise of a favor in the future?"

"Hah!" the large one snapped. "Typical. That is nothing more than the standard, the baseline we would require for normal interaction. Garnering a sample of our most precious possession requires something far greater. Humility, for starters. And you have been nothing but arrogant with us."

He hoped they couldn't hear the sound of his teeth grinding together. "Have I? Gosh, I'm dreadfully sorry. This is a big deal, though, so tell me what I have to do to… uh, prove my humility."

All of them smirked in unison, and he wasn't at all sure he liked where this was going.

"You must," proclaimed the big kahuna, "demonstrate your humility not only before us but before your own people as well. While we watch."

· · ·

Washington Heights, Manhattan, New York

Remy cleared his throat. "Well, I might as well get started," he announced loudly enough for the hovering mass of gleeful winged spectators to hear. They whispered and chortled behind him, eager for the show to begin.

Then, in a lower voice directed at Riley, he added, "You said the glamor will make it hard to tell if I'm completely naked or not, right? People will see me and kind of do a double-take like they're confused if it's actual indecent exposure or merely a fruity guy in peach-colored underwear?"

"I think so, yes," Riley answered. "It's hard to achieve these kinds of subtle half-enchantments because I still don't completely understand how humans think. It might not work if they look at you too long and hard."

He nodded. Fortunately, it was a chilly day, and he wasn't in the mood to be long and hard, anyway, so that ought not to be a problem.

Once they'd decided on terms, he'd walked—with every last inhabitant of the entire goddamn colony floating at his heels and magically cloaked from human sight, to be safe—out of the park and into the closest neighborhood where it looked like a fair number of people ambled around. They weren't far from the Armory, so there were a few tourists in addition to various locals.

They were all adults, fortunately, or at least teenagers. It was hard to tell in some cases.

"All right, gang," he grunted and suddenly wished he were extremely drunk, "let's fucking do this."

He stripped his clothes in record time, tied them into a bundle with his tie as a handle, and slung it over his shoulder. Only his boxer shorts remained free, and he slid them over his head. An old woman, seeing him get naked, stopped and stared for a second, then turned and hurried back the way she'd come.

Remy pranced forth into the street. "La, La, La! Hey, everyone, look at me. Ha-*haaaa...*"

A car swerved to avoid him and a few pedestrians froze and gawked or cried out and turned away. He skipped on one foot to the sidewalk, close enough for the small crowd there for them to see him but not so close that they'd think he was coming at them.

"Row, row, row your boat, gently down the...uh, spleen!" he cawed and deliberately made his voice crack as though he were intoxicated and very emotional. "Merrily, merrily, merrily, merrily, life is but a peen!"

"Oh, my God!" a fat guy gasped and shook in horror as he fell back against the nearest building, his face ashen.

Something struck him upside the head. He wheeled his arms and made noises as he turned to see that it was a purse.

"Bastard!" screamed the woman who'd hurled it. "There are children who sometimes walk through here."

"Aww!" Remy shouted in response, although he did not look at her and was already rapidly hopping away, "but Mom, I'm only seven! Also, uh, one thousand bottles of beer on the wall, one thousand bottles of beer..."

While all this was happening, the cluster of Fair Folk squawked and cackled in near-hysteria. They might well have been the most appreciative audience he'd ever had for a comedy routine, come to think of it.

But the mood on the street began to turn more and

more hostile and a couple of tough-looking barfly types scowled at him with belligerent contempt.

"Riley," he whispered, "I'm very sure they can see the family jewels. Why isn't the glamor working?"

"Sorry," she apologized and trailed him closely. "I'm trying. I don't think it's going to work on that...scary, ridiculous, beastly thing." She gestured at his groin.

"Thanks," he replied, "but I'm about to get in trouble. Can you go see if the colony is satisfied yet? Oops, here come some more people. Hey, folks! Do you have a moment to talk about our Lord and Savior, Cthulhu? Stranger aeons, even death may die. Isn't that precious? Ha-ha, ho-ho, heee..."

He stuck his tongue out and did a Russian squat dance as he moved down the sidewalk and finally came face-to-face with a tall, sour-faced Wall Street type guy who stared at him, shook his head, and pointed behind him. Then, he turned and walked away.

Remy stopped. *Did that guy see the fairies? Or is it...*

From over his shoulder came a couple of low, grunting chuckles before a loud voice commented, "Well, well, look who it is! It's about time this guy came to see us again."

With a deep breath, he put on his best "my innocence is the source of my self-confidence" face, and turned.

Naturally, the two men who believed he was specifically seeking their company were patrol officers of the NYPD. The tall young black guy and a short, pudgy, slightly older Greek or Turkish guy clearly knew who he was.

He did not specifically recognize either of them but then again, so many cops had arrested him over the years that there was no way he could keep them all straight in his head. Especially since most of the times it had happened, his neural functioning had been impaired.

"Good evening, officers," he greeted them and casually removing his boxers from his head and bent slightly to slip his feet through them and return them to their intended position. "I'm finishing up one of those performance art pieces for the...uh, college. Can I help you?"

The shorter man moved around to flank him while the taller one closed in from the front.

"Sure," the former said, "although you already made our lives a hell of a lot easier by putting your pants on."

Remy scratched behind his ear. "You're welcome. Are you planning to escort me somewhere warm and safe? Spring hasn't really altogether sprung yet and I'm worried I might catch a cold."

"Something like that," the black cop stated and retrieved a pair of handcuffs. "It must have been a hell of a party. Classic David Remington. We're gonna throw one of our own to view the results of your blood test, you know. Invite the whole family, have a potluck. Real science fiction shit, combining that many chemicals."

He recoiled as if slapped and his eyelids fluttered. The officers tensed briefly and hands moved toward their waists.

"I—" he stammered. "That's—I've been clean for months. On the straight and narrow, aside from...well, you know, this. Which, again, is performance art. I think that's covered under the First Amendment, right?"

"You have the right," the Mediterranean cop informed him, "to remain silent. Anything else you say can and will be used against you..."

With a sigh, he allowed the indignation to slough off him and extended his hands to receive his new loan of two beautiful silver bracelets. Again.

Riley was about twenty feet away, perched on a lighting fixture, and the two of them exchanged a quick glance. They knew each other well enough that he trusted her to do what was necessary—fly off at once and tell one of his other, larger friends what had happened so they could rescue him from the slammer for the umpteenth time.

As the officers led him away, though, he puffed his chest out and strode purposefully with the air of a man facing the bullets of a firing squad and determined to do so with courage and splendor.

"Because," he added aloud, although in a rather low voice, "mark my words. This is neither the first nor the last time I get completely humiliated on the evening news."

CHAPTER TWENTY

Taylor's House, Harrison, Westchester County, New York

Two cars headed toward Harrison, and Bobby's was one of them. Volz rode with her. Agent Gilmore drove the other and was alone.

The dwarf was somewhat restless since he'd taken a short nap before they'd left the office.

"When are we gonna be there?" he asked and squirmed in his seat. "I wanna see Taylor. She's pretty. Does she have gems at her house? This is boring. Are we there yet?"

"Almost, Volzy," she told him and tried to be patient. In a way, he was probably having as much trouble as she was, what with the effects of the spell. "We're in her neighborhood now. See all the big, old, gorgeous houses? Man, I knew she'd live in a place like this."

It took a few moments of navigating the winding, labyrinthine streets before they came to a gate, as expected. Someone buzzed them in and after another short, serpentine drive up a low hill, the mansion came into sight.

"Wow," he marveled.

"You said it," she agreed. She'd seen bigger houses, but Taylor's was so...ornate and so well-aged, a perfectly preserved relic of a time that had been more barbaric in some ways and more sophisticated in others.

She parked near the far edge of the broad paved area in front of the massive garage. A moment later, as she helped Volz out of his seat, Kendra's car pulled up behind her.

The agent stepped out and surveyed the premises. "Well," she stated, "the private investigation business is clearly far more lucrative than I thought. Then again, this looks like seventh-generation money."

Bobby shrugged. "Taylor isn't all that forthcoming when it comes to her personal life. I guess we're about to learn more, though."

The trio approached the front door, which opened for them as they mounted the steps. Standing beyond the threshold was a dignified-looking elderly man in a black tuxedo and white gloves. He would have seemed out of place—and out of time—in the doorway of most houses, but not there.

"Good day," he greeted them, his voice tinged a slight upper-crust English accent. "Ms Steele is expecting you, of course. Mr Remington is out on an errand. Mr Warfield is here as well. My name is Presley and do let me know if you need anything to make your stay more comfortable."

Kendra laughed in a dry but good-natured way. "We will do that. I don't think any of us are used to the...uh, royal treatment, though. We're fairly self-sufficient."

With a nod, the butler stepped aside for them to enter and closed the door.

The foyer beyond was noticeably dark although beautifully furnished in a somewhat archaic style. Bobby was suddenly and harshly reminded of the revelation that Taylor Steele was one of the undead. She only hoped everyone there knew that Kendra hadn't been initiated and would parse their words accordingly.

"Whoaaa," Volz drawled, "a piano. I wanna play it."

Bobby tugged gently on his wrist. He was strong enough to have broken her arm, but he seemed to trust her even in his befuddled state and usually responded to her urgings. "Sorry, Volz, but that's Taylor's and we have to be careful not to break it. Maybe after we ask her, okay?"

Kendra cast odd sidelong glances at the dwarf and clearly wondered why being "sick" would cause him to behave like a child or a developmentally disabled person. Even with her augmented brainpower, Bobby didn't have an answer for that yet.

As the three guests removed their coats and shoes, light footsteps approached and Taylor entered, accompanied by another woman.

"Hello," the vampire said. "I'm glad to see you made it safely. And I'd like to thank you for working such long hours last night. I've been up since yesterday evening myself. I'll probably retire for a few hours of rest soon but first, we have things to see to."

She turned to the other lady. "This is Alice Pendlebury, an expert in the occult. We've consulted with her on some of the stranger elements of the Moswen case. Alice, this is Roberta Diaz—you may call her Bobby—our office assistant and Kendra Gilmore, who is in much the same line of work as ourselves."

The woman waved. "Well, hello there, both of you.

Lovely to meet you." She was slightly older than Bobby but slightly younger than Kendra, with large, thick eyeglasses and wavy hair the color of a ripe tomato. Her demeanor was a strange combination of friendly and guarded. She seemed slightly unnerved by Kendra's presence and more than normally curious about Bobby and the dwarf.

Well, Bobby told herself, *that's our witch. She looks normal. Can she tell what happened to Volz and me simply by looking at us?*

Presley, standing off to the side, cleared his throat. "I'll make a pot of tea and I can show you to your guest rooms. You should find them adequately prepared."

Conrad wandered in at that moment. "Don't worry about me," he said and smiled pleasantly. "I'm perfectly comfortable on the couch."

Taylor smiled, then squinted as something occurred to her. "Where is Alex?"

"The bank," Bobby replied. "I sent him to deposit cash before we left and told him to call us when he was done. If the rest of us will be here, he probably should as well, don't you think? He's not very nice, yeah, but I wouldn't want anything to happen to him."

The vampire nodded. "Agreed. If he calls you instead of me—which is likely—tell him he may come over."

Alice, meanwhile, had drifted over to Bobby and Volz.

"You two are an interesting case," she quipped, leaned close, and almost seemed to sniff the air around them. "That's quite an impressive hex you've collected. Someone with real talent and power, I'd wager."

Bobby almost panicked when she felt Kendra's eyes on them all.

"Ha-ha." She fake-laughed, "I guess I'd expect an occult expert to put it that way. Volz is sick—we think he might have MS or something—and I get like this when I'm stressed. Let's talk, though. I read a fair amount of...uh, paranormal stuff, so I bet you can explain some things to me."

She put a hand on the witch's shoulder and led her away down the hall, hoping Taylor wouldn't object to her barging deeper into her house like this.

The vampire, though, made no comment and only stepped between them and Agent Gilmore, making small talk and vaguely asserting that they were making progress on the case.

The two women reached a door that opened into a lovely formal sitting room and Bobby continued to urge Alice along until they stopped in the far rear corner.

"Sorry about that," she whispered, not wanting a sorceress angry at her, "but Kendra hasn't you know, had the talk. She doesn't really know what's going on. We have to be extremely careful. She's an FBI agent, too. She's on our side and has even bent a few rules to help us, but I think she's already suspicious that something weird is going on. She's seen things I'm not sure how she even rationalizes."

Alice blinked a few times but seemed to take the message in stride. "Ah, I see. Not a problem, although in my opinion, you might as well try to initiate her. That might make her more sympathetic if anything."

Bobby frowned. "I think we should leave that up to Taylor. Until then, as far as Kendra is concerned, Volz is merely short, Riley doesn't exist, and Moswen is merely a foreign mafia princess hopped up on PCP. Understood?"

The witch shrugged. "Aye. Well, I suppose it's partially my fault, anyway. I put a glamor over New York City and its suburbs a few years ago—a potent one, too, if I may say so. That is probably part of why she's remained a skeptic even if she's seen unusual things. Being a fed, she has to be the observant type so blame magic, not her. But yes, yes, I'll keep my big mouth shut until the Queen Bee says otherwise."

She closed her eyes and sighed with relief. Alice seemed like a reasonable type of person. Although she had only the vaguest idea of what the witch was talking about with this glamor thing.

"You were right, though," she continued. "Volz and I were hexed. Someone sent a mail bomb that...affected our intelligence. He got dumber and I...well, became way smarter." She blushed.

Alice nodded slowly. "When there's time, I can look you both over and advise you on how to deal with that. There are multiple things to consider. I'm sure you've already touched on many of them."

That was an understatement. In more ways than one, the universe had turned inside-out and she was no longer certain of her place in it.

The two women wandered back toward the foyer, where almost everyone had sat and now conferred over their next course of action. Bobby felt like her brain was being overloaded. She'd met a real, actual witch on top of everything else.

"Excuse me," she said gently to the group. "I'm going to get some fresh air for a minute. I'll be right back."

Taylor gave her a nod and the others watched her for only a second before they returned to their conversations.

She stepped out onto the front steps, pulled the door closed behind her, and released a long, whistling sigh. Her gaze drifted to the slate-colored clouds overhead that hovered above the grasping claws of the brown trees which were still a good month from producing green buds.

Her eye caught something moving through the air and she tensed. For a second, it had looked like a bird, but she soon realized it was a fairy.

Riley flapped up, her face drawn and her eyes wide. "Remy's in trouble!" she blurted. "He got arrested again."

"Arrested? What for?" Bobby hadn't expected to hear that.

The fairy spread her small hands. "Something to do with being naked and dancing around singing. My colony made him do it in exchange for fairy dust. They thought it would be funny."

The receptionist put both hands over her face. "Oh, no. Great. Well, thanks for telling us. This sounds like a job for Kendra, though. She's a fed and can probably throw her weight around to get him bailed out."

"But," Riley protested, "she doesn't understand what's happening."

She shrugged. "We'll think of something."

They went inside. Everyone except Agent Gilmore noticed the fairy but did not let their gaze linger on her nor say anything to acknowledge her.

Bobby raised a hand. "Okay, excuse me, but while I was

out there, I had a phone call." She breathed deeply. "It turns out that Remington is in jail. We need to bail him out."

Taylor slapped a hand to her face and her usual composure cracked. "Again? For fuck's sake."

Almost in unison, Kendra and Conrad asked, "What for?"

Bobby's mind cycled quickly through the possibilities that each response was likely to bring. "He didn't say, exactly. While working the case he had to do something he wasn't supposed to, and the cops caught him and took him in. Kendra, do you think you could help?"

The agent frowned. "Possibly. One more abuse of my position isn't likely to matter much at this point."

Taylor folded her arms. "I could handle it myself but that would cost us valuable time and potentially draw scrutiny toward Moonlight. Agent Gilmore, if you think you can spring him, that would be a tremendous help to us."

The agent strode toward the door. Bobby accompanied her out to the front walk, with Riley hovering behind. Presley closed the door.

"I can do this," the agent said, "but I need to know where he is, obviously, and more about what the hell actually happened. Are you sure he didn't mention what he was arrested for?"

They were already halfway to the cars. Riley hovered close to Bobby's ear.

"We were in Washington Heights," she whispered. "So whatever place the police would take people from there."

She relayed this information. "And, to be honest," she added, "he did mention that it involved...uh, public nudity."

The woman stopped in her tracks. "I see. This keeps getting more and more interesting." Briskly, she resumed her stride.

Bobby hung back and turned her head slightly to speak to the fairy. "Go with her. Hide in her car or something and remind Remy that he needs to get those ingredients. Make sure they don't cock it up."

The fairy agreed and buzzed toward Gilmore's vehicle. As she reflected on the situation, Bobby suddenly regretted her choice of words.

34th Precinct, Washington Heights, New York City

Remy, from his cell, had the privilege of overhearing the discussion—really more of an argument—between Agent Gilmore and the precinct chief over whether or not he should be granted his freedom.

"Sir," she urged, "as far as I'm concerned, he probably should be prosecuted for this." She shot him a fiery glance. "But under the circumstances, his presence is required for our operation."

The chief, a hulking man with a sour face, threw his large, meaty hands up. "What the hell kind of operation requires him to prance around naked in the street, shouting gibberish at passersby? I'm curious, Agent Gilmore."

While the agent and the chief had this conversation, Remy looked calmly at them and stood ramrod straight with his hands behind his back. The idea was to emulate the pose that Hannibal Lecter used at the beginning of

Silence of the Lambs. He felt it might make people respect him more under the circumstances.

Probably not the guy in the cell across from him, though. A brooding, malevolent-looking individual scowled and flexed his hands, probably looking forward to the privilege of beating the crap out of sex offenders and other such low-ranking convicts.

At least Kendra was already there. She was almost better than Taylor, after all, given her status as a legitimate public servant.

"We both know," the agent went on, "that there are strange things going on in this city lately and the Bureau is doing whatever's necessary to deal with it. There was a miscommunication as to exactly when and where Remington was to begin his diversionary action. And it won't happen again."

The chief sighed and grumbled his disapproval. "I'd better see documentation for all this. Even if there is an ongoing investigation, we can't have idiots running around bare-assed in public and acting like they're high on goddamn acid. The people have certain standards."

"I understand," she replied, her face grave but empathetic. "This never should have happened. Still, given the seriousness of the operation at stake, we have to demand his immediate release."

He glowered at her, then at the prisoner. "Fine. Pull him out and get his ass the hell out of here."

Kendra did not speak as they walked to her car, which made Remy suspect that she would chew him out as soon as they were safely within the vehicle. What surprised him, though, was to see Riley crouched in the far corner of the backseat.

"Get in," Kendra said and opened the passenger's side door.

He obeyed, and during the few seconds it took her to slam the door and walk around to the driver's side, Riley spoke.

"Remember, we need to get the fairy dust." Her voice, already tiny, was so soft he barely heard it but he nodded in acknowledgment.

As the agent climbed in, he turned to her.

"Hey, thanks, and sorry about this. Trust me, I have my reasons. Also...uh, can we stop at Fort Washington Park? It's only a few minutes away. I need to get something."

She stared at him. "You have your reasons? I cannot possibly think of what they might be. This whole incident makes me question your competence—not only in the sense of how good you are at your job but in the sense of the term 'mentally incompetent.' If you're going to pull shit like this, you probably ought to be languishing in an institution."

Exhaling slowly, he responded with, "I was put up to it. I can tell you all the details later after we've taken care of Moswen. For now, though, there simply isn't time so please, trust me when I say it won't happen again. Also, the park. We need to go there."

"What for?" she snapped.

"Some friends will drop off a package I need," he explained. "It will help with the situation."

She scoffed and shook her head. "A package? What is it —drugs? Black market weaponry? Non-prescription

Viagra for the next time you plan to run around naked on a cold day?"

Remy pinched the bridge of his nose. "None of the above, although those are...uh, fairly good guesses. But please, do this for me. Taylor would approve. In fact, she insists. If this isn't worth it, she's as guilty as I am."

Kendra had been heading north. Now, she took a sudden turn to the left, presumably to loop around to the south and the park. "Sometimes, I wonder if all you people are simply plain nuts," she grumbled.

Moments later, they arrived and Remy directed her to park near his usual place but slightly farther away to reduce the chances that she'd see any of the details of his transaction.

He thanked her, stepped out, and paused to say "Thanks, and I'll be right back," which left the door open long enough for Riley to slip out.

"Oh," Kendra said coldly, "no problem at all."

Leaving the agent's car, he trudged across the park, as he'd done many times before with the fairy floating nearby. As they approached the nest, his ears picked up a sound wafting across the grass.

"What is that?" he wondered. "Oh, wait, it's a cacophony of laughter. Clearly, your people got hours of quality entertainment out of that little stunt."

"Yes," said Riley.

"That's good to know. I'm glad that something like that is considered an all-ages community event amongst your kind."

They were practically on top of the two holes to the colony's depths when the squeals and guffaws quieted enough for the fae to notice that they had visitors. A few drifted out from under the earth.

"Oh!" one exclaimed. "Ha-ha. It's Remy. Look at him, pretending like everything is normal again! Ha-ha-ha."

Remington waved. "Yeah, hi. I fulfilled my end of the bargain. So, now—"

"Look!" another cried, tears streaming from its small eyes with barely controlled mirth, "the ungainly stupid human is back. He's wearing clothes now. Oh, but we'll never forget what he looked like earlier. Ha-ha-ha-ha."

Others flew up and out, most of them already chuckling, then pointed and shrieked with laughter when they saw him.

He coughed. "Okay, yeah, it was a good show. Now give me the fairy dust. I did what you asked, so do as you said you would."

A few of those who seemed to be in charge, including the especially large fairy who'd set the terms earlier, gradually gained control of their hysteria and regarded the human with a steady gaze.

"So be it," the big one announced. "You have demonstrated—amply—your humility before us. And so we shall bequeath to you our most precious possession. Use it wisely, human."

"Oh," Remy intoned, "I shall, don't worry."

The throng parted and two fairies emerged, carrying a pouch between them made of much the same gossamer green material as Riley's dress and about the size of two or three matchbooks pressed together.

He nodded and accepted it. It seemed awfully small, but

if the stuff was as powerful as its reputation suggested, they probably wouldn't need much.

As he turned away, one of the Fair Folk cawed over his shoulder, "Don't waste it on making your backside bigger! Ha-ha-ha-ha. It was so small and flat."

The others began to laugh again and didn't stop.

His jaw muscles had a good workout on the walk back to the car, although his teeth began to ache by the end. Riley rode on his shoulder and put one of her minuscule hands on the side of his neck.

"You got it. That's what's important," she observed.

He tucked the pack deep into his pocket well before he was in clear sight of Gilmore's car. When he climbed in, her mood seemed to have improved.

"How'd it go?" She arched her eyebrows.

"Fine." He buckled his seatbelt.

Kendra started the engine and added, "I must admit, I'm curious. If you all aren't insane, then this has at least been an…interesting experience."

Her fascination seemed genuine but now, he was the grumpy one.

"Like I said, I'll tell you about it later. For now, don't ask."

Bayside, Queens, New York

"Damn," Colonel James Russel swore. The lights were off in his townhouse and he stared into the deep gloom that blanketed his living room, which still bore the marks of the tussle the other day. "So the Feds really are in on it. Although I don't think this Gilmore realizes what she's gotten into." He rubbed his nose and suddenly wanted a stiff drink.

Seated on either side of a low table on which some equipment hummed were two friends of his—one a soldier and the other a civilian employee of the Department of Defense. Both were trained as analysts and neither was retired.

And yet, there they were because he'd asked them for a favor. Both held earpieces to the sides of their heads and listened to the feedback they received from the bug.

A hell of a big favor.

Joe Conason, the civilian currently seated on the left, clenched his jaw. "They said they were Company. The guys who came here, right? If the FBI is cooperating with them, then either they were lying and they're actually some kind of crooks whom the Feds are protecting for the time being, or they really are from the CIA and we've stumbled onto something beyond serious."

He took a swig of coffee as the other two men chewed on his words. Then, he continued. "The thing is, I almost think a real Company field agent would have realized by now that he'd been bugged. I'm not entirely convinced."

Russel inhaled. "You make a good point, Joe. The guy seems sloppy. Either he's a brand-new agent in way over his head with deep-cover stuff, or he's a shiftless goddamn moron."

"Well," quipped Rory Valdez on the right, who was Army, "whoever these people actually are, this is some crazy, ridiculous shit. I mean, come on. Witches? Fairy dust? Ancient Biblical spells to control vampires? These people are insane. And aside from Gilmore, they actually seem to believe all this."

The colonel did not respond and merely pushed his glasses up his nose. Something had happened to him, and it was damn hard to explain. Scary stuff, yet it was, at least, the most action he'd seen in years. His ass had been parked in a chair at a desk for too long.

Even slipping Remington the bug, to begin with, felt like getting something done to a greater extent than he'd accomplished in the last decade.

"Gentlemen," he told Joe and Rory, "I'll make another pot of tea. If I have to run this kind of operation—if you can even call it that—out of my own home, it's the least I can do."

Valdez nodded. "Thank you, sir."

When he returned a few minutes later and refilled all three of their cups, Conason turned to him with his brow furrowed.

"Sir, what exactly will we do? We probably ought to report all this crap to the higher-ups and let them make the decision."

Russel's eyes were distant but sharp. "I'm not sure yet, Joe. But whatever we do, it sure as hell won't be nothing."

CHAPTER TWENTY-ONE

Cochran Mortuary Services, New Rochelle, New York

Riley was in a pestering mood, Remington decided. Then again, after what he'd gone through, he supposed he was easily pestered.

"How long," the fairy inquired, "will you try keeping Kendra in the dark about all this? How long do you think you can?"

Remy kept his hands on the steering wheel and his eyes on the road. "I'm fairly sure we've had this conversation before."

"Yes," she conceded, "but we never finished it. I still don't understand, and I don't think you're making the right choice. Why are you so determined to keep the rest of the world hidden from her? Why not simply tell her about the preternatural so she knows?"

He shrugged. "She's seen things that are almost impossible to explain according to normal human knowledge. If she paid enough attention to other shit we've said and done and opened her mind a little wider...well, she's smart enough to work it out."

"Maybe she only needs a little push," she suggested.

"She might push back," he responded. "You know, a backlash—an equal and opposite reaction. She'd get angry, totally deny everything, and finally decide that we're all wackos and she should report us to her bosses and let them swoop in. If that happened, our hands would be tied while Moswen took over the city."

The fairy folded her arms and hunched on the dashboard to pout in annoyance and confusion. He left her to her thoughts for now.

After Kendra had taken them home, they'd managed to ditch the agent and fobbed her off on Taylor and Alice.

"I think," the witch had stated, "that it might be helpful, Agent Gilmore, for you to know more about the occult foundations that we suspect are involved in Moswen's cartel. Now, you might not believe in magic and such, but they certainly do. Know thine enemy and all that."

While Remy watched, Alice and the vampire had exchanged a quick glance.

"Agreed," Taylor had said. "Come, let's head to the library."

The agent might have realized that she was being separated from him by design, but her curiosity had become more important, so she'd complied. Then, Bobby had moved in and guided him by the shoulder to the other side of the house.

"Okay, you have it, right? The dust?" the receptionist had asked.

"Of course." He made himself smile.

She'd nodded. "Good. Leave it with me. The were-wolves"—she'd nodded to Presley and Conrad—"will stay here for our protection. There's one other thing you can get, though. Dead man's blood. There's a mortuary in New Rochelle, fifteen minutes down the road, that should be perfect."

"Thanks," he'd responded. "It's so comforting to know that my friends are doing their part to send me to the morgue."

So, after he'd swallowed a half-cup of coffee and splashed water on his face, he'd set off once more, again accompanied only by Riley—and a syringe with a nice plastic cap for the needle.

Now, they were almost there.

"Ugh," he lamented, "mortuaries are such depressing places. They're like a cross between a hospital and a museum. I'm surprised we didn't have to take a field trip to one back in school."

The morgue came into sight, a building of pale sepia stone with lightly decorated, carved accents near its corners and entrance. He drove past it to do a quick scan of the place, then looped around and parked in the lot of a nearby shopping plaza.

They got out and locked the car—the Lincoln, this time since Taylor hadn't given him permission to take a Tesla.

"Okay," Remy stated, "we'll kind of circle it on foot like we're confused where to go in and maybe go to the front desk, then—"

He stopped as he noticed the fairy gazing intently at the line of stores across the asphalt.

"Riley," he said, in a gentle but firm voice, "please remember what you said. We have a job to do here."

For a few seconds, she was quiet.

"No," she whispered.

Remy felt the beginnings of tension and anger before he realized she was talking to herself.

"No. I'll do what I know is right. What will really make me happy." She turned toward him in midair.

He smiled and extended an arm. She perched on his hand, climbed up to his shoulder, and sat there, holding the collar of his jacket.

A short walk brought them to the morgue. He strolled around the north side, pretended to be confused as if he'd expected the entrance to be there, and returned to the south side before he approached the front door on the east face. There were at least a few nice big windows on each side.

The investigator stepped into the formally furnished lobby and a receptionist greeted him at once.

"Hello," the young man behind the counter said, "welcome to Cochran. How can I help you?"

Remy glanced quickly around. A woman in a suit dress waited in a chair off to the left. Somewhere behind the receptionist, it appeared that a few other people bustled to and fro.

"Hi," he said and almost smiled but deciding it would be inappropriate here, "I have a family member who's near the end of her life and I'm looking for someone to provide the necessary services. I was a medical student for a while, though, so my standards are exacting. Would it be possible for me to tour your facility?"

The receptionist frowned a little. "Um… That's not a common request, but it might be possible. I'll have to talk to someone, okay?"

"Sure, fine." he straightened his tie.

The young man got a message on one of his screens and looked over to the woman in the chair. "Ms Halpern, you can go in now." He reached down and pressed a button, which resulted in a beeping noise.

The lady stood and opened the door leading into the rear of the facility. As the door swung shut, the receptionist released the button. He looked at Remy.

"Please wait here while I consult with my manager." He stood and left.

As soon as he was gone, he whispered to the fairy, "Fly through that slot in the glass and push the same button he pressed. Keep it down until I'm through that door then release it right away."

"Okay," she agreed, flapped off his shoulder, and vanished behind the desk.

He positioned himself near the door, and the beeping sounded only a moment later. Quickly, he turned the knob and stepped through and the noise ceased.

Beyond the door was a small maze of hallways. A sign reading *cold storage* pointed left, so he went that way, Riley fluttered up to him as he made the choice.

"Riley. If you can detect…uh, dead human bodies, point me in that direction."

They started to turn a corner, but it looked like someone was walking through the hall beyond so they ducked back and waited. Silence settled around them. He crept around and the fairy pointed him toward a particular door about a third of the way down.

Remy put his hand on the lever and waited a moment in case anyone was nearby, but the coast was clear. He sidestepped into the room and shut the door gently behind him.

The chamber was, predictably, kept at a cool temperature. Still, it contained no fewer than four human bodies on tables covered by sheets, so it nonetheless smelled a little dank.

He whispered to his minuscule companion. "Keep watch at the door. Or...uh, listen, I mean. Let me know if anyone comes."

She nodded and levitated off his shoulder to remain where she was as he advanced into the room. He withdrew the syringe from his pocket, uncapped it, and advanced on the first corpse.

There's no reason to be picky, he concluded and aimed the needle toward the bare, withered foot that protruded from under the covering. *One dead person is as good as another, right? The spell recipe only said it had to be a dead man's bl—*

He stopped. The tag on the cadaver indicated that this had been a woman in life.

Shit. Does it actually have to be a man's blood, or were they speaking euphemistically? The spell was probably written in the days when humankind was referred to as "Man," I would think.

He opted not to risk it and advanced to the next corpse. This one was definitely male. Hurriedly, he stuck the needle into the center of the foot, pushed it in, and pulled back on the plunger. The liquid that filled the tube was dark, cold, thick, and sluggish, so different from that of a living thing.

A shudder rippled down his neck and back as, unbidden, he wondered if Taylor's blood was like this.

Riley's small whisper sounded behind him. "Remy! Someone's coming."

Jolted from his brief rumination, he pulled the needle free, capped it, and put it down his pants, willing himself to not be grossed out by having it so intimately close to his body.

He hurried to the door but froze before it. If whoever was coming was merely passing by, it would be better to remain there rather than emerge and be seen. If they planned to enter the room, though, he'd have to think fast.

The footsteps stopped in front of the door and the handle turned.

"Whoa!" he exclaimed as the door swung open and did his best impersonation of someone who was embarrassed by their obvious error. "Sorry. I obviously have the wrong room. I was looking for the crematorium. Excuse me."

A short man of about sixty-five with a bushy white mustache stared at him, dumbfounded, as he pushed his way past, stepped over the threshold, and ambled down the hallway. The fairy clung to his collar.

He looked up, about to congratulate himself on his quick thinking, when he noticed a beefy orderly at the end of the hall blocking his exit.

"Hey!" the man called and pointed at him. "You're not supposed to be here. What the hell are you doing?"

Crap. It was nice while it lasted.

His arm snapped out to open the nearest door and he

practically teleported himself into the chamber beyond before the orderly could react. Still, by the time he'd slammed the door shut, the heavyset man was already pounding the hallway floor as he advanced.

He was in some type of office with desks and chairs and file cabinets. More importantly, it also had a nice big window on the far wall, which even faced in exactly the direction he'd need to run in order to get out of sight and reach his car.

The orderly's brief jog came to a stop and the handle clicked as it turned.

The investigator was already beside the window. He unlatched it and heaved it upward. It rose easily at first but seemed to get snagged about halfway to fully open. There was still enough space to crawl through, however, so he ducked and stuck his head and arms through.

The orderly was in the room and only a few feet away.

Speaking to the fairy, Remy urged, "Put that guy to sleep."

Out of the corner of his eye, he saw Riley dart out of sight while he forced his torso through the gap. The angle of his body was as awkward as hell and made his head almost spin.

Behind him, though, he saw the edge of a silver flash.

The orderly's voice rose and fell. "Hey! Whuh? Uh..." The protest trailed off and his body slumped with a thud.

"Hah!" He laughed. "Good work. Now, I only need to get—"

The words seemingly fell straight down his throat into his stomach as he pitched forward, having tilted his balance slightly too far in that direction. For a split second, the earth below blitzed toward him before he landed and for another second, the world was nothing but weird spots in his vision and a vague stinging in his face.

He made himself scramble to his feet, wobbled, and almost fell again, but his vision was already clearing. Thankfully, he'd only fallen about three or four feet. Riley streaked past and turned to face him as she drew ahead. He followed her in a rambling, awkward sprint across the lawn, the street, and around a couple of buildings.

The fairy seemed overjoyed. "We did it. It wasn't even that hard."

Angling toward the lot where his car was still parked, Remy felt the half-numb sting turn into a sharp ache. "It was hard enough," he grumbled. "Is my face messed up?"

She squinted at him. "Yes. It looks like someone punched you."

With a scowl, he whipped his keys out and pressed the remote starter. In another half a minute, they were both in the car, had pulled out into the street, and were a good quarter-mile away.

He didn't hear sirens. The mortuary had probably called the cops by now, of course, but they most likely treated it as a minor incident to be resolved later via security cam footage or something.

"Well," he admitted, "that was easier than getting the fairy dust, at least."

CHAPTER TWENTY-TWO

Kingsbridge, The Bronx, New York

Taylor's love for her Tesla's self-driving function was never more evident than when she had no wish to be followed.

She smiled in contented relaxation and merely rested her fingers on the lower part of the wheel. The car conformed to the convoluted and irrational course she'd plotted to her destination.

Hours before, Alice had spoken the truth. Eccentric rich people did collect such things as the Apples of Eden. They merely didn't necessarily keep them in their own houses.

Before Remy and Kendra had returned, she and Alice had discussed ways of undoing Volz's enchantment. The witch was confident it could be done, but it might take some time.

"We have to crack the spell open," Alice had described it, "and let it slowly run dry."

They hadn't yet asked Bobby whether she wanted to be cured. There would be time for that later.

They'd been obliged to distract Kendra for a while Bobby accepted the fairy dust and sent Remy and Riley off to their next objective. After that, finally, Taylor had trusted that things were moving along well enough for her to pursue her leads on the apple and the twig.

She had a moderately high estimation of her chances of success. Of course, she also had a well-concealed derringer at her hip, loaded with two .45 caliber silver rounds plus two to spare and an eleven-inch hunting knife strapped to her leg.

A sword would have been a comfort, but the one she'd used for years had broken in her fight against Starik Grey-hammer, and the smith to whom she'd sent her specifications had only started work on a replacement. It would likely be another two months before she received it.

The vampire drove down a side street in an unre-markable commercial district of Kingsbridge across from Manhattan and not far from the freeway. The street was a dead-end, and almost at the very end was a small, chalky-colored, nondescript storefront with a larger warehouse-type building slightly behind it. There was no parking on the street itself, and she would rather have her car sighted elsewhere than her actual destination, anyway.

Taking manual control of the vehicle, she retraced her route and parked on the last perpendicular street facing away from the business. From there, she walked to the storefront at the dead end, carrying only her hidden weapons and a purse with her personal ID info—and an empty plastic baggie.

The sun itself no longer hung in the sky. Only the scarlet, amber, and purple glow of its recent presence remained.

The thick glass of the door was tinted almost jet-black, and nothing advertised that the place was even open. There was a buzzer, though. She pressed it.

Above her, she heard the faint whiz of a small dome camera examining her. The door swung open and she stepped inside.

Almost the entire store consisted of the lobby, a spacious room paneled with marble and limestone of grey, off-white, and rich brown. Thick, square, blocky marble benches lined one of the walls, opposite the low front desk. It had a stone façade, too.

On the façade, square, runic letters read "Gurnshagg & Smithsire."

"Hello," Taylor greeted the person behind the desk, a long-faced dwarf with silver hair and a huge nose. "I'm here to collect something."

He leaned forward as he looked at her. His bushy eyebrows and even bushier mustache bristled and twitched. "Madam, I do believe I recognize you. But we must go through security protocols. All customers are treated equally."

She let herself scowl a little. "Very well. I had hoped we could skip the most time-consuming ones, as I am a repeat customer and have my documentation with me."

In fact, she was fairly sure she recognized him, too. The last time she'd been there—the most secure bank in New York—someone else had been training him.

A guard—a large dwarf holding a heavy diamond-edged ax and with a revolver that fired shotgun slugs hanging from his belt—drifted out from behind one of the pillars to watch the proceedings.

As she approached the desk, the teller suddenly produced a stack of papers along with a thick, old-fashioned ink pen. "This is our new standardized withdrawal security form. After you've filled out all the required information, we'll run this documentation of yours." Almost as if he anticipated her protest, he quickly added, "If you have time to come here and retrieve something so important, then surely you have a few minutes to write down important information."

With a frown, Taylor accepted the papers and the pen. "The last several times I was here, all of this was expedited via your computer system. Why the regression to inefficiency?"

"Security reasons," the teller stated. "There have been so many unnecessary acts of violence lately. It's almost as if the people in charge like to promote an atmosphere of paranoia, backstabbing, and plotting against each other."

Glancing up, she saw that the dwarf's nametag read *Kelldarm.*

"I see, Mr Kelldarm," she responded and her hand flitted across the pages to inscribe all the redundant details they required. "Next time I speak to Mr. Gurnshagg himself, I shall have to ask him for more details."

The teller almost fidgeted in discomfort at this but stopped himself. Instead, he turned, made a quick phone call, and muttered words in the dwarvish tongue in a low voice into the receiver before he hung up.

She finished the documents in minutes and displayed her documentation. He made a show of slowly and carefully examining each piece of ID and checking the account numbers against what was displayed on his computer. Then, he made another phone call.

Finally, he turned to her. "All right, Ms Steele, you've passed the first step of the protocols. Before we allow you into the vaults, are you armed?"

She nodded. "I have a derringer pistol and a knife on my person."

The dwarf stiffened. "Why didn't you declare them when you first walked in?"

Taylor shrugged with exaggerated casualness. "Weapons aren't taken until the first gate is about to be opened, anyway. It would be pointless to declare them prior to that."

With a scowl, he directed the guard to move closer and remain alert as she removed her humble implements of death and place them in a plastic box, to be returned to her before leaving.

"Of course," the teller could not help adding, "one such as you, who intimidates the council even when unarmed, hardly needs these little things anyway. One suspects that part of the reason so many other entities keep trying to overthrow you—destabilizing our city in the process—is merely for the challenge."

Stony-faced, the vampire said, "I had thought that dwarves valued forthrightness over bitter sarcasm, Mr. Kelldarm." She thought she could see a faint smirk on the guard's face at that one. The clerk did not respond.

Finally, they opened the first gate, an archaic contraption of stone and metal, to reveal a cart that ran along a rail into the depths beneath the nearby warehouse. She stepped into the cart. It faced the second gate, which only opened after the first was shut.

The contraption wheeled forward, slowly at first but picked up speed as it descended the incline. The air grew cool and musty once she was underground. The cart scraped to a halt in front of the third gate.

Here, a dwarf and a gremlin came out of two doors on either side of the rails. The former was another beefy armed guard and the latter was dressed in a robe, armed with a wand, and held an open book in one hand.

"Stop," said the dwarf, although Taylor was already still.

The gremlin passed the wand over her while reading an incantation from the tome. A faint tingling spread across her skin as though something teased it and tried to gain access to her deepest core.

"Ohhh," the gremlin sighed and its eyes rolled around in their sockets. "Dark magic! Not super strong but all over her."

Taylor folded her arms over her chest. "I'm a vampire," she pointed out. Somehow, she'd come on the one night when the staff was composed entirely of new guys.

The gremlin made a whining sound in its throat and flipped through a few pages of its book. While he did so, the dwarf guard listened to someone speaking to him via earbud. He nodded as the diminutive mage found the right passage.

"Yes!" the gremlin exclaimed. "Uh...you okay! Go now."

"Thank you," she said.

The third gate's central mechanism rotated in a circle, then split down the middle to reveal, at last, the vaults. The cart moved ahead another hundred yards before it stopped at the end of the tracks and the gate closed behind her.

Beyond was a stone labyrinth like an underground tomb complex with heavy steel doors of varying sizes in the walls, each bearing a circular lock.

A particularly short and rotund dwarf wearing suspenders over a white shirt and with a blue-black beard and bright violet eyes appeared to greet her.

"Good evening, Ms Steele." He waved and smiled. "I hope you didn't have too much trouble with the recent hires. We've had to buff up security of late."

She stepped forward but stopped a few paces beyond him in the direction in which her vault lay and politely waited for him to lead. "The inconvenience is an acceptable price to pay, Mr Gurnshagg, but I don't understand why filling out paper forms is now required."

"Oh." The dwarf chuckled. "That's only to waste time while our computers run a few extra scans of the security camera footage. We have better measures in place now to detect forged records in the public databases, not to mention telltale signs of face-stealers posing as legitimate customers."

She smoothed her eyebrows with her fingertips. "Fair enough. I'm here for the apple."

He was already waddling in the proper direction. "Really? Fascinating." He did not ask what she planned to do with it as his bank never interfered in clients' personal affairs, but it was clear that he would not mind if she chose to discuss the matter.

She did not, however. Until the spell was cast, it was better to remain tight-lipped.

Hers was one of the smaller compartments in the rear corner of the complex, above another and toward the ceiling. Mr Gurnshagg fetched a stepladder and climbed it to reach the locking mechanism, which only he and his closest associates knew exactly how to operate.

"Mkayyyy…" he said to himself. His tongue stuck out slightly over his beard as he fiddled with dials and counted fractions of seconds, his small but thick hands working with surprising deftness.

After about two minutes, the door clacked loudly and came loose from the stone around its edges. "Ha, success." Gurnshagg chortled. "Your possessions are within, madam."

Thanking him and helping him move the ladder without having to dismount it, she glanced into the dark stone cavity before she reached in to take hold of the apple's stem. She drew it out into the light.

By now, it was mostly rotten and dried out, a shriveled brown lump that resembled a prune—or perhaps something like a pinecone or a bee's nest more than an apple. She fluffed open the plastic baggie she'd brought with the other hand, dropped the ancient fruit into it, wrapped it up with the extra slack, and tucked it into her purse.

"That is all," she said. She pushed the stepladder back so that Gurnshagg could shut and re-lock the vault. "I or my estate will contact you in the next two to three days on the matter of whether I'll need the vault again."

"Quite right," the dwarf acknowledged and quickly sealed the door.

Fortunately, getting out was a much faster process than getting in had been, and not even Kelldarm could find a way to impede her. As she passed through the first gate and into the lobby, he peered at her as if to discover what she had retrieved, but the single small object in her purse did not catch his attention.

"My weapons, please," she told him.

In silence, he handed them back to her and she strapped them into their appropriate places. Then she nodded and strode out.

When the vampire emerged into the frosty air, her shoes lightly tapping the damp pavement, the sun was entirely gone.

She almost wanted to stop, spread her arms, and hurl some kind of prayer skyward to whatever deities governed the night, such was her relief. She'd never spent as much time having to operate continuously during the daytime as she had these last few days, and it was taking a toll on her. And she'd not really rested since the plane back from Israel.

Only about twenty steps away from the bank, her senses discerned subtle movements, both above and around her. They were quick, stealthy, and deliberate.

It was no great surprise. The setting of the sun had made things easier not only for her but for others too.

Taylor turned right down the first alley she came to. This technically moved her farther from the sounds, so it ought to give the appearance that she simply tried to sneak away. In fact, her goal was to move the impending confrontation to somewhere out of public sight and potentially, with fewer innocent bystanders.

A few hundred feet into the dark corridor, she reached a slightly wider area where the back corners of four unequally-sized buildings receded from a dusty space containing a dumpster, a sewer grate, and not much else.

She stopped in the center, put herself in plain sight, and pulled her coat more tightly around her as if frightened. Her purse still dangled from her right arm.

The barely audible movements grew in strength, and faint chattering and whispering noises seemed to converge on her position. In the next moment, the attack came.

Four figures burst out at once. Two bounded from the shadows on the ground, while two swooped down from the surrounding structures.

The vampire took a split second to assess the situation. The two land attackers were thralls, probably higher-end ones. The two airborne ones could only be full vampires.

She darted forward, seized the arm of the smaller of the two thralls—both had been strong thirtysomething men— and flung him into the legs of the other to trip him. Without slowing, she pounced upward to seize the clothes of one of the undead and hurl her against a wall. The other passed her and landed near the grate.

The woman Taylor had thrown was a little larger than she was with long, flowing black hair. The man's hair was shorter and white. Both would have been dark-complexioned in life but were wan and sallow in undeath.

Of the two vampires, she recognized the male as Oroche, a peripheral member of Scalion's coven. Since she hadn't heard anything from the group in months, she'd assumed that by now, Moswen had either destroyed the coven or taken control of it. But perhaps neither was true.

The female looked vaguely familiar, but she did not know her name and assumed she was probably another castoff of Scalion's. She'd already recovered from her tumble and now circled her prey.

"Taylor," Oroche whispered, "we followed you. You've been up all day, haven't you? You must be tired."

The thralls were back on their feet and advanced from different directions, the larger one taking the direct approach. Taylor's foot lashed out, caught the big man in the chest, and thrust him stumbling back into the dumpster.

She turned her head to the vampires. "Only two thralls, Oroche? You're moving down in the world."

"They're not mine, you idiot," he snarled. "Besides, we've upgraded from Scalion."

That answered all her questions. This was Moswen's work.

He and his lady companion half-leaped, half-floated to flank her from each side while the second thrall attacked from the rear. She took a step back, whirled, and seized the human to hurl him into the female vampire. Both tumbled aside.

In seconds, Oroche was upon her and swiped at her with a small, sickle-like blade as well as his nails and feet. Anticipating his next step, she blocked it with her foot and in an instant, drew the derringer and fired both rounds point-blank into his face.

He fell back with a scream and pawed at his eye and cheek. Silver could only kill vampires in large quantities, but two silver bullets would cause him enough pain and nausea to keep him out of the fight for a precious moment or two.

The big thrall returned to the action and stepped in

front of her as she strode toward the other two foes. The man tried to trap her in a giant, crushing bear hug. She did not move but drew the knife from her leg-sheath and slashed the arteries and tendons running up his torso and down his arms.

He gasped and groaned in pain as his arms fell limp. His eyes bulged when she stabbed him in the skull before she roundhouse-kicked the side of his head. He catapulted seven feet to the side, already dead when he crashed to earth.

The female vampire hurled the remaining thrall at Taylor. She sidestepped, ducked, and vaulted high to slice the knife's blade through the man's collarbone and about half of his neck. He fell to his knees and gurgled.

The vampire drew back and hissed. "You bitch! You think you're so—"

Taylor kicked her in the knee with sufficient force to crack it. Her adversary shrieked and crumpled but launched a claw-attack toward her breast. She dodged it with an easy swivel of the hips, grasped the woman's hair, and rammed her knee into her back to break her spine.

She flopped limply, although her head was still suspended by the length of hair in Taylor's hand which made it easy to saw through her neck in two quick motions. The body sagged and she tossed the head aside.

By now, Oroche had recovered, although his left eye looked milky and amorphous. In the unlikely event that he lived that long, it might take half the night for his eyeball to completely repair itself. His cheekbone was still a little warped as well.

She hitched the purse up slightly on her shoulder. In

the tussle, she'd almost dropped it.

"Oroche," she stated, "I'm sure you know what Moswen will do to you if you try to flee from your responsibility. It's best that you simply stay and fight."

His lips drew back from his fangs. "Agreed."

He advanced in the same sidewinder motion he'd used during his earlier strike. Understanding its trajectory now, she flicked the knife. It spun half a dozen times before the blade buried itself halfway in his right eye.

"No!" he cried and raised his hands to his face again.

By now, Taylor was already toe to toe with him. She plunged her right hand through his ribs, found his heart, and removed it. He clawed feebly at her arm as her hand crushed the organ, but he was already collapsing. She dropped the lifeless heart and retrieved her knife before he fell completely.

Wasting no time, she continued down the alley parallel to the street she'd been walking on and intended to approach her car from the opposite direction.

Another bungled assassination attempt on Moswen's part, she reflected. *But this must mean that we don't have much time. She's getting ready to close in soon. The big assault is coming. We must have the spell ready by the end of the night, if possible.*

They needed a thrall's blood but now wasn't the time or place. She had nothing to store it in properly. Fresh was best for these kinds of operations. Trying to transport old, contaminated blood could interfere with the functionality of the spell.

She picked up the pace. Even besides the blood, there was another ingredient she had to collect that night.

CHAPTER TWENTY-THREE

Cresskill, New Jersey

The Tesla stopped before the massive black iron gates. They were taller and more theatrical than the ones barring the public from Taylor's mansion, and the security cameras more numerous and obvious.

She rolled her window down and pressed the button on the small console.

A deep, velvety male voice came through the speaker. "Who are you and what is your business here?"

"Taylor Steele," she stated simply, "and I've come to ask you a favor."

It was likely that her voice alone would do the trick, but to be safe, she removed her dark glasses to allow the cameras a better view of her face.

There was silence for perhaps ten seconds before the man replied, "Very well. Are you alone?"

"Yes."

"Come in, then." The speaker went silent and the gate buzzed before it swung open.

Taylor closed her window and drove beyond the iron portal. The plot of land was not as impressive as hers, but between the gate and the house itself, the owner of the place hadn't done too badly.

The mansion rose beyond a dense strand of birches and firs, paneled in ebony and deep red brick. It was narrower than her house but taller—three stories, plus two towers that added another miniature floor.

The ground floor was lit, she saw as she approached. Otherwise, only a single dim orange light burned at one of the third-story windows.

She parked in a broad area beside the garage and approached the second gate in the second fence, which surrounded the house proper. Beside it was a booth and a brawny security guard emerged with a handheld metal detector.

"Ma'am," he greeted her. "I'll have to scan you for weapons before you can go in."

She held a hand up. "I have a pistol and a knife. Mr. Danforth knows me and will not be shocked or threatened by this. You may call him to verify it."

The man squinted and wrinkled his nose, perhaps detecting the lingering scent of Oroche and his cohorts. After a moment, he backed away a few steps, set the metal detector down within his booth, and retrieved his direct-line phone by its cord with his left hand. His right remained near the pistol he wore at his side.

"Hi, Mr. Danforth," he said into the receiver, "it's me. There's a lady here—obviously, you already admitted her— but she says she has a pistol and a knife and that you—"

"Yes." The smooth voice from the first gate was audible

to her ears even from eight paces away. "That is fine. You may let her through."

He seemed confused but only responded with, "All right sir, no problem. Let me know if you need anything." He hung up and punched a few keys, and the second gate released.

"You're free to go." He waved her through. "I'll...uh, keep an eye on your car in the meantime."

"Thank you." She nodded to him, walked past the iron fence, and quickly mounted the steps to the wraparound porch and the red double doors.

They were unlocked. As she stepped over the threshold, her host descended a staircase at the opposite side of the foyer.

The room's aesthetic was an Art Deco style that would have been popular with the rich in both America and Europe almost a century before. The staircase broadened as it neared the ground, and both it and the floor were covered with thick, deep-red carpet.

"Taylor," the man said.

He was tall with dark brown hair that fell to his broad shoulders, and a mustache and pointed beard that were about half a shade darker. He wore a long robe the same color as the carpets. In his left hand was a crystal glass filled with what appeared to be red wine.

She looked at him and a faint, gentle smile came naturally to her face. "Hello, Gerald."

Her host continued down the stairs rather than invite her up. The hem of his robe trailed behind him as he walked across the foyer and stopped about three paces away from her.

"You smell of blood," he observed. "Spilled not long ago. It's soaked into your clothes. You came here straight after killing…someone."

She did not deny it. "Two vampires and two thralls who tried to ambush me. You know I prefer to avoid feeding on living things, whether mortal or preternatural."

"Of course," he intoned, his dark eyes momentarily distant. "Killing at will on the one hand and drinking blood harvested humanely on the other, but never the two shall meet." He raised his glass and took a long, slow sip.

She cleared her throat. "The second gate is new, I see. I remember the first and you keep a guard closer to the house but don't have an inner gate."

Gerald Danforth finished his drink. "One can never be too careful. How are things in New York? I don't get across the Hudson much these days."

"New York," Taylor explained, "is under a certain amount of extra strain of late. You might even say it's in danger and the source of that danger will be all too happy to expand to all surrounding environs. That is why I've come. So that you can help me and be free of your obligation."

The man's eyes didn't open beyond their almost sleepy, two-thirds lidded state. He turned, strolled to the nearest table, and set the empty glass on its ebony surface.

"I seem to recall," he remarked suddenly as he rotated back toward her, "that once, you had an obligation to me. A mutual obligation. One which I did not try to cheat."

She almost cursed because she ought to have known that they'd end up rehashing ancient history before she could get down to business.

"That was a hundred and fifty years ago, Gerald," she observed. "And I have already apologized. You have every right to still harbor a certain subdued anger, I will concede that much. But what amends could be made have already been made. Taking me to task in the present year is pointless."

He laughed in a low, almost rumbling fashion. "That is such a detached, almost scientific way of speaking. Analyzing the situation rather than experiencing it. The notion of feelings hardly enters the equation, does it?"

The vampire folded her arms and drummed the nails of her right hand against her arm. "That is immaterial. What concerns me tonight is the fact that I require your help. And as it still stands, you would likely not have come to possess this"—she gestured at the spacious and beautiful house with her chin—"without me."

He stepped closer to her again. "Yes, too true. Helping you is rather near the bottom of any list I might make of things I want to do. But I also dislike languishing in debt. Eliminating that particular responsibility once and for all makes the prospect far more attractive."

"Good," she stated. She arched her thin black eyebrows. "May I have a drink?"

"Certainly," he almost grunted. "Come to the drawing room. It's on the third floor as I've always favored high places."

Taylor almost tittered at that as she followed him, walking a little to the side as she took care not to step on his robe. "Our kind belongs in the depths of the earth, but you've always been…atypical."

He didn't disagree.

They ascended two floors to the drawing room off the third-story landing and behind another ebony double door. The chamber was furnished mostly in reds and golds, with accents of black and the deep iron color of the two suits of armor which stood at the eastern corners as if guarding the house against anything that might cross the Hudson River.

At the far end of the room was a full bar, including an ice compartment as well as many wines and liquors and a tap with a slight rust-colored stain around the spout.

Taylor smiled. "I'll have a Historical Bloody Mary. If you do not have celery, that's fine."

"Quite right." He set to work, selected a glass, and added trace amounts of tomato juice and the necessary seasonings. Finally, he poured a generous but not excessive splash of vodka in before he topped it off with blood from the tap.

She accepted the drink. "Thank you." She sniffed it and her appetite, dormant for some time, roiled within her.

He nodded and fixed himself another wine-and-blood. "Don't drink yet. I think it would be proper to make a toast first."

"Very well, although we must discuss business directly."

Once Gerald's beverage was complete, he spun toward her, his drink raised. "A toast, then, to a temporary reunion of the very best people in both New York and New Jersey." He lowered the glass to bring it within Taylor's reach.

She extended her own. "To a productive alliance," she said and clinked hers against his before she took a sip of the Bloody Mary. It was excellent. Danforth drank enough that she'd had no doubt of his skill as a bartender.

Gerald himself was still in the midst of a rather long draft of wine, and she did not wait for him to finish.

"I require the twig from the Burning Bush," she stated.

The other vampire startled and almost choked on his drink, and for the first time, his eyes opened wide as he struggled to not spit blood and fermented grape juice across the drawing room table. After a second or two, he swallowed his mouthful and the lump moved visibly down his throat.

"What? Why? That's the one piece I refuse to even show! You appear, with no warning, on my doorstep after years of silence, and immediately demand the most precious—"

"Gerald," she cut in and raised a hand, "I'm sorry. Believe it or not, I truly am. But this is important, and not only to me personally. I don't think you know what's going on. Allow me to explain."

He brushed a lock of hair away from his face. "Please do."

Taylor leaned against the table. "You may have heard of an ancient Egyptian vampire called Moswen Neith. She was imprisoned in the Negev Desert in southern Israel at least two hundred years ago, and released only recently."

She went on to relay the whole story—minus the most intimate or tedious details—of how she became aware of Moswen's presence while the elder vampire was still in the Levant. It included how Moswen sent her thrall Alex to try to prepare New York for her coming. He listened quietly while she described how she'd since come in person to finish the job and already had tentacles spread throughout greater New York's underground, business society, and political structure.

Finally, she explained how she had tracked her the whole time and opposed her every step of the way.

Gerald did not interrupt and simply listened with an ever-increasing, slack-jawed amazement. He said nothing as she reached the conclusion of her spiel.

"And now, I have acquired the dagger of the Coptic magus Teremun al-Harb and a spell from the Sinai Peninsula which is likely to be even older. This spell requires a component of the Burning Bush in order to function. With it, we can bind Moswen once again and bury her beneath our feet, ending the threat she poses to the entire balance of the preternatural world."

Slowly, Danforth shook his head, his eyes still wider than they'd been at first but almost glazed over.

"I'll be damned," was all he could muster in a near rasp. He sat suddenly in one of the cushioned chairs lining the east wall. "I'd heard rumors but I don't pay much attention to such things. And it was decades before I was even sired that Moswen was bound."

Watching him—his shock, his distance, and his seeming lack of enthusiasm to leap to her aid—gave Taylor an idea.

She put a hand on his arm. "Gerald, please," she said softly. "Don't make me invoke your sire bond."

Honestly, she doubted whether she was capable of actually pleading but right now, she came about as close as she could. The time she'd spent with Gerald was not time she'd regretted and her need was great. He could be the one who gave them the final and perhaps most important component.

Blowing air from his nostrils, the tall vampire stood and seeming to pull himself together in a moment. "This is a lot to take in," he commented. "But, yes, let us view my collection."

She smiled. "Thank you."

As he led her out of the drawing room, he asked, "And what will happen to this twig during the spell?"

"It's likely," she admitted, "that it will be incinerated and there will be nothing to return."

He almost stumbled as he advanced toward the staircase, and she could feel a new surge of anger rise in him.

"Would you prefer I lied?" she asked.

"No." He said nothing further but she guessed his thoughts—that she was still too blunt and insensitive.

They descended to the second floor and made their way into a great central hall which acted as Danforth's personal museum. She doubted the twig would be kept there, but assumed that they were obviously moving in the right direction.

The walls were lined with bronze and marble busts and statues, rare oil paintings, weapons collected from archaeological digs, and even exotic plants. Interesting items, she conceded but still rather pedestrian at the end of the day.

They moved through the hall and approached an elevator, and she nodded approvingly. The basement must be where he kept the really good stuff.

Gerald stood before the security pad beside the stainless-steel doors. "Look away, please."

She did as he asked and turned back to examine a macabre Expressionist piece by James Ensor, while her host punched five digits into the pad. She turned back when he finished and as the elevator doors slid open. They both stepped inside.

He reached out with his thumb—she noticed that he still kept his nails trimmed impeccably short—and pressed the *B2* button.

"The sub-basement," he explained, "is only accessible from this elevator, the doors of which are virtually indestructible."

"That's wise," she acknowledged.

The lift took them deep into the earth and opened onto another hall like the one above. It was, however, far more sparsely decorated and of dark limestone rather than blackened wood.

Danforth walked forward slowly, and Taylor wondered if he were deliberately giving her time to ogle his famous collection. Not that she minded.

Several were kept in safe boxes or were too obscure to draw her interest, but others seemed to leap out at her and demanded attention. And in some cases, she doubted this was mere metaphor. There were relics in the world that possessed their own wills and agendas.

One was an ornate jade chalice, well over two thousand years old and, judging by the inscriptions, probably intended to contain the elixir of immortality which China's fang shi sorcerers had worked on before Qin Shi Huangdi, the first emperor, ordered them buried alive.

Another was a roster of scrolls on which hints of old Greek writing could be glimpsed. Taylor had heard whispers that Gerald might possess this—an ancient treatise on lycanthropy which was one of the only volumes saved from the Library of Alexandria before it burned down.

A third—the small skull of an animal—was mysterious to her at first before she noticed the Arabic symbol burned into its bare scalp and realized it must have belonged to Abu Hurairah, companion to the Prophet Muhammad and Father of Kittens.

"Gerald," she quipped, "you have a veritable treasure trove here. It exceeds my expectations."

He glanced at her and smiled. "Thank you, Taylor. You didn't think the twig was the only thing of real value I possessed, did you?"

She shrugged.

Near one of the side halls, they stopped. An airtight glass cube contained a thin forked stick that looked almost petrified with extreme age. Taylor waited as Danforth put a pair of elbow-length rubber gloves on and opened the glass box with what seemed a great exertion of strength.

In contrast to this, he was extremely gentle in his handling of the twig itself. He drew it out with great care, placed it on a wad of tissue paper, and wrapped it with precise movements.

"Come," he said, "I can find you a small padded box upstairs."

He did not offer her the item yet and carried it himself on their ride up the elevator shaft and through the second-floor museum. He went to a closet nearby and found a box, placed the twig within, put the lid on, and secured the whole package with two lengths of twine.

"Now," he proclaimed, "it is yours. May it serve you well since I'd far rather surrender this object to you now than surrender my entire collection to this usurper, Moswen, two months from now."

She gave him a long nod that was almost a slight bow and accepted the box.

"Would you like another drink?" he inquired.

"No, thank you," she replied. "I must be off to work. Another night, when I have more time, though, I might enjoy that."

He escorted her to the mansion's front doors and held them open as she walked out.

Taylor gave him a final glance. "Farwell, Gerald. Be well."

"Farewell." He smirked and raised his voice as she had already hastened off the porch and halfway down the foot-path. "And don't forget—this makes us even now!"

Without turning, she waved a hand casually as though it were no big deal at all.

The security guard greeted her and watched as she climbed back in her car with her precious cargo, turned the engine on. and steered it down the driveway through the woods that would take her back to the security gate and the real world.

CHAPTER TWENTY-FOUR

Taylor's House, Harrison, Westchester County, New York
The black Tesla soon reached home, having veered north to cross the Hudson at the Tappan Zee Bridge before it returned to Harrison via a patchwork of back roads. Taylor pressed the button to open her gate seconds before it was visible.

She was pleased to see that no vehicles were missing as she pulled into her garage. Having everyone present would make their final preparations much easier.

Tonight. It would happen tonight.

Presley opened the door before she reached it, his timing impeccable.

"Hello," she greeted him. The apple and the box containing the twig were both in her purse. "I was successful."

"That is very good to hear, madam." The butler stepped aside as she entered. "Everyone is in the library awaiting you, except Agent Gilmore, who is napping upstairs."

She nodded. This sounded agreeable. It would be better

to have Kendra out of the way at first while they discussed the more arcane elements of the plan.

Taylor handed her coat to Presley and strode directly into the library. Alice sat in the corner and flipped through a book, but the others were gathered around the reading table, engaged in a couple of interlocking sub-conversations. Everyone stopped talking, turned, and stared as the vampire made her entrance.

She nodded to them. "It's good to see you all again. Remington, what on earth happened to your face?"

"Oh—uh," he answered and returned the ice pack in his hand to the angry red lump, "I fell out a window." He cleared his throat.

She felt her face lengthen in horror and already tried to imagine the medical complications.

Alice added from across the room, "A first-story window, don't you worry. He plummeted a vast distance— all of about, say, three feet. Maybe three and a half."

"Oh." She was almost disappointed. "It's still impressive that he acquired such an ugly shiner from such a minor injury. Remington, did you also acquire…"

He picked up a syringe from the table, mostly filled with a blackish-red liquid. "Yeppers. And the dust."

She closed her eyes a moment. No one had failed. They might triumph over the would-be tyrant and her mindless servants yet.

Andrew Volz trudged up to her. "Hi, Taylor. They say you were getting something important? And there's…uh, a spell we need to cast? I am still trying to understand everything that's happening…" His brow wrinkled and his reddish eyebrows bristled.

The vampire looked up as Bobby walked over and put a hand on his shoulder. "Alice did some work on him while you were gone when we had a little free time. She did something right since the hex seems to be wearing off. He's not completely back to normal but she said it would only be a matter of time."

"Excellent." Taylor looked at Volz again. "You have been under a spell yourself, in case Alice or Bobby didn't tell you. You'll be better soon, though, and we'll make sure that this never happens again."

The dwarf nodded and comprehension seeped slowly into his face as his reawakening brain began to put things together.

"All right," the vampire announced and raised her voice enough to make sure everyone grasped that she was speaking to all of them. "I have acquired the apple and the twig. We are almost ready for showtime. I want everyone to gather and tell me, in an orderly fashion, exactly where we stand on every current issue."

As the others drifted back to the table or adjusted their positions to face her, Bobby spoke again.

"Kendra is catching a couple of hours of sleep upstairs in one of the guest rooms," she explained. "She was tired anyway, and we thought it would be much easier for Alice to work her magic on Volz without her around."

"Yes," Taylor acknowledged, "Presley mentioned that and good thinking. We'll need to update her on the broad outlines of the plan but will let her sleep while we discuss certain of the details."

Alice took her place within the circle and Riley, who'd drifted around the upper stacks somewhere, descended and perched on Remington's shoulder. Conrad also appeared from the hallway. He'd apparently been guarding Kendra on the second-floor—which presumably meant protecting the rest of them from any sudden intrusion by her.

The vampire regarded them with a serious expression. "Thank you all for your hard work thus far. I already possessed one of the Apples of Eden myself—I'd kept it in a private vault and it was a simple matter to retrieve it."

She reached into her purse and produced the long-dead fruit in its baggie, mildly amused when Remy and Bobby wrinkled their noses at the sight of it. Neither commented on it, though.

"Second, a twig from the Burning Bush lay with the personal collection of an individual who is known to me and furthermore, who owed me a favor. I have now collected on that debt."

They craned to look closer as she pulled the small box out, untied the string, and removed the lid to expose the nondescript ancient stick within.

"Wow," said Riley. "There's a strong aura coming off both of those."

Alice agreed. "Yes, I might not have recognized them in the wild, so to speak, but I'd definitely have realized they had some significance."

The vampire nodded. "We now have all we need."

"Except," the witch added and raised a finger, "the final ingredient—the blood of someone already under control."

"Yes, I know," Taylor countered. "We may be able to deal with that one on the spot or possibly even beforehand. It will, in any event, be the easiest ingredient of them all to come by. First, let us focus on how we will lure Moswen into our trap."

A brief discussion ensued, in which Taylor and Remington explained that they'd chosen the New York Public Library, Main Branch, as the site of the Egyptian vampire's tomb-to-be. Alice, Bobby, and Conrad voiced their concerns, but the vampire quickly convinced them.

"The Library," she explained, "will not be bulldozed next year to make room for an apartment building. It's an iconic New York landmark. Furthermore, the deepest vaults are seldom visited. And carrying out the operation tonight means that almost no one will be present. Our abilities and Agent Gilmore's authority will be more than sufficient to deal with any security guards or a single librarian working late."

When everyone finally agreed, they turned to the subject of how to lure Moswen there.

Bobby sighed. "Alex hasn't arrived yet, and we thought about going to look for him before you did. The idea seems to be that we can use him to indicate our position and Moswen then tracks him to try to kill us, right?"

"Exactly," Taylor confirmed. "Where could he be, though?"

Remy snorted. "I suspect I know. We'll pick him up later. If he's not there, I don't know where else he could be besides the office, but that doesn't make much sense."

She flapped a hand. "Yes, check the pub once we're done. I seem to recall someone mentioned a spell we could send through his brand to taunt his former mistress?"

"Yup," said Bobby. "Riley and Alice both have something

to say on the matter." She gestured toward the fairy and the witch to indicate for them to speak.

Riley went first. "I broke the brand on that colonel that Remy and I talked to, and I think I can use Alex's to find out where Moswen is. So, if she doesn't come to us, we might be able to go to her."

Alice followed this up almost immediately. "However, I do believe I can perform an adaptation of that which will also ping Moswen with Alex's location in a way she'll find completely insufferable. It will be like an itch she'll need to scratch, more than a traditional thrall-bond, but, hey, it will solve the problem of getting her to where we want her."

Taylor considered this. "Yes, let's do that. Of course, Moswen knows that we are not pushovers. She won't come alone. We can expect a significant entourage of her strongest thralls."

Grim nods followed around the circle. Remy spoke next.

"Maybe we'll get lucky and Colonel Russel and his men will arrive for the party," he began, "but I wouldn't specifically count on it. We also might be able to get Kendra to bring her team and at least secure the exterior—you know, to keep the battle from spilling out onto the streets."

The vampire drummed her nails on the reading table. "Hmm. We will discuss that after Kendra awakens or wake her up ourselves if need be. More backup is always better, despite the risks involved."

There were still things they needed to know before their plans could be set in stone and even then, flexibility and adaptability would always be required.

She turned her mind to another subject. "Bobby, Volz, do you have any updates on tracking down important people found in the vicinity of Moswen's supposed hideout in North Queens?"

"Yeah," said the receptionist, "Kendra and me had some hits once we managed to find out how to use some of Volz's software. It's facial recognition stuff, mainly. We turned up about half a dozen people sighted near that warehouse. There were a couple of politicians, a cop, a few business people, and some guy we had no information on, but he's probably some kind of criminal with underworld ties."

Taylor frowned. "Yes, that is disturbing. I almost wonder if Moswen might try to dispatch them to make our lives more difficult in other, less obvious ways at the same time that she rushes to kill us herself. It might be best if Riley, supported by Remington and perhaps Bobby or Volz, goes off to de-thrall these individuals while Alice and I cast the spell. A two-pronged attack."

Most of the group's faces fell at this—or squinted in confusion—and for a moment, she experienced doubt as to her own wisdom. It was a rare occurrence.

Then again, she was tired and full of fear at the prospect of what defeating Moswen might do to her personally. Both of those situations were rare, too.

After a moment of awkward silence, Remington stood, adjusted his tie, and grimacing stoically the way he sometimes did. "Hey," he said and spoke directly to her, "can I talk to you for a minute?"

He inclined his head toward the library doors. He meant talk alone, obviously.

She folded her arms over her chest. "Fine."

Taylor's House, Harrison, Westchester County, New York

There was, Remy decided, no getting around it anymore. Taylor was stretched too thin lately, and it had finally begun to affect her judgment. No one else was about to step up and say anything, but everyone expected him to be a cocky loudmouth with minimal tact or self-control.

Thus, of course, the responsibility fell to Remington Davis, the man with no reputation to risk.

Side by side, they walked out into the far corner of Taylor's beautiful foyer. With the lights out and only the dim residual glow from the kitchen seeping in, the room had a lovely, peaceful atmosphere. He would have liked to simply stand there for a while, relaxing and enjoying the evening.

But there was no time and that wasn't why they'd come out there.

He took a deep breath. "You're wrong," he stated and paused when she tensed as if mildly shocked by his impertinence. After a moment, he plowed on.

"Listen, we need the whole team there to defeat Moswen. Splitting up right now would not be wise. Please, hear me out on this. I know I seem like an idiot, but think of how often I turn out to mysteriously be right about things."

Her eyes narrowed and her jaw tightened, but all she said was, "Go on."

"Okay, then." He extended a hand, his index finger out.

"First, committing all our resources to deal with Moswen will be more efficient because, as you yourself pointed out, when she goes down, the thralls fall, then rub their eyes and wonder what caused such a strange nightmare."

Taylor barely inclined her head, and he continued.

"Second, you need all the backup you can get. You admitted that you and Moswen were, at best, evenly matched. So if the two of you cancel each other out, that means you're talking about Alice trying to fend all the thralls off on her own and work the spell at the same time. Even if you also brought Conrad, that's cutting it close, don't you think?"

Her gaze flicked to the side and she nodded again.

"Third," he concluded, "you need us, specifically. It doesn't make much sense to push away the people you care about while you go off on this endeavor with a complete stranger. I know, Alice seems nice and she's been helpful so far, yeah, but we barely know her. No one cares about you the way we do. That...changes things."

He trailed off, suddenly afraid he might be blushing. For a perhaps a full minute, they stood there in the darkness, neither speaking nor looking at one another.

The vampire finally broke the silence. "I have two counter-arguments to those points," she said.

"Of course you do." He sighed. "But I hope you're considering what I said."

"I am." She extended her hand. "First, the spell is to bind Moswen, not to kill her. We don't know if her power over her thralls will be entirely vanquished. At least she won't be able to command them if she's insensate, but they might continue to try to mindlessly dig her up and bring her back to life even without direct orders. There are no guarantees."

Remy almost flinched. He hadn't thought of that.

"Second," the vampire went on, "it is precisely because I care about all of you that I'd rather not have you in harm's way unless necessary."

She was being her usual aloof self, but he could detect the emotion slipping through the cracks.

"Damn," he breathed. "I believe you on the latter point, actually. But we're already in harm's way. She's tried to have us killed on multiple occasions—anywhere we happen to go in the New York area, remember? I think now is the time for all of us to face this together, and end it, once and for all."

Taylor leaned back and closed her eyes. Sensing that he was getting through to her, he pressed his advantage.

"You have to let us in, Taylor. Let us help you. No one thinks less of you for needing a little assistance with something like this. A joint effort is the only way we'll win."

She didn't open her eyes for a few more seconds, then she nodded slowly with a deep, deliberate motion.

"So be it," she stated. "You're right. I...had considered both options. But the single strong front is...very likely the better one."

The vampire extended her elbow, a borderline mischievous look forming around her mouth.

Smiling, Remy hooked his arm through hers and escorted her back to the library. When they entered, everyone looked up expectantly.

Taylor made the announcement. "Change of plans. We'll all go. Victory is better assured by a larger force and one way or another, Moswen's thralls will be less of a problem once she is dispensed with, anyway."

Most of them looked relieved to hear this, and he had to bite his tongue to keep from leaping forth to take credit for saving the day. As he'd told Taylor, it was a joint effort.

"Okay," said Bobby, "that's great. The blood, though—we still need that. What if, by some chance, Moswen doesn't bring her thralls? Or we can't...uh, draw any from one of them?"

"Good point," he conceded. "Unfortunately, Colonel Russel isn't a candidate since we broke Moswen's bond with him. And I'm afraid it didn't occur to me to stick a syringe in him when we invaded his home and beat him up a couple of days ago. You know how it is."

"Right," the young woman quipped, "but what about Alex? I know you guys mostly broke the link, but the fact that Moswen can still sense him means that he's still partially under her influence, right?"

Taylor put her fingernail to her chin as she contemplated this. "Yes, but some of my influence is on him as well. His blood might trigger the spell to affect both of us. If that is the only way to stop Moswen, then so be it. But I'd rather not. Let us collect some of Alex's blood as a backup plan and try to use one of her true thralls first. Either way, we need Alex to lure her. Remy?"

"I'm on it," he agreed at once. "Riley and me, that is. Not a problem."

The vampire folded her hands together. "Someone rouse Kendra and let's make our final preparations."

CHAPTER TWENTY-FIVE

Taylor's House, Harrison, Westchester County, New York

"Riley," said Remington, "get my car started and wait there for me. I'll be out in a couple of minutes. I need to ask a last-minute question or two."

The fairy agreed. He tossed his keys to her and she "caught" them telekinetically in midair. They sparkled with silver light alongside her as she floated out toward the Lincoln.

Fortunately, Kendra Gilmore was discussing security issues with Conrad in the kitchen while both ate a quick meal, so she wouldn't have been able to see his keys float down the path.

He hesitated and closed the front door. Presley stood between foyer and kitchen, looking at him.

"Have you forgotten something, sir?" he enquired.

"Sorta," quipped Remy. "You'll be holding the fort, right? As nice as it is to have backup, I know you're getting a little long in the fang for combat. Plus, Moswen might send some of her pet dickheads back here, so…"

The butler smiled. "That is the plan, sir, yes."

He gave the old man a thumbs-up, trod gently down the hallway, and paused near the door to the library. Bending forward, slow and steady, he could see Taylor seated at the reading table alone, her back to him.

She turned her head halfway, the corner of her black eye making contact with his gaze.

Of course, she could hear you coming down the hallway, he chastised himself. *She probably even recognized the meter of your footsteps.*

He went ahead and swung his head through the aperture. "Hey there. Is...uh, everything okay?"

"Yes," she responded and turned away. It didn't appear that she was reading or doing much of anything except staring at the polished wooden surface of the table.

Again, he decided to intrude—to exceed his boundaries a little. They were going to war here, and if it took a little forwardness to get her to open up to him with anything he should know, then that was that.

He entered the doorway, ambled to the table, and sat down across from his partner, technical boss, and friend.

Faintly, he detected a hint of annoyance on her part, and yet there was something she was holding back—something she wanted to say or do but still struggled with. Rather than pester her, he simply sat, and waited, keeping his own face calm and neutral.

Finally, the vampire released a short, sharp sigh. "David," she almost whispered. "I am...concerned."

"That is understandable." He adjusted his cufflinks. "We all are, and I imagine you've burdened yourself with the issue of our safety. I had a taste of that when I had to run the agency while you were gone."

She closed her eyes for a second. "No. Well, yes, that too. But what I mean is... I worry about...what will happen to me during the fight. Like we talked about. I may...begin to lose control. It has been so, so long since that last happened that I...don't know if I'll be able to bring myself back. I may hurt someone without meaning to, exactly like the monster some people already think I am."

He listened to her speak and made sure he'd heard and comprehended her words before he offered an answer.

"I will be there," he stated, and he reached across the table to put a hand over hers. She didn't try to stop him. "To watch over you. To make sure that does not happen— no matter what."

Taylor took his gaze into hers. She had always had that ability to not only hold someone's gaze but practically engulf it. "No matter what," she echoed. "I will hold you to that, Remington."

The vampire slid a hand into her jacket, which she'd not taken off since she arrived, and produced the small blue bundle she'd carried when she first returned from Israel. Suddenly, he wasn't sure he liked where the conversation was going.

"This," she explained and unfolding the cloth, "is the Al-Harb Dagger. The weapon was sanctified against vampires over a millennium ago. We are primarily interested in its magical abilities, but the very construction of its blade makes it far more deadly to our species than a normal knife or sword."

"Oh," he replied, sweating, "that's...uh, good news if Moswen tries to—"

"If," Taylor cut him off, "I lose my...humanity...I want you to promise to take this dagger and kill me."

That was exactly what he'd hoped she didn't say. His abdomen felt like it had collapsed around a miniature black hole.

She continued to talk as he struggled with a response. "It may be difficult to slip this into my heart in the thick of things, but that would at least wound me badly enough to be finished off by other means. This would also be far easier than trying to take my head off in straight combat. But if I become a danger to innocent people, you must."

Steeling himself and inhaling deeply, Remy insisted, "It won't come to that, Taylor. Shit, I can practically feel it. But...if it makes you feel better, then yes. I promise that in that very unlikely event. I'll do it."

He almost cringed. It wasn't the kind of vow he could renege on. But it wouldn't come to that. It wouldn't.

"Thank you," she said.

"Right, right," he drawled, stood, and smoothed his hair. "Anyway, I'd better get to it. We'll kick ass, though. I'll see you at the other, even bigger library." He touched her shoulder as he departed the chamber, realizing he'd lost track of time and probably kept poor Riley waiting.

Lower Manhattan, New York

The fairy had seemed perplexed by something all through the drive, but it wasn't until they were on their way out of Greenwich Village that she finally spoke.

"Remy," she asked, "how will we find Alex? I thought maybe you knew where you were going so I didn't try to track his scent. Do you need me to?"

"Oh, right," he stammered and snapped out of his somber reflections on the promise he'd made to Taylor. "Nah, I don't think that will be necessary—unless I'm wrong, of course. And how often am I wrong? That's right —almost never."

He reached for his phone, drew it out, and after checking carefully for nearby cops, dialed the number of a business.

"Hi, it's me," he said into the receiver. "Is Alex there? Yeah? Mkay. Okay, yup. I'll be there in ten to fifteen minutes." He hung up.

"Who was that?" the fairy wondered.

Remy smiled, supposing that it looked almost rueful in a way. "I've had someone keep an eye on Alex lately. And by someone, I mean Porrillage, mostly, since his bar is the only place where our friend from Down Under really drinks these days. Since he likes to complain about work incessantly and even in New York you can't really rant and rave about vampires and dwarves in a bar too long before someone will start giving you shit."

To his pleasant surprise, Riley tittered. "That's funny. I haven't seen him drunk before. I wonder what he's like?"

"He's not a happy drunk," he said. "But that would imply he was sometimes happy, so it's no great surprise. I might have to have a talk with him about how substance abuse isn't exactly a great way to deal with your problems —something I happen to know a thing or two about—but at least his increased drinking habits have made it easier to keep tabs on what he's up to lately."

The fairy rolled over on the dashboard and began to kick her feet into the air for no particular reason. "That makes sense. Do you think he would...help Moswen?"

"No," Remy stated. "Maybe if she cornered him and threatened him enough—since he already did that once, after all—but for all his bitching about, well, everything, he hates her and looks forward to being rid of her as much as we do. Perhaps a little more, even. It might mean he can go back to the University of Melbourne and ambush the freshmen to lecture them about what a great place it is."

Remy wove his Lincoln through the evening traffic and soon reached the inconspicuous little corner of Manhattan where Por's Bar lay hidden more or less in plain sight in the basement beneath a shop.

He parked in the next alley over, locked the car, and had the fairy throw a quick protective enchantment over it, just in case. That done, he walked toward the iron staircase leading to the pub with her flapping over his head.

Minutes later, he pushed through the door and stepped into what had always felt rather like another world.

Standing against the wall to his right and sipping drinks so pungent he could smell them from ten feet away were two withered, desiccated humanoids. They gave off a dry aroma of dust and spices and were bundled up save for their faces—probably mummies, he reasoned. Remy wondered if they'd ever bumped into Moswen during their original lifetimes.

Meanwhile, the pool table had seemingly been taken over by trolls, who were sufficiently loud and aggressive that the other patrons gave them a wide berth. He didn't blame them and still recalled how one Mr Shauckburn had almost throttled him after he slightly misspoke while investigating the troll's wife's infidelity.

And at the bar itself was the usual smattering of elves, dwarves, gremlins, and shapeshifters, along with a single average-looking blond man hunched over the surface and yammering away in a low voice as he gradually drained a mug of beer.

"The quality control here," Alex said vaguely to the space behind the bar, "isn't up to snuff. Did you know that Melbourne has produced some of the finest craft breweries in the world? Not to mention that we're already in the running as one of the planet's best coffee cities, on par with Paris. Or New York, for that matter."

Porrillage the gnome darted within his domain, dispensed beer from taps, dried freshly washed glasses, and mixed drinks. He hadn't noticed Remington yet. It was a busy evening.

"Por!" he shouted. "Hey there."

The gnome caught his gaze briefly and waved a hand before he disappeared behind an ice machine with a half-complete daiquiri in hand.

Alex turned his head slowly toward the new arrivals. "Whuh? What are you people doing here? Come to deliver my check, have you?"

"Alex," said Remy, "we need you. It's time to finish your drink. We'll buy you a cup of coffee on the way to the library."

"Library?" the man sputtered. "Who gives a shite about a library? Well, the one at the University of Melbourne did have an excellent film selection, not simply all this direct-to-video crap from the last ten years that you see on Netflix."

The investigator exchanged a quick glance with Riley. "Uh, yeah. Standards have declined. It looks like your beer is almost finished. Por, he's done after this one. Sorry! We'll make it up to you after this is—"

Alex interrupted him with another slurred rant. "And, of course, they need me, which is to say you plan to use and abuse me again, right? Send the intern to get everyone coffee and donuts, no matter that he still has a fucking piece of evil itself lodged in his chest. The A-Team never calls me to do anything cool. It's all merely availing themselves of my utility as a homing device. Isn't there some word for that like 'dehumanizing?' Meaning no offense to other species. 'Depersonalization?' You know what I mean."

For all his usual barely suppressed snobbery, Remy had to admit that he felt bad for the guy and even vaguely understood where he was coming from. He was only in the United States, to begin with because Moswen had forced him there on pain of death and now, he was the lowest man on the totem pole. It would help if he wasn't so bitchy all the time, but still.

"Well," Remy said to him, "you have, in fact, been help-ful. And think about it—when this is over, you might even be able to go home."

The Australian drained the rest of his beer mug. "I'll believe that when I see it, but I suppose I'm willing to believe anything."

That doesn't even make sense, Remy grumbled inwardly. Fortunately, Riley intervened.

"Aww," she said in a cute voice dripping with sympathy. "Poor Alex. You haven't tried to...uh, kill any of us ever since we freed you from Moswen, and that does count for something. And Melbourne does sound like a wonderful place. I'd like to visit it someday. But help us this one time. Please? You're the only one who can."

She hugged the muscle that joined his neck to his front shoulder area.

He sighed and looked at her. "Very well, I guess," he drawled and attempted to hop off his stool. He stumbled immediately, and Remy caught him but almost ground Riley between their bodies in the process.

"Sorry," he grunted and heaved the man to his feet.

Por called to them from behind the bar. "I'll send his tab to the office, okay? Have a nice evening."

"Yup, great," he said. "Thanks for keeping an eye on him, Por. Next time I'm in, I'll order, like, three Bloody Marys. Modern, not historical."

Holding the intern's arm, he helped Alex the rest of the way across the pub floor. Riley then used a little light levitation magic to help him up the stairs and soon, they staggered their way into his car. Alex slumped in the passenger seat and didn't even attempt to look sober as Remy fastened the seat belt over him.

"So," Alex asked as Remy took his own seat and fired up the engine, "which library are we going to?"

He smiled. "The library. You know, the one that was in *Ghostbusters*."

CHAPTER TWENTY-SIX

New York Public Library Main Branch, Midtown Manhattan, New York

The distinctive structure came into sight, less recognizable at night but only slightly.

"We're here," Remy announced. "Elvis has...uh, reached the building. And will leave it later."

"What?" Riley asked, her wings moving out of sync.

He flapped a hand. "Never mind. It's a classical reference. Treat 'we're here' as the important part of the statement." He pulled into a parking space near the opposite corner from the library.

After they hauled Alex out and made sure he was able to stand, they performed the usual routine of locking it and having Riley put a protective magical shell around it.

"That reminds me," he said to the fairy, "once we get inside the library, can you do that thing with the soundproof barrier? I know it's a big building but perhaps at least with the vault area we finally choose."

"Hmm," she responded thoughtfully. "Probably. Let's look around and I can tell you afterward."

"Aye." He hooked an arm under Alex's shoulder and urged him forward, pushing, pulling, or steadying him as needed, given that he still swayed randomly. They'd poured most of a cup of coffee down his throat but it hadn't had much effect yet.

As they left his car behind, he hoped Riley's rather basic spell would be enough to protect it from Moswen and her dark army of douchebags.

They're out to kill us, not vandalize our rides, he reminded himself.

A group of people stood on the steps that led up to the library's main entrance. It seemed they'd noticed the approaching trio but were content to wait for them to arrive.

First, though, Remy saw a black van parked on Fifth Avenue with *MOONLIGHT SECURITY* stenciled on the side. That was a new one on him. He dragged Alex along as he approached its driver's side window.

"Hey," he called, "Volz. It's good to see you back to being capable of safely operating a motor vehicle again. How do you feel?"

"Hi, Remy," he reciprocated. "Um, better. They had me park here, behind that," he pointed toward a couple of orange and white barricades, "and gave me this thing, which will control traffic lights so no one drives past here for a while." He hefted a heavy black device from his lap, laden with switches and blinking lights.

Remy nodded. "Right, that thing. You actually invented

that. I'm not sure if you remember, but you did. Do you know how it works? Still? Again?"

"Yeah," he grunted and adjusted his position in the seat. "It's a little…complicated…but I got the hang of it."

"Okay." He shrugged. "Keep fighting the good fight, and ask…uh, probably Kendra if you need help."

It was clear that Volz wasn't completely restored yet, but he'd probably recovered a good seventy percent of his intelligence. That ought to be enough for now, given how smart he was normally. Part of the problem might be the disorientation he must have felt as the curse wore off.

Alex mumbled something as he continued to drag him along, and when they reached the base of the stairs, Riley used another slight levitation spell on the Australian to essentially reduce his weight to the point where Remy could manipulate him without struggling.

All the faces gathered on the first landing were familiar. Their group was there, along with Kendra's usual crew, whose names he had mostly forgotten, but at least he recalled seeing them a few times.

"Sorry we're late," he stated. "I had to get Alex a cup of coffee. You know, for medicinal purposes."

Taylor looked mildly irked but all she said was, "You're just in time, really. We're finalizing the roles each of us will play. We've already shuffled the security guards off to their homes, not to mention a grad student who had permission to study late. We have the library all to ourselves for the night."

Alex, for some reason, responded to this. "That's encouraging. We wouldn't want to have to fight the crowds. Ha, ha. What time is it?"

Agent Gilmore's face was stern. "Late. We'd best not waste time. The longer I have to keep this place off-limits to the public, the more suspicious it gets."

She glanced between the nearby rows of buildings. "By the way, I contacted Colonel Russel. He texted me asking where we'd be, and I told him as we arrived—the goal is to take him into our confidence, after all—but he hasn't replied yet. There's an off-chance he'll simply report us so we might have company."

Remy winced. He hoped it would be the welcome kind of company, if so.

Taylor raised a hand. "We shall burn that bridge if we come to it. Now, let us review. First, Agent Gilmore, I understand you will form a second perimeter around the library. The first perimeter will consist of the rest of us inside, of course. Gilmore's team will ensure that no one gets in—besides Moswen and her followers, obviously."

Everyone nodded their assent.

"We should know by Alex's reaction when Moswen is close," the vampire went on. "Now, everyone else—inside. We will discuss the rest of our roles within."

They took a moment to look at the sprawling, well-aged building with its imposing Classical architecture. The iconic lion statue seemed to watch them from the side.

Remy tapped his lips. "In a way, it's the perfect tomb," he remarked. "It already looks like an ancient Roman mausoleum or something. And it's full of old things."

"Very highbrow," Taylor riposted. "Come. We have one more thing to do tonight."

She led the way and Remy, Riley, Alex, Bobby, Alice,

and Conrad followed. The front doors were open and they did not lock them.

"You know," Alice said with a slightly mischievous smile, "Kendra really looks good in that tactical gear, doesn't she? It flatters her. It makes you imagine that she must be good at...uh, taking charge of situations. All kinds of situations." She giggled.

Oh, Remy thought. *Somehow, I missed it earlier. Well, maybe I can use her as a human shield against Taylor's and Bobby's strange assertion that I'm on the verge of asking Kendra out myself.*

Their footsteps clattered as they walked the length of the Rose Main Reading Room. As he recalled, their destination was this very chamber, but at a point near a basement room that housed a collection of old, boring records that no one really cared about. Moswen might well be safe and sound for a millennium there.

"Now..." Taylor resumed her speech. "Alice will supervise the casting of the spell as well as perform it. Remington and Bobby, you two will be her assistants and protectors. Do whatever she tells you to without exception. And if any hostiles get past the rest of us, eliminate them immediately."

Remy nodded and Bobby gulped. She'd never been in combat before, he realized. He wasn't exactly an expert himself, but the simple fact that he'd survived quite a few battles by now had left him a changed man.

He wondered, though, if it was right to make her participate in all this. She was their receptionist, not a field agent, and did not have experience with violence. But she might well have volunteered while he wasn't paying attention—after all, being involved in spooky shit had seemingly been a lifelong dream of hers.

"Alex, if you're sober enough to understand," the vampire continued, "we'll need a little of your blood as a backup for the ritual. Otherwise, your main role will simply be to draw Moswen to our position. Don't hold back from her. We want her to know that I'm here, that you're scared, and exactly where we are."

"Uh…" The intern moaned miserably. "Why do we want to see her again? I hoped I'd never have to. Do you people even realize what an awful c—sorry, uh…bad person. Vampire. Whatever."

"Yes," Taylor agreed, "she is. Conrad, Riley, you two will handle Moswen's thralls, aside from the ones I can spare a moment to deal with. We don't know how many of them she'll have—anywhere from four to fifty. If we're lucky, Kendra's team will sight them as they enter and give us a quick warning. Riley, use magic to slow and disorient them. Conrad, and possibly Remington, can deal with them after that."

"Okay," said the fairy.

The werewolf grimaced. "That should be doable, madam, but even I can only do so much against fifty if she does have that many."

"Understood," she replied. "Remember, you only need to keep them busy long enough for the spell to work. Finally, I will keep Moswen herself busy. She won't turn down the opportunity to kill me personally, I suspect. And no offense, but none of you would be capable of going toe to toe with her."

No one was offended. They all had varying degrees of

understanding of who and what they were up against.

Alice had Bobby and Riley help her set up a small folding table to serve as an altar in the rear corner of the hall near the taped-off staircase leading down to the basement addition. The witch also gathered the four vital components, along with a few other minor ones she'd already collected and a black-bound book.

Watching them, Remy was glad that Alice and Bobby seemed to have gotten along well since the witch had arrived. Riley had worked with her on a couple of spells already. They couldn't ask for a better team, really.

Meanwhile, he, Conrad, and Taylor selected a long table nearby on which to lay their duffel bags and remove and assemble their arsenal.

He was impressed by some of the hardware they withdrew and he also noted—with slight jealousy—the easy way the vampire and the werewolf worked together to put shotguns together, load pistols, draw crossbows, charge tasers, and sharpen knives. Again, he was morbidly curious as to exactly how much history there was between the two.

Then again, Taylor allowed them to help her.

"So," he quipped, "it looks like we're all in this together. Everyone leaning on everyone else."

Alex leaned against the wall at the moment, but that was beside the point.

The vampire looked at him. "Yes, David. We all need help sometimes. And I think we will all have ample opportunities to pay back any favors incurred, besides."

He nodded, not about to argue, and took to loading one of the revolvers.

Alice approached. "We're set up for the spell. The

dagger spell—the binding one, I mean. That will be the longer, more complicated one, so I almost wonder if we should start it first and then perform the beacon spell on Alex."

"Mm, no," said Taylor. "Once the dagger is activated and the binding spell is engaged, Moswen might sense its power and realize the trap. We want her to come here as soon as possible. Ideally, the dagger should activate at the moment we see her so she doesn't have time to change her mind about fighting me again."

"As you say, madam," Alice conceded, and Remy detected a trace of the woman's earlier resentment of the vampire's authority. "Since we have no idea where she is, though, well… What if she's only two streets over? We might not have enough time."

"We'll risk it," the other woman stated firmly. "We can handle Moswen and her minions while you complete the ceremony. Now, draw some of Alex's blood—remember that we'll try to get some from one of her thralls, preferably, since his blood may not work—as backup, and ignite the proverbial beacon."

Alex protested as the witch came over to him and despite her soothing words, his eyes bulged in horror for a moment as she slit his thumb with a small scalpel-like knife and squeezed about a teaspoon or so of blood into a tiny saucer.

"There you go," she told him, "that's enough. All done now. Here, let me wrap that." She tied a strip of gauze around his thumb as he muttered incoherent sentence fragments. Remy worried that the man might pass out but the spell ought to snap him back to attention.

Once his blood was safely next to the altar, Alice and Riley converged on him.

"Alex," the fairy began, "we're sorry, but we need you to think about Moswen. About the mark she left on you"

"Uggghhh." He groaned and his head jerked. "Fuck that. Why do you think I'm drunk? Because I don't want to remember. Having her poking around inside my mind. Setting my heart on fire. Jesus. You'd be a mess, too, if…"

He trailed off and again, Remy felt a twinge of pity for the man. He was probably dealing with some degree of PTSD after all that. Then again, no one had forced him to choose tonight of all nights to get hammered.

As the Australian unwittingly recalled his bondage, Riley seemed to find the residual link to his former mistress and faint light, mingled silver and gold, shone from his chest.

"There," Alice whispered, excited. "You've got it. Now…" The witch closed her eyes and twisted her hands into odd configurations and the light grew stronger. A deep mossy green added itself to the two hues already present.

Alex began to tremble violently as the golden light threatened to overwhelm the silver and green. "No," he groaned. "Dear God, no. She's coming. She sees us!"

Taylor stepped forward. "Where is she, Alex? And how many are with her?"

"Near." He gasped and his eyes snapped wide open, although he seemed to stare beyond them. "Fuck. She was already on the prowl for you—near! Very close. She'll be here, uh…five minutes? Ten?"

Shit, Remy thought. *I hope the dagger thing is a short*

procedure. Suddenly, he almost felt ready to piss himself and he was glad he hadn't shared the coffee with Alex.

Taylor put a hand on the Australian's arm as Alice and Riley continued to manage the spell with their minds.

"Alex," the vampire repeated, "how many thralls are with her?"

"I don't know," he sputtered. "Too many. Uh—shit, a dozen. Twenty? Around that. Oh, God. She's coming! And she'll kill all of us."

Taylor turned to Alice, who looked drawn and pale. "Begin the ritual," she ordered. "Now."

New York Public Library Main Branch, Midtown Manhattan, New York

Colonel James Russel permitted himself to smile for a few seconds. It was dark and none of his men with night vision goggles were looking at him right now, so no one saw. That was probably for the best.

He was back in action. And, now that he had begun to recall more and more of what the Egyptian crime-queen had made him do, he looked forward to getting some payback.

"Colonel," one of his men whispered and move closer. "The FBI already has a perimeter of their own set up. Do we hang back or approach them?"

Russel locked gazes with the man. "You hang back, for now, Sergeant. I, on the other hand...I think I'll take a walk and maybe see if they have a light."

"Yes, sir," Sergeant Buford responded, his tone almost unnaturally soft.

The colonel, his hands folded behind his back, strolled forward and across the street. Remington and Taylor and their cohorts had blocked the road off in addition to clearing any loitering civilians, which would make the whole operation far easier when—if—push came to shove.

There was no getting around it, though. It felt good to be back in action and to have men around him with rifles and submachine guns in their hands and consider the prospect of actually needing to use his own sidearm.

He walked out into the middle of the street and made no effort to stay out of the cone of yellowish light generated by a nearby streetlamp.

Predictably, two feds materialized to welcome him.

"Excuse me," one said loudly and raised a badge, "this area is off-limits. FBI investigation."

"Hi," he responded. "Colonel James Russel, US Army National Guard. I'm here to assist. Is Agent Gilmore on duty?"

The two agents, a black guy and a white guy, had clearly not expected to hear this and even in the dark, he could see their startled expression and the tension rippling through them in their partial confusion. The black man stood closer to him, his hand resting on his pistol. The other man, who'd greeted him, took a step back.

"Uh, Gilmore?" he said into a mouthpiece and kept his gaze on Russel and his hand near his gun. "There's a gentleman here who claims to be a Colonel Russel and says he's here to assist us. Do you know anything about that?"

He listened for a moment and then spoke to his guest.

"Colonel Russel," he began, "we'll have to ask you to wait here for a couple of minutes. Did you come alone?"

"Of course not, agent." He grunted scornfully. "I have a squad hanging back on the other side of the street. Maybe you've already seen them. Once your boss arrives, we'll get this cleared up, though."

The two men looked skeptical but did not question him further. It only took about another minute for Kendra Gilmore to arrive.

Russel watched her approach. She was a fit, attractive woman, perhaps twenty years his junior and probably of mixed black and white parentage. The vibe she gave off was one of toughness, seriousness, and professionalism.

"Colonel Russel." She extended a hand.

He took it. "Agent Gilmore. We spoke briefly over the phone. And let's say a little bird told me a few other things about what's been going on. We're here to lend a hand in neutralizing the enemy."

The woman raised an eyebrow. "My civilian allies are already committed to that very goal, Colonel. It's a sensitive business. They may not appreciate interference."

"Well," he retorted, "the more sensitive the business, usually, the more it helps to have big guns waiting in the wings. And we brought some of the biggest ones we could find." He motioned behind him and signaled his team to approach.

She looked uncomfortable, even though she seemed to be considering his proposal. "I can radio them and ask. This whole operation is, however, my responsibility, and the last thing I need is a few trigger-happy Guardsmen blowing up the goddamn New York Public Library."

He uttered a dry chuckle. "We know what we're doing.

The building will be safe, possibly barring a couple of holes. I assume it's been cleared of bystanders already."

His squad emerged from the darkness behind him. In addition to Sgt Buford and two other men with assault rifles, there were another two with top-of-the-line SMGs, two more with automatic shotguns—one loaded with slugs and the other with buckshot—and one with a high-powered sniper rifle for good measure.

Kendra nodded. "That's a good amount of firepower. May I ask what convinced you to bring it all? And to show up in the first place?"

Russel smiled grimly. "To be honest, I think your friends in there are a few yards short of a football field. Have you heard what they talk about when you're not around? I have, as a matter of fact, and maybe we can talk about that later."

The woman's face showed a dark uncertainty as though she had her suspicions but had kept quiet.

The colonel went on. "But I don't think they're bad people. And our boy Remington, in particular—who did get me the hell out of whatever goddamn spell that Egyptian had over me—is in over his head. I thought he could use people with proper training and proper hardware. Not to diminish your contribution, of course. But let's say you guys hold the fort outside here and make sure no innocents wander in and we'll penetrate the building itself to shoot anyone if they really, really need to be shot."

Gilmore took him aside by the arm. "I'll tell them that you're coming in, with or without their permission. They probably will need all the help they can get."

"Good," he replied.

He motioned again, and his men shuffled quickly past the incredulous FBI agents, half of them toward the main doors and the others toward a couple of windows where they'd be able to breach in a less obvious fashion.

The agent leaned close to his ear. "Don't let me find out I did the wrong thing."

"Oh," he commented, "I wouldn't worry about that. The impression I have is that there's bad shit afoot that needs to be dealt with. Bad shit that comes from far away and no one fucks with America on my watch."

CHAPTER TWENTY-SEVEN

New York Public Library Main Branch, Midtown Manhattan, New York

Taylor was afraid. She hated to admit it or even consider it, but denying facts did nothing to change their reality. She had to acknowledge that she'd not been this terrified since...since...

She couldn't even remember a single instance of this kind of fear.

Even one mistake tonight would result in her own death, she knew, as well as the death—or worse—of the good people now present. All of them had willingly joined this endeavor, knowing the risks but determined to help her anyway.

And after that, New York would fall. The city she had worked so hard to protect and to keep functioning with a modicum of civility would become another barbaric fiefdom populated by almost nothing but Moswen, her sycophants, and millions of slaves whose only destiny would be to suffer.

With New York under the monster's merciless heel, the rest of the United States might follow. Then the West and possibly even the world.

"*No*," she stated under her breath, so silently that perhaps only Conrad might have heard.

The dagger of Teremun al-Harb was in her left hand and a loaded, short-barreled carbine was in the right. The gun would be all but useless against Moswen, but she hoped to pick off a couple of thralls before the main event began. There was no sense leaving them all for Conrad and Remington if she could assist them.

She looked behind her. Alice had begun to cast the spell.

"Light and Dark, Goddess and God, Chaos and Law, witness us now and bestow the protection of your eternal balance..."

While she spoke, Alice crushed the ingredients together in an earthen bowl with an old-fashioned wooden pestle. The various herbs and purified water—the simplest ingredients to acquire—gradually disintegrated, along with the precious primeval apple, the petrified twig, and the dust of Faerie. The dead man's blood, too, lost its individuality amidst the pasty concoction.

The vampire could only hope they'd be able to draw blood from a thrall in time to activate the dagger before Moswen herself entered the fray. If not, the witch would employ Alex's. That would probably work, although she had her reservations.

It presented a danger of its own. When she had first struggled against Moswen's magic to remove the man's brand, some of her own had remained in him. The cosmic powers behind the spell might well interpret Alex to be under Taylor's control or a joint thrall of both vampires.

If that were the case, the dagger would work equally well against either or both of them. Moswen only needed to seize it in mid-battle, and she would be finished and the evil vampire triumphant.

She'd avoided discussing this possibility at any length so as not to alarm her friends. But it was something she thought about constantly.

"Now," said Alice, "light first the black candle on the left and then the white candle on the right of the altar."

Bobby and Remington scrambled to obey. The former clicked an electric lighter next to the black candle, then Remy struck a match for the other. A soft orange glow spread from them to bathe the small table and the wall and floor around it.

The witch raised a simple wooden wand and used it to trace a protective circle around her workspace. That complete, she spoke over her shoulder, addressing all of them generally.

"I am about to begin reading the incantation. It will require intense concentration and take about four to six minutes. I must have the thrall's blood before the incanta-tion is complete—my voice will rise greatly in volume at the final passage, so you'll know. If we haven't wounded one of Moswen's by then—"

"Yes," Taylor acknowledged. "Use Alex's."

Remy stepped away from the altar, looked around, and snapped his fingers. "Oh, volume. That reminds me. Riley? Where are you? Do the soundproofing spell around the perimeter of this room. The last thing we need is someone coming to investigate gunshots and then hearing weird chanting and animalistic snarls. They'd probably call in a goddamn airstrike."

The fairy wafted out from behind Conrad. "Yes, you're right. Give me a moment."

As the witch began to voice the arcane words from the book in her hand in strange, droning vocalizations, Riley flew up to inspect the borders of the reading room and get a feel for them before she worked her own magic. After a moment, she spread her hands and cast faintly shimmering silver light all around the walls, ceiling, and floor.

With a smile, she floated toward Remington. "I think I got it," she reported. "Even though I've never done it on a room this big before."

He stroked her head briefly with the tip of his index finger. "What would we do without you? Thanks awfully —again."

Bobby strode up to Taylor. "She needs to touch the dagger," she said and held a piece of paper on which Alice had written the procedural instructions to be followed. "Only for a second."

With a nod, the vampire hastened to the witch's side and extended the weapon, hilt first, toward her. Alice did not look at her. The witch's eyes were glazing over as she focused totally on the book and the strange words that poured slowly from her mouth. She extended her right hand and tapped the center of the knife's golden hand-guard near the base of the thin sharp blade.

Taylor drew it back to herself. For the moment, she decided to stay beside Alice in case the sorceress needed anything else. It was very likely that the dagger would have to be anointed with the substance in the bowl at some point but not yet. Not until they had the final ingredient.

Conrad took a few steps back and half-turned toward the vampire.

"I have weapons arranged on the seats under all those tables—there and there," he explained and pointed to the reading surfaces closest to them. "They won't know how well armed we are at first. I'll remain in human form to start with. We'll shoot as many as we can before they get close, then bring the weapons back before we engage them hand to hand."

She inclined her head. "Good. That ought to work well, provided they come through the front. Moswen lacks subtlety. However, we can't discount the possibility of flanking." She gestured toward the high, arched windows to either side of them. Rail-guarded walkways ran along the walls under the windows. They might help in keeping the battle away from Alice but they were too narrow to be effective positions for an extended fight.

She frowned when she realized that damage to the beautiful structure and its impressive collection would be almost impossible to avoid. If they failed to defeat their adversary, however, New York could expect far worse.

The incantation rose and fell in intensity, but the witch did not yet seem to have reached the ultimate passage.

The air grew colder. Temperatures did not bother Taylor much one way or another, but she was still highly sensitive to changes in the air. Tension boiled through her and gave way to the limber relaxation she always tried to cultivate before a deadly struggle.

Their radio device crackled softly. "Someone appeared

in front of the main entrance," Kendra's voice reported hurriedly. "I don't know how they got there. They might have dropped off the roof."

Taylor pressed the button to respond. "Only one?"

"Yes. And I should mention—"

"Not now," the vampire said brusquely. "I need to focus and make sure I'm ready when Moswen appears."

The agent made a sound of protest, but Taylor turned the volume on the radio down and ignored it.

The front doors opened, footsteps ascended the stairs, and a moment later, a single figure strode toward them down the central aisle between the broad reading desks. It was not Moswen but rather an average-sized if muscular man and no one Taylor recognized.

"Hi!" he called and waved. "Parley? I have a message for you. It's kind of important, ha-ha. You might want to listen."

This is a trick, Taylor surmised. *Little does the bitch realize that she may, in fact, be helping us.*

Conrad gave her an uncertain glance as the strange man approached and continued his spiel.

"So, I happened to be in the neighborhood," he went on, "and word out on the street is that you people need to learn to negotiate properly. So—"

Taylor darted forward. By the time the man realized what was happening and switched to a combat stance, the vampire had already caught him in a headlock and dragged him toward the altar.

"Hey!" he protested, his voice thin and strangled. "You can't—"

"Be quiet," she snapped. "Conrad, hold him."

The werewolf seized the man's arms and pinned them behind his back as she ripped the front of his shirt open. There, over his heart, was a faintly glowing golden brand. The stranger's eyes widened in fear.

"I think," the vampire stated, "that we already know what this 'message' will be." She thrust her hand out, seized the man's head, and twisted it sharply to break his neck. He slumped in Conrad's arms.

Bobby's hand flew up to her mouth. "Oh, my God," she whispered. This was probably the first time she'd ever seen a person die by violence.

Alice, too, seemed disturbed, although her back had been to them the whole time as she tried to concentrate on the spell. And, crucially, the volume of her voice was rising, the stream of ancient words reaching a crescendo.

Taylor seized the extra, empty saucer on the altar with one hand. With the other, she drove her fingernail into the messenger's jugular. As he'd been dead only a second or two, the blood pumped out, thick and red and hot. She ignored the crude hunger she felt as she caught the fluid in the bowl and then returned it to the table.

The witch did not miss a beat. Still chanting, she poured the blood into the earthen bowl and mixed it with the rest of the sludge, grinding the pestle with her right hand while the book trembled in her left.

Remy glanced around nervously. "Okay, so, does this mean that—"

The four windows closest to them all shattered at once. Dark shapes streamed into the library, scuttling and darting to spread out along the walls while others flew directly to the central floor.

"Oooookay!" Remy interrupted himself and his eyes went wild as he smoothed his hair. "Surprise boss fight, no save point. Let's fucking do this."

Alex, slouched against the wall in the extreme rear corner, groaned and gibbered in abject drunken terror and covered his face with his hands.

Conrad had already seized the nearest gun and opened fire on the thralls near the windows and on the walkways. Eight of them, two per window, had penetrated the building.

To everyone's unpleasant surprise, the thralls returned fire. Moswen had finally caught up with the modern world and armed at least some of her servants with pistols. Taylor pivoted to catch the bullets with her own body— even if they were silver, they would only slow her down so it was better to absorb them and protect the humans. Chunks of regular lead struck her in the chest and thigh, stabbed her with pain, and made it momentarily harder to shoot, but her regenerative abilities were already dealing with the problem.

She aimed her carbine and fired ten shots at the thralls on the right side of the hall. Conrad focused on the left. Three figures screamed and fell amidst the bookcases lining the wall. A fourth dodged behind a table and surged toward her.

More streamed in through the windows along with three figures who, during all the excitement, had come in through the third-floor doors and the stairs. There were probably more who'd flown or jumped onto the roof from other buildings, thus bypassing Gilmore's people.

Conrad had gunned down two thralls himself, and

Remy had picked up a revolver to wound another and send him scrambling toward cover.

Furthermore, Riley worked magic of some kind from her position near the ceiling to create walls of viscous light that the thralls had to slow down to a quarter of their usual speed to pass through.

Taylor saw one of the attackers, a lithe woman with stringy hair and crazed eyes, struggle through one of the transparent barricades. She raised her carbine and squeezed off a single shot. Half of the woman's head burst apart in a spray of red chunks and she toppled without a sound.

The trio approaching from the front stopped halfway down the hall. On either side were two men, huge and strong, with dark glasses and shaven heads, one white and one black. In the center was Moswen Neith.

"Taylor Steele," the vampire hissed and her voice somehow filled the hall even amidst the chaos, although she had not shouted. "This will be our last meeting. Your impudence shall be punished with agony and death everlasting. Whatever paltry enchantment your servants are enacting will not save you."

As Taylor drew a bead on one of the bodyguards, both men suddenly whipped out submachineguns and opened fire.

"Shit!" Conrad exclaimed and flipped the nearest table over to form a barricade, but most of the hail of bullets pierced through the wood.

Again, she leapt directly into the line of fire and held up a heavy chair as a shield. It seemed the two men were mostly aiming for her and the werewolf, anyway. A dozen or more bullets drilled into the wood. A few pierced through and struck her flesh, momentarily paralyzing her with pain and shock.

As she twisted in agony, she saw that behind her, Remy and Bobby had fallen prone. By some miracle, Alice had not been hit. Riley hovered before her, maintaining a shimmering screen with her hands to deflect the stray rounds.

The bullets had only been of lead but the pain they inflicted gave Moswen's remaining thralls—at least ten of them—the time they needed to move in for the kill. The Egyptian now advanced, too.

The witch's voice, grown to a raw-throated shout, finished the incantation and fell silent.

A fountain of light, radiant white and tinged with blue, erupted from the bowl and brightening the whole chamber around them.

"Taylor!" Remy shouted. "The dagger!"

Two thralls had already closed on the vampire's position and she was only now recovering from the barrage.

She raised her carbine and fired four shots into the nearest thrall. He shook as blood spurted and he collapsed, and she fired the last five in the magazine at the bald white guy on Moswen's right. He dodged behind a table but still took two rounds in the arm and shoulder, which made him drop his SMG.

"Kill them!" their adversary shrieked and strode forward at a deliberate pace.

Remy appeared beside Taylor and pulled her back, urging her toward Alice and the bowl as he raised his revolver and delivered a volley the other thrall, now mere feet from them. It was a small but scrappy-looking man, and in trying to protect himself, he took a round through the hand and another in the knee. He fell and writhed in anguish.

Taylor reached the witch's side and extended the dagger.

Alice, who looked simultaneously zoned-out and terrified as she tried not to look at what was going on behind her, drew the luminous white substance up and rubbed it along the blade and guard of the knife.

As both women watched in wonder, the dagger seemingly absorbed the holy ointment and now, the light emanated from the weapon itself.

"Go," the witch said.

Taylor turned. Conrad had shifted into his wolfen form, his suit discarded beside him, and ripped the head off a thrall while three others piled against him, seeking at least to busy him enough for Moswen and her servants to strike at Taylor.

The two vampires locked gazes.

"What is that? You coward!" Moswen raged. "You know yourself to be the weaker. That trinket will not be enough."

Taylor's lips drew back from her fangs. "We'll see about that."

Putting all her strength and speed into the act, she launched forward to dart, weave, and barrel directly at her enemy, seeking to simply overwhelm her with a single overpowering strike and surprise her when she probably expected that she would be hesitant to fight her directly once more. In a fraction of a second, she closed the distance between them.

Moswen's hand, already twisted into a bestial claw,

lashed out and caught her full in the face. She tumbled aside and crushed a table beneath her, although the dagger stayed in her hand.

Her roll put her back on her feet. Before total wrath and bloodlust consumed her, one final lucid thought emerged from her brain.

This won't be easy, after all.

Holding the glowing dagger firm, she lunged.

CHAPTER TWENTY-EIGHT

Remy drew in a sharp breath as he watched Moswen knock Taylor aside like a Doberman resisting the charge of a housecat. His sight of both vampires was blocked by a ravening, hatchet-wielding thrall, a man with a buzzcut wearing a long coat.

Rather than draw back and fight defensively against the hatchet, he stepped into the man's attack and launched a fast side-kick squarely into his solar plexus. With an explosive "oof," the man staggered back.

That was enough time for the investigator to pick a chair up and swing it onto the thrall's head and shoulders. The wood shattered and the man dropped, unmoving.

"Never bring a hatchet to a chair fight," he stated.

He nonetheless picked the ax himself up and ran back to where Alice, Bobby, and Alex waited in the far rear corner.

"Bobby," he said, "take this, just in case. We've dealt with most of her minions, but it's definitely not over yet." He handed her the ax and she accepted it, wide-eyed but surprisingly calm.

Conrad had wrought terrible havoc on Moswen's thralls, killing six or seven of them and knocking out a couple of others. Now, he struggled against the huge black guy who'd stood to the Egyptian's left. The man had wrapped a massive arm around his neck from behind, but the werewolf was so strong and ferocious that he was quickly losing his grip.

A female thrall raced toward the combatants. Remy picked up a loaded crossbow, aimed, and fired. The sharp bolt caught the woman low in the back and narrowly missed her spine, but ruined her day quite effectively all the same. She squawked, fell, and rolled under the nearest table.

Their radio crackled again.

"Colonel Russel is here," said Gilmore's voice when Bobby quickly turned the volume up again. "His team is coming in to assist immediately."

"What?" Remy almost screamed. After a second of mental chaos, he wondered if that might be a good thing but he still didn't exactly have time to explain what the fuck was going on to a team of National Guardsmen who'd decided to crash the party.

By now, Conrad had the upper hand in his struggle against the bodyguard. He'd freed himself and shoved the man to the ground, his jaws open to bite his head off.

I'm sure he's fine, Remy thought and raced past them toward the front doors. *I need to make sure the whole operation doesn't get blown out of the water.*

As he sprinted to the center of the hall, however, he glimpsed Taylor and Moswen.

The two slashed and lunged at one another, circling at speeds his eye could barely follow. Both bared their fangs and occasionally tussled at clinch range. At no point was Taylor able to plunge the dagger into her foe.

She needs a leg up. We have to think of something.

He ran on and almost collided with Colonel James Russel himself, along with four of his men.

"What—" he stammered, "what are you doing here? A routine book security inspection?"

"Mr. Remington," the officer greeted him, "it looks like a hell of a scuffle. Do you want me to waste time explaining, or do you want help? Where are the hostiles? I have more men coming in the back and through one of the windows."

Remy froze, almost flabbergasted, and gestured vaguely over his shoulder. Then, he protested, "Wait! Taylor—you can't hit Taylor. She's trying to fight Moswen—"

Russel was already beside him and examining the scene. "There she is. Oh, I recognize her. Time for a little—whoa, shit!"

Spinning around, Remy immediately saw what had startled the colonel.

The vampires had separated, and Moswen had begun to grow. Her body elongated, her hands became animal-like claws, her face stretched into a monstrous snout, and her feet became cloven hooves. A tail like a serpent's burst out the back of her brown dress and swung behind her.

It almost looked like Taylor, watching her in the total focus of battle frenzy, was about to shapeshift, too.

"Jesus." One of the Guardsmen gasped. "Is this for real, Colonel?"

Without looking at the man, Russel replied, "I'm reasonably sure it is, Corporal. Like I said, this isn't exactly a normal operation."

"Correct," Remy interjected. "We might actually be able to use your help. But you won't be able to do much against that...thing...even with all those guns. Not unless certain other forces are involved. This sounds crazy but trust me."

"Nothing," the Colonel shot back, "that you could possibly say could sound any crazier than what I see right now. Hell, we thought we saw forms moving around in here, but we couldn't hear anything. That's already damned strange by itself."

Conrad ambled up—back in human form and having quickly pulled his pants on. "What's going on?" he demanded.

"Conrad," Remy snapped, "help Taylor get Moswen out of the way, and clear any thralls. We need to get these men through. Alice might be able to tell us what the hell to do next."

The lycanthrope didn't linger to ask questions. He located a thrall rising from behind a table close by and turned, punched the man in the face, and tossed him into the nearest wall. Without hesitation, he raced toward the duel between monsters which was already working its way toward the front corner of the hall.

"This way," Remy beckoned and jogged toward the rear with the Guardsmen close behind. "Feel free to shoot anyone who attacks us. A few of Moswen's guys might still be alive."

They passed the corpse of the black bodyguard, missing the top half of his head courtesy of Conrad's jaws. He wondered where the other one was—the guy Taylor had shot in the arm.

There was no time to contemplate this since the man himself suddenly lunged from between two overturned desks. He'd finally reloaded his submachinegun one-handed and now aimed it at the troops.

Russel's men were faster. An SMG and a shotgun blazed to life, gouged chunks out of the bald guy's broad torso, and hurled him against the wall, already dead by the time his other arm fell to his side.

"Nice shooting," Remy complimented them.

When they reached the altar, Alice and Riley already seemed to be conferring on what to do. He somehow suspected that the men could see the fairy, now—they'd certainly seen Moswen, so it was very likely.

At that moment, two of the other four Guardsmen rappelled in through the window and another two emerged from the cellar, having snuck in the back and worked their way up.

Alice, Riley, Bobby, and Alex all looked confused.

"It's okay," Remy told them, hurriedly, "they're cool. What we need, though, is to know what the hell they can actually do. Besides...I dunno, maybe shoot Moswen enough to slow her down before Taylor stabs her with the dagger."

Riley perked up and her wings flapped faster than usual. "What if we can transfer the spell to those?" she suggested and pointed to the Guardsmen's guns.

The troops, for their part, looked antsy but otherwise

resigned to the fact that they'd walked into something completely outside their past experience.

"Well, ah..." Alice began, "I don't know. The spell is mostly spent. There's some residue left that still seems ethereally active. But the blood is the active ingredient and we'd need more, and even then, I'm not sure if the magical effects can be stretched like that."

The fairy was almost bursting with excitement as she said, "We have a way to extend spell effects. I could combine our magic and maybe make it work."

The radio crackled. The voice that came over, though, was not Kendra's but Volz's.

"So," he grunted, "I've been following the discussion, and I recalled that dwarven magic has some similarities to what you're discussing, also. I might be able to advise you. Yes, I think it could be done. I'll be right in."

Remy shrugged and his gut clenched as awful howls resounded from the other side of the hall. "Okay, let's try it. Gilmore, if you hear this, let the short guy through."

"Roger," Kendra acknowledged.

"And," the dwarf suddenly added, "I won't even charge the agency extra for the service!"

Wow, Remy thought. *He's growing more and more like his old self by the minute. Awesome.*

The girls leapt to work to gather any leftover spell components and pitch them into the earthen bowl, while the fairy and the witch discussed magic in technical terms he couldn't even understand.

Colonel Russel cleared his throat. "While we're waiting for this divine boon or whatever it is, are you sure you don't want us to simply shoot the damn monsters?"

"Yes," Remy said instantly. Conrad had wolfed out again, but Moswen handled both him and Taylor with disturbing competence. "Two out of the three are good monsters. Trust me."

"Crap," Alice interjected. "Someone spilled the spare blood."

Remy snatched the bowl they'd used previously and scuttled over to a nearby thrall who was unconscious but bleeding copiously. He held the container under the flow and hurried back to her with a reasonable amount.

"Good," said Alice and returned to work with the pestle once she'd added it to the other mixture. The blood started to glow with the same white light that shone from Taylor's dagger.

A squat form barreled through the doors and ran with surprising speed down the length of the hall toward them.

"Volz," Remy exclaimed, "my man! I'm glad you could—"

Conrad careened toward the dwarf and they almost collided but Volz ducked and rolled at the same time and narrowly avoided him. The werewolf whimpered and collapsed on a pile of rubble and fell unconscious.

Now, it was only Taylor and Moswen.

The dwarf, the fairy, and the witch hastily conferred in low voice over the bowl as Remy watched the duel of the vampires and the Guardsmen fidgeted in their half-terrified awe. Impressively, they maintained trigger discipline but were obviously eager to do something.

In horror, Remy saw that Taylor had changed. Her white skin had turned a shade halfway between midnight-blue and charcoal-grey, and her eyes were totally red, her skull gargoyle-like and distorted. Her hands were webbed and sprouted blood-colored talons. A pair of leathery wings tipped with hook-like protrusions extended from her back, and the voice that emerged from her throat was not human.

No longer a petite, dark-haired woman, she now resembled a demonic, humanoid bat-creature.

Is this what she feared so much? Becoming a monster and not being able to come back? he agonized. *Don't make me have to fulfill that vow I made.*

"Ha!" Alice's voice announced. "Success! You military guys, gather around, now. I don't think you've ever seen firepower quite like this."

Remington glanced back as the men popped the magazines out of their guns and Alice and Bobby dabbed the bullets within with the enchanted substance. It only took a speck of it for each weapon, and when they reloaded, the entire weapons began glowing faintly with a bluish-white light. He merely hoped the bullets would confer enough of the power that they didn't have to run up and club Moswen with the butts.

And that they'd have a chance to take a clear shot.

CHAPTER TWENTY-NINE

New York Public Library Main Branch, Midtown Manhattan, New York

Remy looked at the troops. Russel and his men were, for the moment, awed by the effects of the spell.

"Man," said the guy with the repeating shotgun, "this is trippy. These are still going to...uh, fire, right?"

"They should." Alice shrugged. "It's not like I plugged the barrels or gummed up the internal moving parts."

The colonel stepped forward. "Right, then. Prepare to take 'em out."

Remy spun toward him. "No, goddammit! You'll hit Taylor. The one who looks like a...bat-woman-thing. She's on our side!"

Russel's jaw muscles tightened. and his eyes narrowed. "They both look like godawful monsters from hell who have no business in our goddamn library," he stated flatly.

With a glance over his shoulder at the pair of vampires, he saw, with mounting alarm, that Moswen had brought an elbow down on Taylor's neck to half-crush her on the floor and that now, she looked toward the humans.

Her eyes, blazing yellow, glowed with an even more awful intensity and she suddenly gestured with a clawed hand.

All around the hall, her thralls—the five or six who were only wounded or unconscious—sprang up, once again animated by her malicious will. The Egyptian had realized that Russel's men were there to kill her, and she intended to neutralize them while she killed Taylor herself.

"Shit!" Russel growled. "Remington, out of the way!"

One of the servants pounced on him, and he realized it was the guy with the buzzcut whose head he'd used to disassemble a chair. The bastard wasn't dead, after all. He wound his arms around Remy's neck and chest from behind and grunted while he blinked half-congealed blood from his eye.

The investigator caught his arm and tried to throw him over his shoulder, but he didn't quite have the right angle and the man headbutted him in the side of the face. He didn't manage to put much force into it, but he happened to connect with the shiner he had acquired earlier at the morgue.

"Fuck!" he exclaimed and struggled to free himself.

The guy was strong, but he had been injured badly enough earlier that now, he was running on proverbial fumes. Moswen's command literally forced his body to do things it ought not to be capable of.

Remy jerked his right foot back, twisted it behind the man's ankle, and threw himself straight back to trip the man and crush him as they both impacted with the floor.

He rolled off immediately, slugged the thrall hard in the jaw before he could react, and managed to send him back to dreamland.

His opponent successfully thwarted, he dashed toward the rear of the hall and cleared himself from the line of fire as the other thralls circled the walls and columns. Russel's men took potshots but were unable to cut loose as yet.

From this new vantage point, he finally had a clear look at Taylor and Moswen, and his gut roiled with tension and primitive dread at the sight of their battle.

This, then, was what had happened in the depths of the subway tunnel near the warehouse. It was the awful clash between ancient and terrible monstrosities that had left his partner almost dead and driven Moswen into remission for weeks. Finally, it had inspired Taylor to fly halfway around the world simply to put an end to her own nightmares.

The slavering jaws drooled. Knife-like claws slashed and jabbed. Bizarre protrusions from their mutated bodies whipped or joined in the effort to slay one another. Not only could his eye barely follow the speed and ferocity of the movements, but his brain constantly tried to reject the horror of what he saw.

He soon identified another problem. Taylor, in her increasingly maddened and frenzied need to rip Moswen limb from limb, had almost forgotten about the dagger. Stabbing the Egyptian with it did not seem to be a priority.

In that moment, the thralls pounced. Their dark forms moved in but the Guardsmen's guns blazed and roared as they tracked their movements, and clouds of vaporized blood filled the air as half of them were annihilated.

It looked as though the bullets, like the guns themselves, glowed with luminous ether.

The surviving thralls retreated as quickly as they'd attacked. In the opening, Remy ducked out into the hall and stared at the vampires, waving his arms over his head.

"Taylor!" he shouted, desperate to get her attention. Somehow, he had to pull her enough out of her battle-rage to take notice of him and to bring back enough of her humanity to reason with her.

Another thrall—one of those whom Conrad had knocked unconscious earlier—lurched from underneath a reading table to Remy's right and shouted in fury.

He pivoted away and to the side, evaded the man's powerful but obvious swing, and seized his arm and collar in the same motion. With as much strength as he could muster, he hurled the thrall head over heels behind him. As he jogged forward, the air cracked behind him when one of Russel's men opened fire to drop the thrall where he stood.

The space before his vision opened again to disclose the terrible struggle between the two vampires. Both become almost totally bestial and their strange and ungainly forms thrashed and stamped around. The white glow of the dagger flashed now and again amidst the movements of the dark forms.

The taller form of Moswen, a terrible Egyptian tomb-statue come to life, seemed to gain the upper hand and almost crushing the other while she loomed above. Her jackal's ears perked up while her snake's tongue trailed hideously from drooling jaws.

But the smaller and even more energetic shape that was Taylor shifted from under her adversary. Her barbed bat-wings slashed at Moswen's arms, her red eyes crazed and wolf-like snout snarling in defiance.

They'll kill each other. Remy was close to despair.

"Taylor! Taylor!" he shouted again. "Don't make me fulfill my vow because so help me, I will. You're better than that, though!"

Behind him, the few remaining thralls converged on Russel and his men. "Hurry!" one of them yelled between well-placed gunshots.

The undead bat-creature finally looked at him. As she turned her head, she withdrew the dagger and held it before her breast.

It saved her life. Moswen, seeing her opening, plunged her claw toward her opponent's heart, but the twisted hand stopped as if it had struck an invisible boundary and seemed to flash with white flame. The jackal-beast shrieked in awful pain.

"Now, Taylor!" Remy bellowed.

The hand holding the dagger lashed out in the next moment, the sacred knife was no longer in its mistress' hand but buried to the hilt in the center of Moswen Neith's chest. Air seemed drawn from every corner of the room in a brief silence like that which came before a thunderclap.

He raced toward Taylor, held her gaze, and mouthed the words, "Trust me."

The Egyptian screamed when she recognized what had befallen her, the sound so cacophonous that it almost knocked him over. It was terrifyingly suffused with hate and pain and mindless animal panic.

Remy launched himself at Taylor, his arms out.

The vampire cringed and hissed as he bowled into her,

wound his arms around her arms and wings in a warmly powerful hug, and pulled her away. She did not resist, thankfully. Understanding seeming to dawn within the ruby eyes, and the two of them catapulted a few yards and rolled away.

As they moved away from Moswen, Remy briefly saw the other vampire claw desperately at the dagger, but she seemed unable to touch it of her own volition and moved as if underwater. Coils of blazing white light encircled her body to trap her and burn away her strength.

"Now!" Colonel Russel ordered. "Open fire!"

The deafening roar of at least half a dozen guns fired at once filled the chamber and drowned out even the Egyptian's final scream of agony. Remy came out of his roll on the floor beside Taylor and snapped his head up.

Their adversary staggering back as streaks of white light—the trails of Teremun al-Harb's holy power clinging to bullets and pellets and slugs—tore into her, cut through her, and destroyed her like the rabid animal she was.

Then, as Russel himself drew his pistol and fired it into her forehead, she exploded. Her demoniac body simply burst apart into a thousand burning chunks that already turned to the ash and dust that millennia should have reduced her to.

An angry, yellowish-amber light seemed to rise from the shower of debris like an avenging phantom, only for the white glow of the binding spell to engulf and dissolve it and blot it out. In an instant, it was gone forever.

Silence filled the library.

"Oh," Alice gasped, far away in the corner. "Oh, my. It's over, isn't it?"

One of the soldiers began to laugh, a low, dry sound as the adrenaline in him crested and crashed to leave him glad to simply be alive.

"Yes," said Russel, "I think it is."

The investigator sat and his face suddenly split into a big, stupid grin. "Holy shit!" he exclaimed. "Six out of five stars. Better than expected—would recommend!"

He extended a hand, his thumb sticking straight up.

CHAPTER THIRTY

New York Public Library Main Branch, Midtown Manhat-
tan, New York

The smoke cleared and Remy heaved himself to his feet, groaning with the efforts of a long day. The partial beating he'd taken from Buzzcut the Thrall and his bump on the head earlier also seemed to come back to haunt him now that the adrenaline was wearing off.

The National Guardsmen and their commander were chuckling, clapping each other on the shoulders, and in general, admiring their handiwork.

Russel's face had taken on a wistful, almost dreamy cast, and his nostrils opened wide to receive the aromas. "Ahhh," he sighed. "The smell of gunfire. It's been too long, my friends."

Remy turned to the side, looking for Taylor. He saw a dark form, briefly, crawling behind a column and then up the wall, seeking refuge in the farthest, darkest corner of the hall.

Is she okay? She's not badly wounded, is she? Damn. She

probably only needs a minute to herself after everything that went down.

For a moment, he was almost sick with worry and concern. But Taylor had recovered from both severe physical damage and massive psychological trauma before. He would check on her soon. But for now, he trusted that she had herself under control.

He trudged toward the rear corner where everyone had congregated in a loose crowd.

Bobby stepped forward. "Well, Mr Remington," she commented and shook her head slowly, "I never thought I'd see anything like this when I signed up to be your receptionist. Even the Inquirer couldn't have predicted this. It's been…interesting."

He smiled and put a hand on her forearm. "That's one way to put it. I wasn't sure how you'd handle all this, but, well… I don't think we could have done it without everyone doing their part."

Moving past her, he came to Riley and Alice, who were already in the early stages of another magical discussion.

"I don't know," the witch admitted. "It was only supposed to be a binding spell, but it seemed that it weakened Moswen severely in the process. That probably had something to do with it."

"Yes," the fairy agreed, "I think so. We mixed different kinds of magic—yours, mine, and Volz's—but on the same frequency, so it probably tripled the power of the spell and made her completely defenseless."

Volz grinned. "Once again, dwarven ingenuity turned the tide. Hah!"

Remy added his two cents' worth. "And a barrage of

that kind of firepower, besides, would have done about the same thing to a normal human without magic involved. I don't think we'll even need to worry about entombing her, after all. Correct me if I'm wrong but I'm pretty sure she's flat-out dead."

Alice's eyes went distant for a second, then she nodded. "Almost certainly. There's no way she can physically revive in her current, uh…state." She glanced at the pile of cinders across the hall.

Looking back at Remington and Riley, she added, "And the residual effects of the magic seem to have completely dispersed her spirit. Still, I'd suggest we bury her remains as originally planned, just to be safe."

"Okay." He shrugged. "Someone will have to find a push-broom and a nice big bucket."

He glanced at Alex, who had basically passed out by now, slumped against the wall and drooling on the floor. He would have been an excellent candidate for the job if he wasn't intoxicated beyond all reason. Hell, he might even enjoy being able to personally confirm that Moswen Neith was now fertilizer and well past the point of ever hurting him again.

Remington decided he ought to talk to Russel and his men—debrief them, essentially—but first, he wanted to check on Conrad. He worked his way over to the side of the hall where he'd last seen the lycanthrope

He was there, crouched between the base of a pillar and a shattered table, back in human form and mostly dressed. Bruises covered his body and blood stained his clothes, but he was definitely alive.

"Conrad," he said cheerfully, "are you okay? You don't look that bad, but you took a hell of a beating back there."

The man nodded. "Yes, sir, thank you. I wasn't too severely wounded. I'm merely, ah, thankful that none of those thralls tried to finish me off while I was unconscious."

Remy helped him to his feet. "Fortunately," he reported, "there were only a few thralls left by then, and Moswen concentrated them on us. As for M-Lady herself, she's toast. Almost literally. We managed to enchant Russel's team's weapons and they completely obliterated her."

A look of relief crossed the werewolf's handsome face, and he blew out a short, soft breath. "That's excellent news, sir. A vampire that powerful who refuses to play by any rules but her own... Well, it's not something we want to deal with ever again."

The two men returned to the others and Colonel Russel stepped forward to speak to them.

"Mission accomplished," he stated, "if I'm not mistaken. Frankly, we have only the vaguest idea of what the hell we actually saw. However, all the men I selected for this job— which, by the way, is completely off the books—were chosen in part because they know how to keep their mouths shut. We can count on them. And it's very clear to me that there's—how does that Shakespeare quote go?— more things in heaven and earth than dreamed of in our philosophy. Something like that."

Remy squinted. "Wasn't that some guy named Horatio? Whatever. But yeah, we call it the preternatural. In case you hadn't realized it yet, our job is to keep it contained and well-managed so that most people don't have to deal with it or even dream of it. But sometimes"—he gestured expansively around the chamber—"we need a little help, I suppose."

The colonel smiled grimly. "Full disclosure—for a while, I thought you were all fucking nuts. And I base that on having heard most of the conversations you've had these last couple of days. I like to know exactly what I'm getting myself into."

Now, Remy was confused. "What does that mean? You've been tailing us? Alice is a mole or something?"

"It's much simpler than that," said Russel. "I slipped a bug on you at my apartment. It's probably still there although I haven't checked recently."

"What?" he demanded, suddenly feeling violated. "A bug? You can't do that! I—uh—I would have noticed! You're bluffing, obviously. Seriously, come on." He immediately slipped off his watch and began looking for it.

The colonel uttered a short, almost bitter laugh. "No, sir. When you guys released me, I couldn't help noticing that you had briefly taken off that nice gold watch of yours. And as it so happens, old habits die hard. I wasn't always a bald-headed desk jockey, you know."

"Habits?" Remy wondered. Did the guy put a bug on everyone he met?

"Statistically speaking," Russel explained, "putting a bug on the underside of someone's watch is probably the best place you can stick it, provided you kind of squeeze it into the crack so the person doesn't feel it. It lasts the longest. People wear their watches all the time but then again, they also take them off when they jump in the shower or change clothes, which reduces the chances of the bug being destroyed or accidentally removed."

Remy clenched and unclenched his hands, clenched his jaw, and, although it took him a minute to realize he was doing it, clenched his sphincter. And of course, the colonel made him look like a fool while Conrad was watching, although the werewolf looked at the floor and remained silent.

"And why," he enquired, his voice seething between his teeth, "did you feel it was necessary to do that, may I ask?"

In a matter of fact tone, the other man stated simply, "I needed to know what was going on. You didn't think I would simply take your word about everything? You lied to me about being from the CIA, for example, after all. I have to know everything in order to do my job properly, to keep myself and my information secure, and to make certain I haven't compromised myself under duress or altered states of consciousness."

He calmed slightly, although he still kind of wanted to find a large cardboard box and punch and kick the shit out of it. "Fair enough," he muttered.

"Anyway," the colonel went on, "there came a point when my analysists and I had heard enough. Agent Gilmore there clearly felt you were worth working with, even if she wasn't in on the full truth of what's been happening. And you guys clearly believed all this, as insane as it might have sounded."

The younger man nodded and waited for the officer to continue.

"And finally," Russel concluded, "I knew that something of a very fucking uncanny nature had happened to me before you two barged in. Memories have come back of doing things that made no sense, of always thinking of her and what she wanted me to do. And your story about that woman who'd used me being the greater evil...well, that much I could believe."

The colonel exhaled and adjusted the hem of his uniform. "I take my responsibilities for the safety of our country seriously, gentlemen. So, I took the initiative, although I've kept it firmly in black ops territory. I haven't been active in the field for a long time, and I don't feel like trying to explain...this"—he gestured toward what was left of Moswen—"to the powers that be."

Remy scratched his chin. "Well, that's certainly understandable. I'm sure you can imagine that we didn't want to explain it to you, either. No offense."

"None taken." His smile crept back. "Having as much responsibility as I do now means I can get more accomplished, but it also means I spend too much time shining a seat with my ass. In any event, the ordnance we fired here will be written up as having been used in training exercises. This incident at the library will be portrayed as a bungled terrorist attack. There've been enough real ones that people will leap to believe that, even if the whole thing looks fishy on closer inspection."

"Right," he agreed. He thought about mentioning Taylor's mindwipe abilities but thought better of it. "Well, despite the bug thing—which you'd better not even think about trying again—I'm glad you showed up, Colonel. We all are. And New York is the better for it. Thanks for your help."

He extended a hand, and Russel took it to give it a good shake.

The man's gaze wandered toward the doors. "I'd best take my men and go speak to Gilmore again...let her know it's over and help her deal with New York's finest in case they've arrived already."

"Good idea," Remy assented. "Maybe we'll see you again sometime if we get in over our heads."

Russel laughed. "Hopefully not, Mr Remington. Hopefully not."

He turned and walked away and motioned for his men to follow him. The troops jogged to meet him and threw the group a strange glance or two as they departed.

"Conrad," he began, "go help Alex and make sure he's not on the cusp of death or something. Make him drink water. I'll be along to help with the rest of the cleanup shortly."

The lycanthrope nodded. "Not a problem, sir."

Remy wandered over to the far corner. The one where, a few minutes before, he'd glimpsed the black form crawl away to safety and privacy. He paused and looked into the shadows.

"Taylor," he called and his voice echoed faintly. "If you're up there, somewhere, take whatever time you need. But we want to make sure you're okay. So, you know... please talk to us when you feel up to it. Anyway, we won. It's over. Glow-in-the-dark banana stickers for everyone!"

Silence was the only response but he somehow knew that she'd heard him.

He walked over to the pile of blasted debris, the only thing that remained of their most powerful adversary to date. The Al-Harb Dagger lay amidst the blackened chunks, still shiny and clean-looking although it no longer glowed with power. He picked it up and slipped it, hilt-down, into his pocket.

Touching the damn thing reminded him of his promise to Taylor. The last time he'd seen her, she had still been in her monstrous form—yet the Taylor he knew and trusted and cared about was still there in her eyes.

He glanced around and sighed. No one else seemed to have volunteered for the task, so he decided he might as well start looking for a push-broom.

New York Public Library Main Branch, Midtown Manhattan, New York

Kendra Gilmore was glad she'd had her team form a perimeter around the library and maintain it, even with all hell breaking loose inside. There'd been curiously little noise, but she had glimpsed commotion through the windows and there had been far more noise over the radio when she'd called. As such, she had very nearly ordered her people in to help, but she trusted that Taylor and Remington and Colonel Russel and their allies could handle it.

And they had, but in the meanwhile, their operation finally began to draw the public's attention.

Curious random citizens had started to wander up, closely followed by officers of the NYPD, who were even more curious.

"Hey," one cop enquired, "what's going on here? We had reports of weird flashing lights, people climbing all over the building, stuff like that. No gunshots, though. Do you wanna tell us what's up?"

"Officer," she responded and flashed her FBI badge, "at this point, I cannot divulge all of the details. Suffice it to say there's been a serious incident, but we have it under control. More information will be forthcoming. You may also have the opportunity to speak to Colonel James Russel, Army National Guard, who works for the DOD. He's been assisting."

A white guy with dreadlocks in the growing crowd threw both hands up. "This is crazy, man," he remarked. "We're lettin' the Feds destroy the Library. They're trying to take knowledge away from the people."

"Sir," she told him in her best PR voice, "the Library should be fine, mostly. Possibly barring the need for minor repairs or replacement of furniture. This entire operation has been undertaken in part to protect the Library."

She'd begun to grow tired of this kind of conversation when Russel and his heavily armed team emerged from the front entrance and marched in formation down the steps to where she stood in front of the stone lion. Seeing them, most of the civilians dispersed quickly, while the cops waited for their cherished explanation.

The colonel nodded to her. "Agent. Can I speak to you off to the side? I'm sure your men and mine can handle crowd control for a minute."

She sighed in relief. "That sounds great, Colonel. I take it we won?"

He grinned. "We did indeed." The man extended a hand in an *after you* gesture and she ascended the steps to a sheltered corner near the doors. He joined her presently.

"So," Kendra began and positioned herself to where she could stop him if he tried to slip away before he'd answered her questions. "First of all, I'd like to know exactly what happened in there. I'm sure I'll hear it from our friends in the private sector, but I want to hear your side of the story first."

Chuckling, Russel told her. He did not speculate as to the exact nature of what he'd seen but he didn't spare any details, either.

When he'd finished, she needed a moment to put a hand over her eyes and breathe deeply a couple of times.

"Jesus," she whispered. "I knew something was...wrong. Or if not wrong, exactly, then at least really fucking weird. I...I saw things myself, over the course of these last few months of working with them and tracking Moswen—things I barely managed to explain rationally."

She looked up. The Colonel's face was calm and accepting.

"But," she added, "I don't think that, even then, I really believed it. And now...well, you, a goddamn colonel and DOD asset, are telling me you saw something out of a horror movie or a fantasy video game in there. And that your men saw it too..." She shook her head and looked aside and off into the distance. The city seemed so dark and mysterious, even with its myriad electric and neon lights.

Russel nodded. "That they did, and those men aren't crazy. I'd be curious to hear Remington and Taylor and their motley crew explain exactly what all that was, but for now, I'd say it's good enough to know that it sure as shit wasn't all in our heads."

She looked at him again. "Well, we'll both have plenty of cleaning up to do—tying this whole event off in hundreds of yards of red tape and hoping no one tries to cut through it to look too closely. Once I'm caught up, perhaps we can have a cup of coffee while you tell me how it is that you know these people and how you got mixed up in the whole mess."

"Affirmative," the man replied and smiled again. "I think we could both use a good debriefing. Obviously, therefore, I expect quid pro quo, especially since it sounds like you've dealt with them for longer than I have."

She confirmed his assumption. "Since before Christmas. Originally, what I thought I was dealing with was an international crime syndicate. Now...I'm not sure anymore."

They stood in silence for a moment and looked from the library to the perimeter where the men did a fairly good job of getting rid of the civilians and stalling the police.

Russel spoke first. "Remington used a term in there while he tried to fill me in...the preternatural. That seems to be their catch-all word for this kind of thing. It makes me wonder if any other of ours—servants of Uncle Sam—are in on it. If so, we ought to get them all together. 'Preternatural Virgins Anonymous' or something like that."

Kendra laughed gently. "I think 'novices' might be a better term, but I like the idea." She looked toward Fifth Avenue. "All right, back to the grind for both of us."

· · ·

New York Public Library Main Branch, Midtown Manhattan, New York

Taylor breathed in, then out. Pain stabbed her in too many different places with each breath but the damage would heal, albeit slowly. Her vision changed. She no longer saw everything as though through a translucent screen of fresh blood. Her eyes were shifting back to those of a human being or something close enough to pass for human, at least.

The bat wings had retracted into her shoulder blades as well, and her limbs had begun to shorten, smooth out, and return to normal. Her head and clawed hands were still distended. Those seemed to take a while to adjust.

She didn't want her people—her friends—to see her like this. They'd already seen enough but she wouldn't dwell on it too much. There were two important facts that trumped any such concerns.

First, Moswen Neith was dead. They had not only incapacitated but totally destroyed her. Never again would she threaten the world. They had won.

And second, even if it took time and concentration and centuries' worth of mental discipline, she was reverting to her old self. The darkness within her was receding.

It hadn't gone entirely, though, and she did not trust herself to get too close to humans. She had only the vaguest idea how she'd resisted the urge to rip out Remington's throat when he'd grabbed her—to drink his blood and go on a rampage.

After hiding in the shadowed upper corner for a few moments, she'd crawled out through a window and now clung to the exterior of the building. A crowd was forming, of course. And down below, the other employees of Moonlight Detective Agency now emerged.

She watched them go and made no move. Finally, Conrad appeared in the rear of the group. He lingered for a moment in the deep darkness behind one of the marble columns and she crept toward him and dropped almost soundlessly.

None of the humans noticed, but he turned his head for a second. He was smart enough not to draw attention to himself by greeting her openly and only spoke in a low voice and out of the side of his mouth.

"Taylor," he whispered. "It's good to see you're okay."

"More or less," she replied. He, of all beings, would be sympathetic to the difficulties involved in shifting one's form. "I need time to…return to my normal self. I'll be fine. Go home and I will meet you back at the house."

He pretended to crane his neck so he could flash her a quick smile. "As you say, ma'am."

She darted up the wall and onto the roof and slipped away into the night.

Before she left the library entirely to slide between or above the other buildings of night-shrouded Manhattan, she glimpsed a single person looking up at her. David had noticed her. He did not gesture or say anything but merely watched her leave before he turned to the general chaos around him.

CHAPTER THIRTY-ONE

Taylor's House, Harrison, Westchester County, New York

Remy laughed along with the others. Volz had said something clever and apparently funny. He hadn't actually heard it but for the moment, he was swept up in the general mood. Everyone was happy.

They were also sweaty, dirty, tired, and in some cases, caked with blood. Conrad's suit was a complete mess, partially due to the stains and partially because he'd ripped it in places when he couldn't get it off in time while wolfing out. Blood had spattered on almost everyone else, and Alice and Bobby still had some residue of the bizarre magical pâté they'd made on their hands and shirts.

He hadn't even noticed that the headbutt he'd taken to his bruised face had split the flesh open and spilled blood down his suit jacket. Bloodstains were an absolute cocksucker to get out of garments, so the jacket was essentially doomed, but he decided he'd keep it, anyway.

It had become a trophy of sorts—the jacket he wore the day they finally defeated Moswen.

Alex was asleep upstairs. He clearly needed rest while his liver did what it needed to do. Come morning, the hangover would be easier for him once they raised the subject of shipping him home to the upside-down part of the world.

Taylor still hadn't returned, though. He wondered where she'd gone.

Presley wandered in with a large bowl filled with ice cubes. "Since you've already taken to raiding Miss Steele's liquor cabinet," he began, "and, under the circumstances, I don't think she'd mind too much. I've taken it upon myself to aid you to properly chill your drinks if such is your taste."

Smiling subtly—as though secretly, he was almost as ecstatic as they were—he set the dish down on the foyer's central table.

Remy raised his glass, which was already half-full with a lovely brandy slightly older than he was. "Thanks, Presley. You're the best," he stated. "So good, in fact, that I'll make a real, serious effort to keep calling you Presley instead of Jeeves. Even if the latter is traditional and all."

The butler straightened and folded his hands behind his back. "Why, thank you, sir. Did I hear some mention of pizza? If you're all busy, I can take your requests and place an order myself."

"That," urged Alice as she sloshed some of her brandy and barely avoiding a spill, "sounds like an excellent idea."

Everyone interjected with their preferred toppings. Out of the chaos of this vast profusion of choices, Presley created order and suggesting three variations in a combination that ensured that everyone would find something to their liking.

Bobby raised her hand, and Remy wondered if he ought to suggest to her later that she didn't need to keep doing that when she wanted to make a comment. "You know," she mused, "it's funny that pizza has become basically the world's most popular food and the go-to for parties and such. It's weird when you think about it—a base that can have anything on it, but almost always seems to include unrecognizable tomato guts and fermented cow's milk."

Conrad cracked up laughing at that for a second before he caught hold of himself again and Riley cringed. "Did you have to put it that way?" the fairy complained. "I like pizza. I don't want to start disliking it."

It occurred to Remy in that moment that Bobby had made another of the kind of curious, thoughtful—albeit weird—comments that often came from highly intelligent people.

"Hey," he commented, "have we discussed how to handle the spell on you yet? As in, will it simply wear off eventually and you'll be—" He almost said stupid but stopped himself in time. "Uh, back the way you were before?"

He looked at Alice, who merely shrugged. Then, he noticed that Bobby looked at him with a subtle hint of hurt on her face.

Damn, he chastised himself. *I'm glad I didn't use the s-word, at least, but that still would have been a good time to plan what I was going to say before I opened my mouth. High-quality brandy will do that to a man.*

Fortunately, the witch broke the awkward silence when she turned to the receptionist and posed a few questions.

"Along that line," she said, "have you felt any...different lately?"

Bobby stared at her and said, "No, not really."

"Any slowdown in consciousness? As if, for example, it seems more difficult to reach conclusions or parse information, or seems to take longer than it has been these last few days, or you find yourself forgetting things that you thought you'd remember? Anything of that nature?"

"No," the receptionist went on, "not really, as far as I could notice. Hell, if anything, I think I feel a little sharper after all that excitement but that might only be the adrenaline. It must be an evolutionary advantage, speeding up our thoughts in times of desperation and struggle."

Everyone nodded and her face suddenly went blank. "Unless...shit. Maybe all the stress is what's kept me smart. Maybe if things go back to normal, I'll wake up one day and be dumb again. That day might even be tomorrow."

She looked downright forlorn.

"Well," Remy interjected quickly in an attempt to cheer her up, "you could always stop sleeping. It's basically a waste of time, anyway."

Volz looked at him with amusement. "I do not think it works that way. Your species—like most—requires sleep to survive. And as I understand it, it's rare for an enchantment of this kind to simply vanish overnight."

Well, Remy thought, *the spell sure as hell wore off in his case. Then again, Alice sabotaged it, so that's different.*

"Okay," the witch snapped, "I'm hungry. If we get back

to the business of ordering pizza—if—I promise I'll look into it in the morning. Fair?"

No one argued.

She furrowed her brow. "Although I cannot make any promises as to the outcome. My suspicion is that Moswen had the spell concocted by someone far away and through multiple intermediaries, so I can't comment on its properties based on the caster. But I can try."

Remy noted how easily Alice had already become part of the group. Her standoffishness when they'd first met her was obviously a defensive gesture. Beneath that veneer, she was a sweetheart, if a little individualistic and eccentric.

Presley cleared his throat. "Very well. I will place the order." He produced the house's cordless phone.

No sooner had he hung up than the front doors opened. Standing upon the threshold, silhouetted against the night beyond, was Taylor.

"Miss Steele," the butler intoned. "Welcome home. And congratulations."

"Thank you," she said quietly and trudged in.

After his initial elation to see her again wore off, Remy was almost alarmed. The vampire looked about as worse for wear as he'd ever seen her. The monstrous form she'd worn had disguised how badly Moswen had hurt her and the stress of the fight, not to mention the transformation, seemed to have taken its toll, too.

He almost jumped out of his chair when she stumbled against it.

"Jesus, Taylor!" he exclaimed. "Are you okay?"

She nodded. "Mostly. I will heal. Presley, please prepare my tea."

The old man bowed. "At once, madam." He was already halfway to the kitchen.

"Well," Conrad remarked, "the danger should be over, at this point, so she'll have time and breathing space in which to recover. Her remaining thralls will have snapped out of it. Any other preternaturals riding her coattails will probably panic and scatter. Her outfit wasn't the sort of organism that can live without a head."

The vampire closed her eyes. "Yes. We won. And..." She coughed. "I wanted to thank you. All of you. I could not have done it alone."

"Aww," Alice quipped. "Humility. From the great queen of New York? Seriously, though, it's been both a pleasure and an honor."

Riley buzzed over, landed on Taylor's shoulder, and hugged the side of her neck. Not too long before, Remy recalled, the fairy was afraid of getting too close to her out of fear of being eaten.

The vampire opened her black eyes again and seemed to drink in the sight of them all. "In truth, you saved my life along with many others. I had spent a long, long time assuming that what I needed to do could only be done by me, alone. I grew used to being self-sufficient. But now... you all stood by my side, holding the fort even when I rudely departed and left you to your own devices without warning."

He had never seen or heard her behave quite like this and slid his hand over hers. "I think, Taylor, that we're mostly glad to have you around. Knowing you're back and seeing that we're all alive."

The others agreed and all of them smiled to varying

degrees. The smallest smiles, though, were the ones on the faces of Remy and Taylor herself. They exchanged a brief, knowing look.

Then, it struck him. Remy understood, finally, what had happened during the terrible struggle. Before they'd gone to the library, his talk with her—his assurance that everyone was with her and that they were all in this together—had planted a seed in her mind that had germinated just in time. That knowledge had stayed with her and allowed her to trust him at the final moment when he tackled her out of the way.

Without it, she might have killed him and Russel and his men would have had no choice but to send Moswen and Taylor to hell together. And they both knew it.

"So, then." Volz grunted and shifted in his chair. "what do we do next? Besides eat, drink, and be merry, of course."

A few joking suggestions went around as Presley returned and handed Taylor a steaming cup of red salt tea.

"You know," Remy interjected, "it's actually kind of nice having everyone together like this at the same time. It's almost like a family gathering. Of course, we all get tired of our families." He thought briefly of his own, who didn't seem to miss him much. "But for now, let's all stay here a little while. If Taylor's okay with it, obviously."

She half-smiled and half-grimaced. "That is fine."

Bobby asked, "Will we close the agency for a day or two? We had at least two outstanding cases but then again, the last time I talked to them, they weren't expecting a resolution until next week, anyway."

"Yes," Taylor agreed, "I think we all deserve a little time off."

The vampire straightened her posture and her gaze grew distant before she went on. "There have been reports that the Vampiric Order in Europe had thrown its support behind Moswen. We don't seem to have encountered any of their agents, but they could have provided her with money, guns, contacts... It's a disturbing prospect."

"The Vampiric Order?" Remy marveled. "That sounds like one of those horrible mail-order fan clubs. Just when I think the rabbit hole has gone deep enough—"

Taylor waved a hand brusquely through the air. "They are not supposed to interfere in our affairs. We can hope that, with their champion dead and her operation essentially powerless without her, they will realize that New York is not in play and leave us be. Still, we must be vigilant."

"Right," he said. "But not tonight. First, we party, then we pass out, then we do basically nothing for most of tomorrow. And if anyone needs any advice on how to do that," he proclaimed, "I am definitely the man to ask."

Taylor sighed as the others snickered.

"But of course." She squeezed his hand. "David."

EPILOGUE

Sub-Basement Beneath a High-Rise, Midtown Manhattan, New York

The building above them that scraped the sky was impressive if not excessively distinctive, and those who met far below ground level preferred it that way. In the unlikely event that someone saw them going in and out of the place, they would grasp instantly that they witnessed people of power and influence on their way to discuss important things.

At the same time, it did not draw undue amounts of attention from those with a more discerning eye. Regular businesses, legitimate affairs that operated in the sunlight where all the mortals could see, were located in its many high-stacked offices.

Now, the seven members of the Preternatural Council were meeting again. The general understanding was that, for once, the gathering would not be a mere formality. Something big was happening.

Each member of the council represented a different preternatural species—the most numerous or at least most influential of those found in New York. Elves, dwarves, lycanthropes, shapeshifters, gnomes, and fairies each had their spokesperson, who was understood to advocate for the overall welfare of his or her species.

The one exception was the Council's de facto leader, Taylor Steele. Vampires never seemed to get along with one another. Like cats, they were territorial and usually regarded others of their kind as their greatest potential foes.

This was the one saving grace of Taylor's lopsided dominance of the organization. No one really believed that she abused her position on behalf of the rest of her kind. It made it easier to tolerate her.

She now sat in the middle of the crescent-shaped black table, itself located in the center of the glossy black marble chamber. Dim lights gave the room an intimate feel. Plants sustained by sunlamps—always aimed carefully away from anywhere she might walk—bloomed in the corners, and the chairs were large, plush, and comfortable.

Taylor folded her hands in front of her, her gaze moving from side to side to collect the attention of the other six members.

"Ladies and gentlemen," she began. "I will assume you've all heard the news. The would-be usurper Moswen Neith is dead. It is possible that some of you may have been privy to ill-conceived whisperings that she would repre-sent some kind of improvement for our domain, but nothing could be further from the truth. She came as a conqueror, and when she could not conquer purely by open force, she aimed to subvert through the mental enslavement of humans. In essence, she represented a return to the bad old days of outright vampiric tyranny, beside which my own tendencies would seem very lax indeed."

They all nodded. She had no reason to suspect that any of them were truly sympathetic to Moswen but she also knew well that they resented the fact that their own power on the Council was effectively a privilege that she allowed them.

Margda Helfschmer, a stoic dwarven woman who always wore a chestnut-colored hooded cloak, responded first. "Congratulations on your victory, Taylor. My people were not pleased when the details of what Greyhammer's cartel was involved in leaked out. That this Moswen was also involved in distributing Snow White did not endear her to dwarfdom."

The vampire nodded. "I am glad to hear that."

"Yes." Oliryan Shelluvis, the willowy but dignified elven representative, sighed. He ran his narrow fingers through his long, straight hair. "It would seem we dodged an arrow and no one on this Council is prepared to challenge the justice of destroying Moswen. We have, however, been led to believe that there is some further announcement you have in store. Much eagerness and a speedy revelation of the news would do wonders to quiet the gossip."

Taylor readjusted her position slightly. Her wounds, still not entirely healed, ached terribly. She ignored the pain.

"Very well," she stated, "I shall cut to the chase. I am

temporarily stepping down as head of this council, effective as of the coming dawn. Frankly, I need a vacation."

The gnomish member, Dossemant, chortled. "Why ever might that be?"

Clearly, it was a rhetorical question, so she did not bother to answer it.

"Furthermore," she went on, " a series of events, conversations, and personal reflections have led me to believe that a more democratic approach may be beneficial, particularly since I've had ample opportunities to demonstrate during this last half a year that wanton breaking of the rules shall not go unpunished."

She spread her hands wide. "You have governed well enough when called upon to do so, and your people trust you. Until further notice, I leave the preternatural affairs of Greater New York in your care. Do not abuse that trust."

As she'd expected, the six were quiet for a moment, all stunned by the revelation.

Shelluvis was first to break the silence. "Taylor, thank you for your confidence. We appreciate the notion of... movement in a more equitable direction. At the same time, only the willfully blind can question that New York has remained at relative peace in part thanks to the example you've set. We shall keep that in mind."

She thanked him. He was something of a double-talking bloviator, but not an evil or untrustworthy man. Merely a highly diplomatic one. There was a place for such people in the world of modern leadership.

Taylor pushed her chair back and stood. "As I have things to do, I shall depart and leave the six of you to the rest of your business—namely, your plan for governing our city for at least the next month or two and quite possibly longer. You will have updates before I return."

Almost in unison, the others said, "Thank you, Taylor."

She smiled and walked toward the elevator. Before she reached it, she stopped and turned to face them. "Thank you, as well. And remember—I'll always be watching."

AUTHOR NOTES FROM ISOBELLA CROWLEY (AKA ELL LEIGH CLARKE)

WRITTEN DECEMBER 9, 2019

Thank Yous

I'd like to start by thanking the team of suppliers and collaborators for making this happen: Nathan, Brittany, and Chiara, as well as our team of beta readers and JITers. Thank you for all your efforts... And of course making sure our jokes not only make sense... but are also at least a little bit funny ;-)

I'd also like to thank my collaborator, MA, and for his encouragement. You have no idea how much it helps to get back a section, or a set of beats and have him laughing because it was entertaining. It also makes me more confident we're on track if he finds it amusing. He's a good humor barometer! Thanks MA!

Brittany, JIT and Beta

Huge thank yous also go to Zen Steve and the JIT and Beta teams who work tirelessly to make sure that all slips are caught and corrected, the files are uploaded on time.

Thank you so much folks. I truly appreciate all your efforts. :)

Reviewers

Massive thanks also go out to our Amazon reviewers. It's because of you that we get to do this full time. Without your five-star reviews and thoughtful words on Amazon we simply wouldn't have enough folks reading these space shenanigans to be able to write full time.

You are the reason these stories exist and you have no idea how frikkin' grateful I am to you.

Truly, thank you.

Readers and FB page supporters

Last, and certainly by no means least, I'd like to thank *YOU* for reading this book... and all the others. Your enthusiasm for the world, and our renegade, broken characters, is heart-warming. Your words of encouragement, and demands for the next episode, are the things that often stay in my mind as I sit down to write.

Thank you for being here, for reading, for reviewing, and for always brightening my day with your words of support on the fb page. You're best!

This is my last set of Author Notes...

...

...

For the year. ;-)

Yes, that was cruel of me.

But as 2019 draws to a close I'm forced to reflect on the progress this year. For a start it feels like January was only five minutes ago. And yet looking at the manuscript we published and laughs we've had, as well as my Goodreads challenge I've realized that something has been accomplished.

This makes a change. And I think realizing this is a function of being able to look back on all of these tangible things that are traceable. I have never really been in a position in my life to be able to track progress in the same way. Obviously in education it's a case of just getting through the year and doing the best you can. But this isn't the same as being able to point to say a catalogue of work you put out, or a library of books you've read. This is new for me. But I'm sure if you're reading this this isn't a new concept the you! I've spoken to a number of readers over the last few years and I am continually blown away by the number of books you can consume in any given time period! I think I still have a very long way to go to catch you up.

On the writing front, it's been a wild ride. I had Brittany do a count for the number of books we've published this year, because my NINC re-application asked the question. (NINC is a writing association. I'm pretty sure I mentioned it in a recent set of author notes, in conjunction with the recent conference in Florida. They have pretty strict rules about us needing to qualify each year I guess, hence wanting to know the numbers).

Turns out we've done 40 in total, and 19 this year. (She may have counted from November to November, for any sticklers who want to go and check....!)

This includes titles under my alter egos: Oscar Andrews, and Isobella Crowley.

As I mentioned to the folks on my email newsletter a few months ago, they've been received with varying degrees of success. Oscar Andrews started as an experiment to see whether a male pen-name would generate more traction than my Ell Leigh Clarke name. Unfortunately, probably due to bad covers that miss the mark, the series didn't take off. My plan going into 2020 is to take these books and put them wide on other platforms like Kobo, Apple, Google Play, B&N. With new covers! At the very least it will be interesting to figure out how these other platforms work and evaluate the opportunities there.

And that brings me onto the subject of publishing as a whole. Not to get too in-depth into the magic behind the scenes but as you may have already seen I've switched my mindset from being a sci-fi writer to being a publisher. You might also have noticed that this is exactly what MA has been trying to get me to do for at least the last year! No doubt he'll jump in here and re-iterate this point.

But I think it's a valid course of action. Life as a writer is tenuous. You never know if the next series is going be a hit, and to what degree it will work or not work. Not only that but you can no longer be just a writer. There is a ton of marketing and brand management and business that needs to go with it - all of which takes time and focus. Short of somehow regaining the energy and drive that I had as a 20-year-old - which is an interesting story premise now that I come to think of it - I need to figure out a way of going about things differently in the coming year.

For those who take an interest in astrology, and the psychic weather that corresponds with the movement of the planets, it looks like there are big opportunities coming as Jupiter moves into Capricorn. Jupiter is about possibilities and potential. Capricorn is about hard work and doing the things that are necessary. I read this as an opportunity to meet with potential by doing the things that are necessary. If you're interested in this kind of archetypal insight then I strongly encourage you to check out the work of Robert Ohotto. I've been following his work for many years now. Recently taking one of his online courses I realized a couple of shifts that I can make going into the New Year.

1. Adrenal fatigue is real, but I'm at the stage in my healing now where I have control over my energy levels. This is a huge step forward. Yet I still have work to do. I'm taking this Jupiter in Capricorn energy to mean that I can use discipline in order to heal better. For example, I know that that second cafeteria of coffee in the day is probably putting too much pressure on my adrenals and causing periodic relapses. I can certainly cut back. I can also work more diligently in the early hours of the morning and probably increase my productivity in the few hours of focused attention I have in a day.

2. I also know that I also have to protect the energy that I do have. Some of this means less time on social media, although you might have noticed and pretty good that already. Some of it may also mean spending less time on calls, and more time in meditation and in just being quiet. I've noticed that this really helps me in general, but also creatively.

3. I have an hypothesis that this new found discipline will allow me to increase my health and energy levels, which in turn will give me more energy to be focused and productive. This means I can do more writing, more

stories, more projects, and more fun stuff the patrons and readers. All of this is positive stuff, right?

4. While you'll never hear me say that I have control over adrenal fatigue, there are no doubt small things that I can do that in helping my healing. Small things that I *do* have control over. I really believe that I'm at the point now where I can leverage these small things, and no longer be completely at the mercy of my health, or lack thereof.

(Okay, so that's my 2020 plan, AND my homework for the online course with Ohottie! BOOM. Multi-tasking. Efficiency. Yay – go 2020! HA :D)

Goodreads

You have heard me talk about Goodreads. Normally it's in conjunction with tracking the reading I do, and the reading challenge set forth by my author-friend, Claire. However, it was recently pointed out to me that not only are all our books reviewed on that platform, but that actually people are liking them. I stumbled upon this in conversation the other evening as I was navigating the platform with a friend.

Ellie (looking at page and realizing that people have been rating the Ascension Myth): Oh my god… Is that real? Are they really giving Molly 4.8 stars on Goodreads?

Friend: that's unusual for Goodreads. The ratings are normally about 20% lower than on Amazon. (*Friend scrambles to look up the series on their computer.*)

Ellie: I think I'm reading this right. I had no idea so many people are rating the books over here. They have an author profile set up me and everything. I didn't do any of this.

Friend (finding page): oh no… that's right. Wow. That's unusual.

Ellie: oh gosh, look! I wrote that. They're quoting stuff that I wrote! I don't believe this. This is incredible!

Friend: that is pretty cool. Hey, you should claim your profile.

(Next 20 minutes is Ellie jumping through hoops to claim her profile and prove she is who she says she is.)

20 minutes later…

Ellie: well, that was tedious. And they didn't ask me for anything that revealing. Anyone could have filled that form out.

Friend: no, they have checks and approvals and stuff. They'll probably get you approved in a couple of days…

Ellie (clicking back to the Molly quotes): I can't get over it. People are quoting Molly! That makes me so happy!!

Anyway, discovering that was the highlight of my week. Thank you to everyone who has left a review, or shared a quote, or added anything to do with the books on Goodreads. I was blown away, and I'm so grateful for all the love and support. Thank you.

++

In terms of the Goodreads challenge, things are going well. If you remember I set my goal at 50, not 100. I'm still debating whether I should increase it for next year. I'm not sure. If the purpose for me is not to get through volume but to assimilate the information that I want to learn, and increasing the volume will make me want to read shorter books and not necessarily take the time needed on one difficult texts. With an easily achievable number it will keep me moving forward, but also taking the necessary time and reading the important books first. Okay, I just talk myself into not increasing my goal, but keeping it at 50 next year. Thank you for helping me figure that out!

I'm currently at 59 of the 50 books. I have two audiobooks that I'll get through before the end of the year, and another two or three that I just need to finish off. I'll probably close out at around 65 all being well. I'm going to try not to start any new books until next year now. (Reading that is, not writing! Lots of writing to do still!)

The problem with all of this though is the more I read, the more I learn and the more I learn the more I realize I don't know... and the more I want to know. I find that this thirst for understanding is insatiable. What's more – there are too many good books, and too much awesome information so easily available. I was born at a time when we have to go to the library for books, or had to physically buy them from the bookstore which meant walking into town. If you wanted to learn something there was no internet to just search for an immediate answer. You had to somehow acquire books that had the information in them. If those books even existed. This age of Kindle and Google and audiobooks and Amazon Prime has me continually in awe of how blessed we are to have this information our fingertips. My mind is blown every day. The only constraint on information consumption is how much time in a day I can focus! Needless to say I'm also continuously overwhelmed.

Good Reads

Okay so no discussion of Goodreads would be

complete without a discussion of my favorite reads this year. What follows are my top 7.

1. I Am That, Sri Nisargadatta Maharishi. Profound. No matter where you are in life or what you're going through – I thoroughly recommend reading this from cover to cover. Twice. And then again. In fact, I'm putting on my "I'm reading this at least every year until I'm enlightened" list, which currently consisted of the *Bhagavad Gita* and *The Power of Now*.

2. The Tibetan Art of Living and Dying, Sogyal Rinpoche. Fascinating. Reading this will be prepare you for dying. We're all going to have to face death one day, no matter what our faith – or lack of it. My basic opinion on this the same strategy I advocate for investing. You can't start early enough ;) These two spiritual books (1 & 2) have been immensely helpful to my development as a human being this year.

3. Long Walk to Freedom, Nelson Mandela. My father fled from South Africa during this period in history. My great uncles were teachers and rebels and resisted apartheid. I mostly pass as white though, so in both England and the US I have all the privilege of being seen as a white person. I struggle with this conflict. On the one hand my father's family left to give their descendants a better life. On the other hand I was born into the socio-economic class of the oppressor. I haven't quite reconciled these two things yet, and my heart isn't at peace with it. I feel like I have a lot more reading to do around the British colonies, and colonization in general, to fully grasp what happened.

4. We Were 8 Years in Power, Ta-Nehisi Coates.

Profound and insightful. After reading this I also realized that my favorite type of books are written by essayists. (*White Fragility* and *Men Explain Things*, were two other books I read this year, which I found emotionally triggering, but ultimately essential to living in this age. I'd thoroughly recommend all three of these titles, but be compassionate with yourself and others as you explore these ideas. There's a lot of "high voltage" material in these books.)

5. Radical Candor, Kim Scott – made me a better boss. I've recommended it to everyone on my team and will be re-reading it every year until I feel like I've "got it" engrained in my psyche!

6. Attached, Amir Levine and Rachel Heller. Changed my relationship to relationships! It also helped me understand a lot about why people behave in the confusing ways that they do: a little insight which has changed me profoundly.

7. The New British Constitution, Vernon Bogdanor – infinitely fascinating, and ironically helps me understand the American political system a little better. It also helped me understand the root of the key challenges which laid the groundwork for Brexit to come about – even though it was written before Brexit was even a thing. (I plan to read the follow up next year, as well as the one by the professor at Liverpool university I've talked about in the past).

Rex and Hexe

Okay, one final thing before I let MA take over.

We've been releasing Hexe over the last several weeks. We're about to put book 4 into KU. However, we've realized that it might be better suited to other platforms – just because of the sub-genre and style of writing. As such, we're going to be pulling it from KU in the coming weeks and months, and republishing it wide – over those other platforms. You'll still be able to get it from Amazon – it just wont be in Amazon's exclusive program. Sooooo…. If you want to use your KU membership to read it, you'll want to do that now, before it disappears from there.

End of PSA ;)

Again, thank you for reading and for reviewing. I really hope you've enjoyed this series as much as we have had creating it! Have a great holiday season, and 2020 – and I'll look forward to writing to you again in the coming year.

Ellie x

<<Ellie edit: okay, I have to say up front – I'm reeling from shock. I've just gone to hand my author notes in to teacher (Zen Steve) and here are MA's notes in the channel. THREE hours before mine. I feel like I've slipped into the Twilight Zone! >>

Thank you for not only reading this story, but all the way through to our author notes, as well!

So, just the other day I was recording author notes with Ellie for our story Deuces Wild 5 and it went a little…

Long.

Like, real long.

We had two hours to produce two sets of author notes and we should have had plenty of time if Ellie hadn't diverted us so often. Ok, well, that's not totally true.

We just sat and caught up for the first half hour since we hadn't spoken much lately and then when "I" was the bad guy and started pushing us to read the author notes, I realized we had a *BOOK* to record and I had a 9:00 AM hard stop.

<Ellie edit: hahhaa. This is HILARIOUS reading his version of events. Ladies, you'll be able to read between the lines and know exactly what's going on here!>>

Holy S$%T the book's first author notes (Ellie's) was like 3,000 words or something. More like a small story in and of itself. I'm looking at these pages of author notes thinking…

There is no way we are going to get two books done today. Not if you have a burning hot brand waiting to sizzle our hindquarters – we were well and truly screwed.

I had so many troubles getting the pagination correct during our hour long first author note reading that I started worrying if I was going to get a chance to read my author notes. (spoiler, we did.)

The problem (ok, one of the problems) is Ellie is constantly reading and learning (as opposed to my reading and enjoying) and then she mentions the latest knowledge. Well, that's like throwing me catnip if what she is reading has anything to do with something where I have an opinion.

And it usually does.

<< Ellie edit: I'm glad you're confessing your part in this! >>

So, off we go debating into the future as we both argue our sides. What is nice, is it really IS a debate. Sure, I want to win but I don't feel like I have to win. She is so damned logical, I feel 'ok' admitting if I'm wrong.

Well, actually I think I come to the conclusion that I KNOW I'm wrong and am not too bullheaded to just keep arguing.

Damn, now I realize that isn't true all of the time. I

might have been known to argue once...maybe twice... when I just didn't want to give up.

<<Ellie edit: OMG, MA! My how you've grown over this year! Props, man. I'm impressed :D >>

This Story

So, we conclude (for now at least) our little story about a rich dude who needed to grow up, and an old Vampire that maybe needed to accept a little love and both of their lives are changed for the better.

I hope you have enjoyed our stories and we promise to provide a few more.

<<Ellie edit: Yeah, I feel like we've got a momentum going with this tale-telling thing, eh? We should defo do some more in 2020. I'll clear my schedule! >>

Ad Aeternitatem,

Michael Anderle

with Michael Anderle

Darkest Before The Dawn (3)

Dawn Arrives (4)

Interplanetary Spy For Hire

with Michael Anderle

Expelled

Exposed

Deuces Wild

with Michael Anderle

Beyond The Frontiers (1)

Rampage (2)

Labyrinth (3)

Birthright (4)

Resolution (5)

The Sword-Mage Chronicles

Awakening

Taken

Heist

Resistance

Legba

Storm

CONNECT WITH MICHAEL ANDERLE

Michael Anderle Social
Website:
http://www.lmbpn.com

Email List:
http://lmbpn.com/email/

Facebook Here:
www.facebook.com/TheKurtherianGambitBooks/